THE WORLD GAME

THE WORLD GAME

J. H. CLEARVIEW

© E. R. Hill, 2019

J.H. Clearview is the pseudonym of James Hill, the author of *The World Game*.

Published by E. R. Hill

All rights reserved. No part of this book may be reproduced, adapted, stored in a retrieval system or transmitted by any means, electronic, mechanical, photocopying, or otherwise without the prior written permission of E. R. Hill.

The rights of J.H. Clearview to be identified as the author of this work have been asserted in accordance with the Copyright, Designs and Patents Act 1988.

All the characters, and the events in this story are fictitious. Some of the dialogue reflects local pronunciations. There are some explicit descriptions of sex scenes and violence. Some language may be considered offensive.

A CIP catalogue record for this book is available from the British Library.

ISBN 978-1-9996913-0-1

Book layout and cover design by Clare Brayshaw

Cover image © Alphaspirit | Dreamstime.com

Prepared and printed by:

York Publishing Services Ltd
64 Hallfield Road
Layerthorpe
York YO31 7ZQ

Tel: 01904 431213

Website: www.yps-publishing.co.uk

"If you keep your mouth shut about things you think important, hell, I don't see how you can expect the democratic system to work at all."

(Harry S. Truman, 23rd President of
the United States of America)

ACKNOWLEDGEMENTS

I would like to give my gratitude to the Swedish Football Association for arranging an open-ended telephone interview with former Swedish national team manager, Georg Ericson, who was with the Swedish squad in the World Cup Competitions in Mexico, 1970, West Germany, 1974, and in Argentina, 1978. With amiable succinctness and profound footballing erudition, he answered every question I could think to put to him concerning the running of a national side.

Gratitude is due to the U.S. Information Service and the United States Soccer Federation for making available to me the complete details of the 1983 U.S. bid for the World Cup Competition.

My thanks, also, to former football international, Ronnie Hellström, who kept goal for Sweden in Mexico, 1970, West Germany, 1974, and Argentina, 1978. His experience and observations from the viewpoint of a playing member of a national side in international and World Cup football were both useful and reassuring.

For reading and criticising the manuscript, I thank you each appropriately: R.W. Garner, Angela Edenborough, Ingegerd Varda St Vincent, B. Varda St Vincent, Gunnel Rågvik, D. Austin, H. de Soto, E. R. Hill. The copyright holder would also like to thank others who have re-read the book more recently.

ABOUT THE AUTHOR

J. H. Clearview was born in Marton, Gainsborough in 1938; and died in Stockholm in 2016. Middle son of a family of nine. He went to the local village school, Queen Elizabeth Grammar School in Gainsborough, and the London School of Economics. He had lived in the U.S.A., Canada, and for the last 49 years of his life, Sweden. He started writing seriously in the second half of the 1960's with historical, and later, more modern plays; and has a large portfolio covering novels, poetry, and essays.

CHAPTER 1

Who am I? Where am I? He felt he could break through to awareness. Tried. Could not. Did not panic. So long as he stayed still, he was safe. Fog tendrilled the darkness; shadows of buildings all around held enemies. The sky hinted inchoate dawn. Sunlight meant freedom!

His joy betrayed him to a black-haired goat-faced thug who sprang kicking for his knee from the alleyway on his right. Laughing silently above his fear, he moved instantly clear: no man living was fast enough if he was ready: only when they came at him from behind. He whirled: the aggressor's shoe grazed his kneecap. He zigzagged in five-yard bursts, exulting. Over five yards, no one could catch him. No one.

Who was he? Who was he? He was near to knowledge. Merely the tiniest effort left.

If they came at him in twos and threes, simultaneously from different directions. He twisted, leapt evading their kicks as they closed in. The goat-faced attacker's foot struck his knee.

A nun at his bedside; pale green walls; big window with drawn, white gauze curtains, leafy trees and evening light; the left side of his head was swollen, aching almost sharply. The nun was smiling. He smiled back. Angelo had kicked him when he had dived to head to Jim Arrowood.

"Did we win? **I'm** in hospital, aren't I? Anybody from the team waiting?" His nod at the room door winced pain.

The nun showed concern. Her posture and hands motioned him to stillness. Gesturing reassurance, she left the room.

Jacky closed his eyes. Mary would be anxious, his mother, too.

Headline stuff: DAY IN HOSPITAL.

"You are awake?" the youngish doctor's tan accentuated his white coat.

"Yes."

"Your head, how does it feel?"

"Rough."

The doctor told him he had concussion. No fracture.

"Did we win?"

The Italian spread his hands and rolled his eyes in a sympathetic negative.

Jacky closed his lids, pushing back disconsolation. "Anybody from the England squad out there? Send them in. And I'd like to ring my wife."

The doctor said he should rest; the hospital would take care of everything.

"Let 'em in. For two or three minutes. I'll live," Jacky's smile became a grimace of pain. The doctor grew instantly serious. "Send them in," Jacky ordered firmly, "or I shan't be able to relax."

So we lost. No World Cup for us in the U.S.A. Not that we could have won. Too many weak spots. Jim Arrowood and Benny Cawthorne are world class; Richard Trelawney's near; Joe Berrigan in goal's okay. But the rest. Maybe next time, if some of those new kids who beat Young Italy four-nil last night measure up.

His head hurt; he felt sick; would he play again? Angelo had broken his leg when Nottingham Forest had beaten Juventus in the European Champions Cup. It had taken all summer to regain fitness. His mother had worried. She would afresh. She was a sick woman. Had been since her stroke three months previously.

"Look at the li'l bagger – lazing his life away in idleness!"

Jacky grinned faintly at the tough-faced Cockney, spruce in his England tie, dark blue blazer and grey trousers. Behind Benny Cawthorne, Jim Arrowood, fair-haired, blue eyes smiling, six foot of easy strength; Richard Trelawney, dark, gaunt-cheeked, the biggest of the three. "Now, lads. We lost then."

"Three-one," Jim Arrowood said.

Benny Cawthorne informed him lightly: "I got sent off, Jecky. Your mate Angelo kicked me from behind, so I give him one wiv my elbow and kneed the bastard in the balls. Evened fings up for you, eh?"

Richard Trelawney's displeasure was heavy: "Behaviour like yours and Angelo's brings discredit on the game, Cawthorne. You both deserved being sent off. If you're not picked again for England, I for one will understand."

The Cockney was unperturbed: "Alright, Preacher, you ain't in your Methodist pulpit now. A lot of people will be glad I gave the bastard what he got. He started it. I don't turn the other cheek. I'll break their facking jaws and kick their heads in if they bagger about with me!"

Unnoticed by the disputants, Jim Arrowood showed amusement.

Jacky's grin became pain.

"What's the matter, Jecky boy?" Benny Cawthorne was alarmed. "We call the doctor?" he sidestepped quickly towards the door.

"No. It's alright," Jacky stopped him. "My head hurts like hell."

Richard Trelawney was decisive: "We'll leave."

"No, stay," Jacky was calm. "A couple of minutes won't matter. Where's the Boss, and Joe Berrigan? I'd've thought they've been here."

"The Boss ain't the boss no more," said Benny Cawthorne. "He was in the bog when the doctor came and said we could have a couple of minutes, so we left him to his diarrhoea."

"He's got a job in Canada, Jacky. He's resigned as England's team manager," said Jim Arrowood.

"And Berrigan's gone to see the Pope," said Trelawney.

Benny Cawthorne was grinning: "He took wiv him twenty little gold crosses for his kids and wife for the Pope to bless. He reckons he's going to get 'em all into Heaven, old Joseph."

Richard Trelawney grunted disgust. "Superstitious rubbish."

"I thought you was a Christian, Richard, you, a preacher, and all that," the Cockney teased.

"Popish mumbo jumbo!" the Devonshire man spoke quietly yet with passion. "Bowing down to one man and priests in fancy dress! Burning candles and incense, worshipping saints and graven images! It's wrong! One man and his God and God's word in the Bible, that is enough."

"The other lads send you their best wishes, Jacky," Jim Arrowood said.

"Who'll be team manager now then?" Jacky wondered.

"We'll have to wait and see, shan't we?" said Benny.

"Whoever it is, he'll make changes in the squad. He'll have to," Richard Trelawney was definite.

"Some of those new kids who won last night," said Jacky. "Young Milburne from Newcastle."

"That big-mouthed black guy from Brixton what got three for the Arsenal last Saturday, and Tottenham's new boy, Lewis," said Benny Cawthorne.

"Eddy Corelli, Aston Villa," Jim Arrowood observed.

"Jed Lennox, Manchester United," Jacky said.

Disagreement churned Richard Trelawney's tone: "They're too young! Milburne's scarcely seventeen! The others aren't much older. It's one thing to have two or three good League games at the end of the season and win one Young England match, it's another to play in a real England side."

"I did," said Benny Cawthorne. The Preacher was silent, not wishing to acknowledge the genius of the Cockney defender. "Age ain't got nuffink to do wiv it: if you can, you can, and if you can't, you can't."

The doctor entered and, holding the door open, told them it was time to leave.

"Watch out for all these nuns, Jecky," Benny Cawthorne joked. "They're all sex-starved, you know. One or two nice looking ones wiv big tits and nice arses on 'em out there. Get them in bed wiv you, you'll be alright. They'll smother you, you li'l' bagger!"

Richard Trelawney was disgusted: "You crude –, Cawthorne. Take care, Jacky."

"Get well, boy," said Jim Arrowood

"We'll be seeing you, Jeck," said Benny Cawthorne.

"Jim." Jacky's Nottingham Forest team-mate paused in the doorway. "Ring Mary. Tell her I'm okay." Arrowood's fair head dipped acceptance.

Who would be England's new team manager? Some forelock-touching yes-man on good terms with everybody, basically an arse-licker to the Establishment? Or somebody who knew football and could put together a good team? Some of the top club managers could. But they had too much jealousy against them.

Wyckliffe of Lincoln? He had taken Stoke into the First Division. Then they had sacked him. He had taken the Wolves into the First Division. Then they had sacked him. He had taken Sheffield United into the First Division – and had resigned over a point of principle. Now he had lifted Lincoln from the bottom of the Fourth Division to fifth place in the Second Division within three seasons. They would never choose Wyckliffe. He spoke English like an Englishman and not like a public schoolboy. He said what he thought. About anything, anybody, anywhere. A Socialist. They would never have him. The conservative Establishment did everything they could to blacken a man's character, belittle him, sneer at him, do him down, if he crossed them in any way. He had found that out these last two weeks when he had agreed to support Robert Jarvis, the Labour candidate in the Workfield by-election.

Footballers should not get involved in politics, they said. His mother thought that, too, poor old Ma. The Tory press had made fun of him. He was jibed at every day on television and radio. As if being a professional footballer made you an idiot.

Jacky's father had been the Labour Party's local agent for twenty years before lung cancer killed him. Robert Jarvis had been in the Upper Sixth at Danethorpe Grammar School when Jacky had been in the First Form and had protected the diminutive Jacky against the bullies. So now when Rob Jarvis asked for support, Jacky gave it willingly.

Would Robert Jarvis win?

Mary thought maybe.

Would he be back in England for their election meeting on Friday?

Tiredness coiled thickly, suddenly, relaxing him down.

Mary and himself and little Jessica walking along a sunny lane, with week-old lambs baaing in the fields, birds singing about leafy hedges and bare trees.

Peace, contentment, security.

Security?

Through approaching sleep, pain and unease wavered dully.

Yes. Security. Mary smiling. Jessica trotting and serious in her new pink and white dress. His wealth. Twice European Footballer of the Year. Forty-five caps for England.

CHAPTER 2

i

"Don't let them bully you."

"I won't let them bully me."

"Keep your scarf on in the car, and your woolly cap." Mary raised her 5'1" on tiptoes and nose to nose kissed Jacky's lips. "You've got your speech all prepared?"

"In my head."

She rubbed her nose against his and, grinning, winked her right eye: "My hero," she murmured. Jacky grinned back, and pulled her to him. They kissed hard on the mouth, each snuggling to the other, hands and arms caressing. "I wish I could come."

"Jessie needs you here."

"I've got my textbooks and computer for company. Hurry home, Jacky." Through her dress, his masculinity was hard. "Maybe tonight Jessie will get her little brother or sister."

"We've time now," he said, and stepped back enough to bend and lift her hem to her waist. Mary held it there with both hands and parted her legs to give him freedom.

"You'll be late if we do," she murmured, then shuddered as he stroked her.

"You're right." He held her pubes in his palm, its hair soft against his thumb. "Stay as warm and wonderful as ever, won't you, wife?" he breathed in her ear, and kissed it. "Promise."

"Promise," she whispered. Then chuckled in normal tone: "Sexy!"

"That's me," he responded lightly, and gave her a sloppy sounding kiss on her lips. "I'd better be off then."

"Mm," she smiled into his eyes, friendly and peaceful. His hand moved to stroke her flank, both luxuriating in the contact. "Speak kindly of Sir Alec 'Sinjin' spelt St John Frobisher and his supporters. He can't help being a stupefied, wrongly-educated public schoolboy, taught to obey his social betters and despise the hoi polloi. They whipped his bum and bullied him at prep. school and public school where his mummy and daddy sent him because they couldn't be bothered to take care of him themselves and didn't love him. So it's not his fault he's a flog 'em, jail 'em, hang 'em reactionary now."

"It's a good job you're not going instead of me," said Jacky, grinning into her innocent big blue eyes. "You'd have 'em shedding tears and voting for him."

ii

"Yaah! Why don't you stick to football instead of politics?! What do you know?!"

"What does anyone know?" Jacky countered the heckler. "If you're a free man, you've a right to your opinion. Anybody has. I've told you already why I'm here – Rob Jarvis came and asked me to speak on his behalf, so I did and I do because he's a good man. He was at school with me when I played in the Under Thirteens and he was in the First Eleven. He stuck up for the little kids against the bullies. He went to university and studied economics and he's done well at everything he's put his hand and mind to. He speaks French and German and he'll soon be as fluent in Spanish. He's straight and fair and he's a good man and just right for us in this constituency as our M.P.!"

A mixture of cheers and clapping and "Good old Jacky!" "You tell 'em, boy" mingled with jeers, boos, and shouts of "Never!"

The ultra-refined cockney of public school dialect drawled from a tall man in the front row, superciliousness a-sneer: "Do you agree with the Socialists' intended programme of pump-priming obsolescent and inefficient industrial enterprises in depressed or decaying sectors of the economy? Perhaps you could enlighten us on your position vis-à-vis the main alterations proposed in the current Social Welfare Bill and their legal and social ramifications? Or maybe you'd care to comment on the strategic military, political and economic implications inherent in the policies of the party you're giving your backing to?"

"Rob Jarvis can do that better than I can," said Jacky.

"I'm not asking Jarvis – I'm asking you!"

"It's alright, Rob," Jacky stopped the lean, dark haired man on his left from rising to his feet. "I support Rob Jarvis because he's a good 'un and I trust him. You want to know if I'm acquainted with all the present Labour Party policies and facts about everything. No, I'm not. And I certainly shan't agree with everything that's proposed to be said and done by any man or any party. But I do know that Rob Jarvis and most of the people in his crowd have got more sympathy for the working man and the have-nots than any other party has."

Boos and cries of "Rubbish!" were countered by cheers and shouts of encouragement.

"What do you care about the working man and have-nots? You're rich!" a fat man in a tailor-made suit called out.

"Working men fill the grounds on a Saturday to watch me and others like me play football," Jacky spoke above the hubbub. "Before I made it as a footballer, I was a working man. Like my dad before me. Who worked all his life and hardly had anything to show for it at the end of it! Like the majority of people in this world!"

"You're rich!" a red-faced man in the third row blared. "If you're a socialist, give it all away!"

"Yih! Give it to me, Jacky!" urged a whisky voice from the back of the hall, provoking laughter and similar requests.

"Socialism's not about giving all your money away or taking everything off people and making 'em poverty-stricken," Jacky began.

"Isn't it! I thought it was!" "You could have fooled me!" "Yes, it is!" "Gerr off!" "No!"

Jacky continued: "Socialism is about fairness, seeing that the people who don't have anything are given something!"

"What about you then? You've got more than your fair share! You're rich!" shouted the red-faced man.

"Yes, I'm rich! Whether I've got more than my fair share, you may be right! I don't know. But socialism isn't about begrudging the rich their riches! It's about getting rid of poverty! giving the have-nots a decent standard and everybody a fair deal. It's about helping those who can't take care of themselves, stick up for themselves, fight for themselves, watch out for their own interests – and for that, we need men like Robert Jarvis," Jacky flung his arm at the Labour candidate, "to represent them and see that they <u>do</u> get fair shares and a fair deal, because Robert Jarvis is fair and straight, and that's why he's getting my vote, and, I hope, he'll be getting yours! That's all I have to say, ladies and gentlemen. So I'll sit down, and shut up."

Loud cheers and clapping burst forth and shouts of "Good old Jacky!" "Up the Forest!" "Come on, England!"

Robert Jarvis was on his feet. "Thank you very much, Jacky." Cheers, cries of "Bravo!", whistles and shouts for Jacky rendered him inaudible.

"Who'll be England's manager, Jacky!" "Are you fully fit again, boy?!" "Cm'on, Forest!" "Show 'em, England!" "Good old Jacky!" "Who'll be England's next Team Manager, Jacky?!" Calls for Jacky to talk on football coming from every row and side predominated. Jarvis sat down, Jacky stood up.

"Somebody asked me if I was fit." Shouts of encouragement, handclapping and appreciative whistles crescendoed, then quickly stopped. "I'm in full training." Fresh applause.

"Is your concussion better?"

"The doctors say so. I feel alright," he repressed memories of pain. "I'll be fully match-fit for the season's last fixture, against West Ham, if I'm picked," he pushed aside fear of hurting himself heading a football.

"It's all that tobacco and booze, Jacky," the hoarse whisky voice called from the back of the hall. Jacky joined in the general laughter.

"I never touch tobacco," Jacky answered. "It's poison, and a killer. It helped put my dad into an early grave with lung cancer. As to booze, I don't need it. I'm not fanatical about it either way. I'm a professional athlete and I keep myself in as good a condition as I can because I feel best that way."

"What about women?"

"I'm a happily married man. Any more questions?"

"Yes," drawled the public school man in the first row, "whom would you like to see as England's team manager from the current power struggle now waging – Wyckliffe your controversial man and fellow Socialist who is being backed by the Players Association and some of the big club managers? Or Nigel Smythe, the so-called Soccer Establishment's safe candidate?"

"No comment. Except that I hope England's next team manager will want me on his squad for the Friendly against Sweden in Stockholm."

"Are you sorry England yet again won't be playing in the World Cup?" Jacky recognised the Nottingham journalist.

"What do you think? We still have a theoretical chance, of course, if Norway beat Hungary in Budapest." Disbelieving laughter and comments spattered the audience. Jacky spoke on: "Naturally, that's only a slim possibility since Norway lost at home in Oslo, 4-1."

"Who do you think will win the World Cup now that England are not going?" the reporter asked.

"The Italians have probably the best side in Europe at the moment. The Germans can never be discounted. The French. The Soviet Union and the Dutchmen could be in there with a chance."

"The South Americans? Brazil's new wonder team. They beat the Germans three-one, then the Italians two-one in extra-time in that tournament in Uruguay last month when Angelo half-crippled their new marvel man, the Black Prince, Zezinho."

"Brazil are always good. Argentina have one of the best teams in the world at the moment, by all accounts. And Uruguay have a useful side."

"Brazil have won 24 of their last 25 games. They beat Costa Rica 7-0 last Saturday with the Black Prince and Barboza the Bomber each getting a hat-trick," the journalist commented.

"I've got that match on tape. Both players you mention are skilful. And there's a fellow called Vivi Machado who is exceptional."

"Better than you, Jacky? You're the best, aren't you?" a lad of twelve was anxious.

"You can never say who's best. It depends upon the team you play in, your opposition, how fit you are, what form you're in at the time."

The boy insisted: "But you can do all the tricks of all the greatest players who have ever lived, can't you, Jacky? can't you?" Jacky grinned and shrugged. The boy insisted: "You can, though, can't you? You've got 'em on video."

Jacky told him: "You've got to learn from the best if you want to better yourself."

The lad worried: "You're the best, though, Jacky, aren't you?"

Jacky answered him: "I do *my* best, that's all anyone can do." He addressed the entire audience: "And the best tonight and in this election, ladies and gentlemen, is supporting Robert Jarvis, who, I hope with all your help, will be our next Member of Parliament!"

iii

Mary kissed the side of Jacky's throat gently: her arms and legs and body moved against his in their double bed; contentment in mutual warmth. Rain tapped the window spasmodically, varying the rustle from the wind.

No sound from Jessie in the next room. Affection. Longing for a second child. Ebullient impatience seethed a passion so intense she almost woke Jacky to assuage it; thighs parting, pelvis raising, absorbing the cool sheet's inadequate appeasement, intellectual detachment twitched, laconic and shrewd: pregnancy for nine months, then motherhood's torments and bondage. A second child would diminish her laboratory time at Bio-Veracity, impede her research on Ageing.

Fresh, big ideas, however, flitter as vividly as memories from a re-encountered scent. Dainty in diction, she indulged herself. A tiny son would be a multiplicity of stimuli, a gallimaufry of newness, a chiliad of quotidian marvels, any one of which could flick forth that huge intuitive insight she and her researcher colleagues so rarely enjoyed.

Jacky murmured and stirred as her leg touched his. Mary lay still. Footballer, she thought tenderly. Consummate performer in a sphere scorned by conventional intelligentsia. Your physical skills are rated lower than a ballet dancer's, the ingenuity and emotions of your game judged trivial against those of classical music or literature, the drama of your ninety minutes worthless against a theatre play or a night at the opera. Yet such judgements are as right or wrong as they are arbitrary. Products of the human cortex. Neuroses and psychoses twirling with reality in the giddy complex of present society and its modes. For your game encompasses almost every human quality in movement as intricate as strong currents in limpid water. To the mass millions and many an intellectual, football is an art-form equal to any.

A soft bump in Jessica's room. Mary listened, ready to investigate; propped on one elbow; partially uncovering Jacky. Jessie's teddy bear fallen on the floor, she decided. The air was cool on her semi-nudity. Jacky stayed supine. His head injury had been a worry. And yet he talked about signing for an Italian or some other foreign club! Not while I can stop him, she thought fiercely. She had her own life and interests, too! And Jessie needed the security of a settled home. Bad enough with Jacky being away so often. He would soon be off afresh if the new England manager, whoever he might be, picked him for the Sweden Friendly. In that respect, she was glad England was not going to the States for the World Cup. So was his mother. Jacky's mother did not want him to sign for a foreign club, either. Even more so since her stroke. They were going to see her tomorrow. She had improved these past few weeks. If only she could stop worrying about her son Harry's taking his Finals at the L.S.E., and about Jacky's latest injury.

Mary eased carefully down, adjusting the bedclothes.

Her husband heaved abruptly up.

"Nightmare?" she inquired after a few seconds.

"Getting crippled," he agreed. Explaining: "The new England Manager."

"It won't be Wyckliffe."

"It might!"

"No, he's too honest. He's offended too many bigwigs by telling them home truths."

"Most players think he'd be a good man as manager. Even Benny Cawthorne and the Preacher – and they don't often agree. Berrigan thinks so. And Jim Arrowood."

"Just because England's best players think so, the brilliant F.A. strategists and guardians of our national reputation won't pick him. They'll select one of themselves."

Jacky chuckled in friendly exasperation. "You know what you are, don't you?"

"No. Tell me."

"A little shit-stirrer," he rubbed his palm over her breasts' softness and hard nipples.

"Typical coarse, vulgar language, John Day. Exactly what one would expect from a member of your crude sex," her hands stroked his flanks.

"A female chauvinist, hey? There's only one thing to do with you."

"And what's that, you masculine brute?" she taunted yet invited him in a tiny, female voice.

"This," said Jacky, and did it.

CHAPTER 3

The coal fire crackled in Mrs Day's front room grate, a black and red fragment puffing yellow rapped onto the fireproof hearth and scribbled smoke. Jessica's excited laughter and shouts mingled with Mary's friendly calls as they played hide-and-seek among the bushes around the house.

Outside the front garden, two hundred yards of grassland sloped down to Trenton village. Fields beyond, some with cattle, one with a tractor ploughing. Glimpses of the Trent curling through the valley. Distant huge power stations, north and south. Across the river, stray houses and hamlets were tiny amid the springtime.

"These headaches. I get all hot in my head, yet my hands are cold. Feel," Mrs Day's partial paralysis of her left side slowed and slurred her words.

Jacky, concerned, took his mother's work-worn right hand in his, then felt her forehead: "Shall I put some more coal on the fire, Mam?"

"No. It usually goes over after a bit."

"Is there anything I can do to help? Anything at all? We can get some more specialists to come."

"No. It's alright, Jacky. They can't help. All I can do is rest, and try to get better." Jacky smiled, worried yet reassuring, and patted her hand. "You've done more than enough for me. You've done well. All my children. I worry about you."

"You've no need to, Mam."

"I do, though. I can't help it," talking was difficult for her. She began to cry.

"Don't cry, Mam."

"You've done everything for me. Bought me this house and done it up. Paid people to come in and stay with me all the time and help."

"I wish I could persuade you to have a proper nurse."

She calmed down: "No. Those two girls from the village take it in turns to help out everyday and do whatever needs doing. The doctor comes in the morning. And Pete Gregg who you used to play football with in the village team, drops in off his tractor for a word every day. And sometimes he brings eggs and stuff off his farm. He always asks about you."

"When the season's finished, we'll come over and stay for a day or two, Mam, and I'll go see old Pete and all the rest of the locals. Look, Mam, if you need anything, anything at all, don't hesitate to tell me straight away."

"What I would like is for you not to get mixed up in politics. The girl reads about you in the paper to me. And I see you on television. Your dad was like that, always running off to meetings and sticking up posters and delivering election stuff around the villages."

"Rob Jarvis will make a good M.P., Mother."

"You're like your dad, Jacky. Politics," her slow, slurred voice dwindled in disapproval. "Poor old Johnner, he'd have been proud of you," she was looking at Jacky. "You're not going to the World Cup now, then, Jacky."

"Seems not, unfortunately."

"I can't say I'm sorry. You shouldn't be footballing so soon after that bad head."

"It's better now, Mam," he repressed anxiety.

"The newspaper said you might be playing on Saturday. I hope not. Just the thought of you heading that ball," she wrinkled her face in first imagined, then real pain and sucked breath through pursed lips.

"I shall be sitting on the reserves bench. They're giving a local young black kid his first full game try-out, since it's our last match and we're going to finish third in the League anyway."

"That means you'll have all summer to rest and not have to head a football, does it?"

"I'm hoping to play in the England Friendly International against Sweden in Stockholm a week next Saturday, if the new England Team Manager picks me."

"Has England got a new team manager then?"

"Not yet. They're going to announce it on Saturday night, after all the League games are finished."

"I'm worried about our Harry. Has he said anything to you?"

"No."

"I think he's in some kind of trouble. He won't tell me. I worry about him."

"Don't. He's big enough to look after himself."

"He's not, you know."

"A man who looks like getting First Class Honours at the London School of Economics should be."

"It don't matter what you read in books," she persisted in her tired, slurred voice. "I know he's got something on his mind, but he won't say."

"Don't worry, Mam. Whatever it is, it's not that bad. It's certainly not worth worrying about."

"I do worry, though. I can't help it." She lay unmoving, eyes closed. "My head hurts." Mary, Jessica and Mrs Day's helpmate, laughing and exuberant, clattered in through the back door. "I can't stand the noise or excitement now, Jacky, it makes my head throb. Give me one of those pills off the table, there's a good lad."

Jacky did as bidden, then opened the hall door and shushed the noisy threesome.

Mrs Day murmured, protesting: "It's not right to keep the little girl quiet for me, Jacky. It's just that my head's so bad." She put her right hand over her eyes. "I've got into the habit of having a little sleep in the afternoons."

"We'll clear off and leave you in peace, then, Mam."

She objected weakly, worried: "I don't want to drive you away, Jacky."

"You're not driving us away, Mam. It's time for us to leave anyway, and get Jessie fed and bathed and into bed. And I've got to put in a training session. You need your peace and quiet and rest so you can get better. Mary and me'll be giving you a ring every morning and night. And you can always get me at the Forest if you need me urgently."

She lay on her back, hand over her eyes, a little, grey haired, prematurely old woman, inter- spacing her gasping with longer, shuddering breaths. "Pull the curtains to, Jacky, will you? It's better when it's nice and shady in here. That's it. Thank you. You're a good boy, Jacky. I wish Harry would ring me. He's not on the phone. He only writes. He never rings. You'll come and see me next week, will you?"

Jacky said he would.

"Take care of yourself. I don't want you getting a bad head like mine. I do hope you don't have to play on Saturday."

CHAPTER 4

"One-nil! One-nil!" bawled liltingly from five thousand Cockney throats. The Nottingham Forest goalkeeper picked the ball disgustedly from the back of the net and slung it towards the centre spot. Nine minutes were left of the match, plus possible injury time.

The Forest Manager was decisive: "That's it, Jacky. Warm up. You're on at first chance."

The City ground and environs filled with the roar of the Forest faithful as Jacky jogged up and down, did knee bends and sprinted.

Benny Cawthorne beat the black lad to the ball and sent his left winger away to centre from near the corner flag: the Forest goalie palmed the Hammer centre forward's header over the crossbar.

Noise exploded as Jacky ran onto the pitch and swelled and rolled when, following the corner kick he emerged from the goalmouth mêlée, dummied two men, sprinted twenty yards wing-wards upfield and drove a high, forty-five yard diagonal crossfield pass for Jim Arrowood to run onto and curve a distance shot which the Hammers' goalkeeper had to dive to save.

Benny Cawthorne's tough face was a big grin: "You li'l bagger, Jecky, how are you, then? 'Your head better?"

"Doctor says so."

"I'd've rather you kept sitting on that bladdy bench. We need these points if we're going to play in Europe next year."

During the next few minutes, the two men opposed skills again and again. Jacky's freshness gave no advantage. Difference in reflex speed was unobservable. Solid tackle met brilliant dribble. The Cockney's sure positioning and long, quick legs thwarted Jacky each time.

Jacky's presence, however, eased pressure off the Forest players. His few precision passes disturbed the Londoners and created chances from which Jim Arrowood forced goalkeeping saves.

Joy in speed, at having a body which responded perfectly to judgement, energy bubbling laughter in his mind, Jacky throve, probing the Hammers' defence, darting and arcing, changing and following the patterns of play, snatching sustenance from Forest's cheering, singing fans.

A full-power miskick from fifteen yards away by the Hammers' centreback aimed head high two strides to Jacky's right. Jim Arrowood sprinted for the open space near the corner of the Hammers' penalty area: an excellent goalscoring chance should he receive the ball.

Jacky thrust for a bullet header: but in that tick of time between reflex and deed, recalled his mother's damaged brain: he jerked back and twisted to take the ball on his chest: Benny Cawthorne cleared into touch. The crowd groaned; everyone had seen Jacky's reluctance.

Jacky dipped his head, then instantly sucking in a deep breath, sprinted towards the throw-in. He lobbed the mid-air ball over Benny Cawthorne and surged round the Cockney's left, swayed right then went left past a second defender, kicked sharply towards the goal-line fifteen yards from the corner flag, outsprinted a third Hammer player, and, in one movement a foot from the line, spun and chipped the ball high and hard towards the penalty spot for Jim Arrowood running in to score.

Amid tumultuous exultation, many were chuckling and shaking their heads in admiration at the sequence of consummate skill and imagination.

"You l'il facker, Jecky! You li'l, li'l facker!" Benny Cawthorne's face twisted with angry frustration.

"Sorry, Ben."

Two minutes later, the game was over.

"Whoy didn't you soften him up, Benny?" a red-haired West Ham player scowled as he trotted off the pitch.

"Because he's a mate o' mine, ain't you, Jecky?" Benny Cawthorne replied. They stood, waiting for Arrowood to join them. "I don't know what he's worrying about. He's off to play in the States next year, so he ain't bothered about not playing in Europe. Well, Joimes, m' boy, so you've got goal forty-four for the season. We'll just have to hope Derby County lost, if we're to play in Europe." Some thirty yards away, the West Ham manager, holding a portable radio to his ear, suddenly threw up his arms laughing and began jumping around. "Looks like they did. How about coming back wiv me for a celebration tonight? I'll show you lads a good time."

"I can't, Ben," said Jacky. "My wife and daughter are waiting at home with dinner. You're welcome to join us."

CHAPTER 5

"That was a lovely meal, darling," Benny praised Mary. Jim Arrowood concurred. She smiled at them.

Opposite Mary at the dinner table, Jacky had Jessie on his knee. The little girl's left arm was round his neck, fingers loosely playing with his hair. "Top of the Pops has started, Jessie," he said. The little blonde exclaimed, and wriggled eagerly off him and ran beaming out of the room.

"How about that then?!" Benny Cawthorne was astonished. "She likes music, does she?"

"We're free for half an hour," said Jacky. Sound of heavy rock music filled the ground floor. "If we go in there now, she'll be dancing around like the big boys and girls she can see on the screen. She's got a little guitar," Jacky chuckled, "and she stands there bobbing up and down, and jumping about imitating them. And after a time, she takes all her clothes off."

"Striptease, eh?" said Benny. This party I'm going to tonight will see older girls that like to take their clothes off, a Member or two of Parliament maybe, and titled gents and stars of stage, screen and television, etcetera." He looked inquiringly at the other three: "Perhaps this is the wrong kind of fing to be talking about here, eh?"

"We're broad-minded," said Mary.

"In that case, next time you're in Town, you've got an invitation," he grinned.

"Not that broad-minded," said Mary.

"They'll have selected the new England team manager by now," said Jim Arrowood.

"It won't be Wyckliffe," Mary taunted Jacky.

"You don't know," he responded.

"He'd make a good manager," said Benny Cawthorne. "He ain't afraid to take risks and chance his arm. The way he's been hired and fired and quit over principles after making a success wherever he's been has shown that."

"It won't be him," Mary was definite. "They'll pick one of themselves. They always do. A good conservative, a safe man who always follows precedent and the book and never re-writes it."

"Boo," said Jacky.

"We need changes in the present England team, that's for sure," said Jim Arrowood. "So long as they don't drop us three and Richard Trelawney."

They analysed the skills and qualities of England's best players over the past three seasons and illustrated their ideas at first by moving plates and cruets about, then by indicating play-patterns utilising the parquet floor and the pale grey-green speckled walls of the ten by seven yard room, its three-lamped ceiling light, four floor lamps, wall bookcases and cupboards, and finally by shifting the table chairs and the two brown easy chairs about.

Through the westward-facing window, the blossom of the garden apple trees gleamed and birds flitted about. Trees in bud sentinelled plashed and bushy hedgerows. Half a mile away, a copse of pine, birch, oak and sycamore burst wildness against fields varied with spring crops and cattle.

Noise of a single-engined propeller plane low overhead brought awareness of the world outside, bird sounds, the rock music, the white clothed dinner table's empty plates and dishes, the mellow sunniness of the room, their own intensity.

Mary laughed at her stocky husband balancing on one leg kicking a spinning drop-shot as the spare-framed, wide shouldered Benny positioned to counter with the burly, lithe Arrowood crouching for a header.

The men relaxed.

"Anybody for coffee?" Mary inquired. Benny and Jacky preferred tea.

"It'll depend upon getting new young 'uns, if England's going to build a consistent winning side," Jacky summed up the discussion.

Benny said they were all agreed on that, then he commented on the beauty of the countryside.

"That's where I take my training run – behind the spinney and over the fields there, look," Jacky stood at the window, pointing. "I can take a ball with me all the way, and set up posts and obstacles to dribble round. Nobody touches anything out here. They all know me, and I know them."

"Like me in the East End. Sometimes that's a bad fing, sometimes a good."

The television volume lowered: Mary and her daughter's voices were indistinct.

"What about that bank robbery in the East End last week, Benny?" Jacky asked. "According to the newsmen, you're supposed to be friends with all the top villains."

"Benny's one of them," said Jim Arrowood.

The Cockney grinned. "It's common knowledge who done it. Even the Filth know – that is the police to you, Joimes," he enlightened the fair man. "But nobody's talking, of course."

Jim Arrowood wondered why Benny did not volunteer to aid the police.

"What?! Me help the Law?!" Benny Cawthorne laughed with amazement. "Never! Those lads got away wiv a few thousand quid, and all the responsible people say, `Ah! What criminals!' Yet a couple of miles down the road in the City, they steal millions every day, and nobody says anyfink because it's all legal and they own the police and they sit in Parliament and they appoint the judges and they can do what they like, and nobody says a fing." Benny was serious. "Nah, those lads what done that job lawst week, good luck to 'em. They'll piss it up the wall, and spend it on," Mary entered the room with the tea and coffee, "ladies of the night and lose it on dogs and horses and gambling in general, and after a couple of months they'll be as poor as ever they was. Meanwhile, they'll have had a good time and given a few lucky people employment."

"I don't agree with that attitude," said Jim Arrowood. "If you permit people to go thieving and doing what they like simply because they like, nothing and nobody can ever be safe."

"I shall," the Cockney responded. "If not, I'll give 'em a bit of the old Kung Fu," his hands flickered savagery and his left leg kicked high and was back on the floor in an instant. "And if that ain't enough, I'd shoot 'em or get rid of 'em some other way."

Mary was wide-eyed with shocked surprise: "Was that Kung Fu?" she handed out the beverages.

"Yer. Beat a Chinese guy from Liverpool for some sort of championship last year, best of nine, five-two. Grandson of a Taiwanese general he was. My Uncle Ralph got me into it when I was a little lad. Said I had to learn to defend myself. Poor old Uncle Ralph. He was one of the best."

"At Kung Fu?" Mary asked.

"Nah. He had a bad back, di'nt he? Baggered it up at work. Yer, he was a good old geezer was my Uncle Ralph. Brought me up."

"What about your mother? And your father?"

"She was German, wasn't she? Met my Old Man in Berlin when he was in the Army. She came back to England wiv him, and went off wiv some black guy when I was about a year old. The Old Man got run over by a bus coming out of a boozer one Saturday night. That left me and my Uncle Ralph, di'n't it?"

Mary showed concern: "I'm sorry, Benny."

"I was only a baby. I don't remember 'em."

"So your Uncle Ralph brought you up on his own."

"Yer, you might say that, him and an old charlady, Mrs Bellamy, our next door neighbour, together wiv different birds he had living wiv him from time to time. He did his best, old Uncle Ralph. He was a pretty good mate of mine."

"Do you visit him a lot?" Mary wondered.

"I'd have a job, wouldn't I? He was cremated seven years ago."

"Oh, I'm sorry."

"He saw me play for the Hammers two years. Saw me play for England. Pleased as a dog wiv two tails, he was. He loved watching the Hammers, never missed a home game. `Concentrate on football, Benny. And watch your health and your money,' he said. Cancer of the back got him."

Mary expressed sympathy.

"We all got to go sometime, ain't we?" the Cockney was amiable.

"Do you see the charlady these days?"

"Dead – before Uncle Ralph."

"And you're not married, thinking of it?"

"Nah," the Cockney derided, grinning, "I like variety. The more the better. Two's better'n one – keep you warm on both sides. Pardon me, Mary."

She was scornful: "Now, that's a male chauvinist attitude if ever there was one! What do you think your girlfriends would say of that?"

"They love it."

"Then they're not real friends! They're only interested in you for what they can get out of you!"

"Women all are," said Benny.

"What nonsense! If a woman cares for a man, she's not concerned about making a profit off him! She wants him, and him alone! She certainly doesn't want to share him with other women, even though she may lie to him in the beginning so as not to lose him, and even lie to herself."

"You said a true fing there, darling: women are certainly good liars alright. Lead us poor men on by the nose anywhere, can't they, Joimes?"

"I don't know, Benny. I'm not that experienced."

"Why, I thought you was a secret ladies' man! You like women, don't you?"

"I'm taking one to a dance tonight, anyway."

Mary was curious: "Who? Where?"

"Willingby, and you don't know her."

"Serious?"

The good-looking six footer smiled and his blue shirt tightened as he breathed in deep and shrugged powerful shoulders.

"Have I met her? Bring her round, Jim," Mary was bright-eyed and eager.

"Birds, eh?" Benny Cawthorne grinned. "A little romance and they're in their element. Love 'em and leave 'em's best, Joimes."

"I don't agree," said Jacky.

"Play the field, that's my motto," Benny added amicably. "You mean to say you've never been tempted by beautiful women, Jacky? Never wanted anybody except your wife?"

"This conversation's getting a bit too close to the bone for me," Jim Arrowood interrupted.

Mary, sure of Jacky and their relationship, said: "It's alright, Jim. Jacky can answer for himself."

Jacky hesitated, at first worried and apologetic then mellowing into candid affection, all the time holding his wife's gaze: "Yes, Benny, sometimes I see beautiful women I want very much. But it never goes any further than that." He faced the Cockney. "Because, Benny, Mary's not simply a woman to me, she's my friend," he turned to his wife, "my mate," he lowered and cocked his head to smile into Mary's eyes which were wide and moist with emotion, "aren't you?" he put his hand over hers: she leant her cheek against his shoulder.

Mary said softly: "You could make love to another woman if you wanted, Jacky, I wouldn't mind, so long as you were honest, and it was only physical and no more."

Benny Cawthorne spoke easily: "There you are, Jecky. She's given you permission."

Jim Arrowood, brisk and deep-toned, changed the subject: "We shall know who England's new team manager is in a couple of minutes," he stood up, intending to turn on the wireless.

Mary exclaimed: "Is it that time already?!"

As if in answer, her daughter, wearing only a straw hat and a big grin and strumming her guitar, entered bobbing up and down in slow rhythmic circles.

"Here she is!" Benny Cawthorne laughed. "Hello, you beautiful little darling!"

Jessica laughed back and ran to her father holding up her arms. Jacky lifted her to his chest, kissing her and stroking her hair as Mary looked fondly on.

"Married bliss," the Cockney commented, ironic and benevolent.

Jim Arrowood switched on the radio.

"England's new manager is Denzil Wyckliffe, current manager of Lincoln City. He takes up the post immediately."

"What did I tell you?!" Mary, roguishly triumphant, spoke above the Radio Nottingham newscaster. "I always knew Wyckliffe was going to be appointed manager!"

The men guffawed, exclaiming and commenting on the boldness of her lie.

Jim Arrowood stretched to turn the radio off.

"In the Workfield by-election,"

"Wait," Jacky bade.

"...the latest opinion poll published today showed a three per cent lead for the Conservatives. In the last General Election, the Conservatives won with a comfortable majority. Sir Alec Sinjin-Frobisher, the Conservative candidate, is confident of retaining the seat which his party has represented since 1951. Robert Jarvis..,"

"Good old Rob," said Mary.

"...the Labour candidate, is equally sure of victory."

Robert Jarvis's recorded voice spoke: "The Conservative record in Workfield and District is one of consistent neglect and continual opposition to working men's and the ordinary voter's interests."

The newsreader resumed: "Nottingham Forest drew one-one today."

"Turn it off," said Benny Cawthorne; Jim Arrowood did. "I'm surprised nobody's been getting at you for backing the Labour candidate, Jecky."

"They have," said Jacky.

"I mean at your club."

"My dad stopped them," Jim Arrowood spoke. "He's the majority shareholder."

"I wouldn't have thought he was Labour."

Jim Arrowood chuckled and the Days smiled. "No," said Jim. "But he likes Jacky, and wants to keep him playing for the Forest and setting up goals for me to score."

"You backing Jecky's man?"

"I haven't got a vote in this constituency, otherwise I might. I'm not bothered about politics."

"He's a Tory," Mary was direct. Jim Arrowood grinned. "What do you expect when his father is one of the richest men in England and farms half Lincolnshire?" Jim Arrowood's grin widened.

Jessica began calling loudly, squirming and twisting, demanding her mother's attention. When Mary took her from Jacky, the little girl started to cry and struggle, wanting to play and be read to. Jacky explained that after Top of the Pops, they usually tumbled about together for half an hour, sang nursery rhymes and looked at picture books before Jessie went to bed.

"We'll let you get some peace, then, eh, Joimes? It's a nice drive up to London," said Benny Cawthorne. "Alright, darling," he comforted the little girl who hid her face against her mother, "we're not taking your daddy and mummy away from you. We're going."

The men stood outside in the cold, sunny evening, Jim Arrowood in a baggy old Harris tweed coat with leather frayed at the cuffs and elbows, open-neck blue shirt, faded jeans and old brown brogues, Benny immaculate in dark blue suit, white shirt, maroon tie, gleaming black shoes, gold wristwatch and armband. Jim Arrowood's vehicle was a mud-stained battered twenty-year-old Morris estate wagon, Benny's a gleaming new black Jaguar.

"Anybody'd fink you was a poor man," Benny jibed.

Jim Arrowood smiled.

Jacky nodded at the Cockney's suit: "Saville Row, Benny?"

"Nah. Better'n that," Benny was scornful. "Best tailor in England made this, according to the 'Cutter and Tailor'. Went to school wiv my Uncle Ralph. Yer, nice place you've got here, Jecky." The three men gazed at the nineteenth century farmhouse with its discreet modernisations and white-painted windows, comfortably protected by lilacs, fruit trees and bushes, and graced with vegetable gardens and bright green lawns bordered by flowers. Their attention concentrated on the ten-acre field east and north of the former crew yard and stables behind the farmhouse. Two sets of wheelable goalposts on its long sides, one on each short. A thirty-yard stretch of forty-foot high netting behind the farthest posts. "Very nice. Very nice indeed. This is where you train together and perfect your tricks, eh?" They nodded. From the house, the sound of the telephone wafted small yet clear.

"Twice a week," said Jim Arrowood.

"It gives us a goal or two we otherwise wouldn't get," said Jacky.

"Like this afternoon, you couple of cants," Benny was rueful; the others chuckled. "Well, I tell you, lads, I like having you two up there in front of me in the England team: I always know the opposition's got somefink to bladdy worry about. Let's hope this guy Wyckliffe lives up to expectations, eh?"

"Jacky!" Mary was in the house front porch. "Telephone! Your brother Harry!"

CHAPTER 6

Jacky leant against the wall, shadowed from the dim orange street lights paralleling the northern side of Nottingham Midland Railway Station. A double-decker pulsed east along Carrington Street followed by a taxi, a couple of cars going west towards the city centre. Not too much traffic at this time of night. Near midnight. Train due soon.

Jacky hunched into his turned-up raincoat collar and scarf and pulled his cap down further over his forehead as a foursome clattered out of the back entrance of the pub on the corner and came towards him. A gang of youths and girls, shrieking, bawling, laughing, playing football with beer cans, vibrated past the railway station corner, eating fish and chips bought on Arkwright Street, destined for Mapperley and Arnold by their shouts.

The foursome from the pub passed, laughing beer fumes, scarcely noticing him.

What was so mysterious that Harry could not, would not talk about it on the 'phone? What?

Jacky shrugged, looked at his watch. Give it another five minutes. He preferred the shadows' anonymity to the station's sociability. Fame was troublesome when one wished to be alone.

Not that he grumbled about fame. His meant he need never worry about money again. Dan Arrowood's business advice and lawyers' and accountants' directions in the beginning had seen to that, and these last four years, he had Jock Mackenzie, his own business adviser. His best investment, in Bio-Veracity shares, had topped three million and was still climbing.

What good was money, though, when you had enough of it to cover your needs? It could not buy back his mother's health. He had tried. No one could help her. Only Nature. And time. She had been right about Harry. She could often sense things. Mary could, too.

He had not told Mary about his fear of heading the ball that afternoon. He probably would. He usually did. They normally told each other everything.

Another bus went by on Carrington Street.

Angelo kicking his head.

Jacky winced. You could never escape if they wanted to cripple you at any cost. If you were there where the action was, you were vulnerable.

He and Jim Arrowood had video-taped and studied every type of dirty trick and how to avoid, nullify and lessen their effect.

But you couldn't! You couldn't stop them all!

A good referee and linesman helped.

Ultimately, a vicious player who was ruthless or skilful enough could cripple you. Sooner or later. As Angelo had.

He did not want his brain injured.

Not like his mother.

Fear hunched his shoulders and shuddered his spine.

He relaxed, and breathed in. Hint of diesel oil. Petrol.

Three minutes past midnight. Train due.

"Right, Harry. Tell me what all this is about." The car stood quietly in the dark lane. Several miles away across the fields, Nottingham's lights glowed up the sky.

"I'm scared. I know you'll think I'm crazy. I know you'll think –" Harry's head jerked to stare out of his side window. "I am crazy," the tension that had mounted towards hysteria was gone from Harry's voice. "Stupid, ringing you up like I did, coming up here dragging you out in the middle of the night. Idiocy." He faced Jacky: "I was terrified out of my wits in London. That seems unreal sitting here beside you in peaceful Nottinghamshire countryside. It is unreal. But when I go back to London, I shall be frightened again – somebody's going to kill me."

"Why?" incredulity tinged astonishment.

"Oh, it's –," Harry's face wrinkled in cynical self-contempt and fear; he twisted to stare out of his side-window. He breathed in deeply and said in a calm voice: "I did a stupid thing. It was entirely my fault and I'm completely to blame." He faced front, sighed, then went on quietly: "Last

Monday, I was sitting in the L.S.E. refectory, talking with half a dozen others. A Chinese student who's reading the same subjects as I but who has a different tutor came up and asked me if I would do him a favour and put a £110 bet on for him. He was going to a tutorial and he didn't know how long he'd be. Everything was written down. All I had to do was go to the betting shop and place the bet. I agreed, and put the money and paper in my pocket."

"Then forgot about it," said Jacky.

Harry's voice rose: "We were discussing Stalinism! I was so interested! Then my girlfriend came along and said, `Come back to my place, Harry'. Oh God! God!" He was near tears. "I didn't mean to keep the money! I didn't, Jacky! I forgot. That's all. I forgot."

"The bet came up."

"Nearly £20,000." Jacky whistled. "He had a yankee: six doubles, four trebles and an accumulator – all the winners at Newmarket." Harry was extremely upset. "I didn't mean it, Jacky! I didn't! I didn't! I genuinely forgot."

"So you told the Chinese student."

"He went crazy."

"It's a difficult situation, isn't it?" Jacky was thoughtful. "I can understand your not being on good terms with that Chinese after that, but," Jacky was both sceptical and reassuring, "he's not going to kill you for it."

"It wasn't his money, Jacky! That's the point! It was some kind of gangster's! Oh, it's imbecilic!" Harry tried to be rational.

"You mean this gangster's threatened to kill you?"

"I don't know! That's the imbecility!" Harry struggled to keep control, and, with difficulty, succeeded. "I'll take it from the beginning." He sucked in an enormous breath through his mouth, and whooshed it out. He spoke quietly: "When this Chinese kid –"

"What's his name?" Jacky interrupted.

"We call him Billy Woo; but that's not his real name: it's too difficult to pronounce. Friends call him that, and I don't feel very much like his friend at the moment." Harry paused; Jacky stayed silent. "When I found the bet in my pocket that night when I went to bed, it was too late. I didn't have his phone number, so I couldn't ring. And anyway I was going to give him the money back next day."

"Anybody know that? Did you tell anybody?"

"No. It was too late, you see, Jacky!" Anguish broke: "I didn't realise until I took my jacket off! It was in my left pocket and I don't often put my hand in my left pocket! You don't normally."

Influenced by Jacky's stillness, Harry calmed down.

"Anyway, when I told him the next day, he accused me of wanting to keep the £110. I'll never, never, never take responsibility for money like that again in my life!" Harry was savagely determined. "I'll have witnesses, and papers signed, and guarantees. How can you persuade somebody in that situation though? I swore my innocence. But what can you say? Then he got the idea that I'd placed the bet and collected the winnings! Nothing I said could sway him! Oh God," Harry groaned and bowed his head and rubbed his forehead with the back of his hand and sighed. "I told him I had to go to a tutorial and we'd talk about it that afternoon. He wouldn't listen. I'd robbed him and I'd have to pay."

"He can't make you, Harry. Not over a bet, in a situation like that."

"I did see him that afternoon, and he'd calmed down a lot. He said maybe I hadn't kept the money and maybe I had intended giving the £110 back if the bet had gone down, but the bet wasn't his. He'd only agreed to put it on for somebody else."

"Who?"

"I don't know. That's it! I don't know! He didn't say, and it didn't seem important at the time. I could see Billy Woo was in a fix. The bettor – the gambler – would be saying to Billy Woo what Billy Woo had said to me! Anyway, Billy Woo said he would talk to this man and try to explain. I told Billy Woo that he could blame me, it was my fault. It was my fault! Next day he came and told me the gambler said I would have to pay: I had either meant stealing the stake money or I'd collected the winnings! I wanted to know the man's name. Billy Woo wouldn't reveal it. The man and his friends weren't to be played with."

"Why didn't this gangster put the bet on himself instead of asking a young student to do it for him?"

"I don't know. I suppose he knew Billy Woo and that Billy Woo backs horses regularly. Billy Woo is a gambler. I see him playing cards for money every day, and he must win because he's always got a walletful."

"He seems a strange fellow," Jacky was sardonic. "What I do not understand is why he did not place that wager himself – and straightaway, with so much money at risk, and for such a dangerous third party."

"I told you!" Harry was strained. "He didn't have time."

"He should have made time, with a bet like that and for such rough customers. He knows you've got no money of your own, does he?"

"Yes."

"So he will expect you to turn to me for some. Where does he come from? What is his background?"

"He's a boat refugee from Saigon."

"How old is he?"

"Mid-twenties."

"Mm," said Jacky. "Do you know what I think, Harry? I think it is a con. job. This stuff about a mysterious gangster is simply a threat to frighten you," Harry, startled, stared at him, "and to raise some money off me, or whatever part of it Billy Woo is willing to settle for. I don't think there is a gangster, Harry. My opinion is that this Chinese is a very worldly-wise and cunning customer. I don't fancy giving him anything. He's got his money back, let him be satisfied. My advice, Harry, is that you go tell your tutor everything –"

"I already have," Harry cut in. "We've talked to Billy Woo's tutor with Billy Woo present. He denied the existence of any third party!"

"There you are then," said Jacky, relaxing.

"Afterwards, on our own, he said he had to say that, I still owed the money, and he would deny the existence of any third party and he would tell any outsiders, tutors, the Principal of the London School of Economics, the police, anybody, that the matter was forgotten."

"This man is obviously somebody you'll do well to avoid in future, Harry."

"He said that the gambler wanted his money, he would tell the gambler about my bringing in the tutors, and it was up to the gambler what to do next."

Jacky was contemptuous: "He's as full of hot air as anybody I've ever known!"

"The thing is, I've seen a Chinese following me."

Jacky's contempt deepened: "Good God! Harry, you don't need to bother about this nonsense. It's some friend of Billy Woo's doing him a favour. If there were a gangster, hurting a university student like you who hasn't any money wouldn't do him any good. In fact, it'd do the opposite: the police would hunt him till they caught him; the newspapers wouldn't let the matter drop – I'd see to that. If there were a gangster involved, though, Harry, I would probably be tempted at the end of the day to give you the money, especially if there seemed a real risk of your getting hurt. But what you must do now is talk to the police in London. They ought to have a word with Mr Billy Woo, and that friend of his."

Harry, though calm, remained apprehensive. "I'm still frightened, Jacky, deep inside. I feel threatened."

"Because you're not used to threats. And you're all tensed up from studying too hard and worrying about your exams. Try and forget this whole stupid bet business, Harry, and about being threatened. It's not easy, but try. Christ, the times I've been threatened! Death threats, too," he shook his head in near disbelief at human folly. "Nutters and people on the make, Harry, the world's full on 'em."

Both were smiling, Harry nervously.

"I never asked about your head, Jacky."

The older brother's smile vanished, his manner stayed easy: "It's alright. Fully better now. More than I can say about my mother's. She says she never hears from you."

Harry grunted an opposing laugh, and said he had rung her the previous night, that he rang her every week. "I can't do any more for her than I do! If I could, I would! I've been averaging ten hours a day concentrated swotting these last few weeks, Jacky! My Finals start on Wednesday! Then the trouble with this bet –."

"You see? You're overwrought." Jacky's certainty relaxed his brother. "Forget your wager worries, Harry! Concentrate on doing your best in your exams."

"If only they ask the right questions. There's so much luck to it."

"Ay, but in the long run, you make your own. Tell you what I'll do to put the final cap on this betting rubbish. The Chief Constable of Nottingham is one of Forest's firmest supporters. I'll ring him first thing tomorrow. We can get his advice. If necessary, he can speak to the police down in London for you. Satisfied?"

"Yes," Harry was smiling shakily.

"He'll want to talk about football," Jacky, amused, turned on the engine, "the Forest this season, last season, next season!" he eased the car gently off the grass verge, "about Wyckliffe, and about England's chances against Sweden, and our missing the World Cup."

"You think Wyckliffe will pick you? You only played a few minutes this afternoon."

"We'll have to wait and see just who he does pick."

CHAPTER 7

"Jingo Byrnes!" Jacky exclaimed, amazed.

Wyckliffe was businesslike: "He's kept that Bundesliga team of his from relegation two seasons running. My eyewitness reports of him say he's as good as ever."

"But Jingo Byrnes!" Jacky's voice held wonder; he was wide-eyed and pleased. "The Press and television'll go crazy." Rain tapped his gymnasium window, and glistened the training field and hedges like a skilful oil painting; smell of embrocation; polish gleamed on the wooden floor.

"J.N.G. Byrnes is one of the finest midfielders in Europe," Wyckliffe was crisp. "My job is to pick the best England side possible. If he's good enough, he's in. Tomorrow morning, twelve o'clock, the Sincil Bank ground, Lincoln. And don't be late," Wyckliffe was friendly and firm.

Jacky stared smiling open-mouthed at the receiver purring in his hand.

"Jacky," Mary prompted on the extension.

"He's picked Jingo Byrnes! And half the Young England team as well! And he's changed training quarters to Lincoln!"

"Well, they did say Wyckliffe would be controversial."

CHAPTER 8

i

"Hello, lads, I'm Jacky Day." Nervous smiles relaxed into amusement at Jacky's thinking he needed to give his name.

"Jed Lennox," the broad-shouldered, light brown lad, shook Jacky's outstretched hand.

Eddy Corelli was merry brown-eyed, black-haired, thin. David Lewis, a well-built sixfooter, sallow, and wavy black-haired, wore his clothes with the elegance of a professional model.

"Bob Milburne," the fourth muttered shyly and bent his eggshaped head with its thin fair hair to frown at and scrape the turf with his left toecap.

"I saw you got two good goals against Young Italy, Bob," said Jacky.

Not raising up, the fair head jerked indicating Eddy Corelli: "He made 'em," Milburne's low voice and Geordie accent reduced the words to near incomprehensibility.

"Yes! I did!" Eddy Corelli laughed, and all except Bob Milburne shared mirth over Corelli's lack of modesty.

"That's one thing you can be sure of about Mester Corelli, Jacky, he's norr afraid to blow his own trumpet," said the coloured Jed Lennox.

"Well, if I don't, who will?" Eddy Corelli's Birmingham lilt was as pronounced as the brown man's Hull tones were reassuring.

"Where's your fifth man, Winston Jones?" Jacky's gaze flickered searching the Sincil Bank ground for the black teenager.

The four youths looked at one another. Jed Lennox said: "He'll probably turn up late, knowing him."

"He'd better not," Jacky was serious. "Wyckliffe's not a man to fool about with. If he says a thing, he means it. He said get here by twelve."

"It's only a minute or so past," said David Lewis.

"Jecky!" Benny Cawthorne's loud greeting made everyone turn in his direction. "You arrived safe, then?" the Cockney clapped Jacky on the shoulder. "Good morning, lads." He shook hands and the youths gave their names. "Where's Jingo Byrnes? 'You seen him, Jecky?" They gazed about. "Yer, there he is, talking to Joe Berrigan." The two men were sitting on their own in the third row of the eastern stands. Benny bawled: "Good morning, Jingo! How are you?! Welcome home, stranger! What do you fink of this place? Back of bladdy nowhere, ain't it?! Right among the turnips!"

Jacky protested mildly: "I was born only a dozen miles up the road, Benny. And Jim about a dozen that way," Jacky pointed northeast.

Benny bellowed: "You hear that, Jingo?! Jecky Day was born here, him and Jim Arrowood, the poor baggers!"

Richard Trelawney, talking to Jim Arrowood some forty yards away, shook his head in disgust.

"I've been in worse places," Jingo Byrnes said.

"I'll bet you bladdy have!" the Cockney shouted meaningfully.

"Go easy, Benny," Jacky muttered so that only the Cockney and the four youths could hear. "It's his first time back in England since they let him out of jail six years ago."

Benny Cawthorne waved a careless arm at Byrnes and Berrigan: "See you later, lads! That's a big church you've got there on the hill, Jecky. Sort o' dominates the skyline when you're coming into the town. You can see it for miles off."

"That's Lincoln Cathedral, you ignorant sod!"

"Oh, that'll be nice for the Preacher and Joe Berrigan to have a look at while they're here."

"Me, too," said Eddy Corelli.

"Religious?" Benny inquired. The swarthy youth nodded.

"Lincoln used to be a centre for medieval Jewry in England," David Lewis remarked quietly.

"You would know about that, wouldn't you?" the Cockney observed sprightly, and Lewis smiled.

"Used to be a fortress town for the Romans about a couple of thousand years back," Jacky explained. "They dug up some remains a few years ago."

"I'll bet those geezers didn't have much to say for themselves after all that time," said Benny.

"Buildings," Jacky clarified. "They might have found a skeleton or two as well, I don't know."

"Hello, hello," said Benny, "here comes Wyckliffe. Looks like we're going to get some action. We're all gathered."

"Except Winston," Eddy Corelli noted.

"Why, it's gone twelve, ain't it?" Benny said. Jed Lennox's goodlooking brown features began frowning anxiously, he peered around.

The players and other squad personnel moved to group in front of Denzil Wyckliffe.

"Good morning, gentlemen," the England Team Manager began. Sound of someone running and shouting made him turn.

Heavy shouldered, slightly bow legged, carrying his bulging scarlet holdall as though it were an empty carrier bag, the black-garbed newcomer bounded fast and lithely over the grass.

"What a handsome man!" Benny Cawthorne murmured a few inches from Jacky's right ear.

Winston Jones, oozing sweat, gleamed like black, shiny leather. "There was this bird! – we was talking! Then I met the reporters out there!" Winston's rush of broadest Cockney coupled with his manner and appearance caused some of the group to exhibit mirth. "Aw, it's all right!" Winston condescended. "I'm here now. What ' you looking like that for?! I'm here!"

Wyckliffe was hard: "You're late, without reason. I said twelve o'clock, I meant twelve o'clock. When I say a thing, I mean it."

Winston was aggrieved, belligerent: "But it's nuffink!"

"Don't argue. You're wrong – be wrong. Let's hear an apology to everybody for coming late and wasting our time." Wyckliffe's gaze was stern on Jones. The Brixton youth glared sullenly back a couple of seconds, wishing to dispute, then looked aside and mumbled the necessary.

ii

Jacky, panting with exertion, stood in the centre circle and wiped sweat from his eyes. Benny Cawthorne was trotting towards him. At the far end of the factory sports ground, Denzil Wyckliffe and several other players were heading for the changing rooms and showers. On Jacky's right, Jim Arrowood, Jingo Byrnes, Bob Milburne and Winston Jones were outside the penalty box alternately shooting in at Joe Berrigan and practising set patterns trying to dribble round Jed Lennox, the Preacher and Dave Lewis, with Eddy Corelli now helping to defend now attack.

"What do you fink, Jecky?" the Cockney opened.

"Too early to tell yet. Picking the young 'n's was a bold move. And picking Jingo!" Jacky spoke with appreciative near-incredulity.

"The reporters are after him like flies, ain't they? Giving him eighteen months for what he done was a diabolical liberty. He should never have been sent to jail. Never. Not for that."

"I can understand them. But in Jingo's case," Jacky shrugged. pushed his bottom lip over his top and sighed through his nostrils. "Hypocrites, Benny," he summed up resignedly. "This is England. Hypocrisy. One set of morals for private use, another for public. And Jingo, a comprehensive school graduate from the slums of Barnsley, didn't have any friends in high places to hush things up, or defend him like that old public schoolboy the judge let off last week with a warning instead of prison because the judge had been to the same public school and felt sorry for him. I say all honour to Wyckliffe for giving Jingo another chance." They gazed at the Team Manager approaching the changing rooms.

"No messing about wiv our new boss. He seems to know what he's doing. Quiet around here, ain't it?" The sports ground held two football pitches, four empty tennis courts and had plenty of well kept grass to spare. Hedges marked its boundaries. Fields to the east and south where, several miles away, Lincoln Cathedral predominated. Village houses lined the ground's north side, at its west the clubrooms and amenities adjacent to the car park of the light engineering works whose facilities the England squad were utilising.

Both men focussed suddenly some thirty yards away on Eddy Corelli sprawling after a savagely unjust charge from Winston Jones: he ignored the ball which Richard Trelawney was pulling under control, smashed straight into the big Devon man felling him, then whirled making to kick the prone Corelli: Jim Arrowood pushed him off balance.

"Facking cant! Bastards! White bastards, all of you!" Winston's features snarled fury at them all.

"Me, too?" Jed Lennox's manner was mediatory.

"You ain't white! It's these bastards! Corelli, sneering, poking fun all the time!"

Eddy Corelli, doubled up wincing and rubbing his side, gasped: "I was joking, that's all!"

"I ought to smash your head in," the Brixton man's rage boiled into a sudden roar, "you facking cant!!" he lunged towards Corelli; Benny Cawthorne stepped in front of the thin youth and Jed Lennox wrapped his arms around Winston.

"Cool it, chum," Benny Cawthorne's tones were neutral, his blue eyes unblinkingly confronted Winston Jones's insane glare.

"You, too, white shit!"

"Okay, black twat," Benny Cawthorne's bloodlust was as deadly in its quietness as the negro's in its fury.

In one swift sequence, Winston Jones sank at the knees, wrenched free and kicked for the crotch. A moment later, he was face down on the ground with his leg twisted in Benny Cawthorne's grip.

"I ought to break your leg, son!"

The other players protested instantly.

"Children!" the thirty-eight year old Berrigan ridiculed the combatants. "Little boys." He shook his head slowly, and sucked his tongue tut-tutting.

"And we're supposed to be team-mates," Richard Trelawney said with disgust.

"Let him go, Benny," said Jacky.

"You're in the England squad, Winston," Jed Lennox appealed almost plaintively.

Benny Cawthorne released his hold, simultaneously stepping quickly out of striking range.

Winston Jones rolled over, quietened yet vicious. "I'm better than all you white bastards! Faster, shoot harder, jump higher, better! I showed that in training this afternoon!"

"You didn't!" Eddy Corelli denied strongly.

"Those are things we can easily prove," said Joe Berrigan. "Since I'm only a goalkeeper, I'll freely admit you're better at all of them than me. But I think you'll admit I'm a bit better goalie than you." The Liverpudlian's remark induced amusement. "If you think you can kick a ball further than Jim Arrowood or beat Jacky Day and Benny Cawthorne over five yards and Jim Arrowood over fifty, it's easily arranged. We've got plenty of balls here," he gestured at the dozen footballs they had been using.

"Shooting from the goal-line at the other goal," Jacky suggested. They all looked reflexively towards the far goal which was being used by other players, then east towards the pitch recently vacated by the remainder of the England squad. Winston Jones, scowling, with ill-humoured energy thrust David Lewis out of his path and ran at a ball lying some dozen yards nearby.

Jones's rightfoot kick soared to well over eighty yards away, bounced four times and ran past and wide of the one hundred-yard distant goal.

Jim Arrowood's face was serious. He carefully placed a ball where Winston's had been and measured off his run-up.

His kick, though long, was visibly short of Jones's. But its accuracy trickled it over the goal-line and into the net arousing spontaneous appreciation.

Jingo Byrnes's subsequent rightfooter was on line, but several yards short. As was Bob Milburne's.

"Now the left foot," said Jim Arrowood.

"Count me out," said Jingo Byrnes.

Winston Jones, sneering, stabbed a ball into position, ran and kicked with graceful power. It was short of the goal and would have gone wide.

Jim Arrowood, concentrating and measuring all the variables, kept his try accurate, but it, too, wanted distance.

"Go on, Bobby," Eddy Corelli gave encouragement as the expressionless Milburne positioned. "He's a natural left footer, aren't you, Bobby?"

It took ground over eighty yards away, and was in the net at the fourth bounce. The little group clapped, smiling, and congratulated the perturbed seventeen year old.

"Okay, Winston," the green-jerseyed Berrigan accepted challengingly, "you've shown you've got a hell of a kick on you. Let's see how fast you are."

Richard Trelawney and Jingo Berrigan decided not to compete.

Joe Berrigan as starter was approximately five yards from the goal-line, Jingo Byrnes twenty and Richard Trelawney at the centre spot. The others spaced at three-foot intervals behind the goal-line, backs to the direction they had to run.

"Ready?" said Berrigan. "Go!"

At five yards, Jacky was three feet up on Benny Cawthorne, five on Eddy Corelli who was inches ahead of Jed Lennox with the others behind. At twenty yards, he was three clear of the fourth man, Bobby Milburne, with Cawthorne and Lennox having bettered their positions. But by two-thirds distance, Jim Arrowood and Winston were with him and Bobby Milburne a foot back with the others a yard and a half behind abreast. At forty yards, he was a pace down on the three leaders and Jed Lennox and David Lewis were nearly level, Benny and Eddy Corelli a stride adrift.

Five yards from the finish, Jim Arrowood's head went back and he gritted his teeth and surged with all his power to pull back on Winston Jones's narrow lead.

"I won!" Winston Jones was jubilant and danced around. "Yah! What did I tell you?!"

"Dead heat," said Richard Trelawney. "I could not separate you."

"What do you mean?!" Winston snarled. "I won! I won!"

The Preacher spoke quietly: "As God is my witness, I could not separate you."

"Yah," Winston Jones was disgusted, "you're all the same, white men ganging up on the black man."

Jim Arrowood was smiling and panting hard: "It's alright, he won. Congratulations," he held out his hand to the young negro who took it suspiciously, searching the other's demeanour for mockery.

Joe Berrigan strolled leisurely up: "Well run, Winston. Well run, lads."

"You idle sod, Joseph," panted Benny Cawthorne. The tall goalkeeper grinned.

"I don't know how we can decide who can jump highest," Berrigan addressed them. "We all know it's a matter of positioning and timing probably more than height."

"I can clear six-six," Winston Jones challenged lifting his chin, his gaze embracing them with complacent superiority. "I did six-ten in practice when I trained for the decathlon."

Jim Arrowood shrugged: "Six foot was my best at school."

"Five-ten," said Bobby Milburne.

Winston invited further comment. No one spoke. His arrogance was clear: "I told you I was best." He turned to Eddy Corelli: "So you don't have to be poking fun all the time, right?"

"You're not best," Eddy Corelli retorted levelly, "Jacky is. And Jim Arrowood's better than you, and so is Bobby." His serious expression suddenly crinkled in laughter: "And me, too, for that matter, and Benny, and Jingo and Jed, and – and –," his mirth prevented him from continuing.

Winston Jones scowled while the others indulged in various degrees of amusement.

Except Richard Trelawney who decided: "Practice over. Time to join the others."

"You're hoping to see Joyce tonight, ain't you?" Benny Cawthorne was sly.

The Preacher replied crisply: "Yes, I always look forward to seeing my wife, Mr Cawthorne."

The Cockney grinned broadly: "Nuffink like a bit of crumpet to raise a man's expectations and provide nourishment in times of direst need. Mary coming, Jecky?"

"We're going over to my mother's."

"I've got a nice little bird in Lincoln waiting," said Benny. "Caw, look at that!" His erection was prodding up his shorts. "Just finking about it's enough!"

The Preacher's expression seethed disgust: "You are absolutely the most crude, vulgar –!"

"Why, Richard, darling," the Cockney grinned, "I didn't know you cared. It ain't in your league," he nodded at the big man's groin.

"You filthy, disgusting – !" Richard's loathing was beyond words. He addressed the teenagers: "I would advise you boys not to listen to this animal. He has a mind and mouth like a sewer!"

The Cockney said cheekily, grinning broadly: "Richard's got a dong on him – "

"I'm off!" Trelawney loudly gave his tormentor no chance to continue. To the older men, he said: "I'm surprised at you, encouraging this foul tongued – "

"I'll join you, Richard," said Jim Arrowood; Trelawney, Joe Berrigan and David Lewis moved off. Bobby Milburne glanced anxiously after them, hesitant whether to stay or leave.

Benny Cawthorne cupped his hands round his mouth and called after the receding group: "He's got a dong on him like a horse!"

Winston Jones was grinning crookedly, superior: "White men have got little cocks. Not like mine."

Benny delivered judgement quietly, almost indifferent to the Negro: "Not as big as the Preacher's you ain't. He's got a cock on him like a donkey, the poor sod."

"One thing's for sure, Benny," said Jacky, "you are a foul-mouthed, insensitive so-and-so. Richard's basically a decent chap."

"I could promise to improve, but I fink I'm too far gone," said the Cockney.

iii

The hotel lounge was full of England players, officials, girlfriends, wives and children. Mary greeted acquaintances, her bright eyes missing little. "Ho, ho," she exclaimed quietly. "So that's Jim's girlfriend. She has made him smarten up! Joyce Trelawney has spotted them." Jacky changed stance to look; he did not stop bub-bubbing for Jessica as she flapped his lips with one hand and held his hair lightly with the other. A tall, attractive young woman with longer than shoulder length fair hair was holding hands with Jim Arrowood, handsome in medium grey suit, white shirt and England tie. They were being detained by a big brown-haired woman wearing a mauve costume and matching hat.

The girl in the doorway was unusually beautiful, her body displayed rather than concealed in a high necked, sleeveless white dress. Wavy chestnut hair over slender shoulders and large breasts. Little waist and hands, long elegant legs and small feet in white, high heeled sandals.

Noisy conversation and laughter stopped. Only a few continued talking.

"Sexy," Mary lilted murmuring to Jacky who glanced still bub-bubbing as Jessie flapped his lips.

Benny Cawthorne in perfectly tailored light grey suit appeared behind the girl and steered her forward. Conversation recommenced. Most men were grinning, some appreciatively, some self-consciously.

"Booh!" Jacky suddenly punctuated his bub-bubbing and thrust his face with widely smiling eyes an inch towards Jessica's causing her to shriek with laughter and strain instinctively to escape.

"Jecky, Mary. Hello Jessica – not saying anyfink then? Like this girl here," Benny indicated his girlfriend. "She said she wasn't going to open her mouth to speak, and she hasn't. How about that, Jecky? It's Heaven when a woman keeps her mouth shut, eh?"

"We'll merely ignore him," said Mary haughtily, and put her nose in the air, sniffed twice, then smiled at the beauty who grinned back and gave two tiny nods.

"I saw that," said Benny. "But it don't count, do it? – you didn't speak. Funny fing is when we're alone, she can talk the hind leg off a bleeding donkey."

"You've still got both your hind legs anyway," said Mary.

"I ain't a donkey."

"What's that carrot juice on your shirt then?" Mary stared, serious, and laughed gleefully when Benny sought the non-existent stain. The girl and Jacky smiled. Jessica began to struggle to be free.

"I could answer that one, too, but I won't, Mrs Day," said Benny. He felt in his pocket; Jacky squatted to put his daughter down. "Alright if I give your little girl a chocolate?" Both nodded. The Cockney produced a paper-sealed After Dinner mint.

"The gang's all here, but I haven't seen Jingo Byrnes," said Mary. She fluttered a wave to Jim Arrowood and his girlfriend.

"Nah, he's in his room listening to music, keeping out of everybody's way."

"That's awful," Mary said.

"Depends on your point of view," said the Cockney. "The Press and TV are out to crucify him first chance they get. So he's not giving 'em it. Well, we only stopped to say hello on our way out. Shall we be going, darling?"

"Sightseeing?" Jacky asked.

"Yer. We'll ring the cathedral bells while we're at it."

"Jessie, Jacky, and Dr Mary Day, bio-chemist and research worker. Elizabeth Helen Langdale – Beth, my lady love," Jim Arrowood conducted the introductions.

"How did you meet him? Tell me all," said Mary.

"Through the Equestrian Fellowship where I work. A private, rathah special organisation of which Jim and his fathah are membahs. They breed the most gorgeous Shires and Clydesdales!"

"From the sound of you, my dear, you did not grow up in any backstreet slum," said Mary.

"In the countreh, actualleh, with my great-grandmothah, the Dowager Duchess of Brierley. My parents divorced when I was a child. Mothah still lives in Brazil, I think, with her third, or fourth – or is it her fifth husband? Daddeh was killed in a 'copter crash on a N.A.T.O. exercise – he was a majah in the Guards, leaving lots of death duties and debts and me an orphan at twenty-one. I'm twenty-three. Broke. An old maid. Sniff, sniff," Beth touched her nose tip with a knuckle, pretending to cry.

Jim Arrowood, arm round her waist, continued: "She's also a first rate horsewoman, cordon bleu cook, expert on flowers and bee keeping, and about as loopy as they come," he kissed her temple.

"Charming," grinned Mary. "You're the first great grand-daughter of a Dowager Duchess I've met."

"You're my first biochemist. And your husband," her gaze moved to Jacky, "is my first grass roots socialist. Of course, I've met tons of undergrad. socialists."

"Three," said Jim Arrowood. "Her second cousins – Winchester and Cambridge, Eton, Harrow and Oxford. Twits."

"Oh Jim! Don't be so awful! I've met lots. More than ten, anyway. We had a socialist working at the Equestrian Fellowship last summer during his Long Vacation. He was pretty lazy, actualleh, and he used to steal things, too."

"Yes, you've got to watch these socialists!" Mary looked gaily askance at her husband. "He'll have your handbag or anything else you leave lying about!"

"Don't tell her that," said Jim Arrowood, "she'll believe you."

"I won't!" Beth protested.

"They're a rotten lot, aren't they, Jessie?" Jacky complained and raised his daughter to face level. Jessie, laughing, flapped his lips to recommence their bub-bubbing game.

"Isn't she sweet?!" Joyce Trelawney cooed, she and Richard joined the group. Behind the Trelawneys, Denzil Wyckliffe was intercepted from following them. "Hello, Jessie! I wish I had a little girl like you!" Jessica, fascinated by the bright stones and metals in Joyce's South American Indian necklace, touched their gleaming smoothness. "Do you want to try it on? Here. It's yours to keep. Isn't it pretty? Do you want to look at yourself in a mirror? Come on, then, let Aunty Joyce take you. That's a good girl. She's lovely," Joyce pronounced warmly. "Come on, darling, let's go look in that glass over there how beautiful you are." They moved off, an endearing contrast, the big powerful woman in mauve, the little blonde tot in pink.

"She longs for a child. But the Lord hasn't blessed us so far," said Richard Trelawney.

"Keep trying," Mary advised cheerily. Trelawney's serious dark countenance eased, he inclined his head acceding. "Is Joyce going to Stockholm on business?" Mary peered up from her trim five foot one on three-inch high heels at the six foot four inch Trelawney. He nodded. Mary laughed delightedly. "She arranges it every time, doesn't she? Business expenses!"

"She's visiting suppliers. She'll perhaps sell some of their stuff in her stores," said Trelawney.

The Days and Jim Arrowood were smiling. Behind Richard Trelawney, Denzil Wyckliffe came free.

"I'm popping over, too," Beth Langdale volunteered. "Been offered a ride in one of those little twin-engined executive jet things. 'Get you a lift if you wish, Mary."

"I'm not going," Mary said quietly. "I've work to do."

"Hello, everybody!" Wyckliffe greeted the group cheerfully. "Who haven't I met?!"

"Me," said Mary, and introduced herself. "You're lucky to have had the honour! In five minutes, we'll be on our way to see our parents. Your ten o'clock curfew leaves us no time to waste."

"Discipline," Wyckliffe explained the time limit. "Team spirit. They're essential."

"Are you pleased with the team?"

"They're shaping up."

"Equally important, is the team pleased with <u>you</u>?" Mary asked pointedly.

The England Manager was nonplussed, then smiled: "I hope so. I've asked them for ideas and criticism whenever they have any."

"Good," Mary was decisive.

Wyckliffe chuckled: "I'll bet you keep Jacky on his toes."

"On the contrary, Mr Wyckliffe, he keeps me on mine." Mary cocked her head, winked at Jacky and gave him a squeeze with her right arm round his waist. Jacky kissed her temple. Over her head he watched Joyce Trelawney, carrying Jessica, approach.

"Are you travelling to Stockholm with us, Mrs Day?" Wyckliffe inquired.

"No."

"I wish you would, Mary," Joyce Trelawney coaxed, "then I could help look after Jessica, take her for walks, go shopping, it would be wonderful, wouldn't it, Jessie, darling?"

"I'm staying at home," Mary was serious. She took her daughter from the big woman. "If you want to see your mother tonight, Jacky, and be back before curfew, we'd better be going."

CHAPTER 9

Trenton village was quiet in the valley below, its foliage, lawns and gardens lush setting for the grey Anglo-Saxon-Norman church, and the mild hues of its buildings. From a chimney here and there, smoke curled against the pale blue sky and golden, crimson sunset. Red and black bullocks grazed in a couple of fields west of the village; the rest contained late spring crops. A man was walking his dog on the field footpath a mile and a half away. A meander of the Trent glistened to the southwest. The steaming, red power station towers several miles further south and ten miles northeast revealed the hidden river. Sound of a car starting. Glimpses of its northward movement through the village.

"You'll be going when Mary and your little girl get back from Mary's mother's," Mrs Day's speech was slow and slurred.

"They're staying the night there. Her father's running me back to the hotel. Jessie can get to bed early that way."

"Yes. It's a pity your two youngest brothers run off like that after tea without stopping to talk to you."

"They said all they wanted to. The young 'uns working on a car engine down at the garage and the other man's visiting his girlfriend."

"Working on refrigerators or some electrical stuff more like. Her father gets him doing work at that firm of theirs. Mind you, he likes it, and it pays good money. They treat the lad well. They do at the garage. Like a son in the house at that garage. I never see much of him. Neither of them. And Harry, he never –" she interrupted her low slurred complaint, remembering, "oh, he did ring me. He did. He's starting his exams tomorrow. I hope he does well. He deserves to. I remember him at school, squatting in that back kitchen."

Jacky chuckled: "Swotting, you mean. Not squatting!"

"Ay – squatting – I mean swotting. Yes. Not like you, you were always playing football. You were a little 'un. You didn't start growing till you were sixteen. How big are you now, Jacky?"

"Five six and a half in my bare feet, and eleven stone two."

"You're strong as a little bull, Jacky. I wish I were. But I can walk to the end of the pathway now, with my stick, and round the garden."

"That's wonderful, Mam. You'll soon be fit again."

"The doctor says if I keep on as I am doing, I shall."

"Remember, if there's anything I can do to help."

"You're a good boy, Jacky. Your sister's coming up from Wales to see me on Saturday, bringing her two kids. They're growing up. I wish you weren't playing football on Saturday. It worries me, that head of yours, getting kicked like that."

Jacky recalled pain. He suppressed fear. "It's better now, Mam."

"I remember that man kicking you," her face puckered slowly against agony, and she drew in a slow breath through pursed lips. "Awful. I wish you didn't have to play football."

"After Saturday, it looks like I won't till next season, except for summer training."

"Good. Then I shan't have to worry about you."

"You shouldn't anyway."

"I can't help it. Our Harry worries me."

"He needn't, Mam. With all his brains. All he has to do is pass his exams which, on past record, he will, then he's got nothing whatever to bother him."

"I dun' know."

"Believe it, Mam. We had a talk last weekend."

She glanced at him, very interested: "Did you?"

"Yes. We discussed things through. He had a few problems troubling him as you guessed, but we sorted them out."

"What was it?"

"They're finished now. Solved completely. So you can rest easy."

"But –" she was still curious, not entirely reassured.

"Do you believe me?" Jacky asked lightly, smiling yet serious, his alert posture showed he required an honest answer.

"Yes," his mother accepted. She eased in her chair, respiring through her mouth.

Jacky teetered on anxiety: "You alright?"

"Yes," she answered in her quiet, slow slightly slurred way. "My head's not bothered me these last few days. It's your head that worries me."

"Aw, Mam!" Jacky frowned exasperation; inwardly he cut off memory of being kicked, his pain, his fears.

In a hawthorn tree some thirty yards away, a blackbird began to sing. Sparrows chirped and bickered. A thrush hopped about the lawn seeking food. A car was climbing the hill from the village. Sudden breeze shook the greenery and varicoloured flowers a-jig in complex fragrance and whispering.

"How are your new team-mates, Jacky?"

"They're settling in. Except one young black kid. He's very fierce. Chip on his shoulder. Fallen out with half on 'em. Not with me and Jim Arrowood, though. Benny Cawthorne the Cockney would like to thrash him."

"Oh he mustn't do that."

"The team manager's given the lad a talking-to, and he's had a word with Benny – and others – in private. He's sensible, Wyckliffe. Strict, firm, and very fair."

"Mm," she murmured acceptingly. "And what about that politics election thing?" she wondered quietly. "I saw about you on television last night. The Labour man, Robert – Robert Jarvis, said you're going to speak for him at a big election meeting next week with the Tories and everybody there. Sir Something, the Tory."

"Sir Alec Sinjin Frobisher. Yes, I'll be there."

"I wish you wouldn't get involved in politics like your dad did. It doesn't do any good."

"It does."

"That's what your dad said, and it never did. It's getting a bit cool out here, Jacky. Soon be time for that television programme I like to watch. Then you'll be going down to Mary's parents, won't you?"

Jacky helped his mother to her feet and supported her with his arm under hers. "I'll stay with you till about nine, Mam. That'll give plenty of time to get back to the hotel before ten o'clock." He smiled, serious: "Curfew time. We've a hard day's training tomorrow. Then Stockholm, here we come!"

CHAPTER 10

Grimsta Wood's conifers swayed green in the late afternoon sun, and the half-grown foliage of the aspen and birch flickered like tiny glittering tongues chiding yet happy, hailing the tardiness of Östra Svealand's bright though chilly spring. Naked oaks. Mountain ash. Beech. Pigeons and crows, jackdaws and magpies; seagulls from Lake Mälaren half a mile away were whirling and swooping.

"We've trained hard and well this week." Jacky's gaze flicked from the window to Denzil Wyckliffe who continued: "We're beginning to play like a team." Appreciative comments and chuckles came from various players and officials. "We know as much as we can about our opponents without actually having played them, thanks to all the video film supplied by the different television companies and from the information given us by our countrymen here in Sweden. The Swedes are rebuilding their team after not qualifying for the World Cup. And three wins and a draw out of their last four games – and that draw against West Germany – shows that we'll have a job on tomorrow. They've a good centre forward in Gunnar Fast. And one of the top midfield men in Europe, Magnus Magnusson. And Johansson, their goalie, has been voted the best in the German Bundesliga for the past two years. It's a Friendly – and I've told you all week, I want it clean, no fouls. A Friendly, right, Mister Cawthorne?"

The Cockney, palms upward supplicating, amidst differing comments and jests, protested loudly with injured innocence: "What have I done?!"

Wyckliffe leant head and shoulders forward and fixed his gaze on Benny's: "What haven't you done?!" The Cockney smiled slowly, closed his eyes and rolled his head lazily to the left in an accepting, throwaway gesture.

Wyckliffe addressed them all: "Keep it clean. Remember," he spaced the words, giving each significance, "you are England," which produced embarrassed smiles and shuffles, cynical grins and serious faces. "I'll not make a big thing of my being proud and your being proud, and all that sort of stuff, to represent England. But we do. So remember that while you're here. We're ambassadors for England, whether we like it or not. Enough of the serious. The general democratic consensus over-ruled me—" he was smiling, players stamped their feet, smiling and cheery and saying hear, hear. "I wanted you to watch a film or go for a bus-ride together or something else," raucous sounds and meaningful jeers and yer, yer broke out, Wyckliffe grinned, and resumed, "to preserve team spirit, in accordance with usual management practice. But I think our team spirit can permit flexibility and trust in each of you," he summed up the general feeling. "Those who still wish to buy souvenirs and presents for wives, families and friends have the list of places and suggestions Mrs Trelawney kindly prepared. You've got your maps of Stockholm and tourist information. If you run into any trouble, need any help, contact the hotel at once. There's one of us here all the time, and we'll get help to you straight away. Not that we expect any trouble here in peaceful, Social Democratic Sweden, eh, Jacky?" Various squad members jeered and booed good-naturedly at the political reference. "Keep sober, sensible, and be back without fail by ten o'clock. Any questions? None? That's all, then, lads." As the players stood up to leave, scraping chairs, clearing throats and beginning to talk: "I'd like to see John Plumtree, Winston Jones and Jacky Day. Come on, John, Winston, we'll go into the office down the corridor. John will tell you when it's your turn, Jacky."

"What's he want you for, Jacky?" Jed Lennox, the Hull youth, asked and squinted against the sun where he stood on the concrete outside the clubhouse door.

"Probably about the interview Swedish Television wants to do with me." The football pitch, twenty yards from the forecourt, beckoned attention with its greenness. A bushy hedge hid the bottom part of the wire mesh fifteen-foot high fence bordering the west side of the ground. Over the hedge, half a mile of common grassland, with woods to the south and trees and Hesselby Manor House to the north. Hesselby's buildings were village-like among the greenery.

"I know what he wants Ginger Plumtree and Winston for," Jed concluded sadly.

"Roughing up a team-mate before a match," Benny Cawthorne said, "he could have bust old Ginger's ribs, the way he ran into him. Then cursing everybody for saying he should have been more careful."

"They provoked him, though," Jed said.

"Everybody and everyfink provokes our Winston," said Benny. "Who's coming to my orgy tomorrow night? You can come, Gerald. You'd set a bit of colour on the party. Guaranteed no Aids victims present."

"No thanks," the brown youth replied. "I'm off out with that lass from the hotel."

"What about you, Curly?" Benny addressed Colin Greenhalgh, Manchester City's left winger. "That nice shiny head of yours. Sexy."

"Piss off, Cawthorne," grunted the bald Greenhalgh, grinning. "My missis'd kill me if she found out. Besides, I'm too bloody shy."

"Can I interest you, Joimes?" Jim Arrowood shook his head. "You could bring your girlfriend along and all. No? Jecky? We'll fix you up wiv a nice little blonde. They've got some right little darlings here in Stockholm."

"You can have my share, Benny," said Jacky.

"Jingo," the Cockney turned to the thirty-one year old who declined, smiling. "You've got somefink lined up for yourself, have you?"

"With half the World Press after me?" Jingo Byrnes was serious.

"Can't blame you for being careful, I suppose. You've certainly got your fan club out there if you change your mind," the Cockney raised his eyebrows and nodded towards the ground exit where a scattering of young teenagers were waiting. "You're popular here in Sweden, Jingo."

"Sweden, maybe," said the older man quietly, "but not in England."

"Get a hat-trick tomorrow and you will be," said Benny. "And after the game – my orgy." The others grinned at his sprightly single-mindedness. "I'm meeting one or two guys tonight – all you have to do is give me your requirements and I'll get you fixed up. Right? Right. Hello, here comes Ginger and Mr. Innocence himself."

"Swedish Television say they have agreed all terms with your business manager by phone and telex, and they'd like you for the interview at your convenience. I told them seven o'clock would probably be okay." Jacky nodded; Wyckliffe resumed: "So they're going to have a car waiting for you at Bromma Hotel from a quarter to seven onwards." Wyckliffe sat; Jacky did the same. "Well, tomorrow's the big day. What do you think?"

"We're playing as a team. The young 'uns are fast and fit, and Jingo's top quality. The Swedes'll test uz."

"Yeh." Wyckliffe put both hands palm down on the table and looked at the space between them, sighed, then said: "I wish I'd had the team a year ago, when I was shortlisted with my predecessor but got rejected."

"Politics," Jacky referred to the conflicts and deadlock which had preceded the Team Manager's appointment.

Wyckliffe looked up with a quirky grin, palms still on the table: "They wanted me to stand as Labour candidate for Lincoln, you know."

Jacky said he had heard.

"How's your head?"

"Alright."

"No twinges, pains, headaches? Nothing abnormal?" Jacky indicated not. "You should head the ball, Jacky. I've talked to the doc, and a couple of top neurosurgeons. They give the all clear. I don't want to press you, and I won't press you. I can understand your fears about brain damage. Especially since your mother's stroke."

Jacky was earnest: "It's physical. Not psychological," he repressed his doubts.

Wyckliffe slid relaxed palms off the table and eased comfortably straight in his chair. "I shall be playing you from the start tomorrow, Jacky, despite your lack of recent match training. Don't forget to tell the Swedes a few home truths in your interview."

CHAPTER 11

i

"Stockholm is beautiful," Jacky answered, "a place of lakes and forests, rocks and open grassland. With the buildings blending into the natural background. And everywhere is clean, no slums. The Old Town is old but well kept. The people are good looking, and there are lots of pretty girls – like you."

The little blonde interviewer sniffed, tossed her head, and pushed her specs with their three inch wide lenses up off her retroussé nose tip with a dainty forefinger – no man was going to treat *her* as a sex-object! "You're supposed to have been training – not looking at girls. You have a wife and small child. Your wife sacrificed her career as a biochemist for you. Iss that fair?"

"She didn't! She works part-time at Bio-Veracity. Our little girl goes to a day-nursery not two hundred yards from her laboratory and Mary can see her from her window. My money from football gives my wife a freedom to choose and study and think which she wouldn't otherwise have had."

"You have had offers worth millions of pounds from clubs in Italy and Spain. Iss it true your wife hass made you turn them down?"

"I'm happy with my present contract and our home in England."

"Last season you discussed terms with two leading Spanish clubs and earlier this season with three Italian. Multimillion record sums were named. Your wife's attitude stopped those talks. A footballer's career iss short. Can you really afford to turn down such large sums?"

"Money is important. But other things are, also. Let's leave the subject by saying I'm satisfied with the status quo. Next question," Jacky acted amiable, his willpower so totally re-engulfing his disappointment and resentment that the interviewer was deceived.

"You have become a very controversial figure in England by publicly supporting the Labour Party candidate in your local by-election for the Westminster Parliament. Does your wife like that?"

"I don't think I'm controversial, nor does my wife."

"You have been heavily criticised on television and radio, and savaged by the English Conservative press because they say that a footballer at the peak of his active career should not participate in party politics, and especially if he iss a member of the English national team."

"I'm an Englishman," said Jacky, "which means that provided I respect the truth and the law, I can do what I like, and I can say what I like, about anything and about anybody."

"Because you're an Englishman," her pointedness was almost a sneer.

"That's right. In England, you don't get killed or put in jail for speaking your honest opinion. You do in many countries. They don't do that here in Sweden, do they?"

"No," she was obliged to defend. Then slid in: "You seem very proud of being an Englishman."

"I am an Englishman," Jacky was affable. "I'm not fanatical about it. I don't go around waving a Union Jack. Nationalism is daftness. When you travel and see different countries and meet different people, you realise that, if you've any sense. If a man's a good man, or a woman's a good woman, it don't matter what nationality they are. The same applies to customs, traditions, machines, institutions, whatever you like."

"But nationalism iss part of football, and you represent the English nation. That makes you a nationalist."

"No, it doesn't. It makes me a footballer who has been picked by the England team manager who is trying to put together the best side he can from English footballers."

"Yes! To represent the English nation!"

"You can say what you like, I'm not a nationalist! Hitler was a nationalist, and look at him, the madman! Every crackpot dictator and politician out for power, and military men, waving their national flags and mouthing about national pride and national honour and leading the gullible on to sacrifice and suffering, they're nationalists! I'm not! Don't classify me with them! I never have been and never shall be a nationalist!

"But you are a socialist."

"M' dad was, strong. I suppose I am, too, I'm supporting one for Parliament."

"What does socialism mean to you? What things are you in favour of?"

"A high minimum standard of living for even the lowest of the low in society. And fair treatment for everybody, not merely the rich, the well-educated, and the smart, but for the stupid, the ignorant, and the scum as well – especially for them, because they can't get it for themselves. It's up to the government and those in power to m laws and rules that ensure a decent society for everybody! Not one where the rich and the strong crush the weak and rob 'em and keep 'em down."

"The Conservatives do that, do they?"

"Yes," Jacky agreed, then chuckled hard realisation, "and not just Conservatives, either. Look, lass, I'll answer your questions about everything, and give you my honest opinion which any free man – free Englishman that is," he cocked his head at her with a smile, "has a right to. But they're only my opinions. I'm not representing anybody except myself. I want to make that quite clear."

"And so you think Mr Snatcher iss a reactionary?" the Swede approved.

"Yes. He stopped free school milk for schoolchildren. He stopped cheap, good school meals."

"School meals are free here in Sweden," the blonde interjected.

"Oh," Jacky was pleasantly surprised, "you do have the right idea! Anyway, talking about England, for a lot of kids from rough families, that school dinner was the only decent grub they got each day. He knew that. Son of a little Tory grocer from Muckham in Lincolnshire, same part of the country I come from. He'd seen the working men and their kids and he looked down on 'em. He was one small step above 'em. And he didn't want to be down there with 'em! He wanted to be at the top. And when he got to the top – through hard studying – he showed what he thought of the people at the bottom alright! Millions got the boot. You can talk with your mouth, but it's what you do that counts. He was in favour of cuts. Ay, he was that right enough. Straight across the throats of quite a few people, and the backs of a lot more! – figuratively speaking, mind." Jacky sobered. "The cuts in the Health Service meant that people died. The money wasn't there for the equipment and services needed to save them." His mood changed: "When it came to armaments and military stuff, there was money then. Plenty on it. Like ovver the Hawklands business. The American Central Intelligence Agency would certainly have told British Intelligence what the military were doing, preparing seriously to invade. All that was needed to have been done was to have sent a few warships down there on manoeuvres. But no, Snatcher's mob didn't do that. So they fought a war. It cost men's lives, hatred, and thousands of millions of pounds off the British taxpayer."

The pretty interviewer was delighted, yet maintained a modicum of impartiality: "You should be running for Parliament and not this, er, er," she sought the name, "Robert Jarvis."

"Oh, I'm no politician!" said Jacky. "I've got my views, for what they're worth. But they're only my views."

"Those of a free Englishman," the woman put in.

"Right. I don't pretend that they're the whole picture. They're not. They're my way of looking at it, though. Or the part of it that we've talked about. You asked about Snatcher, I told you. Snatcher would have another view – and so would his bootlickers."

In his soundproof control room, the TV producer was grinning all over his face and rubbing his hands with glee as the interview ranged on from topic to topic: Using a young and pretty, political reporter instead of a middle-aged, male sports specialist had proved shrewd and successful. This programme would go down well in England – and not only in England.

"And finally – are you sorry England are not travelling to the U.S.A. for the World Cup?" the blonde concluded.

"I'll answer that better tomorrow night," said Jacky.

ii

In the Bromma Hotel inner courtyard, Bobby Milburne, Joe Berrigan, Jingo Byrnes and Colin Greenhalgh were playing solo whist. Eddy Corelli lounged, watching. About the courtyard at the circular garden tables with their red and white umbrellas, various England squad members sat reading or stood around chatting in groups while the simple three-jet fountain spouted water into its pale green pool.

"Abundance," Bobby Milburne declared quietly.

"He'll gerr'it and all, the jammy young bugger. Goo on then," growled Curly Greenhalgh in his heavy-vowelled Manchester English, scowling at his cards. "Who taught you to play?"

"My father," Bobby slurred in his chipped Geordie. "He plays at the Working Men's Club every Sunday."

"He's a bit of a cardsharp is our Bobby," said Joe Berrigan. "How much have you skinned off us tonight?"

"About four quid."

"Who dealt these cards?" Curly moaned accusingly. Bobby's customarily serious face began a small grin as he stared at his hand. "You can smirk, you young bugger, you dealt 'em. We know. Giving himself a good hand," Curly railed good humouredly, stroking his bald pate with his right hand.

"I hope they play me tomorrow," the seventeen year old muttered, and took a trick.

"They will, Bobby," Eddy Corelli was encouraging and confident. "You and Jim Arrowood, Jacky, Benny, Dick Trelawney, and Joe and Jingo here, are certs. It's the rest of us who need to worry."

"Everybody who's being seriously considered for a regular place will get a chance," said Joe Berrigan. "They've agreed to make up to five substitutes. This Friendly was supposed to be a final try-out before going to the World Cup." He grunted disappointment at not going to the tournament.

"The Norwegians might win tomorrow in Budapest," Eddy Corelli tried optimism.

"Pigs might fly," said Curly.

"Inshallah. If God is willing," Jingo Byrnes was deadpan. "4-1 defeat in Norway. Hungarians only need a draw: they've a better goal average than us. They should win. Your turn," he prompted Joe Berrigan who played the ace on Bobby's ten. The seventeen-year-old laid down the rest of his cards.

"He's won again, the young sod!" Curly grumbled. "There's Jacky Day, look, just come in after ringing his wife and mother. It's a good job Jacky didn't get into this card school, you'd have won all that money he got for his TV programme tonight. I wonder what he said?"

"We'll know in due course," said Joe Berrigan. "They'll be showing it on television in England, no doubt."

"What're you looking so worried for, Jed?" Jacky asked.

"Winston i'nt here," the brown youth was frowning at the clock as though willing it to stop.

"It's not twenty minutes to ten yet. Benny i'nt here either. He's never late, though. Fancy a breath of fresh air?"

The twin-lamped street-lights in the three rows of trees which dissected the near empty carpark in front of the hotel added yellow to the light nordic evening. Across the carpark, near the tunnelbana railway bridge, a large brownish-yellow sculpture resembling a flying tortoise reared on a ten-foot pole. The lights of the closed Metro supermarket shone red, blue and yellow. Beside it, thirty yards to Jacky's and Jed Lennox's right where they stood in front of the hotel's main entrance, Bromma's small civic centre raised its seven storeys above some neatly box-cut trees. A red and white Stockholm Transport bus pulled up at its terminal fifty yards diagonally to their left. A car went by on Drottningholmsvägen's right carriageway heading south.

"I hope Wyckliffe plays me," Jed said quietly. They strolled slowly leftwards under the hotel restaurant's red awning towards the hotel corner.

"He'll play you. That's why you're here." The bus cut its engine. All was quiet. Trees across the other side of Drottningholmsvägen combined with those in the carpark to soften the manmade harshness of the carpark and road surface. They reached the hotel corner and stood near the tree there. Some taxis were speeding along Drottningholmsvägen under the tunnelbana bridge; on the bridge, a green four-carriage electric train flickered lightning as it rattled westwards. The interior lights of the stationary bus at the terminal came on. Its heavy motor coughed, pulsing.

"I still can't believe I'm on the England squad. My grandad couldn't stop smiling all ovver his face when I was selected. He'll be driving his town bus all day tomorrow, down to Hull docks and back again. An old West Indian negro."

Jacky glanced at him.

"Yes. A negro," the brown youth stressed firmly. "That's what he is and that's what I am. It's not easy being coloured in England. I've often wished I were white." He looked at his sinewy brown left hand and turned it over to its pink palm. "But I'm not. I guess you know about me, the stories, and that?"

"I on'y know you come from Hull, play for Manchester United, Young England, and what I've learned from talking to you this week."

"You'll know soon enough. It al'ays comes out. They know all ovver Hull. M' mam was a whore. A black whore, found drownded in Immingham docks a Sunday morning. Murdered. They nivver proved it. 'Death by misadventure.' They reckoned she was drunk and got bruised and bashed about and fell in after 'ooring around the ships there. But she wasn't drunk! Some bastard murdered her!" His good looking face twisted with hate: "Bastard!! Bastard!!"

The bus pulled out with six passengers aboard. They watched it pass within five yards of them, travelling south to the fifty yard sliproad exit onto Drottningholmsvägen.

Jed Lennox spoke quietly: "She wa' twenty-two. I wa' six." He took a photo from his wallet. "Me and m' mam at Skeggy." Jacky studied the photo taken by a Skegness street photographer: a laughing, pretty girl dark as a Madras Indian, with frizzy hair cut short, cheek pressed to that of a miniature Jed holding a stick of candy floss. "I remember that day. She let me ride on everything as often as I wanted. Anything I asked for, she got it. Not like m' granny or m' grandad. 'Course, she'd got the money. They hadn't. I'll see 'em alright from now on. Not that I earn your kind o' money. Defenders don't earn what you get. But I'll do alright if I don't get crocked. I don't smoke or drink or owt, and I'm not starting. And I'll try and look after my money so that I'll ha' some put by when my footballing days are ovver. My grandad and granny taught me that. Why didn' they teach m' mam? I asked that. 'Couple of blacks from Jamaica, escaped from poverty. Glad for wharivver shit they could get. Owt was better than back there on the island. M' mam was born here, went to school here, liked white kids. And they liked her. Just to fuck. Not to marry. That's what m' grandma said: she wanted good looking white lads with good prospects. Her dream. What fucking hope had she in England?" His bitterness was clear. "None. Nowhere in the bloody world had she.

Not to meet a handsome young white bloke with a good job or chance of a career who wanted her like he would a white girl. He wouldn't want her like he would a white girl. He wouldn't want owt to do wi' a coloured lass no matter how good looking and no matter wi' how good a figure. She had me. After that, well. She got gooing with older men, tekking money for it. Bitter. Very unhappy, m' granny said. O' coourse she would be. Not that I remember that. I were too young. What I do remember is that she were al'ys alright to me. Then that Sunday she got drown."

At the taxi station on the far side of the carpark a cab pulled away and wound out of the northeast exit. Both watched. Neither spoke. A black Mercedes sped along Drottningholmsvägen from under the tunnelbana bridge.

Jed Lennox broke the silence: "How was y' mam when you rang tonight?"

"Improving. If she tek's it easy, she'll get well alright." The Mercedes pip-pipped as it drove south. Benny Cawthorne leant with head and shoulders out of the back window, grinning broadly. They raised hands in acknowledgement and followed the vehicle's passage towards the carpark and bus-terminal's southern entrance.

"Hello, lads!" Benny Cawthorne swung beaming from the car. "Had a good night? Get your end in, Gerald?"

"Wouldn't you like to know, you nosey sod?"

"Ho-ho, it's like that, is it?"

The driver of the car was a tough looking muscleman in a black leather jacket and white poloneck shirt. His frontseat passenger was a man in his mid-thirties, with dark tinted glasses, as conventionally well dressed in grey as Benny.

"Thanks a lot for the ride, fellows," Benny bent to look through the car's wound-down window. "See you tomorrow, eh? Cheers." The muscleman was grinning, his companion, expressionless, raised right forefinger in acknowledgement. The Mercedes accelerated smoothly away. "Are we going in, or what?"

"Winston i'n't here yet," said Jed Lennox.

"He ain't all there either," Benny chuckled maliciously. "I'm going to show my face inside and say hello to Wyckliffe. See you later," He paced briskly towards the hotel entrance. They followed slowly, Jed Lennox gazing anxiously about seeking the negro.

iii

"This is the line-up which will start tomorrow." Denzil Wyckliffe read from his loose-leaf folder: "J.P. Berrigan, G. Lennox," Jed threw back his head in soundless joy, "B. Cawthorne, R.G.L. Trelawney, D.S. Lewis, E.P. Corelli," Corelli exclaimed and rubbed his hands gleefully, causing Wyckliffe to look up and smile before continuing, "J. Day, J.N.G. Byrnes, C.N. Greenhalgh," tension left the bald left-winger's face, he exhaled with a whoosh, "R. Milburne," the seventeen-year old remained staring as though hypnotised, "J.D.F. Arrowood."

Some players were smiling, relaxed and glad. Those not named concealed their disappointment. Bobby Milburne sat rigidly unmoving.

"You're playing, Bobby! We're in!" Eddy Corelli pounded the young Geordie on the back and hugged him with left arm round his shoulders which broke the seventeen-year-old's shock.

"Those are the starters." Wyckliffe's words received the squad's full concentration. "We can have up to five substitutes. Whether we take all five or not, circumstances will decide. I've stressed all week we're going to attack. We're playing at top speed. And we're going to challenge for every ball." Wyckliffe spoke clearly and with emphasis. "We've got the velocity, we've got the stamina, we've got the skill, and we're going to win!"

Grins, footstamping, handclaps and yerr-yerr approved the Team Manager's determination.

"This was to be our try-out before going to the World Cup in the U.S.A. Facts have got to be faced. The defeats from last year are in the record books. And you know what that means. However, gentlemen, we are going to play this game tomorrow as if it were a *real* try-out! Because it is!" Wyckliffe's keen gaze sought their eyes. "You are the pick of the finest players in the hardest Football League in the world! England are always a name to be reckoned with in world football. And we are going to make it *THE* name!" He gave time for reactions to settle. "Strategy and tactics. Colin Greenhalgh stays on his wing and floats in the high balls for

Jim and Bobby. Eddy Corelli has been used defensively in his club games and the Young England team. But that quickness, dribbling, fast accurate and imaginative passing he's shown this week makes me want to play him further upfield. I shall be substituting Jacky, probably at half time, maybe before. But first, I want to see how young Bobby shapes up as a target man while Jacky's midfield. When Jacky comes off, I'm pulling Bobby back to replace him because I want to watch Bobby as a midfielder. Jed," he looked at the coloured youth, "with your speed and good left foot, as I've told you all week, don't be afraid to attack. Same for you down the right, David," he addressed the North Londoner. "You have the speed and stamina to sustain those long runs and you have the shot. But your main task is to neutralise Magnus Magnusson down the right. Him and Gunnar Fast, Richard." The big centre-back nodded acknowledgement. "Penalties: if we get any – Jacky, or John Byrnes. Colin Greenhalgh and Jim Arrowood are our other specialists, Richard. Now, before we go on, has anybody seen Winston Jones? Nobody? I'm disturbed. This is his first trip outside England. He's only nineteen. You're on good terms with him, Gerald. Did he say anything to you about where he was going?"

Jed was worried: "No, he didn't, Boss. Well, you know what he is," Jed paused.

"One of Nature's gentlemen," Benny Cawthorne uttered softly from the back row. The squad stirred, some smiling. Wyckliffe deliberately ignored both comment and reactions.

"I think something must have happened to him because otherwise he would have phoned," Jed explained.

Wyckliffe, frowning, nodded. Somebody suggested contacting the police, which was ignored without comment.

For the next twenty minutes they discussed the coming match and the past week, erudition blending with camaraderie. Jed Lennox kept eyeing the conference room door anxiously, hoping for Winston Jones to show.

At ten thirty, Wyckliffe raised his voice: "Okay, fellows, time for hot milk, cocoa and beddy-byes, eh?"

Amid innocuous and ribald comments, the meeting ended.

When the last player was out of the room, Wyckliffe permitted his worry to emerge: "Where in hell has that young Jones got to?" Other England staff evinced similar concern.

Through the open conference room door, scream of an American police siren tore and beat.

"Turn that facking thing off!" Winston Jones growled, and twisted from the young blonde he was kissing to grin savagely at the green and blue hair of the 1963 Chevrolet's driver. The punk rocker sat staring front, jigging his body, bop-bopping and snapping both hands' fingers in time to bawling stereo-taped music, indifferent to all except the cacophony and the disruption and hate he knew his siren and music were provoking inside the hotel. Winston turned to savagely kiss the second teenage blonde beside him while thrusting his hand, baring her legs to clasp her genitals. Sight of other England team members outside the car and in the hotel entrance added arrogant contempt for their womanlessness, lust to demonstrate his superior virility, flaunt his sexual appeal for, power over white girls. He was better than all of them! Best player on England's squad. He would show the bastards and the world the morrow!

He shook the teenage punk rocker's shoulders and bellowed in his car: "Turn that facking siren off!"

"We see you tomorrow, after the match!" the girl nearest the open rear door left her long legs and pubic hair exposed. She was wide-eyed, pretty, wild-faced and coarse, smaller than her equally well-proportioned, big-breasted companion. Two of a kind.

Noise from the car stereo bounced over a hundred-yard radius.

"We fix three more girls like we promise!" the big-breasted girl leant across her companion to earnestly assure the black where he stood grinning with every tooth. "Du är en jävel på att knulla, din lilla skit!" ("What a magnificent screw you are, you bugger!") she yelled at him, then giggled, and caressed with: "We see you tomorrow, elskling. Sweet dreams!" She swivelled to screech at the green and blue-haired driver who sat bop-bopping and snapping his fingers: "Kör för fan! Vi drar tillbaks till festen!" ("Drive, you fucker! We're off back to the party!") The red Chevrolet jumped and slewed with a massive bellow, turned squealing burning tyre rubber and roared across the car park to its north-east exit.

"I want a word with you, my lad," Denzil Wyckliffe was on the top step of the hotel entrance.

"I told you, I couldn't get a taxi!" Winston Jones protested wildly. He and the Team Manager were alone in the basement conference room. "That crazy kid and his siren weren't my idea! He gave us a lift, that's all! The girls know him! I told him to turn the bladdy fing off! He did. I got him to. It's only half pawst ten, just gone! I was at this party in Farsta in the south of Stockholm! It's miles away – like living in Barnet! The police stopped us twice, once in Farsta, and again in central Stockholm. They made us get out, looked at that kid's driving licence and questioned him for Christ knows how long! They were going to run me in if I hadn't had my driving licence wiv me and the girls hadn't told them who I was! White men – they can't stand the sight of me wiv a white bird! It's always the same! Always! That's what it is, ain't it? The sight of me wiv those birds out there!"

Wyckliffe was stern-faced and quiet: "You've been drinking, too."

Winston was loud voiced and aggrieved: "Well, I was at a party, wasn't I?! I had to have a drink, di'n't I?! I only had a couple of pints. That's nuffink!! Nuffink!!"

Wyckliffe frowned; he strove to contain his anger.

Winston Jones protested, boasting: "I can drink ten pints and it don't bother me! I can walk as straight as a die. And next day, I can play a blinder – just like I'm going to do tomorrow!"

"Oh, are you?" Wyckliffe commented, grimly sardonic.

Winston realised. "Why, what?" his forehead furrowed, concerned, his reasonable excuses were not being accepted. "You're not going to -? Aw, for Christ's sake, no!" he was bitter and angry. "I told you – it was not my fault! You're not going to pick me tomorrow for that, eh?! You're not!!" He was almost in tears. "I'm the best man on the team!" his voice rose. "Better than Arrowood, Jecky Day, Milburne, the lot!" he bellowed his belief. "Don't pick me then!!" he bawled, face twisted and unsuccessfully fighting back tears of disappointment with fury and bitterness. "Don't ever pick me, White Man!" he snarled his hate. "White Man! No black ever got fair treatment from a white! You're not going to pick me just because I got back late and had a pint and went wiv white girls!"

Wyckliffe was hard: "Go to bed. We'll talk tomorrow," he dismissed the enraged teenager.

"Don't pick me then! See if I care!" the Winston yelled through scarcely suppressed tears as the Team Manager walked to the door and rested his hand on its handle. "Stick your facking white men's team up your white man's arse!!" He glared wildly, bitterly at Wyckliffe who gazed steadily back and opened the door for the negro to leave. Jones rushed past.

"Mester Wyckliffe," Jed Lennox, nervous, frightened yet purposeful, blocked the top of the basement stairway. Behind him in the hotel vestibule, England team members and hotel guests were attentive.

"Yes, Gerald?" the England Team Manager stopped some stairs away.

"I hope you won't be too hard on Winston."

Wyckliffe, decisive, resumed his climb: "That's none of your business." Gerald stood aside to let the other pass. "Now, goodnight."

Gerald persisted in his strong Hull accent: "It is my business, 'cause I'm black too." Wyckliffe paused. "He was wrong coming back late. If he had a good excuse, tho', give him a chance." Jacky, behind Jed Lennox to the side and between Richard Trelawney and Jim Arrowood, nodded. Wyckliffe observed the gesture. "He's proud o' being here. He's gorra lot o' mouth on him. Burr it means just about iverything he ivver wanted him being here. Me, too."

Wyckliffe, frowning, stern, showed no sign of being influenced by the youth. He noticed the various England players listening. He addressed them all, finishing with Jed Lennox: "We're supposed to be getting a good night's sleep aren't we? We've a match to win tomorrow."

CHAPTER 12

Clap, clap, clap-clap-clap-clap, "England!" repeated from under the few Union Jacks in the sun-spilled east stands and south terraces of Råsunda stadium. The north terraces were empty. The eastern stands were full: no Union Jacks there: only an abundance of blue, yellow-crossed Swedish flags.

At the north goal, Swedes were shooting in with their half dozen balls. England, at the other. Jim Arrowood, Jingo Byrnes and Bobby Milburne jogged and exercised in the southern half of the centre circle. The captains were trotting towards the referee for the toss-up.

Jacky flipped the ball over his right shoulder with his right foot, right-backheeled it over his head, leftfooted over his left shoulder, left-backheeled over his head, rightfooted over his right shoulder, then casually yet exactly leftheeled the dropping sphere to Jingo Byrnes who rightfooted it for Jim Arrowood to head hard to Bobby Milburne who increased its speed with a downward header to Jacky who quickly, without hurrying, caressed the speeding yard-high ball with his right foot and laid it immobile on the turf. The referee at the centre spot beckoned.

"How's it feel, Jingo?" Jacky trotted to take up position.

"Great." Springy grass under his feet, cool clear air, the clap-clap and cry of "England!"; memories of his first full England game eleven years before; old and new joy; determination; the court trial; jail cell and stinking slop bucket; the stench of Turkish towns; the heat of the Gulf, Saudi-Arabia; German grounds. Wyckliffe's 'phone call the previous Saturday night. Jingo Byrnes tipped back his head and breathed in deeply, squinting a grin at the silvery sky.

Jed Lennox tackled possession fifteen yards from the corner flag near the touchline, England's first contact with the ball. He backheeled to

Benny Cawthorne who kicked direct to Jacky. Jacky sprinted past the centre spot, chipped over two Swedes: Bobby Milburne hit the dropping ball twenty-five yards and thwacked the near juncture of crossbar and goalpost. Jim Arrowood challenged the Swedish innerbacks at the bounce, forced a bad short pass which Eddy Corelli's quickness intercepted to touch to Jingo Byrnes who rightfooted instantly and hard towards his near bottom corner. The Swedish goalkeeper full-length saved with Jacky sprinting to utilise possible error.

On the England bench, Denzil Wyckliffe smiled and breathed deeply in.

During the next two minutes, England harassed the Swedes, and constrained them three times to make returns to Johansson.

At the third return, the tall goalkeeper motioned his side into the England half and, from the edge of his penalty area, kicked a long pass to Magnus Magnusson.

Swedish supporters cheered and shouted encouragement to their best player.

The blond, yellow-jerseyed, blue-shorted Swede jinked and feinted, starkly contrasting with the dark-haired, motionless David Lewis poised gaze on the ball. Magnusson leapt to the left, then staggered and fell as Lewis locked the ball.

Wyckliffe sighed, and relaxed back on his bench.

Jacky beat two men and sidefooted to Jingo Byrnes who stared shaping to kick towards Curly Greenhalgh sprinting clear on the left wing: Jingo's unexpected fifteen yard flick diagonally right surprised the defence: Jim Arrowood outran the backs, his fullpower kick passed two inches inside the near post.

England's players registered their joy, their few hundred supporters cheered and sang. Wyckliffe, beaming, commented: "Now *what* do the critics think of John Byrnes?!"

Jingo put back his head and closed his eyes, smiling, and breathed in deep, happy for more.

"Yer," said Benny Cawthorne laconically, running beside Jed Lennox to congratulate the goalscorer, "I fink old Jingo can come to my orgy tonight." The youth was too excited to hear anything except his own thought and passions.

"You nearly missed," Jacky joked, and clapped his fellow Lincolnshireman on the biceps.

Jim Arrowood grinned.

England had the next ten minutes. Their speed, positioning and ball control kept play continuously in the Swedish half, forced seven corners, a dozen throw-ins, five free kicks and numerous saves, three difficult from headers by Arrowood, Milburne and a lob from Jacky.

Curly Greenhalgh's bald head gleamed and sweat ran down his red face. Defender blocking way ahead, defender inside him. Half-headturn – Eddy Corelli seven yards back right; yellow-and-blue figures positioning in defence; Jim Arrowood running right drawing attention from the middle; Bobby Milburne hanging back.

Obscured from view by three defenders, the Swedish goalkeeper first focussed the seventeen-year old Geordie's thirty-yarder when it was ten yards from his top far corner. He tensed to dive, realised, swore, the ball hit the meshing, and Bobby Milburne hopped five feet upwards.

Denzil Wyckliffe leant back with arms folded, smiling, contemplating the cluster around the young Tynesider. Yes, he thought with controlled excitement and cautious joy, it looks like we could have a team going. He eyed the scoreboard: Sweden 0 – England 2: time on the clock, twenty-two minutes. Seven minutes into the Norway-Hungarian game. Had he been wrong in asking the Swedes not to show scores from Budapest? No. Nothing must be allowed to distract from the game afoot.

Magnus Magnusson and David Lewis fell together. Magnusson sprang off all fours chasing the ball; Lewis lay writhing holding his leg. Joe Berrigan palmed Magnusson's leftfooter over the bar. The England physiotherapist ran towards Lewis.

"Your job is purely defensive, Johnny," Wyckliffe instructed; over the ginger-haired Plumtree's right shoulder, sight of David Lewis being borne off the pitch on a stretcher worried him. "Give Magnusson no chance to start anything. Mark him out of the game, exactly as David did."

For six minutes, England were in and around the Swedish penalty area. The big black-and-green jerseyed goalkeeper punched clear, saved with legs and feet, was beaten four times and succoured by defenders blocking the goal-line. A twenty-five yarder from Jingo Byrnes to the bottom far corner elicited a diving save and relieved Sweden.

Johansson motioned his men upfield, walked bouncing the ball to the edge of his penalty area and kicked to Magnusson.

Oh God! thought Wyckliffe. Ginger Plumtree, awkwardly wrong-footed, whirled vainly to chase the speeding Magnusson. Joe Berrigan beat down the blond man's shot.

Again and again, the Swedes utilised their expert's superiority over his ginger adversary, slowing the game's tempo, keeping possession, relieving pressure after each frantic defence against England's speeding, skilful attack.

The ginger-haired man's incapacity compelled Richard Trelawney to cover for him, drew Benny Cawthorne in from the left and England's midfielders into defence, thus permitting the Swedes more freedom to attack.

In the forty-first minute, Magnusson scored. The Swedish crowd cheered and sang. And Denzil Wyckliffe frowned and bit his lip.

"You're doing a magnificent job, boys!" The England players sat around the dressing room sweating, drinking sports drink. "There's nothing wrong with our strategy or our tactics – they're good. Keep your speed up, straight for goal each time but varying your play so they don't know where or how you're going to hit 'em – that's the style! That's what's going to win this match! I won't single anybody out for special praise because you're all worthy of it, the way you're playing!" Wyckliffe's exuberant encouragement quietened to practicality: "Colin," he eyed the bald leftwinger keenly, "you're doing a fine job on the left wing. I'm fully satisfied. No problems. But I'm probably going to substitute you. Not immediately. I'd like to see Sid Garner in action down the right wing. Jacky," he held his breath for a fifth of a second, then exhaled, "I'm taking you off. As planned. Well played. Bobby, you take Jacky's place. Which leaves us in need of another forward." His eyes strayed over everyone in the dressingroom, then darted to Winston Jones sitting in the far corner scowling glumly at the floor between his feet. "Winston Jones."

Winston's head snapped up and his atavistic savage face laughed, amazed.

Wyckliffe was hard, almost bullying yet not unfriendly: "Do a good job! Good luck! I'm making one other substitution – Keith Pilbeam for Johnny Plumtree." The ginger-haired defender was sitting with bowed head, containing his disappointment which had him near tears. He, like everybody else, knew his first England try-out was also his last.

"What's the score in Budapest?" Jacky inquired.

"One-nil to the Hungarians after half an hour," Wyckliffe replied.

Winston Jones snarled and struggled: Jim Arrowood, arms round the negro's waist, held the powerful black off the ground while Eddy Corelli, Bobby Milburne and Jingo Byrnes stood in a half circle in front of them blocking all possibility of Jones reaching the two aggressive Swedish backs who were being restrained by their team-mates. Behind the Swedes, their central defender was convulsing in agony from the hard knee-blow to his genitals which Winston had delivered.

The German referee waved aside Jones's team-mates and demonstratively extracted a yellow card from his left breast pocket to wag it forcefully.

Wyckliffe, frowning, squeeze-stroked his chin with his left hand, his right a clenched fist on his knee. The blond Magnusson running free of his English marker, Richard Trelawney was yet again obliged to cover the right, Benny Cawthorne and Eddy Corelli defend the middle.

Jacky's gaze flicked from his team manager's countenance and saw that Magnusson could shoot inside his nearside post, that Joe Berrigan would block it if Richard Trelawney did not. But a quick back pass would let Fast score!

Wyckliffe's curse at the goal went unheard amidst Swedish jubilation. His frown deepened. Substituting Keith Pilbeam for Plumtree had been an improvement. But not enough. Sweden's counter-attacks had become frequent and dangerous. Now this.

"Oh God! Don't let him be sent off!" Wyckliffe groaned three minutes later. Winston Jones, successfully tackled by the central defender, charged wildly not caring whether he kicked the ball or man and scythed the Swede's legs from under him.

Other England officials were reacting with similar anxiety.

The referee blew for the foul, and ran backwards, ignoring Swedish imprecations to dismiss the negro.

Wyckliffe sighed relief. He turned to his remaining midfielder, the bow-legged Stan Troop. "Okay, Stan, warm up. You're going to replace Eddy Corelli and Eddy's to take care of Magnus Magnusson."

Winston Jones eyed Stan Troop running on and the man he had replaced departing. Jed Lennox is the best of all these shit-houses! he thought viciously. His brown team-mate was waiting to throw-in. Winston glared at the yellow and blue garbed Swedes: All these bastards hate me, are out to get me! He eyed his countrymen: And they'd like to see me fail. Bastards!! Bastards!! Not one decent pass have they given me!

Magnusson jinked left-left-right. Eddy Corelli neatly, without body contact, flicked the ball from him, spurted five yards and delivered sharply to Jingo Byrnes who touched upwards for Stan Troop to head to Bobby Milburne. Bobby rounded one man, and, confronted by three others, stabbed a hard pass through a two-foot gap and gave Jim Arrowood a twenty-yard race against the defence.

Arrowood reached the ball some yards from his right corner of the Swedish penalty area. He lobbed hard and high over two Swedes to Winston Jones who outjumped the 6'3" central defender by at least a foot and headed left, hit the turf and departed with a fourteen-foot bound and lashed the ball at the goal and hurtled after it.

The keeper was perfectly positioned; but the enormous acceleration tore the missile from his grasp.

From four yards out, Winston struck it at full speed with every vestige of power in his right leg.

Only those watching the television slow motion repeat for the second time saw the ball's passage to the roof of the net.

Winston Jones did seven scissor kicks in his leap which took his waist parallel to the crossbar. Then he sprinted bounding and dancing towards the left corner flag where Curly Greenhalgh was the first to congratulate him.

"He ain't coming to my orgy, in spite of that," Benny Cawthorne said, and made no move upfield.

Wyckliffe relaxed, and breathed in deeply and leant forward to add his smiling delight to that of the rest of the England squad.

Deprived of benefits from their best player, Sweden, in spite of four substitutions, were compelled into the pattern of the match's first twenty minutes: England's superior quickness and skills forced Swedish errors. Yet fine defensive positioning and teamwork with every yellow-blue player producing his best and never giving in redeemed the home team.

Each chance for a Swedish counter attack was taken with all ten yellow-and-blue athletes participating.

Richard Trelawney and Gunnar Fast tussled hard outside England's penalty area. Benny Cawthorne deftly flipped possession, sidestepped a midfielder and pushed towards Jingo Byrnes. Jingo, with two Swedes in front of him, lifted over both for Jim Arrowood at the limit of the centre circle to head diagonally right, into open space behind the left back.

Winston Jones, bunched in by two big Swedes sprinting alongside and slightly in front of him, fought savagely with his shoulders to break their blatant obstruction.

The referee prepared to whistle.

Winston sent the two Swedes staggering with his shoulders, stumbled, fell, leapt sprinting without losing motion to overhaul the ball outside his right corner of the penalty box and lash it the instant he was in kicking distance.

The ball, travelling at something over ninety miles an hour, curved into the goal's extreme top corner.

"Gawd!" said Benny Cawthorne in disgust. "We'll never hold the big-headed bleeder now!"

Jones the magnificent! the supreme! the greatest! the king! Best in the world! The one and only! the finest! I am Winston! Winston! Winston Jones!!

With twelve minutes left to play, Wyckliffe substituted Sidney Robert Garner on the rightwing for Colin Greenhalgh on the left. Sidney's splay feet, knock-kneed right leg and piano-key toothed grin turned him into a well known television personality after he had outdribbled the Swedish left back half a dozen times, succeeded with each pass and had two tries at goal.

Wyckliffe was on the touchline near the entrance to the dressing rooms congratulating each of his men as they passed. Out on the Råsunda turf, players were exchanging jerseys and comments.

The attractive young reporter who had interviewed Jacky the previous evening approached the England Manager. Wyckliffe immediately inquired about the Hungary-Norway match.

"One – nil."

Winston Jones stood naked glistening with water and soap in the shower room, laughing and shouting: "Two goals! Two facking magnificent goals! And I had to fight for 'em! Nobody helped me there! Headlines tomorrah – Jones the magnificent! Jones the giant!"

"Bobby's and Jim's were good goals, too," Joe Berrigan let the spray hit his face.

"Yi-ih! Good, good! But I got two!" Winston danced out from under his shower. "And the way I got 'em! Did you see the way I got 'em?!!"

"Well played, Bobby! Well played young Milburne!" Curly Greenhalgh from the far stall reacted against the Negro's boasting.

"Good old Jim! Smashing goal" shouted Eddy Corelli, showering between Curly and Jim Arrowood. "Next best goal after Bobby's!"

Winston Jones was indignant: "What do you mean?! Mine were best!"

Jeers and catcalls greeted him, some good natured.

Winston grew angry: "Mine were best! Mine!! Mine!!! I had to fight every inch of the way for mine! Make my own! Nobody set mine up! You hardly gave me a decent pass." His voice was overwhelmed by boos, jeers and laughter.

Benny Cawthorne entered. "What's all the row about?" he stepped under a vacant shower.

"I'm best!! Best!!" Winston Jones shouted. "And tonight when I get those white girls!" Lust stiffened his flaccid five and a half inch penis to a thick nine-inch truncheon. He gripped it in his right fist and wagged it up and down and peeled back its foreskin and danced around shouting: "Look at this, white men! Look at this!"

They all looked at the grinning, muscular youth, glistening with water, bouncing around waving his stiff member. Some laughed, others looked away. Bobby Milburne stared, then turned his back to conceal his arousal.

"What are you going to do wiv it?!" Benny Cawthorne derided. "Stick it up Jingo's arse?!" which comment provoked general risibility and ribaldry. "I wasn't going to have you at my orgy, but now I fink you could be the main attraction: We can see what staying power you've got."

Winston Jones threatened with right arm raised and forefinger levelled: "I'll smash your face in for you before you're finished, Cawthorne! I'll get you, back in London. We'll be waiting for you."

"Who's we?" Benny stayed under his shower soaping himself. "Sonny Nichols? terror of the Saturday morning Brixton street market and all the little clubs where the black brethren hang out?"

Winston Jones's erection was drooping, his expression apprehensive.

Benny Cawthorne, shampooing his hair, kept voice raised above the hiss and splash of the showers: "Sonny ain't interested in helping you against me. You want to settle any account you fink you've got wiv me, just ask anybody around the East End, they'll tell you where to find me. Then you'll wish you hadn't."

Winston Jones was scowling, indecisive.

Richard Trelawney entered the shower room. Benny, back to the newcomer, called: "Last chance to come to my orgy! Anybody want to come to my orgy?! Guaranteed Aids free and healthy! Last offers!"

Richard Trelawney displayed revulsion: "You are a contemptible and degenerate animal, Cawthorne! There are young boys here away from England for the first time! Keep your corrupting filth to yourself!"

"Aw, c'mon, Richard!" the Cockney cajoled. Then addressed Winston Jones, pointing at the big, hairy Devonian: "You fink you can match that, eh?!"

Trelawney lost his temper: "You are a despicable, immoral man! with your glorifying physical parts and lust! We are all made in the image of Almighty God, and shaped as He, Our Heavenly Father, has seen fit to make us here on Earth! Whatever our bodies look like, or any part of them, is unimportant in the Eyes of God! He judges us for what we are, by our souls, by the cleanness of our lives and of our purposes!"

"Alright, alright," Benny was placatory, "no need for a sermon."

Joe Berrigan above the hissing, splashing water said he thought there was.

"You would, wouldn't you?! you Roman Catholic father of eighteen!" Benny called. "What is this?! Some kind of a religious meeting?!"

"You are a godless atheist, Benjamin Cawthorne, for which you will surely pay the worst price when the Day of Reckoning comes!" Richard Trelawney passed judgement.

"I'll take my chances," said Benny.

"Consorting with whores, wallowing in debauchery with all the moral destruction and risks of sexual and physical disease involved! I have put up with your foul-mouthed jibes and jeers for the sake of the team. But in trying to get these boys to go to your orgy, you have gone too far!"

Jed Lennox cut in: "You needn't speak for me, Richard! I'm not interested!"

"Nor me!" Winston Jones snarled. "I wouldn't go anywhere wiv that bastard!"

Eddy Corelli said he was off to a jazz club in the Old Town.

Richard Trelawney was slightly mollified: young Bobby Milburne was shy of girls; the other players had demonstrated lack of interest or disapproval. "I'm making an official complaint, anyway, Cawthorne. Something has to be done about you." He stepped under a vacant spray. The Cockney jeered wordlessly, and left his and began to towel down.

Laughter and exclamations, cheers and whoops of delight reached into the shower room from outside. "What?!" "Two-one?!" twirled through the hullabaloo. Wyckliffe entered, followed by others. "Lads!" he called. "Listen! Are you listening?!" The only sound to be heard was that of running showers. "Norway beat Hungary two-one!"

Incredulous shouts and cheers stopped him from continuing.

"You're kidding, aren't you?" the Cockney was prepared.

"About this? Never."

"How?" Jingo Byrnes inquired quietly.

"The Hungarians scored after twenty minutes and spent the rest of the match shooting in until eight minutes from time when the Norwegians got a break-away goal. The Hungarians played safe for a draw, got jittery and gave away a penalty in the final seconds. I love Norwegians! A beautiful people!" Amidst the cheers, Wyckliffe remembered: "Oh, Jacky, message from the hotel – your brother Harry wants you to ring him at seven o'clock."

CHAPTER 13

Harry's voice was thin with strain: "I got this phone call about two this afternoon. Chinese. You know how they talk. Not Billy Woo. I'd have to pay. 'Or you suffer'," he said.

Jacky grunted contempt. "He's got some mate of his to threaten you, Harry," he assured his brother with heavy good humour. "'Or you suffer!' Ugh!" Jacky growled disdainfully. "What rubbish! He knows you're doing exams and he's being spiteful to upset you so you'll do badly. You're stopping indoors studying, aren't you? So nobody can get at you. In Passfield Hall, you're among people who know you. Tell everybody there what's happened. And when you go down to the L.S.E., see that you've got people with you all the time. The next thing you do, Harry, is inform our friend the Chief Constable. Say I think it's time for the police to have a quiet word with that young Chinaman. He's a rank wrong 'un."

Harry Day's voice held relief: "Yes. I guess you're right, Jacky." He laughed, embarrassed, freed from fear. "Talking to you makes me seem such a fool!"

"No," Jacky assured him. "When you're under a lot of pressure as you have been the last few weeks, you do tend to blow things out of proportion. How are the exams going?"

"I don't know. I haven't done well. I've forgotten so many things! Missed so many points I could have made!"

Jacky was amused: "That's what you always say. And you always come top. Just like Mary. She's exactly the same as you. When I did my A Levels, I was damned glad I could find anything at all to write about."

Calmed by his brother's common-sense and reassurance, strengthened by his own academic superiority, Harry congratulated Jacky on England's victory and commented how fortunate England were over the Hungary-Norway result.

"That's football," said Jacky. "We had our bad luck last year. This evens the balance. England *should* be in the World Cup. Anything else, Harry?"

"No."

"Good luck then. And don't worry! Things will turn out alright."

Jacky laid the half-read biography of Harry S. Truman beside his thigh on the pale green counterpane: Arab music from Jingo Byrnes's tape-recorder-radio curlicued through the wall to his left. "Come in," he called out.

Joyce Trelawney led: "My supplier's wife asks if you would come to their garden party and meet their neighbour, the Swedish Finance Minister. He knows Robert Jarvis."

"Up you get, boy," Jim Arrowood ordered. "You can read that on the plane tomorrow."

"Lots of interesting people there," Beth Langdale said.

"Show jumping jockeys!" her boyfriend scoffed, eliciting a lip-biting, eyebrow-crumpling, skew, merry, intimate glance from Beth.

"All sorts of fine and odd types from all professions and callings," Joyce added. The Arab music wailed twirling to a thin crescendo, then sobbed thickening, sinuous as an androgynous mullah's prayers.

"Let's invite Jingo," Jacky swung off the bed. "The poor old lad hasn't been out all week."

"He may not want to," Jim Arrowood was reluctant.

Joyce Trelawney was opposed: "Richard wouldn't like it."

"Then I'll stay here, and you can tell them why."

CHAPTER 14

"Will Robert win his election?" The Swedish Finance Minister's dark grey eyes were bright: a smallish, chubby man with thick grey brows, thatch and mild grey suit, a human otter.

"Touch and go. We're having a big public meeting this week with the Tory and Liberal candidates on the same platform with us. I'm apprehensive about it."

"You need not be. You will acquit yourself well, I think. I saw your programme late last night. Front page news in every Swedish newspaper today and mentioned in the news bulletins! You don't like Mr Snatcher!"

"He'd be alright as a prison warder or running a concentration camp," said Jacky, making the Swede laugh. Some thirty yards behind the Finance Minister, on the south-west of the lawn, Jingo Byrnes, hectored and admired by exuberant, near and early teenagers, was joyful. Jim Arrowood and Beth Langdale, beside the lilac bushes at the lawn's north-west corner, were chatting to the middle-aged chairman of Sweden's largest agricultural machinery and chemicals multinational and to a slim person whose straight legs and small bottom appeared to belie her title of Scandinavian Horsewoman of the Year. A tall, thin bishop sipping apple juice and a short, fat prima donna grasping half a litre of lager strolled, clucked about by brightly clad, bejewelled older ladies and a plump hermaphrodite in a pink suit.

From the open French windows of the white stuccoed house with its granite foundations, hubbub flittered and stretched. Around the gardens and everywhere beyond, pine and spruce posed dark amidst sparse wild grass and rocky outcrops of the Baltic Shield. Lawns and parterres patched about the pale grey, ochre and dull red houses, visitors on a natural Nordic landscape tamed scarce sufficient for human need and comfort.

"You will be slaughtered by the Conservative Press in England for that programme," the Swedish Finance Minister warned him.

"I'm afraid so. I said what I think." Two pretty girls raced giggling towards the house from the group around Jingo Byrnes; one perhaps sixteen, the other some months older, both in tiny black miniskirts, pumps, and red and white hooped sleeveless T-shirts whose wide necks and armholes exposed well-developed naked breasts that bounced for liberty at each stride.

"The Bishop's daughter and our host's," the Swede explained. Richard Trelawney, emerging through the French windows, thrust his glass hastily upwards and swivelled sideways to avoid the leaping sylphs. Jim Arrowood raised his drink to Jacky who nodded acknowledgement. "It calls for moral courage to criticise Conservatives in power and to speak for reform and those who champion the underdog. Celebrities like yourself reach hundreds of millions all over the world in ways politicians such as Robert and I never can. International improvement and international co-operation are vital. Robert iss strongly engaged there. He spoke very well about British Trade Union reforms last August at Bergendahl, a few miles from here, when the Swedish Trade Union movements were host to an international trade union conference. I talked about Wage Earner Investment Funds, Company Democracy and Worker Co-Determination."

Joyce Trelawney, a raddled film actress, a sinewy sculptress smoking a cheroot, and a Moslem African diplomat in a fez and green and white robes strolled from the house towards Richard Trelawney who was glaring at the spectacle on the lawn: Jingo Byrnes, boyish equal among the exuberant adolescents, was humbly, roguishly yielding to a maternal lecture from a dark-haired fourteen year old.

"I don't know much about those things," said Jacky. "Are you saying Robert might bring them up at our meeting?" The other youngsters added their good-natured bullying to that of the dark-haired teenager; Jingo submitted, mock-cowering and grinning, making his coterie laugh and Richard Trelawney take an angry pace toward him.

"He might. He had reservations about Wage Earner Investment Funds but wass much in favour of Company Democracy, giving workers the right to share in making decisions that affect their jobs and places of work."

"That, I do like," said Jacky. "There are far too many little Hitlers chucking their weight about. I remember that well enough before I turned pro."

The black-miniskirted girls in their skimpy T-shirts galloped kicking a football across the lawn towards Jingo's clique. Joyce Trelawney introduced her husband to her companions.

"Tell me – I ask the same question of all Englishmen –, why iss it that so many British working people vote for the Conservative Party, when that party so obviously represents the rich and the privileged and iss usually vigorously opposed to the interests of the working class and the ordinary man in the street?"

"Brainwashing, that's why," Jacky told him. "The Conservatives own practically all the newspapers, and control all the radio stations and TV. They favour only *their* opinions, and belittle any others. Ridicule them. Treat 'em as if they are those of idiots, or little better. And at school, all that is taught is conservatism. It's built into the system. All the standard textbooks, especially history books, are written from the conservative's viewpoint. The radical never gets a chance: he's kicked in the head straight away. All English society is controlled by conservatives. All the judges and lawyers, all the top Civil Service people and local government officials, police, army, navy, airforce, all the businessmen and bankers. You name a power organisation – apart from the Trade Unions, and not even always there," Jacky's humour was dry, "- and it's run by conservatives. So naturally many working men and women get brainwashed. And many others like to have a big opinion of themselves and identify with the people in power – even though they don't have any themselves and are looked down on by those who do -, and so they vote Conservative. Will that do you for an answer?"

"Very well indeed," the Swedish Finance Minister said. Jingo Byrnes was demonstrating ball control techniques. "When I wass their age," the Swede indicated Jingo's admirers, "I longed to be a football star. But I did not have the speed, the skill, nor could I kick a ball. I wass a good student, however," he consoled himself. "And now I play each year for the Social Democratic side in the annual match for Swedish M.P.s, Government versus Opposition. Right back. I cannot kick a ball with my left foot or I would play left back, a more fitting position for a socialist, don't you think?"

"Left winger, leading the attack?" Jacky suggested.

"Very good, yes. At fifty-six, however, I am too old, and the position iss already taken. Indeed, some of our rearguard would like to throw me off the team altogether."

Jacky grinned, appreciating the other's whimsy.

The Swede glanced at his watch. "I wish I could stay longer," he sighed, "but I'm flying to Brussels early tomorrow, and I've papers I must read and prepare." He nodded at Jingo Byrnes, now encircled by exuberant ball-feeders keeping him busy: "Superb footballer! Do you think you could give me your autograph before I leave – for my grandson? Do you think the other players would, too?"

Jacky took the proffered notebook and pen. "Jim!" he called, beckoning Arrowood to him. "Richard!" Jingo Byrnes, darting about the lawn, was being tackled on all sides by eager opponents.

"Has he solved all the world's problems for you?" Jim Arrowood's eye-corners crinkled.

"He hass left one or two for us," said the Finance Minister. "He says he iss apprehensive about his coming public political meeting, but I do not think he needs to be, do you?" For answer, Jim Arrowood grinned sideways at Jacky; Richard Trelawney was scowling, nervous to still the prancing, shouting bevy ten yards away. One of the girls shoulder-charged Jingo, another shunted him from the other side, a third leapt to barge him in the back; staggering, laughing, he dribbled on, tackled and hacked at from the front by the boys in the group; the bishop's daughter grasped his outflung right arm, her friend his left. "England have a world class team again, I think," the Swede addressed Richard, busy scribbling his name. Through the adolescents' shrieks and shouts, a piercing scream stopped all conversation; the hostess's daughter, hugging Jingo Byrnes's left shin tight, was tumbling silently backwards splaying him, her friend, legs twined round Jingo's other leg, skirt a thin roll about her waist, T-shirt under her armpits, was a lithe curve undulating from hysterical screech to excited laughter. Jingo hit the turf with his shoulders and outflung left arm, his right round the girl, clutching her near nude buttocks.

Richard Trelawney exclaimed gutturally and started forward, face savage. Jacky swayed across his path, forefinger pointed at the bishop five yards to their left: "The girl's father, Richard. Let him."

Fixed blue-eyed attention, sparse frame in clerical collar, purple shirt, black suit.

Trim ample breasts, nipples pink and pointing, child's face with woman's self-awareness in its bold, assured stare.

The young, teenage girl, retaining her father's gaze, lowered to kiss, with skill worthy of a passionate courtesan, the dazed and supine Jingo Byrnes. Jingo's intensity instantly equalled hers.

The bishop, emotionally fascinated, morally repelled, turned his back on them, and, under strained control, resumed conversation with the pink-garbed epicene, the opera singer and entourage.

CHAPTER 15

i

Somebody in the room – Jacky sprang out of sleep.

"It's only me," Benny Cawthorne murmured through the dark. Around the edges of the blind shone daylight.

"What time is it?" Jacky dropped his head back onto his pillow, eyes closed, relaxing.

"Quarter past five."

Remembering the previous day's victory, England's participation in the World Cup, Mary at home, Jessie, Jacky sank contentedly towards dozing. Benny Cawthorne sucked in breath and swore in pain.

Jacky was alert: "What is it?"

"Bashed arm."

Jacky sat up, fully awake, curious: "What are you doing?"

"What's it look like, you silly little bagger?! I'm packing," he said goodnaturedly.

"Early, ain't it?" Jacky turned on his bedside light, Benny the ceiling light. The Cockney checked to see he had forgotten nothing. "What have you done to your arm?"

"I knocked it. And if anybody awsks you, that's all you need to say. And the less you say, the better I'll like it. Okay?"

"Okay," Jacky was puzzled.

Benny continued: "When anybody asks about me, I've gone back to England."

"What about Wyckliffe?"

"Let him sleep peaceful. He' done a good job. I'll leave a note for him at the reception desk, apologising for leaving so sudden and telling him how some urgent, very important, personal business has called me back to London." Benny turned off the ceiling light. "Remember, Jecky, if anybody awsks any questions, you don't know nuffink, except that I came back and left. Right? And you don't have to tell them about my arm unless they awsk you direct – okay?"

"Okay," Jacky suppressed curiosity.

The Cockney grinned broadly and winked: "See you back in England, you li'l facker. Yankeeland here we come, eh?"

ii

"And that's all Benny said?" Wyckliffe asked.

Jacky nodded, and eyed the third occupant of the hotel basement conference room, a beefy, middle-aged Swede in a wrinkled grey suit and navy blue shirt. "What's this all about, Inspector?"

The detective stayed serious for a couple of seconds, then relaxed and shrugged. "Since Mr Cawthorne have already left Sweden," he decided that he could reveal details. "A man iss badly hurt in hospital. He have broken ribs and broken arm and broken jaw, and he have damaged – I do not know the English vord, – vhere all the blood collect. It does not matter. It vass serious. He have lost much blood."

Jacky recalled the Cockney's injured arm. He controlled his suspicions and emotions.

Wyckliffe spoke: "Let's get it straight, Inspector. You said you wanted to speak to Benjamin Cawthorne as a possible witness at this party where the man was injured." The Swede nodded. "No more than that? You don't suppose he had anything to do with this man's injuries?"

The detective shrugged. "An ambulance vass called out at three o'clock this morning by a voman who have been drinking and vass frightened and a little hysterisk. She say she vork in a hospital and a man have been injured in a fight at a party and need help. Ve get there before the ambulance. The house iss empty except for the man and voman who live there, and the injured man."

"How do you know that Benjamin Cawthorne had been there?" the England Team Manager wondered.

"Because the people in the next villa hear him and the owner of the house and some others talk in the garden."

"They could have been mistaken," Wyckliffe protested.

"Yes. But the owner of the house iss a man ve have reason to keep our eyes on. I vill say no more than that. And Mr Cawthorne have been seen vith him on Friday night. And again last night at some nightclubs."

"What about the injured man?" Jacky spoke.

"He say nothing." The Swede grinned. "He fall down, he say. 'Screw you, Copper,' he say, and one or two bad svearvords I not translate. Whoever do this to him, it must have been a gang. He have black belt in karate. He have been in prison for Grievous Bodily Harm. And tvice ve try to get him for murder, but he have good friends and lawyer and alibi. Vell, I not take up any more of your time, yentlemen. Very good match yesterday. Good luck in the Vorld Cup in America."

CHAPTER 16

I don't want to go the U.S.A.!!! Jessie and I shall stay at home!! I'll work in peace at Bio-Veracity and here! Mary stared through the attic casement at Ursa Major and Polaris. In front of her on her writing desk, illuminated by a single reading lamp, her open journal and some Sunday newspapers. About her in her workroom, textbooks, works of reference, scientific periodicals, rows of files. Computer and accoutrements. Cabinets. At the other north-facing, triple glazed window, a camera-mounted astro-telescope; a red fire extinguisher hung on the wall beside it. A second extinguisher centred the eastern side between its two large windows and floor-to-ceiling bookshelves; beyond the black hulk of the outbuildings, across the night-concealed training field, light from the bedroom of the couple who worked part-time for the Days and whose presence safeguarded the area. "I don't wish to go to America," Mary stated aloud, and swivelled further; the kitchen lamp came on in the lane-end cottage a quarter of a mile south; darkness and remnants of Sherwood Forest through the western glazing. Mary regarded Ursa Major afresh. At Bio-Veracity, she was in the midst of several interesting projects. Security arrangements for the England squad in the United States would be extremely restrictive. Jacky would be continuously preoccupied with training and football. Jessie and she would be caged up in hotels, shuttled from city to city every few days. Jessie would need constant attention; she would whine; she would miss her little playmates. She might fall ill. Better for Jacky to concentrate undistracted on his tasks, Mary decided, and for Jessie and herself to stay safe and happy at home.

I wish I were pregnant, she thought.

Ursa Minor gleamed, bared of clouds. Mary twitched her mind from galaxy to galaxy, peeping at details as diffuse as energy and the edge of knowledge, snapped back to the Big Bang, and the nothingness before the Big Bang.

No thing. Not even a vacuum.

Non-existence before existence.

Her unconceived child.

A little boy to make the pair. For Jacky to teach football to. To become a scientist. To be whatever he would.

And if the baby were a girl, or twins, or triplets. Triplets! Oh-oh-oh! Scre-e-e-eam! One baby would suffice, thank you! Jacky wanted a boy. Jessie, companionship. Two pregnancies were her limit. She had her research work, aspirations of discoveries as profound as Darwin's or Newton's. Motherhood and family must come first, though. Not that there was any conflict. Jacky had always respected and encouraged her scientific bent. Was proud of her. He had not insisted she and Jessie accompany him to the States, merely suggested it might be a good idea.

Mary contemplated her computer. The bedroom light across the training field went out. She glanced through the southern window: the cottage at the end of the lane was dark. She closed her journal, gaze oblique upon her husband's photographs and the front-page articles about him in the day's newspapers.

Sir Alec St John Frobisher and his clique would watch Jacky's Stockholm interview tomorrow night, perverting it for their own misuse at the coming Town Hall debate. What bullies the Snatcherites were! Obstinacy irrefrangible! Imagination nugatory! Compassion – all for their own and none for others. What execrable judgement they continually evinced! And Sir Alec St John Frobisher, the Conservative candidate in this by-election, was as caustic a compound of romantic reaction and arrogant aggression as ever sizzled for a spot on the Tory benches.

CHAPTER 17

"Wycliffe has certainly shown his ability!" Robert Jarvis did not pause from writing on the flyleaf of his book. "England were world class on Saturday. Jingo Byrnes hasn't lost any of his skill. A midfield strategist in your category, Jacky." He looked up: "Is he still the preternatural penalty-taker? Never missed once all the time he played in England."

"Like Jacky," entering the sunlit lounge, pushing a food trolley, Mary defended her husband's prowess. On the lawn outside the open French windows, Jessic and a girl contemporary were playing ball, a third little girl was building with toy bricks, a boy was jumping on a two and a half metres by one and a half metres trampoline.

"Jingo's as good as ever," Jacky confirmed.

"Are you going to win the World Cup?"

"Apart from possible weakness in defence, it's the best England side I've played in, so we have a chance. Italy and Brazil must be favourites on their records. Brazil won again yesterday, 7-2, in Venezuela, and Italy beat Greece 4-0."

"I hate that Angelo for kicking Jacky," Mary poured their guest coffee, Jacky repressed fear. "I'm glad Benny Cawthorne hurt him. I'm not vindictive, but he should have put him in hospital for a month – poetic justice." The men exchanged glances, Jacky's wry, Robert's amused and shrewd. "I don't mean it really," she beguiled them with innocence. "Your book, Robert?" She read his inscription and glanced through the index. "Looks most interesting, Rob. I shall read it at once."

"I shan't!" Jacky exclaimed. "'Economic Theory and Practice'! Puh! Our Harry can read it for me!"

"How're his exams going?" Robert Jarvis asked, taking a lettuce and tomato sandwich.

"He's sitting them. So he'll do well. He always does." Jacky withstood temptation to mention Harry's trouble with the Chinese. "Have you sent a copy to our friend, the Swede?" Jessie, running top speed, tumbled headlong: Mary tensed.

"I may give him one when I see him in New York next month, if he hasn't read it already." Jessie scrambled up to dash after the ball: Mary began browsing in Robert's tome. "It's definitely his area of interest. I've tried to outline the structures and principles operative in units larger than the self-contained nation-state, that is, in international economies and the world economy."

"What takes you to New York, Rob?" Jacky wondered.

The other ballplayer fell down. The boy descended from the trampoline. Mary considered them.

"A United Nations symposium on Business, Investment and Trade Unions in the Third World. The Trade Union Congress is sending me. I may see you two over there," Robert said. Jacky glanced hopefully at Mary. Her gaze stayed rigid on the children. The little girl was on her feet, clutching the ball: the boy called for it. Robert took another sandwich. "Aren't you eating?"

"This banana milkshake is enough for me. I've another hour's ball control practice first. If you'd come half an hour ago, you'd have met Jim Arrowood. We're in extra hard training every day now."

"Then I'd better get on with what I came to discuss, our nation-shaking public debate!"

Sir Alec St John Frobisher, said Robert, had been influenced over the weekend by his offspring: the youngest, a parson wangling for advancement, the middle son, a Guards officer wanting promotion, and his eldest, a multimillionaire moneylender banking on a peerage for services rendered to his country, that is, the Conservative Party: Robert Jarvis, the boys had argued, was nothing but a hell-bound atheist and gallows-bait republican, and Peter Gladquith, the Liberal candidate, a twice-divorced lecher and periodic toper. The Conservative lead in the public opinion polls was so tiny that an all-out personal attack upon them based on those Tory faithfuls, Monarchy, Morality and Patriotism was all that was required to woo and win the waverers.

"They could be right," Rob Jarvis admitted, "especially about monarchy.

The gutter press and Tory media glorify it so enormously that any politician in a marginal constituency like Workfield who speaks sanely about royalty, could drop enough votes to lose the election."

"Sir Alec Sinjin Frobisher!" Mary exclaimed, "noblest of noble champions of high principle and morality! Public hangings to discourage potential murderers who naturally intend getting caught, or, even better, giving themselves up! Public floggings for bullyboys guilty of assault! Whippings for jailed criminals on their birthdays to teach them to stay out of prison in future! Birch the bare buttocks of thieves, louts and scallywags and thus encourage them to consider others! Fifty lashes for sex offenders to promote morality, then castration to ensure permanent good behaviour! Strict laws against prostitution, homosexuality, lewdness, crudeness and nudeness!"

"You've forgotten to ban communism and send all communists to Russia and China and all troublemaking parasitic foreigners, especially Blacks and Asians, back to where they came from!"

"Oh yes! How could I, Jacky?! Alec, Alec, what a true English gentleman you are! Turpitude disguised as rectitude? Not a bit of it!"

Robert Jarvis was grinning. "He's tough and shrewd for all that. I must see your Stockholm interview tonight, Jacky: the Tories are going to attack you in strength over it."

"I'll stand by what I said. All I can do is tell the truth as I see it."

Jessica clambered onto the trampoline; the brick builder, baby mug to mouth, was taking a lemonade break from her labours; crouched like a miler, the little boy prepared for a five yard run at the ball.

"The truth will do. If any problems arise, let me deal with them."

Mary chuckled deep; Robert looked inquiringly at her. Jacky explained: "She thinks all politicians are liars."

"I'm not."

"Do you always tell the truth?" Mary asked. Jessica was exuberant, bouncing at twice her own height.

"No one does."

"That reveals you for the politician you are!"

"That's what I am now," he admitted. "Sometimes it's not wise to tell all the truth, Mary. In some situations, it can lead to disaster and terrible suffering. Sometimes you're confronted with nothing but bad alternatives and you have to choose the least obnoxious. Politics can be a dirty business, like life. Nevertheless you can clean it up as best you can and stay as clean as you can."

Mary gazed solemnly at her husband. "Definitely a politician. Definitely."

"Our next Member of Parliament," said Jacky.

A screech of terror snatched their attention: Jessica, struck by the ball at the zenith of her bounce, was falling awkwardly. Jacky was across the room and through the window before Mary and Robert moved. The tot struck askew the trampoline, partly smiting its frame: half a second later, her daddy had her in his arms, Mary was running from the house.

Shock and fright, and a bit bruised, Robert at the French windows decided. He contemplated the convulsive yells, the tears, Jacky's kisses and consolation, Mary's anxious ministering. The child would be alright with such parents. Unlike many an unfortunate in the constituency and the world. The thought came: I'll ask Jacky if he's willing to help in any international, humanitarian project.

CHAPTER 18

"No! I won't!" Jim Arrowood protested, ducking his head and instinctively passing his hand for protection across his hair, still wet from its post-training shower. "I'm not interested, Jacky! I've enough on with football and farming and business!" Rock music thumped muted along the corridor from the lounge television.

"I think it's a splendid idea," said Beth Langdale: "You should, Jim, darling, if you're asked – noblesse oblige."

"I'm not noblesse."

"You're the noblest man I know, dearest," Beth kissed his cheek. "Besides, you would have been if your father had accepted the baroneh he was offered last year."

"A barony?" across the tea table, Mary was alert. The rock tune howled and juddered, low and thick.

"I'll play in any charity match you get up, donate money, I'll give you moral support at your town hall meeting tomorrow night, and any other, but I'm not getting involved in international politics!"

"We can fix a game up," Jacky mused. "Benny Cawthorne'd play, and Richard Trelawney. The top foreign lads would come if it were for the right cause, a noble one. Every year there are fresh catastrophes, with huge human suffering, destruction, people homeless: like that Ukrainian disaster last week, with hundreds killed and injured. Then there was the Turkish earthquake too. And the one in Iran. Yes," Jacky was sincere, "we could make it an annual institution – with special, high priced seats for millionaires and top dignitaries! – play it in different countries every year. We could raise millions, with the right publicity, selling souvenirs, giving interviews, making records and all the rest of it."

"After the World Cup," said Jim Arrowood firmly. "Let's concentrate on that first."

"And on trouncing the Tories tomorrow night!" said Mary.

"She'd vote for Frobisher," Jim Arrowood grinned and jerked his thumb at Beth Langdale.

"Jim, darling, he is the most charming man. Awfulleh kind and sweet, truleh."

"His politics aren't," said Mary.

"I know nothing about politics, I'm a complete ignoramus," Beth pleaded. The rock music changed to reggae.

"Tory. High Tory," Jim Arrowood was provocative. "She'd like to go clap with her reactionary relatives and Equestrian Fellowship foxhunters!" he teased. "I will sit with Mary among the socialists. She still has not thrown away the little blue rosette Sir Alec Sinjin-Frobisher gave her yesterday. I saw it in your handbag."

"Well it's very pretty and matches my red, white and blue frock! I realleh am not interested in politics, I do assure you! Honestleh I'm not."

"We'll get you one of ours, one from the Liberals, then you can wear all three," said Mary.

"And when we arrange our worldwide famous, international charity match, you can sell Sir Alec a dozen tickets at a thousand pounds apiece!" Jacky exclaimed. The telephone rang. "I'll take it in the study," he forestalled Mary.

The abrupt cessation of noise seemed to shiver the book-lined silence. No sound from the other parts of the house. Sparrows were chirping about the gooseberry and currant bushes a few yards outside the windows.

Harry's voice came small from the telephone receiver: "Jacky? Is that you, Jacky? Mary?"

"Hello, Harry. How are you?"

"Scared. I told the police, and my tutor about that Chinese 'phone call. Billy Woo denied all knowledge! He tried to speak to me yesterday, but I wouldn't. He did today, after the exams this afternoon. He said he's frightened, and I believe him!"

Gazing through the window at a thrush pecking about the garden, Jacky ordered: "Calm, Harry, calm."

"I'm scared!"

"You've no need to be," Jacky was firm and friendly.

"It's easy for you to talk! It's not you they're after! They're going to maim me, perhaps kill me!"

Jacky's disgust bordered on savagery: "What a vicious little bastard! Can't you see he's trying to ruin your chances in your exams, Harry? Upset you, so you'll do badly."

Harry was earnest, though fearful: "No-no, no, Jacky! He w-was afraid. He really was!"

"He was putting on an act for your benefit, Harry. He's a very cunning, very vindictive man, your Chinese mate."

"No," Harry's voice was small, fading with acceptance that his brother might possibly be right.

"Yes," Jacky was convinced. "He wants you to fail or do poorly and thus wreck your life! What a rotten little animal!"

Harry's fear jittered, yet Jacky's scepticism and reasoning were having effect: "He- he said – he said – he- he was scared that they might get him, too."

Jacky rejected the idea scornfully: "He's a liar, Harry. Don't listen to him. You concentrate on doing well in your Finals."

"He said – he said that – that these people, the man who – who put on the money was dangerous."

Jacky was calm and firm: "There is no man, Harry. It's merely this vermin trying to mess you up, and he's doing a good job of it. How're your exams going, Harry?"

"Alright. I succeeded in putting it out of my mind when I was in the exam. room."

Jacky was steady and encouraging: "Keep on doing that, Harry. There's nothing for you to worry about. Forget what this fellow says, forget it completely. Have you told the police what you've just told me?"

"Not yet. I – I rang you first."

Jacky spoke soothingly: "Tell the police, Harry. And your tutor. And the Principal. Put pressure back on the bully. Don't let him intimidate you. You've nothing to be frightened of. Nothing at all, Harry. Where's the sense in anyone threatening you? a student, without any money. It's stupid! And injuring you would be pointless because the police are involved and would be after whoever did it. It would be in all the newspapers and on television, I'd see to that. They'd be onto a thrashing for nothing whoever touched you! But nobody will. It's merely a very intelligent, very spiteful kid bent on frightening you."

Harry Day sighed hard and quickly. "Ye-ye-yes, maybe you're right, Jacky."

Jacky was decisive: "I am right, Harry. You're not thinking straight because the past few weeks you've been under a lot of pressure studying, worrying about doing your best, and now this Chinese bet business has pushed you beyond your limit. These present two weeks, trying for the highest academic honours, are in a way what you've been studying for all your life: they're crucial."

"Yes," Harry Day admitted quietly.

"Concentrate on your work, Harry, and do well," Jacky encouraged him with strength and warmth. "I'll send you fifty quid tomorrow to cover the cost of all these phone calls. And when your Finals are over, Harry, I'll make it another fifty – with three noughts after it!"

CHAPTER 19

Workfield town hall teemed with movement and hubbub. Jacky grinned widely at Mary, Jim Arrowood and Beth Langdale who were placed immediately left of centre beside Beth's godfather, the Earl of Fossdyke, three knights, two baronets, a baron and various millionaires in the first of the three twenty-chair rows below the platform on which he sat with Robert Jarvis and five others: Sir Alec St John Frobisher, flamboyant with his black hair fringing his brown pate, black handlebar moustache, dark eyes and heavy red cheeks, his six foot six inch paunchy twenty-two stone frame elegant in double-breasted pinstriped grey suit with white handkerchief in top pocket, white shirt, Guards tie and glistening black shoes; Mrs F.O.R. Keepingham-Downe, J.P., the local Conservative Party Chairwoman; Peter Gladquith, the sandy-haired Liberal candidate; Jane de la Potte, actress and glamour girl; and A. Goodman, Master of Ceremonies.

Goodman leant forward and spoke into the microphone, flashing yellow teeth in an ingratiating smile at the two portly purple-faced figures on the first row: "My lords," he contemplated the crowd standing shoulder to shoulder filling the hall, "ladies and gentlemen, pray feel welcome to this meeting at which, may I remind you, no smoking is allowed. I now officially start the meeting by calling upon our first speaker, the Conservative Party candidate, Sir Alec Sinjin-Frobisher!" Cheers and boos bounced about the enclosure.

"My lords," Sir Alec commenced.

"Shoot 'em!" shouted a scrawny little red-nosed, red-faced man in his fifties immediately behind the left of the third row of chairs: his red tie was vivid against his scruffy white shirt and black suit.

"Ladies and gentlemen," Sir Alec continued.

"Scum!" bawled the weed.

"Hanging!" roared the Conservative candidate glaring at the little man, "is too good for some people, many might feel!"

"For you!" shouted the runt. Boos and cheers, encouragement and orders to shut up mingled.

"Flogging!" thundered the Conservative, "as a punishment was once widely used in this countreh and many would like to see it returned! These thugs who beat up old men and women, rob them of their old age pensions, and leave them crippled with broken arms and legs. Why, only this morning, I read of five such instances! Animals who attack innocent people! Rapists who defile without mercy their innocent victims! Perverted vermin who molest young children! Hooligans who wreck properteh, smash windows, street lights, go around intimidating law-abiding citizens, screaming and howling in the middle of the night disturbing the peace! Anti-social scum of this and every other type would, any sane person might think – and reasonableh think I am tempted to add -, merit the soundest of severe thrashings to knock some sense and decenceh into them!"

Cheers and shouts of fury, laughter, and bawls of hatred crescendoed; the little red-nosed man was hopping up and down shaking his fist, his mouth hurling sound lost in the general din.

Sir Alec's loudspeakered voice boomed through the racket: "This milk-and-water modern psychological treat-'em soft sort of stuff may have its uses on occasion! – but not on evereh occasion as it is now applied! No! What is needed for most of 'em is a good stiff jolt of no-nonsense old-fashioned discipline! Put the fear of God and stern measures into them! Knock the nonsense out of them and straighten them out! I'm for hard treatment! The harder the bettah! Hard but fair! All these strong, idle spongers scrounging all kinds of welfare benefits, it's got to be stopped! Out to work with them! And if they won't work, they get nothing! And all those officials in the public sector, now servicing that sort of clientele, could then be gainfulleh employed in private industreh! Privatisation is the word! Private enterprise gets the job done efficientleh! Without all the red tape and job padding with ten doing the work of one which is all too frequent an occurrence in nationalised industries and state financed public services, unfortunateleh! Cut down tax rates to encourage private enterprise and people with initiative and those who will work and can use their brains and money to make money! Let people make money and let them spend it how they want! That's capitalist efficienceh and private enterprise! and freedom! freedom for the individual which trades unions in this countreh, and every othah countreh, do their demndest to suppress! How many trades unions genuinely reflect the democratic views and general interests of their membahs and work for their long-term good and that of societeh as a whole?!"

Shouts slung like spears: "All!" "Up the Unions!" "None!" "Tory scum!" "Filth!" Boos and catcalls. Cheers and handclapping from Conservatives and hear-hears and "Good old Sir Alec!" The red-faced, red-nosed man, fist waving, screeched: "The working class – !"

Sir Alec's loudspeakered voice out-noised the cacophony: "Few! Very few! Most are dominated by communists and left-wing socialists out to reduce us to the dismal egalitarianism of socialist poverteh that suppresses individual thinking and leads to oppression for all except the leftist ruling clique! Capitalism, private enterprise and freedom for the individual are what I pledge to support and promote to my utmost at and outside Westminster when I am returned as your next Membah of Parliament on Friday! Thank you."

The cheers, handclapping and footstamping, the boos and screams of "Scum!" and "Vermin!" catcalls and mirth continued as the M.C. called for order and silence for Robert Jarvis.

"Friends!" Robert Jarvis began, and was promptly cheered and whistled, booed and jeered. "State control and public ownership are essential ways of protecting our common economic and social interests and of helping to create a fairer, more just society!"

"Never!" "Rubbish!" "Idiot!" Conservative shouts spattered angrily. The little man with the red tie was smiling and nodding contentedly.

"Conservative misrule with its deliberate dismantling of the Welfare State, cutting down on public spending, and its tight-money economic policy led to millions of unemployed and untold suffering. with the weak and the helpless crushed and trampled down, scorned and belittled! We reject that society where the rich and strong are allowed to grab and plunder at will! A Labour society is a just society, a humane society, a society that cares for the weak and the helpless, that honours and respects the working man and does not allow the narrow, sectional greed of a privileged and relative few to reign malevolently supreme!"

Jacky, chuckling, wholly in agreement, was unaware of the TV cameras recording him.

"We shall strive to strengthen and improve the Welfare State as never before! Make available money for new equipment, techniques, facilities! We shall spend on research! We shall extend and reform all social services so far as need requires and resources permit! We shall invest in and encourage all publicly beneficial services, industrial, commercial and building activities!"

"Money! Where's the money coming from?!" "Where's the money?!" "Money! Where are you going to get it?!" Conservatives shouted, laughing angrily. "Good old Rob! You tell 'em!" Cheers and clapping.

"Public building, if I have anything to do with it,"

"Which you won't!" called a middle class man. "Gerrout on it!" a working man responded. "Boo!" "Rubbish!" others shouted.

"...will embrace"

"I'd like to embrace Jane!" bawled a young fellow with hands cupped round his mouth, and the beautiful Jane de la Potte smiled and blew him a kiss and everybody laughed.

"...housing accommodation for young people, single people, couples who want a small, inexpensive flat easy to afford! We shall give subsidies to encourage local government housing authorities to build such accommodation! And high minimum standards must be observed. As in Sweden where I was last August! With double-glazing, good insulation, architecture, interior functional planning, and efficient building methods which, in this country, are all too often antiquated, especially among small firms that account for much of our building activity. Reform and education are definitely needed there! A Workers' Charter!" Rob began.

"Up the Workers!" called Jane de la Potte's admirer which provoked a loud general cheer and clapping sliced with many appreciative whistles, and no booing, though numerous prosperous-seeming gentlemen smiled sourly and others looked as if they were eating lemons.

"A Workers' Charter, to democratise the whole of British Industry! The ordinary working man must be given a substantial amount of control over his place and conditions of work!"

"Rubbish!" "Nonsense!" "Balderdash!" "Poppycock!" "You're out of your mind, man!" the wuff-wuff Tories barked and growled.

"The feudal, patriarchal way of the boss giving orders to his workers must, as a point of principle, be strongly modified, and, where possible, replaced. Consultation, consideration, respect for the dignity and human worth and value of the employee must be made central!"

Barracking was non-existent. He had the full attention of his audience. Jacky was nodding keen approval; the other TV camera focussed on him.

"Worker co-determination and industrial democracy shall be of central importance!"

"Rubbish!" "Nonsense!" Tory heckling took off again.

Rob's loudspeakered voice carried clearly: "Instead of the present situation where a boss's report on an employee can destroy a person's career and life, it shall be made an axiom in British business that employees prepare a similar report on their boss, showing *his* merits and flaws as a colleague and as a human being and both reports shall be equally important!"

Tories who had positions of power howled and jeered. Tory working class supporters kept quiet.

"Our aim is to encourage and promote a reduction of the standard working week and an increase in paid holidays per year! The proceeds of the computer age and scientific and technological revolution shall not be the preserve of a lucky few, but shall be for the benefit of all society! I repeat, all society!"

Cheers sounded plus cries of "Idiot!" "Liar!" "Pie in the sky!"

"Government money shall be invested in new ideas and inventions and techniques as a large scale venture! All too often, brilliant and ingenious devices, designs, technology and concepts have in the past, and to this day, been let vanish into oblivion through lack of support and money! That must be stopped! A corps of professional ombudsmen shall be set up to investigate and prosecute abuses of power in Industry, the Civil Service and other public organisations. A permanent Special Investigating Unit to be set up whose investigating officers, *independent of the police*, shall examine all complaints involving possible abuse of power by the police."

Several policemen had guilty grins. Others with clear consciences were non-committal.

"These are some of the policies I have been advocating and shall strive to have put into practice. Thank you very much."

Applause, cheers, jeers and boos sounded. The Master of Ceremonies introduced Peter Gladquith.

Jacky listened and found himself in agreement with everything the Liberal candidate said, and noticed the audience's undivided approval when the sandy-haired man spoke of the need for keeping Nature clean, free from pollution and destruction, of planting trees, nourishing greenery, preserving wildlife. Of stopping the dumping of waste and poisons.

Gladquith finished with a bitter attack on Great Britain's inequitable winner-take-all electoral system and called for the establishment of proportional representation as the only fair basis for a true democracy.

The Master of Ceremonies rose, voiced thanks, then pushed his horse face, leering yellow-toothed at the well-fleshed peers in the front row: "My lords, ladies and gentlemen, our guests on the platform are open to questions from the floor and from each other. Yes, sir?" he acknowledged his bank manager on the first row.

"How do the Conservative and Liberal candidates view a footballer's behaviour who, while representing his country abroad, criticises that country on foreign television to a foreign interviewer for a foreign audience, and launches a vicious and unjustified attack upon a statesman who, in the opinion of all true patriots, has proven after Sir Winston Churchill to be possibly our best prime minister this century?"

Boos thundered and passionate shouts of "Never! Never!" "That swine!" "That vermin!" plus similar musty epithets, as well as clapping and cheers of support for the speaker's sentiments.

Peter Gladquith leant to his microphone: "That man Snatcher never was and never could be a statesman! Well spoken, Jacky! However, the time and circumstances were less than fortunate, I am inclined to agree."

"Disgraceful!" Sir Alec St John Frobisher growled into his mike. "In the Old Days, horsewhipping would have been on the cards, of course." Jacky's head jerked in anger to face his attacker; the news media avidly recorded his reaction.

Robert Jarvis countered with hard scorn: "Typical Tory arrogance! The Old Days have gone! We know you Tories want them back, when you could treat men worse than dogs! – but you're not having them back! Not ever!!"

Cheers, whistles, footstamping and roars of approval rendered Sir Alec St John Frobisher's attempted response inaudible.

"Like all Socialists," the baronet boomed, "you're a liar where historeh is concerned!" Tory supporters cheered wildly. Robert Jarvis retorted immediately: "To that, I can only reply you're a liar, full stop!" Hurrays and laughter and "Good old Rob!" rolled and twirled.

"We'll have none of your Socialist Hell on Earth in this our island home!" Sir Alec roared. "Leftwing rabblerousers should be given a one-way ticket to Russiah where fifty years in one of those once much used, and now quite rightly despised and deserted, Stalinist Siberian labour camps might knock some sense into them! Though I doubt it!"

"And if right wing reactionaries were tortured for even fifty minutes in any one of the world's still numerous autocrats' jails, they would not be so ready to condone such cruel treatment for others!" said Rob.

"Gentlemen, gentlemen," the Liberal candidate was smiling, "are these your pleas for penal reform?!"

Amid the following laughter, cheers and relieved tension, Robert Jarvis and Sir Alec St John Frobisher leant back smiling, tense as two fighting stallions taking a respite.

The Master of Ceremonies said: "Perhaps we should move to the next question."

The bank manager protested: "But Sir Alec has not been let answer mine yet!"

"Sir Alec?" said the M.C.

"I deplore the whole business. Soccah playahs, and anyone else representing their country in sporting events abroad, should be under strict instructions to steer clear of politics."

Rob Jarvis intervened: "Which does not prevent British reporters from questioning foreign sports personalities about political and social conditions in *their* countries."

"Sport and politics!" someone in the middle of the hall called out in prelude. "Yes, sport and politics!" someone near the back cut in. Several people began shouting questions on sport and politics. "Ask Jacky Day!" a group of youths salvoed the phrase.

"Sport and politics, Mr Day," the M.C. invited.

"They should be kept as far apart as possible," said Jacky. The TV cameras registered his face, journalists pointed their directional microphones at him. "Sport is sport. It's for amusement, pleasure."

Jane de la Potte spoke: "It's big business, too. Enormous amounts of money are involved. And politics. Hundreds of millions, thousands of millions are spent on sport. Those spending the money know how important it is as propaganda."

"Yes," Jacky agreed, "yet basically, sport is only a game, for amusement." Jane de la Potte was shaking her head, and Mrs Keepingham-Downe's square face had exchanged arrogance for superciliousness. Jacky continued: "In itself, it's unimportant, except for the people playing it." He realised the subject was becoming too complicated for him. "I can only speak for myself," he stated simply. "What others think or don't think, that's up to them. I can only say what I think, personally, me. In my opinion, an athlete, a sportsman, should be allowed to play his game against or with anybody anywhere in the world. It's up to him personally to decide, nobody else."

Jane de la Potte and Peter Gladquith were shaking their heads firmly. Jacky spoke to the audience: "I don't like politicians forbidding people to play in this country or that, or against those opponents, or in that tournament, just because the politicians don't like the politics or the beliefs or the religion or the colour of the people involved."

"You're wrong!" Jane de la Potte interrupted.

"Yes," Peter Gladquith agreed.

Jacky told them: "They asked me my opinion and I'm giving it." He addressed the audience: "Do you want me to?" The TV cameras panned.

"Yes!" roared back.

"Okay, I will. If you're representing yourself and nobody else, in my opinion, as a free person, you have a right to go where you like and do what you like!"

"Yes, but – !" Jane de la Potte began.

"Each case, you've got to decide on its merits," Jacky went on. "It's difficult to decide sometimes. But, basically, what I've just said, I believe in, and I'll stand by."

Peter Gladquith said: "Unscrupulous régimes and oppressor organisations use political innocents like you to gain good publicity and give respectability to their bad causes!"

"Are you going to let me finish?" Jacky wondered. Peter Gladquith nodded. "If you're talking about a team representing, say, England, then it's a bit different from the individual representing himself. But even so, I'm in favour of keeping sport for sport and politics out of it. In football, we play all over the world. And footballers go act as coaches and managers. And that's good, I think. Now, when it comes to speaking about politics, an athlete has a right to his opinion as much as anyone else. And if he thinks a thing is good or bad, he has a right to speak his mind about it."

"But he doesn't!" Jane de la Potte exclaimed. "In most countries of the world he doesn't!"

"We're in this country," said Jacky. "Here he does."

"Do you agree with what he's just said?!" Jane de la Potte addressed Rob Jarvis spiritedly.

"Not exactly."

"Do you?!" she insisted.

He answered frankly: "No – not about sport and politics. I think they are inevitably linked."

The Liberal candidate nodded agreement. The Master of Ceremonies noticed Sir Alec's disdainful smile and prompted: "Sir Alec?"

"I agree with the football playah, Mr Day. As far as I believe I understood him, I'd say I can endorse his opinions one hundred per cent."

"Hear, hear!" Mrs Keepingham-Downe seized her chance to speak.

Jacky reddened at being in disagreement with his candidate, and drew succour from Mary's smiling, nodding encouragement and Jim Arrowood's slow wink and thumbs up sign.

Jane de la Potte challenged Sir Alec St John Frobisher over his sporting and other links with racialist, white South Africans, and Sir Alec counter-attacked trenchantly with indisputable examples of oppression and injustice throughout the whole of non-white Africa and Asia. The Liberal couple responded vigorously. Rob Jarvis joined with them. Mrs Keepingham-Downe got in many telling cuts about naked painted witchdoctor savages, and eating people for dinner, Middle Eastern madmen, Moslem and Hindu intolerance, etcetera, etcetera. And Sir Alec St John Frobisher, who was nothing if not a realist as to the finer distinctions between which unsavoury truths were politic for broadcasting and which not, was obliged time and again to edit, modify, and even renounce facts which he himself in private related with even greater gusto than his provincial partner.

Jacky felt alienated. He smiled at Mary, and she smiled encouragingly back.

During a momentary lull, the local Liberal Party chairman, headmaster of Workfield's largest comprehensive school, bobbed up from the middle of the front row calling for the speakers' views on Politics and the Arts.

Jane de la Potte was not slow to give hers, and with her flawless face, form and brassiereless breasts commanded rapt attention and even a few marginal male votes for the Liberal cause.

Sir Alec admitted he was no culture vulture. You had to have music, opera, ballet, art galleries and that sort of thing for people who liked it, he supposed. Upon which Mrs Keepingham-Downe said she was one and reviewed Workfield and District's current artistic offerings in much detail and made Sir Alec and others yawn more than a few times before she exhausted her store and Sir Alec was able to resume and say how much he deplored government money being squandered on leftwing groups and so-called artists in order to finance vicious attacks on the British Way of Life and Capitalism.

Robert Jarvis was pungent: "Very few socialist works reach the public because small-time Conservatives in power stop them at the outset! Active government backing is essential to stimulate art beneficial to socialism and change in order to counterbalance the torrent of status-symbol, snobbish bilge flooded out by Conservative-controlled Industry, and by the Conservative Establishment in general!" Mary Day was smiling and nodding lively agreement.

Sir Alec snorted contempt. "I do not wish to see Government control of the Arts as they have in socialist countries where writers and artists have to knuckle under to the ruling party bosses and their dogma!"

"Exactly as we often have to in Britain, except to different dogmas and different bosses," Peter Gladquith observed ruefully, recalling his time in advertising and the film and T.V business.

"Mr Day, you haven't spoken yet," the M.C. noticed. The news media became alert.

"It's not really my area," said Jacky. "I've no strong views one way or the other. I pass."

"And Jim Arrowood gets the ball and scores!" shrieked a bright-eyed wag. "Hurray!" "Goal!" Cheers and shouts rang out. Both Internationals grinned.

"What're you going to do for sport in this country?" a young fellow yelled.

Sir Alec replied: "I'm in favour of private enterprise backing sport. Sponsor money. I'm in favour of sport in general." He leant back in his chair to the approving hear-hears of Mrs Keepingham-Downe who had as little interest in the matter as he had.

Peter Gladquith's comments were almost as brief as the Conservatives'. Jane de la Potte spoke warmly for better training facilities and programmes for girls.

Robert Jarvis deflected the M.C.'s invitation from himself to Jacky.

"Every town with a population of over 20,000 should have its own sports centre," Jacky said, "With a swimming pool, facilities for all indoor sports, such as basketball, and volleyball. I saw a good one in Vellingby in Sweden last week. I would like to see every town with its own running track and provisions for field events. I would like to see close, regular contacts between specialist professional coaches and school sports teachers with wide use being made of video film and sound tapes, with the country being split up into regions: each region with its own set of coaches. I want very much to see every young person who has ability at a sport being helped to develop it, if he or she wants. I'd like to see all people being encouraged to engage in a modest amount of physical exercise in order to keep reasonably fit."

Robert Jarvis said he could easily support those views and would discuss them with the Minister of Sport at the first opportunity.

"Does the educational system need reforming? and if so, how?" the Liberal Party's local chairman asked loudly.

"Certainly," Robert Jarvis got in first. "Abolish all public schools, those children's prisons, deform schools, rat holes of Tory privilege and snobbery!" Sir Alec, public school champion and fanatic, choked and turned purple. "All children should be educated at state comprehensive co-educational schools with a teacher-pupil ratio of no more than one to fifteen, preferably one to eight. Spending on education must be given top priority, with the aptitude and interests of the individual pupil put first, so that the joy of learning is nourished and not destroyed as so often happens today."

"Poppycock!! Rubbish!!" the Tory candidate exploded forth.

They battled it out.

Jacky listened, watched and said nothing till directly invited to speak; then, recalling how everybody at school had genuinely longed to know – and experience – the physical facts of sex life, he said he would like those facts to be taught objectively to every child. Mrs Keepingham-Downe attacked him with condescending sternness: sex education, as everybody knew, promoted immorality, promiscuity, Aids, sexual disease, unmarried mothers at thirteen and lifelong tragedies and ostracism.

Jacky had no need to reply: Jane de la Potte did it for him: with beautiful eyes flashing and shapely head and hair tossing, she left no one in doubt as to her views on sexual education, ignorance, hypocrisy, moral double standards and bigots like Mrs Keepingham-Downe.

"Morality," Sir Alec came in with conviction, "is what Britain and the world needs! The age-old religious values!"

Mrs Keepingham-Downe heard her cue and drew a deep breath to attack the opposition for godlessness.

Robert Jarvis struck first : "What religion?! And what values?! The world has had thousands of religions! And billions upon billions of interpretations of those religions! Honesty! Respect for the truth and for the dignity of Man and for all Mankind, those are the values we should put foremost!"

"You're an atheist, aren't you?!" Mrs Keepingham-Downe rapiered insidiously.

Jane de la Potte intervened with spirited contempt: "And you're a religious bigot, aren't you?!"

"Don't you dare – !! You -!!" Mrs Keepingham-Downe was indignantly furious. She controlled herself and countered venomously: "You're an atheist, too, I suppose?"

"My religion is my business!" retorted Jane de la Potte haughtily with toss of head. "I don't care if you engage in Devil's Worship, or ride off on your broomstick to your witches' sabbath or not!" Cheers and laughter and "You tell her, Jane!" "Lovely!" "Tell the old bag!"

"I do no such thing!" Mrs Keepingham-Downe was shocked. "How dare you accuse me of such – such – ! I am a devout Christian, which is more than I can say for some!" she flung and scowled enmity at Robert Jarvis and Jane de la Potte. Cheers and clapping, jeers and heckling whirled.

"And devout Christians like my honourable colleague, Mrs Keepingham-Downe," Sir Alec intervened, "are the salt of the earth! the finest of old England, typical of those who make our beloved countreh strong and mighteh, who keep her pristine values, her traditions and customs handed down from generation to generation! who fear God and respect His laws, and love their Queen and countreh!"

Tory supporters cheered hurray to the last man, clapped and stamped their feet shouting bravo. The frenetic hate-filled cries of the little red-nosed man with the red tie went unheard.

"Conservatives!" Sir Alec boomed over Robert Jarvis's attempts to speak, "Conservatives are patriots! They love their countreh! They are not ashamed to say that, sir! Yes, you, there, grinning and shaking your heads!" he flung his arm pointing at a group of Labour supporters. "Conservatives *will* fight, and *will* die for Queen and countreh! Let our enemies beware of that! because, though we are prepared to die, we shall take ten, a hundred, a thousand of them with us first! No Conservative would ever appear on foreign television in a foreign countreh and refuse to admit his pride in representing England at soccah as Jeckeh Day did in Sweden!"

"Wrong!" said Jacky into his mike, agitated at the Conservative candidate's misrepresentation. The news corps poised. The tv cameras zoomed in.

Sir Alec roared on: "He would speak well of the land which bred and nurtured him, gave him everything he had! not mince words and confuse every issue!"

Jacky said: "I am not a Nationalist, and I never shall be!"

Sir Alec ignored him: "It is wrong to let football playahs or any othah sporting personalities when representing England criticise our beloved nation! They should get on with their game and leave othah mattahs to those bettah qualified!"

Robert Jarvis came in hard: "Tories like you, you mean! Everybody else has to keep quiet while you spew your Tory garbage!" Conservatives howled protest and Sir Alec snapped into his mike but Robert Jarvis spoke on, "and twist everything to your advantage. Well, you're not having it your way!" Labour supporters cheered, clapped and stamped. "Your bullyboy tactics and bawling down and beating down everyone who disagrees with you are not going to work here! nor your mouthing about patriotism! Jacky Day is every bit as good a patriot as you or I or anyone else who was born and lives in this country – is that right, Jacky?"

"Correct."

The Conservative candidate began: "I -"

Robert Jarvis went on: "Nationalism was what he disavowed – not patriotism." Jacky was nodding agreement.

Sir Alec said: "The two run very much into each othah. And by his particularleh vicious attack upon the finest person it has ever been my privilege to meet in my political life, his credit as a representative and spokesman for England and Britain abroad is less than nil."

Jacky said: "I represent nobody except me – "

Shouts of "No!" and indignant, outraged "You represent England!" "England!" "Liar!" bombarded him.

"and I speak only for me – and nobody else, except Robert Jarvis whom I know is a good man!" Labour cheers and shouts of sympathy and encouragement from football lovers.

Sir Alec would not let go: "I disagree." Mrs Keepingham-Downe said she did, too, and both were hear-heared and clapped by Conservative supporters.

"And as to your patriotism and mine, Mr Jarvis, and yours, too, no doubt, Mr Day, there is a vahst and varied difference! I love my Queen!" The Tories went mad. Stamped and jumped up and down and cheered like lunatics. Fervour overflowed into ecstasy and rafts of fierceness soared on the flood. "Royalteh," Sir Alec savoured the word with reverence, and the cheers soared and soared. "Our noble Queen." The hurrays and hurrahs contained frenzy. "God save the Queen!" Sir Alec was martial: the cheering was so loud it could reach no higher. The little red-nosed man with the red tie screamed his hatred in vain. "I love my Queen," Sir Alec repeated, "her loveleh famileh, our Royalteh, Monarcheh, that noblest of institutions, keystone of our constitution, foundation of our State, symbol of our Nation, the British Empah and Commonwealth!" The Chairman of the Workfield Young Conservatives leapt from his seat in the second row, wild with passion, and bellowed: "God save the Queen! Hip- hip!"

"Hurrah!"

"Hip-hip!"

"Hurrah!"

"Hip-hip!"

"Hurrah!"

General cheering broke out.

Sir Alec pointed accusing right arm and forefinger at Robert Jarvis: "You, sir, are not a royalist! You, sir, are against the treasure house of our democraceh, the Crown! You, sir, would abolish the finest of our countreh's glory, the envy of other lands, the proudest feature of our national heritage, the British Monarcheh!"

"No, sir!" Rob Jarvis's reply was swift and clear, "the proudest feature of our national heritage is the British people itself! with its democratic freedoms, laws and ways hard won over the centuries against the conservatism and prejudice of each succeeding generation!"

"And in that struggle, our Party has always been in the forefront!" exclaimed Peter Gladquith, and his supporters cheered.

Mrs Keepingham-Downe's antagonism was intense: "You want to abolish the Monarchy! Do you deny it?!"

"Completely!" said Peter Gladquith. "Reform the Monarchy, yes! Abolish it – no!"

Sir Alec accused and condemned Robert Jarvis: "But *you* do, sir! YOU do!" Robert stayed silent. "Come, sir, answer! Do you, or do you not, wish to abolish our beloved monarcheh?! A straight answer!"

"From a politician?!" a ginger-haired man's incredulity caused laughter.

"A straight answer, Mr Jarvis," Sir Alec insisted. "Are you or are you not against Monarcheh?"

"Plainly put, Royalty has outlived its time," Robert stated.

Boos and jeers and shouts of "Idiot!" "Disgraceful!" "Go home to Russia!" plus a few cheers and "Well said, Rob!"

The Labour candidate went on: "In the Old Days, you had a strong man who fought his way to the top and ruled by strength and cunning."

"Times haven't changed much!" shouted the bright-eyed wag, occasioning more merriment.

"We have democracy today," Robert was earnest. "Monarchy is not needed."

The Royalists were hostile, booing, deriding, angry with insults.

Sir Alec St John Frobisher was aggressive: "Monarcheh is needed! The finest symbol of our heritage, our nation, our representative in the world and for the British Empah and Commonwealth." Mrs Keepingham-Downe hear-heared. The Liberal candidate and Jane de la Potte nodded agreement. Jacky, content to stay silent, sat unmoving: a tv camera stayed focussed on his face. The Conservative went on: "The Monarch has personal contact with heads of state, government, people all over the world. Governments come and governments go, but the Crown is outside and above politics."

"Not true," said Rob Jarvis. "The Monarch is a Conservative and always has been a Conservative. Royalty are rich, privileged. Their friends and associates are rich and privileged. They are surrounded all their lives by yes-men and time-servers." The boos and jeers contained hatred and unforgiving anger. "The Monarch is very much involved in politics. Every Cabinet decision has to be cleared by the Monarch in person – often at much inconvenience and expense to the country. The Monarch has extensive and very real power. And enormous social influence. Because of snobbery and self-seeking social climbers who are very, very, much in favour of the class structure which our Liberal Party friends most mistakenly proclaim outdated! While there are slums, bad housing, homeless, unemployed, people at the bottom of society who have nothing or next to nothing, while economic and social injustice exist in this country – as they very much indeed do! – then we have a class system, whether you admit it or not!" Jacky, tv camera close upon him, was clapping fierce approval amid the cheers. Boos, jeering and angry hostility persisted but were outmatched.

Sir Alec leant forward in triumph: "There we have him! A leftwing extremist and anti-Monarchist!" Tory opposition roared and insulted; Labour supporters cheered and clapped to a man, shouting affronts at Sir Alec and the Conservatives.

Rob Jarvis responded: "And there we have *him*! A Tory reactionary, out to promote his own and his rich friends' interests!" Labourites and Liberals cheered while Tories booed.

Mary embraced her husband warmly, kissing him again and again. Robert Jarvis spoke earnestly to a group of doting Labour supporters. Sir Alec St John Frobisher, flanked by various aristocrats, Conservative millionaires and celebrities, was exchanging good humoured crosstalk with Jane de la Potte, Peter Gladquith and various local Liberal big shots. Mrs F.O.R. Keepingham-Downe was smiling and nodding unctuously: on her right and slightly in front of her, the fatter of the two peers was lecturing six Young Conservatives who were even more sycophantic than Mrs K.-D.

A few yards to their left, near the window, Jim Arrowood stood amiable and neutral while Beth Langdale chatted in blithe tête à tête with her godfather, the earl.

"I'm glad that lot's over!" Jacky summed up. With a half circle of his head, he took in the three candidates: "A politician's life is not for me!"

"Nor, when the polling-booths close at nine o'clock on Friday night," said Mary, "will it be for two of them!"

CHAPTER 20

"Robert's fate is settled," the big hand of the electric wall clock glided towards five seconds past nine. Jacky looked up from his tome, *AMERICAN PRESIDENCIES*. Opposite him, lying full-length on the sofa with cushions under her head and shoulders, pen and paper in hand, technical periodicals and textbooks on and around her, Mary grinned at him.

Smiling, he put down his book. Pleasantly tired after his final training session for the day, he admired her smooth face and compact femininity, ready to make love if she wanted, content with tranquil domesticity if she did not. "We'll know tomorrow morning," he said.

"I know somebody else whose fate is settled."

"Me?"

"Bighead! Jim Arrowood."

"He likes the lass."

"She's crazy about him."

"Must be. Coming here every morning and night."

"Love," Mary was romantic: she closed her eyes, leant her head back and breathed in deeply.

"Huh!" Jacky grunted good humoured cynicism. She threw a cushion at him: he reflexively stuck his left leg up and caressed it to the floor. She raised her right arm perpendicular; Jacky flipped right footed back to her stationary palm.

"I think they make a beautiful pair."

"Yeh," Jacky settled back to his book.

"The Press think so too. Photos of them together at the meeting in all yesterday's papers." Her mood changed: "What savages the gutter press are! Cheer you when you're on top and winning and tear you to pieces when you do anything they dislike." She displayed contempt. "No attempt to be fair. They merely destroy their victims, knowing they can't fight back."

Realising she did not require an answer, Jacky resumed reading his book's description of the Japanese feudal ways and fanaticism which had made inevitable President Truman's decision to atom bomb Japan into surrender and thus avoid the millions of dead and maimed from continued warfare.

"Look at the way they treat you."

"Swings and roundabouts," said Jacky. "One week they write good stuff, the next, bad."

Mary continued: ""And the manner they go on every day about keeping you quiet in America!"

His longing was clear: "I'll miss you in America, Mary." She stayed silent. "I wish you would come." She stood up. "Mary," he coaxed.

She half-turned aside: "it's better I stay here, Jacky. We've discussed it already. It's decided."

The phone rang.

"You've told the police, Harry?" Mary, silent, watched her husband anxiously.

"Yes. And my tutor. Now you." Harry spoke with quiet resignation: "I believe him, Jacky. Billy Woo would not have come here to see me tonight if they hadn't threatened to beat him up if he doesn't pay by twelve midday on Sunday. The police think he could be telling the truth."

Mary said: "What's the policeman's name and phone number?" She wrote them down.

Jacky was scornful: "He's bluffing you all the way, Harry. Nobody's going to beat him up. At worst, he'll probably get some friend of his to give him a black eye to make it look real. So, he's finally brought my name into it and asked you to get the money off me! He's got a long wait coming!"

Harry's voice was low: "He's scared, Jacky. And so am I!"

"Don't be," Jacky said firmly. "Things have not changed: there is still no sense in hurting you. Nobody can touch you while you're in Passfield

Hall or at the L.S.E. The police have been alerted. When your exams finish next Wednesday, come here. Here, you'll be safe."

"Yes," Harry was relieved, though apprehensive.

"Maybe you should pay the money," Mary sat on the sofa.

"Give in to blackmail?! Don't be ridiculous! If you do that, Mary, you'll be paying for ever to every bullyboy who cares to come at you."

"What if it's true and the threat is serious?"

"It isn't," Jacky was contemptuous. "It's this crooked kid from Saigon, trying it on. He's seen more of life than our Harry has. Growing up in Vietnam with all its harshness and corruption, Chinese boat refugee. He's as hard and cunning as hell."

"Still," Mary was doubtful.

"Harry'll finish his exams and leave London, then he'll be alright. He'll never need to see this Billy Woo or worry about imaginary Chinese gangsters again."

"Ring that policeman tomorrow," Mary urged. Then chuckled tersely. "It's funny. Here we've been wondering all week about this by-election. Yet for the past few minutes, I forgot all about it."

CHAPTER 21

i

"Sir Alec Sinjin Frobisher, Conservative, eighteen thousand two-hundred and twenty-three," the election-returns official enunciated clearly, the wireless was at its lowest audible volume. Jessica lay asleep between her parents. The pink rose-patterned white bedroom filtered pale with 6.02 morning light through the closed, red-gold curtains. Sparrows chirped about the eaves. "Robert Lesley Jarvis, Labour, eighteen thousand nine hundred"

"He's won!" Mary started with delight.

"and eighty-seven. Peter Montgomery Gladquith, Liberal, eleven thousand one hundred and one."

Mary turned off the radio. "He won!" she exclaimed in a whisper.

"Good old Rob," Jacky murmured.

"Jacky," she was thoughtful.

"What?"

"You're going to tell him about this business with Harry."

ii

"It's a difficult situation," Robert Jarvis said. "That detective in London was right when he judged both sides to be morally equal."

"Harry would not cheat anyone," Jacky was certain.

"A stranger can't know that," said Rob Jarvis.

"What do you suggest then?"

"The police you spoke to on the phone this morning think there could be a third party involved and they've a possible suspect," Robert Jarvis mused.

Jacky said flatly: "I don't believe it. He would have confronted Harry face to face with Billy Woo."

"Not necessarily. Not if he did not want to be known."

"I still think it's this Chinese kid, frightening Harry for malice and to get money off him if he can – and off me, now, from what he said yesterday. He's not getting any! In spite of what that detective said on the phone this morning."

"It was wrong of that police officer to even mention the possibility of your paying. However, it was only his unofficial view that maybe, perhaps, just possibly – though he officially advised against it – it might be best to pay."

"I'm not giving in to blackmail," Jacky was decided.

"No." Robert Jarvis sighed. "I'm no expert on this area, Jacky. I'll tell you what I'll do, I'll contact our spokesman on Home Affairs and ask his advice and help: he has access to the best people and information."

Jacky thanked him. Then smiled. "I know what the present headmaster of Danethorpe Grammar School will be announcing on Monday morning."

Robert Jarvis grinned: "I haven't been back to Danethorpe since my father and my mother flitted to Sheffield four years ago." He put papers into his briefcase. "I get the old school mag., though."

Jacky said he did too. They spoke of people they had known at school. The four most outstanding scholars: one a professor of biochemistry in Boston, Massachusetts, another a world authority on laser technology, one a farm labourer in Lincolnshire, the fourth the town drunk in Retford. Bright spirits who had dulled to mediocrity, and dullards who had prospered. The brilliant boy who had tried to succeed as a writer and who, meeting only rejection, had committed suicide. The artist who even in the First Form could draw a perfect circle freehand with one quick movement: dead of a heroin overdose in a public lavatory in Amsterdam. Scandals. Incidents. Accidents. Marriages. Life's inexorable progression and variety.

"You'll be going to the States soon?" it occurred to Jarvis. His briefcase was full.

"We meet on Thursday for a week's training first," said Jacky. "I got the letter this morning."

Robert's gaze checked to ensure he had forgotten nothing. Through the window of the second storey office, the red-tiled roofs, chimney-pots, churches, pubs, shops, streets, lawns and gardens of a small, English country town: his first constituency: Robert Lesley Jarvis, M.P.

"I'll phone our Home Affairs man now, I think, before I motor up to Sheffield and wife and kids. If and when he has anything, I'll ring."

"Not tomorrow afternoon. We're visiting our parents in Trenton."

CHAPTER 22

Jacky filled the battered metal watering can at the tap four yards from the cemetery's rusty black gate. The holly trees, copper beeches and lilac bushes lining the flaking black spiked railing behind him rustled and creaked in the breeze; brownish yellow winter grass ruffled; a withered flower dropped from the waste basket behind the tap. He turned off the water and walked along the central path with the can and the roses and tulips his mother had given him for his father's grave.

No one in sight. Only smoke from a chimney here and there in Trenton village across the fields to the east. A varying grey sky, with stretches of blue. Three magpies flying, a crow. About the hedges, sparrows chittering, a yellowhammer swooping, chaffinches pink-pink-pinking. A blackbird. Always a blackbird. And a thrush. Fresh air. But not so clean as when he had been a little boy. The coal-fired power stations along the Trent had not been built then. Tractor sound from across the fields north-west. Northeast on the Danethorpe road, two cars were going north. The ridge above the village; his mother's house to the right of the hill road.

He stood, all five senses alert. This was home, where he had grown up and played. Many of those in the ground around him, he had known. His paternal great-grandmother and grandparents were buried here: and some of his ancestors in the churchyard. He looked east to where the upper half of the Anglo-Saxon Norman church's tower stood against the backdrop of new-leafed trees. He knew all the old families in the village, and most of the rest except the very young.

"Home," he said. That was his father's grave, thirty yards ahead to the right. "Home," he said again. He felt no emotion at the fact: Trenton would always be home. Though never as it had been when he had lived there. Home now was Mary, Jessie, their place and the countryside near Workfield. Nottingham, too.

He removed the aluminium plant pot embedded in his father's grave mound. A worm moved fat and brown-pink in the dank earth; tiny slugs clung to the vessel. Against the white gravestone in the short, damp grass, a snail crawled waving its antennae. He swilled the container clean, and filled it with fresh water; the worm was tunnelling from view. He replaced the pot and began threading flowers through the holes in its lid, and visioned his father where he lay in his coffin as on the day he had been buried. He recalled the anguish of his grief that had stayed sharp for over a year and lingered for several.

"Flowers for your grave, Johnno, from your wife," he said. "Not that you care now."

Memories of his parents together. Happy times of domestic harmony, trips to Cleethorpes with himself and Harry and their sister. Walks on Sunday afternoons down Roman Lane to the river. Lemonade on the bench outside the pub on summer evenings. Football matches. Delivering Labour Party propaganda. The bad times, also: his mother's nagging, his father's bullying; their quarrels and angry rows.

His mother had always appreciated his sister more than him because his sister was a girl. His mother had discriminated against him, made him turn to his father for companionship and praise because she would not give it. She had favoured his younger brothers, spoilt them, given them everything and him nothing because he was older. If there was a choice as to who was going to get the worst bits or nothing at all, it was always him. Never the others.

Jacky savoured ancient bitterness.

That was a long time ago, though. She was old and ill now.

Yet she had pushed him on to Johnner, when he was little, just to be rid of him.

Still, that was all in the past. She had had her reasons for the way she had been, all the troubles and problems of that time. It had not been an easy life, neither for her nor Johnner.

No, it definitely had not.

Jacky eyed the gravestone's lettering, and read it word for word.

Poor old Johnner.

With his belief in socialism, its better life and justice.

"You wouldn't have cared about 'em criticising you for supporting Labour, would you, Johnner?" he said. "You'd have told them, wouldn't you?" Jacky smiled sadly, recalling his father's devout convictions, the arguments he had had with local Tories, his contempt for each and every Conservative politician, and for Winston Churchill in particular as a warmonger and enemy of the British working man and symbol and representative of the so-called British aristocracy entrenched in power and privilege, living off the labour of the working class.

You never had anything, did you, Johnner? Jacky thought. You were poor all your life. A working man. Farm labourer. Factory labourer. Builder's labourer. Bricklayer's labourer. Roadsweeper. Dustman. At the end, lung cancer.

Memories of his father in his last months of life sitting on the bench in front of the pavilion in the football field watching Trenton F.C. Of his father, healthy, managing the village men's team, and the Intermediates with a diminutive eleven- and twelve-year old Jacky playing against eighteen-year olds. His father's lifetime longing for Trenton to win the Top Four Cup, the major amateur footballing trophy of Danethorpe and District.

We won it for you, Dad, Jacky thought. But you were nine months dead. Still, we won it. Old feelings stirred.

After that victory, Jacky and Jim Arrowood who had played for the team Trenton had beaten had both turned professional with Nottingham Forest.

We've won a lot since then. Done a lot. I'm a rich man now. I wonder what you'd have thought of that.

Johnner would have been glad. He was not against wealth. Only against unjust wealth and unjust privilege.

Jacky stared about him over the fields, and the village Sunday. A dull, mild May Sunday.

Sunday. Twelve o'clock.

The Chinese deadline.

A bluff to frighten Harry, and extract money.

He's getting no money from me, Jacky thought. The bastard! trying to ruin Harry's chances in his exams. After Wednesday, Harry can leave London.

His brother was in no serious danger, but the young Chinese could have Harry beaten up for spite. The rest was rubbish: a gambler who was a gambler would have put the money on himself. Never given it to some young student. And if this man had been as hard and rotten as the young Chinese said he was, Billy Woo would have had that money on straight away! Not taken any risks by giving it to Harry.

And that detective was only guessing about possible suspects because there weren't any – in spite of Mary's fears and Rob Jarvis's doubts.

Rob Jarvis would ring –

"Jacky!!" a vast bellow from River Lane made him turn. He grinned: Pete Gregg, massive and scruffy in his old farm work clothes, was climbing from his Landrover outside the cemetery gates.

"I saw you here, boy, I had to come and have a word!" the burly farmer was grinning hugely. "You'll have to come bring Mary and the little lass ovver for tea! Any time! Any time!"

They talked of the village, old Trenton F.C. team-mates of seven and more years before, several of whom had left the district, one to live in Canada; of the changes in the village, their lives. Pete Gregg, in his forties, still turned out at centre half. Centre half, not centre back nor central defender, but centre half. None of that newfangled terminology for him! And a centre forward was still a centre forward and an inside forward an inside forward! All these young kids with their fancy terms. But none of them could get past him on Saturday afternoons for all that.

"Because you're good, Pete."

"Ay! Second Division Lincoln City in the heyday of my youth!" The big man became serious, remembering when in his teens he had hoped to make the big time, perhaps play for England, before his father had died unexpectedly and left him the farm. "Never had your potential, though, Jacky, yours and young Arrowood's. I didn't think so in those days we played together, but I do now. When I watch you two on the box," he shook his head and smiled resigned admiration. "Are you going to win the World Cup for uz then?"

"Bit difficult to say, ain't it?"

"Yeh. You're meeting the best. The bloody Brazilians can play football! That bugger, Zezinho, the Black Prince, by God, he's good! And Barboza the Bomber! And Vivi!" Pete Gregg displayed delighted approbation at the nicknames. " All those buggers are tho'. And the Eye-ties and the Jerries and the Argies. They're already in America gerring acclimatised. England are leaving it a bit late, I reckon. They say it gets that hot o'er there you can cook ' egg on't street. We could do wi' some o' that weather o'er here, boy. Tho' not that hot, o' coourse. How's your head, by the way? Your mam's al'ays on about it."

"Head's okay," under his calm, Jacky repressed all else.

"We'll be rooting for you! I'll watch every match they send! Even if I've to make the missus do all the farm work," Pete Gregg chuckled. "You and Mary are visiting your families, eh? Your mam's come on summat marvellous these last two weeks, she really has. I always stop and have a word. She din't like you gerring involved in politics, boy!" They walked towards the cemetery exit, Jacky carrying the watering can and dead flowers, Pete Gregg, arch Conservative, jibing at Jacky's political activities, throwing in questions about Stockholm, Wyckliffe the Labourite and the England squad. "Ay, y' mam always tells me about you and Mary and your little girl, Jacky. And about y' sister Joanna and her family. Your two youngest brothers, I see ivery day, o' coourse. Hard workers, good lads. And your Harry, eh?! Sitting his Finals this week! She worries about you all, your mam. I tell her she din't need to – especially not about you and your Harry."

CHAPTER 23

Panic filled Harry's every tone: "They broke his left little finger and three ribs at just gone twelve this afternoon! He's got bruises all over his body where they kicked him!"

Jacky believed reluctantly: "It's not faked then?"

"No!! No!!" Harry's low exclamation was near hysteria. "They're going to get me now! He said! He said!"

Jacky was strong-voiced: "Nobody's going to get you. You've told the police, have you?"

"Yes! Yes!"

"Stay surrounded by friends, people you know. You only have till Wednesday, then you come here."

Harry's panic ran free: "You don't understand! They're going to follow me forever! They're never giving up!"

"Rubbish!" Jacky scoffed.

"It's not! It's not! There's gangster prestige involved! The underworld's laughing at him! He's fit to kill us if we don't pay! Oh Jacky! Jacky! He means it!"

"Calm, Harry. Don't panic. That's the last thing you must do."

Terror sang: "I'm scared! I'm scared! You see he thinks we planned it together with me saying I forgot to put the bet on to save Billy Woo! With my being your brother, nobody would dare touch me or threaten me! Oh God! God! Why did I get into this?! Why?! Why?!"

"Harry," Jacky cut in.

Harry flowed on: "I'll never, ever, never put another bet on nor gamble as long as I live!"

Jacky was calm: "Now listen, Harry," the pips of the pay telephone began.

Harry's hysteria broke: "I've no change! There are people waiting – " the phone went dead.

"We pay the money, and it's finished!" Mary appealed and ordered.

"No," Jacky was frowning and stubborn. He continued dialling the Passfield Hall number. "You don't give in to bullies! You fight them, if you have to! But you never give in to them! because they'll be on your back the rest of your life!" The number was engaged.

"It's not like that, Jacky," she pleaded.

"It is! I'm sorry, Mary, but it is," he began to dial afresh.

Mary was matter of fact: "So Harry gets beaten up, probably crippled, maybe killed because you cling to a point of principle."

"We live in a civilised law-abiding country and it's for the police to deal with these things."

"This crook is not civilised, he's not law-abiding and the police can't deal with him. They don't even know for sure who he is."

"And you want me to pay money to somebody whose name and identity we don't even know?! Be reasonable, Mary!" The number was still engaged, he began re-dialling. "If you give in once, they'll be back again and again."

"No," Mary was decisive, "I think Harry was right. It is a matter of gangster prestige. Once the bet winnings are paid, the matter's finished. That detective as good as told you so."

"Him!" Jacky was contemptuous.

"This gambler may be one of a gang of ten, twenty, fifty, we don't know. You be reasonable, Jacky. And think about the Chinese boy. They've beaten him up. Next, they may kill him."

"Rubbish."

"It's not. Or rather, it's a possibility. This Billy Woo seems to have been right all along and he was quite sure Harry was in danger. I don't think we should take chances – we should pay."

"No."

"We are worth nearly seven million pounds – the money's a trifle."

He was adamant: "It's the principle."

"Damn the principle! I don't want Harry hurt. Nor that Chinese. It's Harry's fault he was beaten up. He trusted Harry and Harry let him down."

Jacky, frowning, glanced sideways at her and stopped dialling.

Mary went on: "And what will happen to him if Harry leaves London for good and this thug can't touch Harry? He might not hurt Harry, but I hate to think what he'll do to that Chinese boy. I cannot envisage any of the Chinese Boat People calling on the English police to help them. Can you?"

Jacky was frowning, indecisive.

Mary reasoned: "The London detective said the thug had a good moral claim – "

"Not to beat people up, nor threaten our Harry, nor try and get money off me!"

"No. Yet Rob Jarvis admitted he had some moral right on his side regarding the winnings."

Jacky scowled: "I'm not being blackmailed. It's a matter for the police," he was defensive.

"They haven't done very well so far, have they? Well – have they?

"What can I do?!" under pressure, Jacky appealed. "I don't want to pay money to some strong arm boy whose name I don't even know."

"You can obtain that from Billy Woo."

"And if he lies?"

"You can find out whom the police suspect. It's probably the same man."

"And what if they won't tell me?"

"You can get Robert Jarvis to find out, put pressure on behind the scenes. Besides, I don't see why that detective wouldn't tell you, when he more or less advised you to pay."

"I don't like it."

"I don't either, Jacky. But it's the best thing, darling. Once the money's paid, that's it – finished."

Jacky turned to scowl out of the window into the twilight. Mary stayed silent, letting him consider.

"If I pay him, I want to see him."

"No. Give the money to Billy Woo. Then it's finished."

Jacky had made up his mind: "If I pay him, I see him. And I don't pay him until I have seen him."

"It's dangerous, Jacky."

He grunted opposition. Then, scowling, angry, disliking his decision: "I'll pay! Alright! I'll pay! I don't like it, but I'll pay. He's not getting a penny piece, though, till I've seen him."

Mary appealed worriedly: "Jacky."

"No, Mary," he was decided. "You persuaded me by pointing out the danger to that Chinese kid. Nobody would have touched Harry, couldn't after Wednesday."

"But –"

"I'll meet this character," Jacky spoke through her objection, "see exactly who and what he is, and make it quite clear why he's getting the money. Not out of fear of him – oh no," Jacky was hard. "If he tries anything in future as regards Harry or myself or any of mine, I'll use every bit of influence and money and power I've got against him!"

Mary was troubled: "Jacky."

"It's the only way, Mary. With bullies, you can't back down and give in to them! You do it once, and you'll do it forever. They never let go. Never. I'm not having that."

"It's dangerous, Jacky!" she was anxious. "Pay the money and leave it at that." Set-faced, her husband picked up the telephone and began dialling. Mary pressed down the receiver cradle. "No, Jacky! Please, think first. You don't know what kind of person or people you're dealing with."

"Scum."

"Dangerous scum, that can beat up people and threaten to kill them, and by all indications, actually do it!"

"All the more reason to let him know exactly where we stand."

"No, Jacky!" frightened, she clasped him locking her hands behind his back fastening his arms at his sides, "I don't want anything to happen to you! Neither you nor Harry!"

"Nothing will," he affirmed gently. "And this way we'll ensure nothing does in the future."

"I'm frightened," she whispered.

Jessica trotted into the room dragging one of her illustrated storybooks which she had been looking at. She grinned at her parents and knelt to peruse her literature, pointing at pictures and practising her storytelling to herself. Mary released her grip on her husband.

Jacky spoke calmly: "I'll tell Harry to contact Billy Woo and set up a meeting on Tuesday night."

"Why Tuesday night?"

"It gives us time to get in touch with Rob Jarvis, find out the name and something about this animal and to consider anything else we've not thought about."

"Don't go, Jacky."

"There's no danger, Mary. He's after money. He'll not get any should anything happen to Harry or me. And no money's going to be paid until later in the week."

"Through Billy Woo."

"Through Billy Woo."

CHAPTER 24

i

Murky waters: Robert Jarvis's words alternated with the clackety-clack of the Inter City express train javelling through London's twilit northern suburbs: street lamps glowed orange, and lights shone in many windows, hoardings with adverts, shop lights, pubs, red London doubledeckers, cars and lorries glimpsed in the evening emptied streets. Rough luck, but you're doing the right thing, boy: Jim Arrowood. Mary, apprehensive, clinging to him, kissing him, telling him to be careful; Jessie playing with her lettered bricks in the garden room.

Lee Kwang Yoo.

Gangster.

Scum.

Beater-up of Billy Woo, threatener of Harry. Extorting money from me now. Identifying mark: half top joint of left little finger missing. Jacky registered change in sound as the train rattled by empty, fluorescent-lit station platforms. St Pancras not many minutes away.

You'll be met at the gate: Harry's voice on the phone.

Tiny exhilaration dulled by forethought: this business had to be executed without emotion: state the facts, make positions clear, leave.

Rob Jarvis: A breakaway faction in the Chinese underworld. Suspected involvement in various rackets. Born in Saigon. Worked for Hong Kong based trading company doing business all over South East Asia. Naturalised British citizen with U.K. passport.

Scum. And we let them into this country. The vaulted brick archways, the profuse sidings and slowing train marked the terminal's proximity.

Rob had wanted the police in.

But for what? Billy Woo had and would not file a complaint. Harry had not been touched. And all he and this Chinese were going to do was talk.

Mary's fear.

Rob's warning of possible danger.

Jacky rejected the notion. He would make matters utterly clear, agree on payment, and that would be it. He was hard, edging fear and anger, completely controlled.

ii

"Mistel Day?" the little Chinese in dirty raincoat, with the top button of his grubby shirt missing under his loosely knotted tie, was no more than five feet tall. His left hand was undamaged.

Jacky nodded. The Chinese gave him a white envelope and began walking away. "Hey!" Jacky stopped him.

The Chinese smiled, showing bad teeth. "I don't know anything, Mistel Day. I give you envelope. That all." He walked off.

An underground ticket. A note: "You are being watched. Run to the Tube station to make sure you are not being followed. Take the Tube to Waterloo. Run from the Tube platform to the taxi rank outside the main station to make sure you are not being followed. At the taxi rank, you will be given further instructions. Do not throw this away. You will be asked for it and will need it."

Jacky grunted contempt and shook his head, smiling scorn at what seemed to him pointless melodrama. He stuffed the letter in his right jacket pocket and walked at normal pace towards the Underground, moderately irritated over being instructed to act like a frightened quarry by vermin who should be more than glad to be getting money, and not trouble, for the whole affair.

iii

"Mistel Day." This Chinaman was about Jacky's height, skinny with big buckteeth. Nothing wrong with his left little finger. "We take taxi."

WATERLOO ROAD: no river, so they were going south. A busy road. ST GEORGE'S CIRCUS. Still going south. LONDON ROAD. The Chinese sat silent at his side.

"Vis is vhe Elephant and Cawstle, gav," said the taxidriver. "Where d' you want to be?"

The Chinaman pointed.

While the Asian paid the cabby, Jacky looked about him; red buses, black took-took-tooking taxis, streams of vehicles; varied architecture, old and new; Cockney, West Indian and Asian voices: typical London.

Halfway down the side street, a black Mini stopped a few yards ahead. Driver, Chinese, late twenties. Wore black gloves. Lee Kwang Yoo? Jacky and his companion climbed in.

The knife blade the grinning, bucktoothed Chinaman pointed close to Jacky's right eye was needle pointed, sharp double-edged, channelled for sticking: a killing knife.

Jacky was apprehensive: a sudden jerk of the car or jolt from the road could send the steel into him. They wished him to show fear, intended intimidating him. Despite his contempt for them, Jacky, for the first time, doubted the strength of his position, then he hardened, lifted his hand and pushed away the Chinaman's wrist. The knife drew back and cut patterns and lunges a foot from his face.

The driver growled and hissed Chinese; the blade withdrew to rest pointing up at Jacky's liver from its grinning owner's knee. Jacky eyed the driver's left glove: was he the one?

For twenty minutes they sped twisting and turning down side streets, through rows of houses.

Every couple of minutes or so, the bucktoothed man, snarling and chuckling, repeated his whirling lunging with the knife, bloodlust and sadism disguised as play. Each time the driver spoke, the patterns ceased. Yet gradually their duration increased, as did the knifeman's reluctance to obey the driver.

Outwardly, Jacky stayed calm. Though doubt and fright nagged him, he realised that scum usually behaved like scum. The gangster he was going to see probably did not know of this treatment.

Or maybe he did. Maybe that was him at the wheel.

Jacky suppressed unease. His position was good. All he had to do was keep calm and get the whole business over with.

iv

A sparsely trafficked minor main street composed of lock-up shops and small office blocks closed for the night.

Side street. New office block to let on the left, next to it, another office block under construction. On the right, an unlit Chinese restaurant with scaffolding in front of it and drawn curtains black against the street lighting, beside the restaurant, big open yard gates.

The bucktoothed Chinese pushed Jacky roughly from behind. Jacky leapt diagonally forward spinning round: the aggressor crouched, blade ready. "Stop that!" Jacky ordered, ignoring the knife.

The driver said: "This way."

The yard smelt of paint. Outside the restaurant's back door was a skip piled with rubble, splintered wood and empty paint tins.

Sharp smell of paint, putty, new wood and varnish inside the building: cream paint-speckled, brown paper covered the floor and sinks.

Jacky followed the driver, his back sensitive to the knife man.

Devoid of all furniture except a kitchen chair, the newly painted seventy square yard dining room seemed very big.

Five Chinese. Young.

"Mistel Day." The gold toothed middle-aged Chinaman looked like a cross between a rat and a frog. Half top joint little left finger missing. "You cally gun, miclophone, tape-lecorder?"

Jacky, amazed, displayed contempt: "No." Three Chinese moved to search him. Lee Kwang Yoo gurgled. They stopped.

"Mistel Day, you cause me tlouble. Not nice. You have got note for me," he held out his damaged hand. Jacky returned the message given him at St Pancras. "You not run like you told."

"No need to run. I came alone."

The Chinese scowled: "We do not know that."

"You know now."

"You do not talk to me like that!" the Chinaman threatened nastily with pointed forefinger. "You cause me tlouble! Your thief blother cause me tlouble!"

"My brother is not a thief. And if you want your money, calm down."

The gangster was irritated: "You not give orders here! I give orders, not you!"

"Not to me, you don't."

The other Chinese moved threateningly. Lee Kwang Yoo snarled and hissed Chinese and they stopped.

"English police cannot plotect your blother! They cannot plotect you! You want your leg bloken? Killed? You disappear, nobody find you."

Jacky was disgusted: "And you expect money from me?"

"Money! Money! – shit, shit! Your blother think he can make fool of me! Steal my money! Everybody laugh, ha, ha! He not touch young blother of big English football star. Ha! We see." He jabbed forefinger pointing at Jacky. "You pay my bet money, twenty thousand pounds, big football star! And you pay for tlouble and expense caused since – ten thousand pounds." He sneered: "You rich, big football star. Thirty thousand pounds nothing to you."

Jacky looked him hard in the eye across the intervening two yards, then started purposefully for the street door. The rat-frog face snarled and hissed. Two Chinese blocked Jacky's path. Jacky stood, irresolute.

"Okay," Lee Kwang Yoo decided, "we bleak your leg. You not play football in Amelica."

As the Chinese moved to surround him, Jacky felt fear, frustration, anger, despair. Shouting for help was useless, fighting, futile. Mary had been right! Rob had been right! He should never have come!

He prepared to defend himself.

The street door smashed open. Benny Cawthorne walked in, followed by six tough-looking companions.

"Nah, Jecky, how are you? He-llo, Mister Lee, what have we got here, eh?"

Jacky's amazement and delight did not stun his judgement: the Chinese were all staring at the newcomers; two quick paces secured him from attack, six more put him beside Benny Cawthorne.

"Alright, Jecky?"

"Yeh. I'm glad to see you."

"What's all this about, Mr Lee?" Benny Cawthorne spoke lightly, good humouredly.

"Me and Mistel Day were talking. About some money his blother owe me, and money Mistel Day make me spend tlying to collect my money."

"Is that right, Jecky?"

Jacky explained succinctly.

Benny's smiling, light and persuasive manner toward the Chinese was consistent: "You've made a mistake, I fink, Mister Lee. Jecky wouldn't lie to you. And if he says his brother ain't lying, his brother ain't lying. Jecky's word is at least as good as mine, Mr Lee, and I'd stake my life on both." Cruelty quirked, then vanished, leaving the Chinaman as impassive as before. "Jecky's brother ain't interested in horses or gambling, Mr Lee, nor in taking your money; he's got examinations and studies and all sorts of fings on his mind."

"A-a-ah," the Chinese crooned, "twenty thousand pounds is a lot of money, Mistel Cawthorne."

"But it's not as if Jecky's brother won the money and tried to get away wiv it, is it? And I don't believe he tried to steal your stake money. He don't need to – Jecky will always give him a few quid if he asks for it, won't you, Jecky?" Jacky nodded. "So you can see, Mr Lee, it's all a big misunderstanding. Everybody realises you've got interests to protect, Mr Lee. But here, two young students, a genuine mistake and nobody taking anyfink off you really. You can afford to be generous, Mr Lee."

"A-a-ah, much tlouble caused," the Lee purred.

"I'll tell you what, Mr Lee," Benny lilted softly, "you're always interested in little contests featuring your boy," he nodded at the tallest of the Chinese. "What say we fix one here and now, eh?" Lee Kwang Yoo grunted, his impassivity softened to controlled anticipation. The Cockney resumed, manner unchanged: "Of course, we can forget all that bet money business for good, now that we've talked it over, can't we?"

"A-a-ah," sang the Chinese man, then began nodding. "Ye-es," he agreed. Smiling, face cruel.

"Let's get on wiv the show, then, eh?"

The gangster barked and spat Chinese: his man prepared for combat.

Benny handed Jacky his coat and whispered: "Get near the door, boy. And whatever happens, you keep out of it. These guys I've got here wiv me are good. Get out in the street if you have to: we've got some back-up forces out there what'll take care of you if it comes to that."

The bright light from the unshaded lamp bulbs probed each detail sharply: the cream walls, the seven Chinese in the far half of the oblong room; the six young white men spaced the breadth of the room three yards from the damaged door where Jacky stood; the two converging contestants, similarly clad in slippers, slacks and tee-shirts, Benny's dark blue, his adversary's black.

Jacky had an impulse to shout stop, proclaim the situation's folly, unreality, let loose a torrent of sensations, feelings, discuss the how and why of it all. But the noise could distract Benny, gaze locked on the young Chinaman's, three yards apart, both men poised, neither moving.

Action – at tremendous speed, kicking for shins, knees, groin, kidneys, head, fingers flickering at eyes and throat and nerve centres, hands chopping, elbows stabbing, each move being defended, exploited, countered.

Benny was down! A kick to the stomach! Rolling, fighting with legs like independent thinking sinuous creatures that whirled and jabbed to chop the Chinaman staggering to one knee scarcely able to defend himself.

Lee Kwang Yoo hissed and barked. His fighter scrambled round and to his feet, retreating simultaneous with Benny's leaping to attack with twirling fingers and savage feet.

They separated, both breathing heavily. Eyes unblinking on the Cockney's, the Chinaman snarled, yelping growls as he circled, continually changing position and stance, feinting to attack with hands and feet.

Benny, expressionless, silent save for his breathing, barely moved.

Several kicks at the shins by both. Parried. A right foot two-handed body/face combination by the Chinese.

Resultless.

A flurry with half a dozen hand and foot blows by each fighter.

Withdrawal.

The Chinaman sprang, arms and legs blurring in total commitment. Benny was hurt to the body, cut over his right eye, retreating, almost overwhelmed.

Lee Kwang Yoo and the other Chinese were ardent in their lust for blood and victory.

Benny was against the wall, dodging to the left, the Chinese giving no respite hit with hard foot blows to the arms and thighs, Benny was weakening, slowing, no longer able to evade, scarcely able to defend.

The Chinese were vociferously triumphant.

A kick to the stomach – Benny Cawthorne was defenceless.

The Chinese struck for the head.

Benny broke the Asian's right arm.

Lee Kwang Yoo exclaimed, and shouted angrily at his crippled champion who had dragged free and stood ready to fight on.

Benny kicked the broken arm, then broke the Chinaman's left leg. The prone warrior growled submission in Chinese.

The Cockney acknowledged with a similar growl, and stepped back.

"That was a good fight, mate," he addressed the defeated man. "You had me worried there for a minute." He accepted a clean handkerchief from one of his companions grunting approval around him and held it to stem the blood from his cut eye. He was friendly and polite: "All right, Mr Lee?"

The Chinese gangster, though scowling and hard faced, gave two sharp, substantial nods, each accompanied by an acknowledging matching acceptance in Chinese.

Benny bent to clasp his erstwhile opponent by his left shoulder to show respect and consolation.

"We'll go lads, eh?"

It was raining in the street. Lightly.

"You come wiv us, Jecky. It ain't safe for you in London tonight."

"I was planning on going home."

Benny Cawthorne grinned, handkerchief held against his cut: "Not very hospitable, are you?"

Jacky, overwhelmingly remorseful, impulsively gripped the other's upper arms to look him in the face: "I din't mean it like that, Ben!"

The Cockney's grin widened: "I know you didn't, Jecky," he lilted easily. "You fink I would have been here otherwise? you li'l bagger! You were finking about Mary and the little girl, and Mary worrying about you. Come on, let's get out of the rain and out of here – fast."

v

"'Place was bugged. We knew they were taking you there." Benny's black Jaguar sped through glistening streets.

"How?" Jacky was baffled, amazed. "I mean – how could you even know I was coming to London? How could you know *any*thing?"

"You fink London's a big place, but it ain't. Not for some fings, it ain't. You get a little whisper here, and a little whisper there. And some people who knew you were a bit of a mate o' mine told me."

"Who?"

"Ah, people. Chinese – Mr Lee ain't all that popular -, others. Mr Lee, in fact, is a crazy facker. He's proved it, trying somefink like this. But you and your brother can forget this after tonight. We can't trust Mr Lee tonight, though. He's a treacherous bagger, and we've got to give him time to cool down, and have a few people talk reason to him."

"Who?"

"You don't want to know, Jecky. I might tell you the whole story in the future sometime. But not now. You can tell Mary what happened tonight. Keep it to yourselves, though, ey? We don't want it spread around. Okay?" Benny glanced from the road to his companion's face, wanting serious confirmation: Jacky nodded.

"It was you, in Stockholm, who put that karate bloke in hospital, wasn't it?"

Benny slowed the car to halt: an old couple shuffled across the drenched pedestrian crossing. "Somebody come round asking questions, did they?"

"Police. What happened?"

The Jaguar purred to thirty mph. "He was a faggot," the Cockney was matter-of-fact, gaze alert on the street through the whirling windscreen wipers, rain pounded the car. "He'd had a couple to drink – not drunk – and he was going round making fellows suck his cock, and sticking it up the arse of those he fancied. He beat the shit out of one guy who wouldn't. Decided it was my turn for a nibble. I declined. One fing led to another, and it sort of broke the party up. Wyckliffe say anyfing?"

"No. You took a risk tonight, Benny. It could have been you who got crippled. You could have missed the World Cup."

"So could you."

"I didn't know what I was letting myself in for."

"*I* did. So that evens fings up. Feel like a little entertainment tonight?"

"I've had enough for one day."

"Don't say that, Jecky. I'm in the mood for some relaxation. I promised I'd show you somefink rather unusual and out of your way when you came up to London to visit me. You'll give me the chance, won't you?" the Cockney was very persuasive.

Jacky, grateful, obligated, did not want to disappoint him: "Okay. But we're in serious training, remember. We don't want to stay up too late."

"Attaboy." They passed a van turning down a side street. The rain, thinning, was steady. "Remember at your place when I was there? Remember what we talked about?"

Jacky said he was not sure.

"Beautiful women. I've fixed one up for you, Jeck."

Jacky, startled, glanced at his companion's face: the Cockney, alertly eyeing the road ahead, was smiling. "You'd no need to do that. Anyway, I can find my own, if I ever want."

"Not like this one, Jecky. She's special." Benny looked sideways at his passenger: "She's the most beautiful woman you'll ever see."

Exultant yearning for sexual adventure struck against memory of Mary smiling, happy, friendly, gentle, Jessie laughing up at him.

Fear.

He would not risk domestic harmony nor hurt them.

"Not interested, Benny. I'm a married man."

"Wait'll you see her. Remember what Mary said? She wouldn't mind you having a piece on the side if it wasn't serious."

Fear beat temptation: "No. Better not. No sense in risking it. I'm happy with Mary."

Benny was amiably neutral, concentrating on driving: "It's up to you. I thought I'd lay it on for you in case you wanted. She's got a flat in the building next door to me, overlooking the river. The best view in the world. You've got a room there for the night."

"Can't I stay at your place?"

"You can if you insist. But wait until you see how fings are, Jecky. She ain't no streetwalker. She's turned down some Arab and Yankee millionaires and a trip to the States to come to our show tonight. I told you we've laid on somefink special."

CHAPTER 25

"Midnight!" the heart-faced, lovely woman in her white satin low cut evening dress, black hair waving over her shoulders and breasts, sang the hit song from the musical, 'Cats', with genuine emotion and exquisite technique. Dragging from her left hand, a full length blue mink coat. The nightclub lamps were out, the only light was from the little platform-stage and its décor of a slum back alleyway. A five-man orchestra provided accompaniment.

No one was eating.

Jacky, enthralled by the music, the atmosphere, momentarily forgot the nigh unearthly beauty of the white-blonde at his side.

The song flowed on and on till the last tinkling piano notes faded. Handclapping and "Bravo! Bravo!" came from every table, and shouts of encore.

Waving and blowing kisses to her admirers, mink on her left arm, the black haired beauty stood bowing and curtseying while the Master of Ceremonies, a one-armed Cockney comedian, took the microphone: "Ladies and gentlemen, our own girl and the finest flower that ever grew on Bethnal Green! Star of stage, screen and recording studio wiv over twenty million records sold, and engagements this summer in New York, Las Vegas and other places in the United States and Canada, Rebecca Serene!" He embraced and kissed her. "Good luck, Becky, darling!"

She walked towards Benny Cawthorne, Jacky and their table companions as the comedian exchanged patter with the band.

Her tones were low and Mayfair modulated: "Hello, everybody." Her glance acknowledged Benny's pretty brunette companion and defensively almost insultingly ignored the white-blonde. She smiled blandly at Jacky: "I trust you didn't find it too disappointing?"

Benny Cawthorne scoffed before Jacky could speak: "Come off it, Becky, you bitch, fishing for compliments like that! Talk proper!"

"Alright, then, Benny, you bagger!" her Cockney was as broad as his. "You miserable bastard! you can't even say nice fings to a working girl what risks her livelihood by coming down here tonight and making the guests up there in the West End wait for half an hour!"

"You were magnificent, darling! Wasn't she, Jecky? Wasn't she, girls?"

They all agreed. Benny nuzzled his face between the black haired beauty's very white breasts, kissing quickly and noisily.

"'Ere, what you fink you're doing?!" she protested, yet stayed motionless, making no effort to stop him.

"You're lovely, darling! Marry me," he freed her left nipple and suckled its stiffness.

"When?" she asked quietly.

He re-covered her breast: "You're too good for me, Becky," he smiled.

"I know," she was as serious as he. She took his head between her palms. "Benny, Benny," she said softly: he smiled wistfully up at her, their gazes searching each other's face. "You're a bastard, ain't you?" she murmured, stroking his hair.

"Grade A."

She removed her hands: "Got to get back to m' show in the West End, love. The punters'll be waiting for me, and m' manager'll be tearing his hair out."

"Go on, then."

She bent her head and wagged her right forefinger at him and said briskly: "See you in America."

He stood up: "I'm looking forward to it, Becky."

She was again the worldly sophisticated star with the Mayfair accent: "Goodnight."

The Cockney footballer's companions replied. Becky hugged herself to Benny with all her strength, cheek to his chest. Then, mink over her arm, walked quickly away, determinedly not glancing back until desire broke her resolve at the exit.

The white-blonde said: "She's right – you are a swine," her voice was pleasant, accent English neutral.

Benny Cawthorne regarded her, undecided whether to agree, defend or attack.

On the stage, a conjuror was putting a torn £20 note from a guest into one of two envelopes.

The pretty brunette placed her right hand over Benny's on the table, pressed her bosom against his upper arm and encircled him with her left arm: "He isn't! He's lovely!" She kissed his cheek and tossed her head at the other woman's blue-eyed gaze.

"Nah, I'm a swine," the London footballer admitted easily. "Britt's right. Where women are concerned, I'm fickle."

The conjuror burned up the envelope containing the £20.

"That's why I like you." The brunette kissed him passionately on the mouth; Benny responded, winking as he did at Jacky and raising his eyebrows in resignation to the blonde.

The orchestra, playing softly, paused for a drum roll: the conjuror performed sleight off hand with a pack of playing cards and juggled five golf balls while making magic passes at the guest. The drum roll stopped. The illusionist requested the owner of the borrowed banknote feel in his inside pocket. The guest produced the envelope, and, smiling amazement, from it his torn £20. The orchestra struck up triumphantly. Everyone applauded.

"That magician was superb, wan't he?!" Jacky was chuckling and clapping. "Are you enjoying it?" his England team-mate asked.

"Yes! It's good! Very good! It's a smashing place, this!"

The Cockney grinned, and leant back in his chair and nodded at the white-blonde: "I told you the fräulein, Britt Anderson, was beautiful."

His brunette companion reacted instantly: "Ain't I?"

His palm moved to her cheek: "Of course you are, darling." They kissed. The compère was introducing the World Champion guitarist. Jacky studied the blonde who gazed unblinkingly at him with wide set, large and unusually beautiful eyes: their iris rims were violet, the irises themselves entirely blue, the whites very white; long, dark blonde lashes and eyebrows. Her skin was unblemished. Each feature was in perfectly balanced harmony with the rest; a tip-tilted small nose, two and a half inch wide mouth with thick, shapely lips permanently curled up at the corners as though ready to smile. The thick, long wavy hair was naturally white-blonde. Slim shoulders under a modest high-necked, long-sleeved black dress which was cut to conceal quite large breasts and not emphasise a tiny waist. Small hands and thin wrists.

"You don't go to nightclubs much, do you?" Britt Anderson was attentive.

"No. Training. Football. Family man."

"Politician," Benny Cawthorne added the jibe.

The guitarist was indeed a virtuoso, his fingers almost turning the instrument into an orchestra in itself.

"I'm glad Rob Jarvis got in. He's a good man," said Jacky. "He'll make a really first rate MP."

Benny Cawthorne said: "We know some MPs, don't we, Britt?" His brunette girlfriend's cheek was against his shoulder, her eyes closed, dreamy expression on her face, not interested in talk of politics.

"Yes. Not all of them very good," replied the blonde.

"They're all bladdy useless! And we know some peers like that and all."

Britt Anderson was silent, appreciating the guitarist. "He's another of your specials, Benny," she concluded.

"I thought Jecky might like to hear him."

"Benny's showing off for you," she explained.

"Jecky don't get out much," the Cockney excused himself. "Why not? I mean – at short notice." He nodded at the guitarist: "He's getting a free meal, a free show, and, besides, he's a mate o' mine," he raised his right arm high and waved, the guitar player grinned hugely, winked demonstratively screwing up half his face and inclined his head in acknowledgement. "He's looking forward to what's coming next!"

Jacky was moderately anxious: "We don't want to be staying here much longer, Benny. It's damn good, I'll admit. But we should be getting off," the guitar player was finishing his number.

"We'll watch the next act, then we'll go. Right?" the Cockney was friendly. Britt Anderson contemplated him, worldly wise.

"Okay," Jacky, concentrating on the guitarist, was applauding enthusiastically.

"And now, ladies and gentlemen," the compère announced, "visions of beauty and desire. The dreams and fantasies of a lovely woman."

All lights were out except the coloured ones dimmed on and around the platform-stage which had been lowered to dance floor level and the angle of its sides altered to give increased area. The orchestra and instruments were gone. A pink-cased double bed mattress; pink and pale green cushions; pink and white and green coverings and drapes; a chair; and a backdrop which created an illusion of distance and spaciousness. Taped, soft music.

A tall, copper haired, pretty woman in her mid-twenties who glided soundlessly from the backdrop hangings wore a long white negligée which enhanced rather than concealed her nudity. She stretched her arms, feigning tiredness, then lay on the mattress, her garment, fastened by a white, loosely tied ribbon at her waist, parted off very long, elegant legs, copper pubic hair, and a large, firm right breast with a two-inch, flat, pink aureole. Her skin was very white.

She slept, motionless, breathing regularly. The lights and music faded slowly.

Total darkness and silence existed for five seconds. Then the stage lighting came up quickly. At front centre stage stood a naked, very lovely Chinese Eurasian girl of about nineteen; no more than 4'10". She was perfectly formed with, for her size, large firm-fleshed breasts and dark, erect nipples. Her hair reached her lowest vertebra. Her small pubic area was accentuated by a widespread straight legged stance and, lightly clasping her belly from behind, the right hand of a small, supple-muscled youth who, with his reddish brown hair, long upper lip, cleft chin, snub nose, blue eyes and freckled white skin, was a perfect Irish type. His nudity was mostly concealed by the Eurasian.

The big copper haired woman, right leg and breast bare, stood left stage watching the couple.

The soft music re-started. The Eurasian bent back and reached her left palm to the youth's face as he kissed her neck and slid his hand from her belly to hold her pubes and masturbate her with his middle finger.

She writhed and caught her breath, and after some seconds uttered involuntary whimpers, then went rigid.

Jacky stared, fascinated, lusting after the actresses and acutely aware of the white-blonde. Benny's brunette was excited, too – though her sensations were being heightened by Benny's hand stroking her thigh. The Cockney watched the stage with a little smile, occasionally glancing at Jacky. Britt Anderson, not interested in the brightly-lit trio, contemplated Jacky, varying her attentiveness to register Benny Cawthorne's occasional glances and the reactions of other people about the club. Yearning to indulge in soft woman flesh, Jacky dared not even glance at her.

The Eurasian and her partner engaged in constantly changing sexual play and intercourse, demonstrating not merely litheness and athleticism but imagination as they contorted into almost every conceivable copulatory position except the anal.

Like a hungry little boy in a sweetshop, Britt Anderson thought. Will he want to make love to me, or will he be afraid? Do I want to make love to him? I told Benny I did. But do I now?

The tall redhead hung up her negligée. The little man stood driving quickly at his minuscule partner where she knelt raised with arms and legs on cushions on the mattress.

With mute authority, the redhead ordered him out of the Eurasian and to his knees. Sideways to the audience, guiding his head, she straddled his face and arched her back and neck, and shook her wavy copper mane, hips rocking in sexual symbiosis, pink nipples thick and swollen, their slits like minute, hungry mouths.

Unhappy yet submissive, the Eurasian watched as the big woman murmured, rocked, stretched and finally shuddered with pleasure under her lover's oral caresses.

The old game played, for once, on a woman's terms. And what are my terms for being here with Jacky Day? Those of a free and independent woman? Or those of a prostitute, fixed up by Benny?

The redhead left the little man kneeling and pulled a bell sash, stage right. Through the drapes upstage left, two men entered; one was a big, good looking Viking type, the other of average height, black haired with toothbrush moustache, a handsome Latin gigolo; each wore dark blue trousers and a white t-shirt. The Eurasian covered her breasts with right arm and her pubes with left hand and turned modestly sideways. Ordered mutely to mid stage right, the newcomers stood unmoving, watching while the redhead pressed the little man's face to rub against her belly then oblige her with genital titillation.

The Viking was equally interested in the Eurasian who, uncomfortable under his scrutiny, tried to ignore him.

After three or four seconds, the redhead pushed her partner's head away and raised him up, cupped his genitals in her right hand, then masturbated him hard. Only the pink tip of his glans peeped sometimes visible.

Jacky's lust was yearning for freedom, for tenderness and ecstasy with any appealing woman who wanted him – the actresses. Britt Anderson. Should I stay at her flat now? Should I?!

I do not want Jacky Day. I do not want any man tonight. These casual, sex routines are so tedious and unfeeling.

The little man was too short for upright copulation with the redhead. She stood straddling where he lay on his back on the floor, and, using both hands, stroked and kept opening her vulva, revealing its moist pinkness and large shapeliness below the thick, chestnut pubic hair.

She knelt astride him.

His four and a half inch long, inch thick penis plied strongly inside her, though not displeased her gaze was on the other men. She stood up.

Slowly, she unzipped the gigolo, smiling up at him.

His penis sprang free. She gripped it, and swallowed it slowly and completely while pushing down his trousers. Her head went back and forth, mouth and tongue caressing his six-inch stiffness.

"How about that, then, darling?" Benny Cawthorne murmured to his brunette. "You fink you can do that, eh?" She shook her head, eyes wide and gleaming, lips parted, expression eager. The Cockney opened his mouth to question the white-blonde, then noticing Jacky's concentration on the sex show and the blonde's gaze on both, stayed silent and settled back in his chair.

This performance is better than most because the woman is in control. She likes the gigolo. Her pimp, probably, or husband – or both. No, I definitely shall not sleep with Jacky Day.

Mary said she could accept my making love to another woman if it were only physical. Watching this is sending me crazy! I do want the blonde! I do!! I do!!

Affection, submissiveness, willingness to please permeated the redhead's every move; her moustachioed partner directed firmly, gently, varying occasionally to roughness bordering brutality whenever her countenance and total abandonment indicated that inclination.
They copulated, using all the basic positions, displaying to the full her graceful feminine beauty and his sinuous masculinity.
Downstage left, the Eurasian, partly concealed in the little man's embrace, was troubled by the burly Viking's bright-eyed interest.

How these skin and meat markets bore me. Britt Anderson sighed slightly. And to think the moralists find them pits of iniquity and evil.

I will stay at her apartment, I won't ask to stay at Benny's. I *shall* make love to her! Jacks excitement fought fear.
On the mattress, the Latin withdrew from his partner's vagina, masturbated to climax over her belly, bringing sighs, and caught breath from the audience.
"I always fink that's a waste, myself," Benny Cawthorne commented. "You should always let it come inside." Intent on the scene onstage, neither Jacky nor the brunette spoke. The white-blonde glanced at him, then resumed watching the sex show and Jacky.

The redhead gestured to the small couple. They rapidly fetched bowl, water jug, and paper and cotton towels. The Eurasian cleaned the Latin, her partner the redhead who lay exchanging smiles and affection with her sated lover.

He's staying at my apartment so I can't get rid of him. But I can tell him I've developed a splitting headache" Britt Anderson suppressed a grin.

Mary will have to know: Jacky's lust had lost its keenness; he tried to pretend he had not desired the blonde, that the playlet alone had roused him.

The redhead wanted more. She remembered and eyed the hefty blond and noted his interest in the slant-eyed girl. She smiled, and languidly ordered the little man to suck her genitals. Murmuring and moving in pleasure, she observed the tiny Eurasian's apprehension concerning the big man.

She left the mattress, and unzipped him.

Female gasps and reluctant masculine grunts greeted sight of his two-inch thick ten-inch long erection, dangling testicles and sandy pubic thatch.

"It ain't as big as the Preacher's, though," said Benny Cawthorne.

"Who's the Preacher?" the brunette wondered. The white-blonde glanced interest.

"Nobody you know, darling."

Richard Trelawney would certainly not like my being here! A married man, a happily married man. I shouldn't be here. But it is exciting. In spite of everything. It is.

Maybe I'm being too harsh, Jacky Day, you world's best footballer, socialist and champion for a better world, so single mindedly intent on Benny's inopportune, if, admittedly, better class, sex show.

Impersonal, benevolent mistress to slave, the redhead was appreciatively assessing the big man's nudity testing his muscles and stroking his skin: she cupped his scrotum in her right hand, and, smiling malevolently into his eyes, squeezed slowly, desisting only when his expression registered pain.

She masturbated him slowly, turning to smile at her Latin lover who lay sprawled comfortably across the bed on his back, cushion under head. She noticed the Eurasian was concealing her front in the little man's embrace from the blond's gaze. She gestured the smaller woman to approach.

The girl stood with eyes downcast, legs pressed together in front of the big man.

The redhead, smile tinged with cruelty, stepped away from the Viking and indicated that the diminutive woman was his.

Forefinger under her chin, he lifted the Eurasian's head to meet his gaze. Her eyes went from side to side, closed, blinked rapidly. He stroked her cheek and hair with his other palm till she calmed enough to watch his face.

He caressed her arms and shoulders, admiring their smooth daintiness. Then her back and sides. Her front between her breasts and pubic hair, touching neither.

The redhead became impatient. She silently ordered the Eurasian to suck penis.

Its thickness filled her mouth to stretching. The redhead, frowning, indicated that she use her breasts and hands in caressing the man and his genitals.

With skill and speed, anxious for the big woman's approval, the Eurasian sucked, licked, rubbed, and fondled the thick sex organ whose size was emphasised by her frailty.

The redhead smiled affectionately at her Latin lover.

The little man, downstage left, stood glumly watching the Viking position his girlfriend forward bent, straight-legged, feet wide apart for rear entry. Totally exposed, the dark vulva amidst its black pubic hair was gracefully supreme in its mature femininity, ample in proportion to the Eurasian's trim body, but small compared to the pink glans which tentatively caressed it and to the stiff masculinity seeking ensheathement.

Cautiously, the big man forced entry; the tiny slant-eyed girl squirmed, countenance distorted, mouth working.

"It's almost cruel, ain't it?" Benny Cawthorne remarked conversationally. His brunette and Jacky scarcely heard him. Britt Anderson leisurely considered the nightclub's other occupants.

Two-thirds were inserted.

The redhead, straight legs wide apart, was masturbating whilst regarding the coitus with lustful and somewhat sadistic amusement.

I do want her! I do! But I must not. I'll stay at Benny's. He has his girlfriend with him, though.

With two forward paces, the big woman intervened. Gripping the Viking's scrotum and uninserted portion of erect flesh, she pushed him away.

The top two-thirds of his hardness shone with vaginal secretion. The dark vulva was moist, evidencing the Eurasian's excitement.

The redhead, hips thrust forward, thighs parted, genitals glistening pink, engulfed him without ado, the easy, natural complement of female to male.

"That's it, boy, give it to her, she loves it. Look at her go," said Benny lightly.

Britt Anderson's gaze flickered, then, deciding against comment, resumed contemplating Jacky's wide-eyed fascination with the show: You are not to blame for Benjamin inflicting this spectacle upon us. Benjamin is such a refined person, so exquisitely sensitive as to etiquette and the social proprieties.

Benny won't want me hanging around disturbing things for him after this lot! He's done more than enough for me as it is – too damn much in fact! Jacky ironised over his lust.

The redhead, temporarily relieved, indicated that the small pair resume proximity; she smiled affection at the slim, moustached man who came towards her from the mattress. She met him halfway. They kissed, he her man, she his little girl and obedient loving woman.

He sat on the chair stage right. She imperiously ordered the big man to the mattress, sat erect on him, penis inside, facing the audience, and silently directed the other couple to copy her and the Viking's every move.

All lights were out except those illuminating the mattress area.

I will sleep at the blonde's apartment – but not with her.

He is rather sweet. I think he will live up to his tv image and what Benny has told me of him. I look forward to being alone with him.

Male served female, each act subject to the redhead's command and enhancement of her pleasure. A synchronised duet interrupted several times at the bigger woman's caprice, and taste for disharmony.

All the basic copulative positions were successively employed, varied and accompanied by sex play.

I'll tell the fräulein I'm in love with my wife and ever faithful to her. That will keep me safe and from feeling like a threatened virgin. Jacky covered disappointment and relief with sardonicism.

"Get down to it, lads," Benny Cawthorne urged good humouredly. The men, on top, were into their short strokes approaching climax. The big man's head went back, his neck and face muscles contracted, his rhythm changed to an intensely held injection. "There he goes." The little man thrust busily, then, he, too, emulated the Viking. "And the other. That's it. Lovely. Well done, boys. Give 'em a prize."

His girlfriend sucked in a sharp breath and exhaled a cross between a sigh and gasp. With eyes wide and bright, she watched the naked men lying sexually exhausted atop their partners: "They've already had it, I fink," she giggled, and eyed Benny; he winked at her, his lips fashioning a kiss.

The four actors stood up. Strands of semen dangled from the men.

The lights faded and the sketch's initial soft music recommenced.

The stage became black, the music loud.

At long last, the parody of passion is over, Britt Anderson thought. Oh dear! It isn't! The lamps were glowing again, revealing the redhead in her negligée asleep on the bed, hugging a pillow.

Sound of someone behind the drapes. The handsome Latin lover, work smudged and weary, unshod, big holes in socks, shirt collar roughly undone, entered to eye the scene, incredulous: "The lazy bitch!"

He strode to the bedside and whacked her hard on the backside: "Awake and move!"

Sexually stimulated, she rolled over, stretching and romantic: "Da-a-arling."

"Darling, be buggered! Where's my dinner?!"

"Later, dearest," she was seductive. She held out her arms to him: "Come here."

His indignation was extreme: "We did THAT only last night! What do you think I am?! Some kind of an animal?! You can just wait now till next weekend! You're doing this on purpose to get me mad, aren't you?! because it's my night out with the boys!" he made for the door, not looking back.

Raising her eyes and arms to the audience in resignation, the redhead followed him.

It definitely is over now, Britt Anderson thought. Now begins the interesting part of the evening.

CHAPTER 26

i

Faint smell of fresh perfume, thick, green and white curtains, polished wooden parquet floor, white and fawn carpets, white wallpaper bedecked with different coloured flowers, cushions and chair coverings, a pale dressing table bearing female toiletries. A giant teddy bear sat in a corner wearing a man's red tie. Different knick-knacks and decorations. A very clean, very tastefully feminine room whose wide double bed, with its white sheets and pale green, pink-edged candlewick bedspread, harmonised with its surroundings.

Rain patted the window. Jacky lifted the edge of the nearest curtain enough to gaze out over the lamp lit, shiny people-empty street and the River Thames and the wink and glow and darkness of 1 a.m. London.

A man some fifty yards away in the shadows! Chinese? Had they searched him out? They couldn't know he was here in Britt's apartment. They couldn't!

He looked at the closed bedroom door and listened. No sound from Britt. She was probably in bed.

He stared at the hazy figure. Stupid to get alarmed and jumpy.

Memories whirled vivid: the Chinese restaurant fight, the knifeman, his fear, Mary's, Harry's, the England squad's meeting on Thursday, Benny. The sex show! Lust keened fresh and hungry, gulping at recollection of the beautiful redhead and the pretty Eurasian.

The Chinese outside was moving. Why Chinese? Because if Benny knew about them, they knew about Benny and Britt Anderson.

Sensations seethed anew.

The man approached. A toilet was flushing, barely audible. Britt? A neighbouring flat? He could not see the man's face.

"Admiring the view?" Britt's voice made him jump.

The thin, light green silk dressing gown, secured by a sash, revealed her lack of other clothing and emphasised her loveliness. Her right leg bared to the thigh as she walked. The loose white V from shoulders to midriff showed perfectly proportioned large, firm breasts whose raised two-inch wide aureoles and finger-thick nipples were clearly measurable under the skimpy fabric.

"Yes," he kept his pyjama-clad body turned to the window, concealing his arousal.

She stood close, right breast and thigh warm against him, redolent of violets. Jacky lusted to grab her, thrust into her, kiss her soft white throat, shoulders and breasts hard, nuzzle her, enjoy her with all the sexual brutality and tenderness he was capable of. Mary and Jessie restrained him.

The man went by in the street. An Indian in British Rail uniform.

Britt's hand fondled across his buttocks and stroked his thigh.

Wildness tore his mind. His mouth savaged hers; he bent her and clutched her as though she were strengthless. Her warmth, perfume and enveloping yielding passionate softness matched and moulded to his every action.

He was in her, above her, driving at her. Her softness, warmth, her thick, shapely lips and long lashed, blue eyes half-open, her prettiness tender with pleasure and passion, the tight muscular warmth of her vagina sucking secure.

Mary!

He withdrew, stood up and was two paces away with back turned within a fifth of a second. Frightened, remorseful yet longing immensely to continue making love with the delicious woman behind him.

"What is it?" she asked softly.

"I'm a married man," he stayed back turned.

"So? I don't mind."

"My wife, Mary."

"She need never know. I shan't tell her. You need not worry."

"I shall. I tell her everything."

"Everything?"

"Yes."

"You're afraid of her?"

"I love her."

"And she'd be jealous of me?" the question was a statement.

He faced her: "I don't know."

Her naked beauty was almost unreal in its perfection. Even the pink inner lips of her vulva beneath the neat, fair pubic hair were mutually and aesthetically proportionate. He made no effort to cover his free-jutting erection. He wanted her, but Mary's face held him faster than the strongest chains. His features wrinkled with pain and he turned his head aside, closing his eyes.

"Benny told me that your wife wouldn't mind if we made love."

Jacky stared into her calm, big blue eyes. "What does he know?"

She gazed solemnly back. "You are a good man," she judged him.

She stooped to pick up her shimmering garment. Her blonde waves gracing, accentuating her curvy white slenderness spiralled an added longing and lust whose barely achieved suppression provoked near-physical pain and caused him to twist his head aside murmuring in his throat.

"I wish I had met you years ago," she stood with her gown becomingly covering her from chin to feet. "I want you," she told him quietly, "badly." She smiled. "Let's have a cup of hot milk instead to quieten us down. You get into bed, Jacky, and I'll bring it to you."

ii

"Then my mother married her present husband, an Italian businessman who worked for Fiat in Strasbourg. So I learned Italian," she finished plaiting her hair. Even in the charmless full-length pink quilt housecoat buttoned to the throat and with her face daubed in skin cream, she was exquisite.

"Norwegian from your father. German from your mother, and French from going to school in Strasbourg. Italian from your stepfather. English from being born and living here for the first ten years of your life," Jacky was impressed.

"And Spanish and Portuguese because they were easy for me. Quite good Arabic, and some Russian and Japanese because they are useful in business; I'm learning them and Chinese, currently."

Jacky smiled and shook his head in wonder.

"You have your football, and your family," she observed. He nodded. "Will England win the World Cup?"

"Probably not."

"Benny says you're the only man in the world he cannot guarantee to play out of the game, man to man. That makes you special. None of those artistes at the club tonight were paid. Only invited guests in the audience. Club doors locked. Benny called in a lot of favours, at very short notice."

"From you, too?"

"I wanted to meet you." She eased back in her chair, sipped milk and regarded him propped on his pillows in bed. "Feel quieter now?"

"Yes."

"I don't. Well, perhaps a little. Here I am, rich and beautiful, can have any man I want, and the one I want won't have me," she laughed, bit her bottom lip and eyed him wryly.

"Rich," he curtailed his longing for her and the pain involved, "are you?"

"Yes. I'm a good businesswoman. My old Hanseatic Nazi grandad from Lubeck sitting in his bank director office in Strasbourg is very proud of me."

"Nazi?"

"That's why my mother ran away with my father. To escape family tyranny. My dad was a handsome young Nordic nightclub magician. They decided he needed an assistant. She was nineteen, had long legs, a good figure, and was a beautiful blonde Aryan like him. A perfect match," sincerity and wistfulness were tinged with cynicism. "Till later on. Damn them. That's another story, though."

Jacky was curious: "Benny said you were a model and had had small parts in films."

"That's true. But I have other interests."

"What?" Jacky suspected that she was a high class prostitute.

"Business. Public relations. Advertising. Organising trade meetings, business gatherings. Deals of one sort or another. Investment."

"What exactly?"

"It's not important. I'm very much a free agent." She drank some milk. Jacky, perplexed, considered her. An unusually lovely woman who claimed she was rich, spoke the world's major languages, yet whom Benny Cawthorne had introduced to him as a model and small time actress. She was lying, must be. Wanted to impress. Yet the apartment was big, well and expensively decorated, and the ceiling-high bookcases in the living room contained a lot of foreign books.

"It's a quarter to two," she said. "You told Benny you should both get a good night's sleep. It will soon be morning." She stood up, holding her empty cup and took his from the dressing table. "I'll go to my lonely bed," she said, reluctant though whimsical, "and you can dream of your beloved Mary and little girl, and of training with the England football team and the coming joys of the World Cup Competition in the U.S. of A."

Alone, lust and memories of the past few hours kept him from slumber. Despite Mary, he yearned to couple with the blonde.

He fell asleep, wanting to be safely home, far from temptation.

iii

Britt's soft nakedness wrapping him in, totally compliant, utterly his. Pleasure and lust surged and surged. He knew he was dreaming.

He came out of the dream fast.

Her breasts and front were against his naked back and thighs. He was wearing only his buttoned pyjama jacket! The lust already in his mind lunged and exulted.

Mary!

He moved abruptly. Britt woke, murmuring, curling arms and legs snuggling to him, rubbing her cheek against his chest.

Physical desire surged then floated beyond control: his feelings for Mary were secure below the situation's euphoria; the blonde's scent and soft warmth sucked him to passion.

Triumph, laughter in spring countryside, violets – her perfume –, a good man wanting her, enjoying being with her, hers with his body on hers, in her, she his, with a tinge of envious malice at corrupting him from respectability, domesticity, faith to his woman. She was better than his woman! Any woman! Any man!

No – not this man feeding sensation into her body and brain. She did not want to be better than he was! Only to yield to him, give herself, be his, transcend her loneliness, the barrenness of all the world's available men, meaningless humanity, material things, all and any of which were hers at whim. Women-hating men, handsome men, rich men, men with their lust and longing were useless.

A good man, though, who rejected her because he did not wish to hurt, made loneliness unbearable. Being with him, having his warm body and attention, meant ecstasy.

She shuddered into orgasm.

Jacky, also.

"Are you sorry?" she asked. They lay on their backs, sides touching, he gazing at the ceiling, she his face.

"No," he said quietly, not moving, "it was wonderful."

She kissed his cheek and put her right leg between his and snuggled to his side and chest.

Excitement and lust, carefree and gay; Mary would understand, she had said so.

"I'll do anything you like," her right hand caressed his erection, her lips touched small kisses across his chest. "Anything. You can take me any way you wish, beat me if you want – but don't scar me. I deserve beating."

"No," thought of hurting such beauty was totally alien. "If anybody deserves beating, I do." Mary's face, reproachful, laughing her affection and trust; yet he felt only a hint of betrayal; he did not love this exquisite creature kissing his chest, his neck, whose vulva was rubbing his thigh.

"I was bad. I am bad," she said.

"No," he denied instinctively, then was not sure.

"Yes. I'm to blame."

"I'm as much."

"No. I had to have you. I could not bear being alone. I'll do anything you like. I watched you during the sex show. You'd never seen anything like that before, had you?"

"No. I saw some porno films at a party after a match in Germany once."

Her eyes were six inches above his: "Shall I – ?" she murmured in a tiny, feminine voice, and put the top of her small left forefinger between her loosely closed lips and sucked gently.

Excitement spurted: "But you can't," he was incredulous. She opened her eyes wide and tipped her chin challengingly, slid down his body pushing aside the bedclothes to massage his stiff organ between her cheek and palm, kiss and pluck it sideways between soft lips before swallowing it slowly and completely.

Jacky watched wide-eyed, pleasure rippling. His glans was in her mouth, her tongue rubbing its underside, while she masturbated him.

"Do you like it?" she asked.

"Yes. But it's not as good as the ordinary way. Though nearly." He realised afresh with some awe: "You're very beautiful."

Her muscular smooth vagina sucked sensation rhythmically building in his body and libertine carefree pleasure laughing abandonment in his mind.

As they coupled, he admired her features and contours, firmness of flesh, her thick pink nipples swollen for suckling and kisses.

"It's twenty to six," she lay with her front moulded to his side, her thigh between his.

"I may as well get up and go," he said.

"Lie still, darling, Jacky," she kissed beside his left nipple. "I'll make your breakfast and bring it you in bed."

"No," he sat up purposefully, careful not to hurt her. "I want to catch the first train I can home."

"To Mary," she was calm.

He swung out of bed: "I shall tell her everything."

"Blame me. Because I am to blame."

"No more than me."

"Whenever you want me, Jacky, say, and I'll be there."

"We shan't meet again."

"We shall."

"No! No!" he was almost vehement. "No. We shan't."

She lay on her back against the white sheets and pillows and tossed back bedclothes like a cameo of female beauty idealised, relaxed, motionless, smiling.

CHAPTER 27

"She was some high class Aryan whore Benny Cawthorne purchased for you," Mary was bitter.

"I'm not sure." Sunlight came from behind a cloud and filled the Days' living room.

"Of course she was!" Mary insisted, hard and scornful. "Damn that Cockney guttersnipe!" she tried to make it a joke. She showed real antagonism: "Damn him!"

"It's me to blame, not him."

"Yes," under her curt, matter-of-fact acceptance, she was hurt. She tried to be blithe and reasonable: "Me, too, for saying what I did that time he was here. What happened yesterday was logical enough. Danger, excitement and sex go together, don't they? He risked his life – career, anyway – for you, wanted to show his friendship, his power and influence by putting on a private show with exclusive performers, a beautiful woman -," her emotion broke, "oh damn!" she turned in tears to stare through the window, bend her head and put her hands over her face.

Jacky was upset: "Don't cry, Mary."

"What do you expect me to do?" she sobbed. "I'm jealous!"

"I didn't care about her!" both voice and face held total sincerity.

"I know! That's what's so inane," her voice was tiny with sobs. She strove unsuccessfully for control: "I'm being utterly irrational!" her small body heaved and shook. Jacky stood behind her and put his hands, warm and consoling, upon her shoulders. She was controlled and cruel: "Do you wish I were your beautiful blonde?"

Jacky had no defence: "Mary," he said abjectly.

"Damn you, Jacky!" she was vehement, spinning round; her raging hostility crumpled at sight of him: she hugged herself to him, crying.

Gasping, gulping, she managed: "Stupid woman! Calm, logical, sensible female," she chuckled through her tears.

He held her, ashamed of having caused her distress.

"You do want me, don't you? You're not going to leave me?" she was half-joking, yet serious.

"I love you," he was sincere, gaze on hers.

"A strange way of showing it, making love to another woman. There I go again, being crass."

"No. You're right. I was wrong."

"And you'll not do it again?"

"No."

She recognised: "You must have free choice." She took a pace away. "Will you see that woman again?"

"No."

"Will you see others?"

"No."

"I love you, Jacky," it was in her face. She reached out her right forefinger and stroked his left cheek twice. She changed mood: "All three major American television network companies rang last night. They want you when you go to the States."

"If they pay enough, they can have me."

"The Tory Establishment are going crazy at the thought of you speaking on American television. They are so used to having it all their own way. They never accept and always vilify the fact that over sixty per cent of the people in this country do not agree with them, and not only do not agree but actually despise their bigotry and lying. Yet are denied publicity and acceptance because they have neither money nor power."

"You exaggerate," said Jacky calmly.

"Of course," she agreed easily. "But not entirely," she was demure.

CHAPTER 28

i

"Well, lads," Wyckliffe eyed the twenty players and the England team staff, "to sum it all up, after this past week's hard training, and a deal of brain-searching, you are the final few. The next time we all meet, we shall be bound for our training headquarters in Evanston, Illinois. Has anybody any last questions before we break up camp?"

Richard Trelawney raised his hand. "We know we've got to attend an Anglo-American Trade Exhibition in Chicago. The Press has been full of meetings of one sort or another we're supposed to be at, talking about Detroit, New York, Washington, the British Ambassador, the Foreign Secretary. What's true and what isn't?"

"The Chicago Anglo-American Trade Fair is definite," said Wyckliffe. "Detroit is under negotiation. New York is probable when we're into the second round. Notice I say 'when' not 'if'." Cheering, footstamping, shouts of approval. "Concerning the British Ambassador and the Foreign Secretary, I have no information whatsoever. Personally, I would rather not have any meetings, but we need the sponsor money and we are 'England', so – " he gestured his lack of influence. "Any other questions on this? No? Anybody any questions on anything else? Final questions."

"Yer," said Benny Cawthorne, "you haven't said anyfing about all them beautiful women you've got lined up over there for us, Denzil." Cheers, laughter and floor stamping spattered.

Wyckliffe treated the topic seriously: "Those of you who are not taking wives and girlfriends will have chance to socialise after training's done. So long as the good of the team and security measures are respected, you're free to enjoy the trip."

ii

"I suppose you'll be going to meet your mother and Mary and family," said Benny Cawthorne.

"Yeh," replied Jacky.

"Willingby?" the Cockney asked Jim Arrowood.

"After I've dropped Jacky off at Trenton."

"Hull?"

Jed Lennox grinned happiness all over his brown face: "Yeh. By, lads, it's great, in't it?! Off to 'World Cup!" he rubbed his hands with joy.

Benny Cawthorne patted him on the shoulder. "There'll not be many get past you, Jedder."

"Nobbody, if I've owt to do wi' it!" the coloured youth's utter determination made the others smile. Through the hotel window, they watched Denzil Wyckliffe and other England team officials talking to a group of reporters. A couple of Press photographers were photoing players leaving the building.

"I'll ha' to gerroff mi'sen," the brown teenager said. "M' granny and grandad are waiting fo' me. ' Old Lad's o'er ' moon 'cause I'm off. I'm glad I can do summat for 'em now. They were good to me when I were a kid. I'll see you in London, lads."

"I'm ready for going," said Jim Arrowood. "Are you, Jacky?"

"I want to speak to Wyckliffe first."

iii

"There's big money involved, my business adviser says, and, quite frankly, Denzil, I've no objection to getting some by appearing on American television. My chances of earning top rate aren't going to last for many more years."

Wyckliffe was frowning concern: "Feelings are strong against you in high quarters. You know what this country's like – powerful right wing vested interests and reactionaries not just on the scene but behind the scenes in key positions."

"I want to do that programme anyway," Jacky was frank. "England is still a free country. The Bad Old Days, when you could keep a man down and shut his mouth, have gone for good, surely?"

Denzil Wyckliffe's face cleared: "I'll see what I can do. I agree with you."

Jacky was definite: "I intend signing the contract with those Yanks, Denzil."

Wyckliffe was alarmed: "Don't do that. Not till you've got the all clear."

"Yes. I'm going to." Jacky frowned vexation and disgust. "It's all wrong, this slavery attitude, treating grown men like idiot boys. As regards the team: – training, tactics, keeping fit, doing everything for the good of the lads to produce the best performance from myself and the team – okay. But outside football, my life is my own. What I do with it is nobody's business except mine."

"Not while you play for England," Wyckliffe was firm. "You represent more than yourself as an individual. You represent the country."

"No," Jacky was adamant, "I represent myself as one of the best footballers in the country, just like the other lads in the team" we're some of the best footballers in England playing a game against some of the best footballers from other countries, that's all! And when you try and make it into something big and mystical with nationalism, it's bloody daftness! It's only a game, a magnificent game, the best game in the world for me, but it's only a game, Denzil."

The Team Manager was nonplussed. He gazed at the stocky man's earnest face, then gave his head a single shake and grunted a reluctant chuckle. "Well, I find it difficult to fault your reasoning, Jacky. But a lot of people don't bother about reason, and they're the ones we've got to worry about. Look," he pleaded, "don't sign anything until we've got things settled."

"I'm off to, Denzil," Jacky was decided. "The conservative Establishment is happy enough to crush all opposition to death if the opposition is willing enough to let it. There's too much dogmatism and bigotry in this country, Denzil, and in the world, for that matter. Anybody would think I was doing something wrong in wanting to appear on television. I don't intend breaking the law or doing anything bad. No, Denzil, damn it, I'm off to tell them I'll do the programme."

CHAPTER 29

"Where are our beverages, you male lackeys?!" from the front room, Mary's and their mother's laughter reached Jacky and Harry Day where they stood preparing the evening meal in Mrs Day's kitchen.

"In two minutes, Madame!" Harry called smarmily.

"I haven't seen m' mam so lively and fit since before her stroke," said Jacky, dropping a peeled potato into the pan. "You will visit her regularly while I'm in the States, won't you?"

"Every week. It's not far from Nottingham. By! I'm glad to be out of London free from that bet business and the threat of Chinese gangsters!"

"You feel safe in your mind, do you?"

"The police know Lee Kwang Yoo's identity now, and Billy Woo says there's no danger. I'm apprehensive, but not scared. I'm looking forward to my new job – investment analyst! I'll turn the fifty thousand you gave me into a million in five years, Jacky, and pay you back double! I wonder what old Johnner would have said to that? He never had more than five hundred quid at any one time in his life. Remember how he saved for five years to buy that Morris? Every car he bought, he got cheated on. The Old Man never would admit it, though. Always claimed he was getting a bargain. Poor old Johnner." The two brothers, remembering their father, were quiet for some seconds, Harry scraping a carrot, Jacky a potato. The electric kettle's inchoate murmur croaked and wheezed. "Football and socialism, his life. He'd have been proud of you, Jacky."

"You, too."

"I don't have his dogmatic faith in socialism:- Nationalise everything, have the State run everything. Oh, I understand why! He never had anything, if the State had everything, at least he'd get something. The trouble is, bullies and ignoramuses make themselves at home in any system. Look at the Soviet Union: when Lenin died, the economy was a mixture of capitalism and socialism, a one-party state with an all-powerful, centralised bureaucracy ruled over by Stalin who went on to create a bureaucratic tyranny run by lickspittle murderers utterly cowed to his every whim. And that system of organised oppression became used by leftist revolutionaries everywhere as their model for a better world!" Harry's young face displayed indignation and horror. "What a monstrous betrayal! What a perversion of all that is decent!"

"That's the way it often is," Jacky went to unplug the boiling kettle and make tea. "Get the cups and saucers out, Harry," he requested.

"I want to adapt the techniques of capitalism for use within socialism."

Jacky looked in the oven: "The meat's nearly ready. I think we can put the vegetables on."

"The only way to ensure lasting peace in the world is to blend the best from each system for the benefit and enrichment of all."

"Sounds sensible."

"Tea! you servants!" Mary, imperious, occasioned another cackle of mirth from Mrs Day.

"Making it," Jacky replied. Harry placed the pan of carrots on the stove to cook alongside the potatoes and cabbage. "What d'you think of Rob Jarvis's book, then?"

"He certainly gives Monetarism a hard time. Rightly enough, I suppose. Used as a panacea rather than a specific cure for individual ailments in the body economic, it kills more than it cures. Money is only a function, more or less dynamic, of the system it operates in, and the system is however it be defined. Micro, yes, where the definitions are specific and narrowly limited. Macro, no, the contours are too indefinite and wide, the ramifications incalculable."

"You've lost me," said Jacky. "You carry the tea and milk, Harry, I'll take the rest."

Their mother asked, merry: "Has he been telling you about tax dodge'ems and P.E. training and bandage washing and butterfly bread and stripping his asses?!" Mrs Day's articulation, fretted by mirth, evanesced into silent laughter.

"Oh Mother!" Harry's exasperation at her misrepresentation augmented the others' hilarity. "Tax dodges! P.E. ratios! Bond washing!

Compound interest! Butterfly spread! Asset stripping! She would insist on my explaining my new job, and when I did, she understood nothing!"

"I might have done," she defended.

"I'll read some Shakespeare to you, and get my own back," he threatened.

"Oh, please, spare me!" his mother, tormented, looked to escape.

"You're certainly chirpy, Mam! You've improved since I was here last," said Jacky.

"I feel a lot better. I've got more movement back. The doctor's pleased with me, he says. I'm off to see Harry's new apartment next week, when you're in America." Mary turned to stare to the field beyond the front garden at Jessica playing ball with several small children and Mrs Day's home-helper. "I worry about you being booted in the head again." Jacky's eyes winced, he glanced aside focussing transiently on Mary, then broadened to include the scene in the field. "Every team you play against, they try to hurt you. They'd cripple you, if they could, some of them. Will you be playing against that Italian again?"

"Probably."

"It frightens me. And all the papers talk about terrorists and letting off bombs."

"The security arrangements are top class."

"You're doing well to leave Mary and Jessie at home. They'd only be locked up in hotels. That's no life for them. But you'll miss them, Jacky. You'll be away over a month, near two, perhaps. It's a good job you don't go with other women, Jacky." Mary's head jerked instinctively, fractionally, to confront her husband: willpower stopped her. "You'll be lonely, though. Young man of your age. And Mary will miss you, won't you, Mary? She will. And your little girl. Poor little thing. She is a sweet little lassie, full of life. She's just at that age when she needs you most – both her parents. Especially her daddy. You'll be gone for such a long time. She'll almost forget what you look like."

"That does it!" Mary pivoted round. "Jessie shall see her daddy every day! We'll be there to cheer you for the Paddy O'Rourke Talk Show, and every match, and every waking, aching, willing, thrilling moment along the way!"

Jacky, exultant, clasped and swung her, ending in a mutual, passionate kiss.

"But you can't appear on the Paddy O'Rourke Talk Show!" said Mrs Day, "the F.A. don't like it. It was on television and in the newspapers."

"My business adviser says there's nothing legally binding to prevent me. On business grounds, I should."

Mary said: "We've been approached by an American business consultancy offering different deals with a number of big American companies. Our business adviser's arranged for Jacky's income from them to be kept and invested in America."

"He's set up an American company for you, has he?" Harry was intrigued by the practical details.

"Something like that."

"Politics," disconsolate, Mrs Day shook her head. "I wish you wouldn't get involved, Jacky. It upsets me when they broadcast nasty things about you. It upsets your sister, Joanna, as well. Except she didn't like what you say."

"Because she hated Johnner and is jealous of Jacky," Harry's judgement was conclusive.

"Don't say that. It isn't true," Mrs Day defended strongly. Her head moved, she gazed through the windows beyond the playing children and the village to the burgeoned, verdant countryside. "If only Johnner were alive today..." Memories flittered so poignant that they seemed reality: she and Johnner, teenagers in love, kissing in the warm, darkening, river meadow, fragrant with day-cut hay and the wild roses twining the bushy hedge and the bramble thicket which embowered and hid them; her wedding day, with its terror and delicate, ethereal, evanescent yet permanent sensitivity of every sensation, variegated richer than ever a sunrise and sunset, than light in a flawless diamond. Mrs Day's eyes were wet, her smile gentle. "Johnner," she whispered. Her first childbirth, its feared pain fresh yet joyous, energy endless in wonder and tenderness at the tiny baby, awe at such uniqueness of newborn life. Joanna. Jacky's birth. Harry's. The two youngest boys'.

She blinked, and wiped away the moisture with her forefingers. "Johnner would have been proud of all his children. Especially you two. You for going to university and doing so well, Harry. You deserve to.

You've studied hard." She perked suddenly. "Come here and let me give you a kiss!" Harry, smiling, complied. "Jacky," she said, and kissed him also. "Johnner would have wanted you to win the World Cup. I do, too," she added, surprising them. "But it don't matter if you don't, Jacky. So long as you stay safe and well. That's all I want – for all my family."

CHAPTER 30

"I warned you, Jacky." The American Mid-Western evening sun beamed hotly into Denzil Wyckliffe's room; outside the window were green lawns, flower borders and leafy trees and people strolling. "You should not have agreed to do that programme."

"The contract is already signed," Jacky was frowning.

"You'll have to get out of it. With the public statement issued by the F.A., my hands are pretty much tied. I objected strongly to their making it, but they over-ruled me. They don't

want any publicity or controversy, they want only football."

"But they're using us for publicity at the Anglo-American Trade Exhibition!"

"I know. But that's different."

"I don't see how. If I got drunk or took drugs or neglected my training, or did anything to harm the prowess of the team, yes! But this – no! It's merely political! A pack of bloody Tories, Denzil, saying 'Shut that socialist Jacky Day's mouth!'"

"Now you're being unfair."

"Am I?! I don't think I am! They want the Bad Old Authoritarian Days back again when they could treat players like slaves and keep them down – and they did! It was wrong then and it's wrong now! It has nothing to do with football, nothing at all! And it's certainly got nothing to do with fair play! I see them as a pack of spiteful bullies abusing their bureaucratic power to gag me to silence!"

"As far as I'm concerned, you can do the programme, Jacky."

The stocky man calmed: "Well, tell them, Denzil. You're the boss."

Wyckliffe twinkled a smile: "The way you've been talking to me just now, I'm not so sure."

Jacky was instantly repentant: "If I've said anything that could be interpreted as unfair criticism of you or the running of the team or the sporting side – no, you're the boss, and you're the best. As regards football, I'll do anything – "

Wyckliffe, smiling raising his left palm slowly waving a halt, interrupted: "I know that, Jacky. You're about the most co-operative, hard working, unselfish team player I've ever worked with, as well as the most brilliant." Jacky's head lolled to one side. Wyckliffe continued with a chuckle: "Now we've finished congratulating each other on what wonderful fellows we are, I will repeat that I personally have nothing whatsoever against your going on American television. I enjoyed that interview you did in Stockholm, and the programme they did about you and the Workfield by-election. But here in the States, it could be controversial if you told them home truths they didn't like. Especially when the programme leader's a professional Irish-American with strong anti-British tendencies. You could have some lunatic try to kill you: they don't merely threaten in this country, they actually do it if they can. That's the kind of controversy those bureaucrats, as you call them, are trying to avoid."

"Yes. I appreciate that, Denzil. Nevertheless –."

"You want to do your television programme. Alright, I'll nag those bureaucrats afresh."

CHAPTER 31

"They should have contacted Denzil Wyckliffe by now. They've had twenty-four full hours."

"He'll tell me when he knows. It is the weekend, Mary. They'll have to have discussions, you know how officials are. The tv show isn't till next Friday, so we've plenty of time. You look lovely, darling." Mary, in a white, sleeveless knee length dress with a square cut neckline, patterned in shadows and sunlight near the window, curtsied elegantly. Jacky approached, kissed her and began to lift her dress.

"It'll soon be eight o'clock," she reminded him. "That business consultancy man is coming to see you."

"We've time," he was keen. "Come on."

She stepped back and, gazing continuously into his eyes, pulled her dress quickly over her head and tossed it spryly aside. Right hand behind her head, left propped against her hip in a glamour girl pose, she stuck her tongue out and crossed her eyes.

"You're look'n good, kid," Jacky said in an American accent.

She shed panties and shoes and began a series of extravagantly revealing poses which her rolling eyes, open mouth and protruding, curling tongue made mockery of. Hands on hips, legs astride, she faced him: "Get those clothes off, buster!" she commanded in broad American dialect. Jacky swiftly obeyed. "Stop there," her American accent growled. "Ah godda inspect the goods, buddy!" He stood motionless while she stood beside him, running her hands over him, squeezing his thighs and muscles. "A hard man," her growl continued. She held his scrotum in her right palm as though weighing it. "Yew think yew kin treat a lady right, boy?"

"Yass, m'," Jacky parodied a Deep South squeak.

"Waal, let's see what yew got. Down on your back, boy. That's right. Now you spread 'em." Mary's palms stroked her husband's smooth belly and chest. She licked his erection, then slowly, and very carefully, swallowed it.

Jacky was astonished: "How did you–?! Where–?! When–?!"

In a tiny voice that matched her petite femininity, she said shyly: "I wanted to show you I could do it, too."

"Yes – but– what – how did you learn?" Jacky wondered.

"I practised on a ripe banana," she explained, started to laugh, then stopped. "You said about that sex show." Her head flung back challengingly, defensive and excusing: "If they could do it, I can too!"

Jacky sat up and put his arms round her. "There's no need,"

he said softly. "I love you anyway, darling."

"I can't stand Benny Cawthorne," her husband's heartbeat was still rapid from their lovemaking. Sun rays bounced off the clock registering five to eight. No sound from Jessica in her darkened room. "The sight of him with that Becky Serene tonight." She repented her meanness and was fair: "It's not his fault." Then insisted what she felt: "Yes, it is!"

"What're you talking about?" Jacky was baffled.

"I'm telling you this so you know I want to avoid him."

"Alright."

Aggression flared: "She's too good for him!"

"Who? Benny?" Jacky wondered, "Becky Serene?"

"Let's not talk about him," she dismissed the topic, light-voiced and decisive. "I wonder how Joyce and Richard," warmth and amusement suffused her words, "are enjoying their first All-American Methodist church service?! Good old Joyce! She's got her white Chevrolet for driving to her business meetings!"

"Business," Jacky remembered his appointment and stood up. "Be careful when you're in Chicago tomorrow."

She scoffed: "All these security arrangements are ridiculous! They're so excessive! Nobody knows us here. Nobody's bothered about me."

"Be careful," Jacky repeated, walking towards the shower. The phone rang. "Chicago's not like it was in Al Capone's days, but it's not an English city. Remember, we saw the statistics on murder and muggings and crime in general." He picked up the phone and said hello.

The receptionist told him he had a visitor. "She wants to speak to you, Mr Day."

Jacky, expecting a male visitor, was mystified for a moment.

"Hello, Jacky." Awareness struck shock. "It's me, Britt Anderson. I'm your contact person." Memory of Britt, of Mary's jealousy. "Surprised? I said we'd meet again. Hello? Jacky? Jacky? Are you coming down to see me, or shall I come up?"

He covered the mouthpiece with his hand: "It's Britt Anderson," he said. "She's the business contact." Mary stared at him.

Her face, mobile with strong and changing emotion, became resolute: "I want to meet her."

CHAPTER 32

Mary was polite: "And why Jacky and not Benny Cawthorne whom you knew before Jacky?"

"Jacky has more publicity value."

"Jim Arrowood, England's glamour boy leading goalscorer?"

"Jacky's Swedish tv interview and the Workfield by-election documentary have been shown in many different countries, including this one," Britt Anderson explained. "He's already a recognisable personality with big business potential."

"So that's your mystic charm, is it, Jacky?" Mary's light tones made her husband blush and look out through the hotel manager's office window across the lawns and fifty yard distant roadway glittering with automobiles homing toward the shrubbed and treed residences of wealthy American suburbia.

Britt Anderson's friendly expression remained unchanged. "Appearing on America's most popular chat show next Saturday will add to his publicity value."

"It's not certain the F.A. will let him," Mary remarked tartly. Jacky turned aside, frowning.

Addressing Jacky, Britt Anderson was friendly to both: "From a business point of view, it would be good if you were on it."

Mary was pointed: "Business isn't everything. When you're making your films with Jacky, and getting involved with these various projects," she indicated the files and folders the other woman had piled on the desk, "I don't want him getting near beautiful women, specifically yourself," her tight smile barely eased her bluntness.

Britt Anderson observed blandly: "He's a happily married family man."

"And don't you forget it," Mary smiled. "I didn't think I would ever be jealous. But I would if I had reason."

Britt Anderson also smiled: "A woman who is truly loved by a man need never fear losing him to another woman."

"The operative word is man," Mary riposted. "Put a woman who is enticing enough and often enough in his way, and he might just be tempted in a moment of weakness to take what's there."

"And you're afraid of that?"

Jacky asserted himself: "I'm not some kind of statue, you know! I can hear what you're saying!"

Mary smiled at him and murmured gently: "We know you can, darling. I'm simply making sure this lady knows exactly how things are."

CHAPTER 33

"I'm sorry, Jacky," Denzil Wyckliffe was not happy, "the F.A. still say no."

"Aw, dear!" Jacky turned aside in disappointment and disgust. Through Wyckliffe's window, he noted various members of the England contingent on the hotel lawn.

"I stressed that I was in favour of your doing the programme, but was bluntly told, quote: 'With your socialistic proclivities, you are ill-placed to judge in this matter.' I pointed out that the team spirit of the squad was excellent, that there were no complaints against you whatsoever, that since you already are a 'controversial' figure, your appearance for half an hour or so on American television would make little difference. They still said no. We represent England. The Football Association did not want any controversy attached to the national team."

"I'm afraid they've got some," said Jacky. "My business adviser has had the best legal people examine my legal obligations to the F.A. for this tour. The F.A. has no legal right to forbid me that programme. There's a principle involved, Denzil! It's a bunch of Tories shutting me up out of political spite! Well, they shall NOT treat me like an idiot child to be jeered at and sneered at! They are using us, the national team to publicise the Anglo-American Trade Exhibition advertising British Industry and British goods on Saturday. What better way than for me to do it that on the Paddy O'Rourke Talk Show, nation-wide American television?! I'm going to tell the Press I want to do that programme."

CHAPTER 34

Benny Cawthorne shouted: "Belt up, you geezers!" Hiss and drum of water and voices from the showers ricocheted about the dressing-room; players sat or moved about, some drying down, others dressing. "Listen! Turn those bleeding showers off! Right! Listening? Jecky needs our help. We' got to back him up. All of us."

"No," Joe Berrigan, naked on the bench, stopped towelling his hair. "He got into it himself, let him get out of it himself. I agree with the F.A. We came here to play football, not go ramming socialism down the Yanks' throats. I hate socialism!" he boasted with a wide, aggressive grin. "I'm a Tory! Solid Conservative!" Assent puttered from various squad members.

"I am, also," David Lewis enunciated clearly. "Jacky ought to concentrate on what he's best at – football. Socialism means high taxes, more taxes, restrictions and rules of every unnecessary, interfering and tedious sort."

Eddy Corelli said: "I hate taxes and Trade Unions." He was conciliatory: "We should concentrate on football, it's the World Cup." Others agreed.

"A nice bladdy lot of mates you are, ain't you?!" Benny castigated them. "And stupid! It ain't about socialism!! Money!! That's what it's about – money!! Big money!!" Cynical disdain toned his delivery: "The World Cup ain't just about honour and glory, it's money! We're professionals, right? We ain't got long at the top! We ain't going to be earning good money forever! There's plenty of blokes in their forties and fifties what were good players in their day, and where are they now? On the dole, and scrapheap! And who gives a fack about 'em? Nobody! And that's what can happen to any of us! Jecky's out there right now making money, public relations, wiv that blonde, right? That Paddy O'Rourke Talk Show he wants to do is – money –," he spelled, "M-O-N-Y, big money! What applies to Jecky today could apply to any of us tomorrow."

Jim Arrowood spoke: "What Benny says makes sense. I'm supporting Jacky," he stated simply. He looked at the avowed Conservatives: "I, also, am a Conservative. Mostly by circumstance and upbringing, partly by choice, exactly as Jacky is with his views. He's an obstinate little sod," affection for Jacky showed through, "wrongheaded, charges at brick walls, jumps 'em, flattens 'em or flattens himself," he shook his head in exasperated amusement. "I sympathise with the F.A's viewpoint. But Jacky is what he is," Jim Arrowood's tone dropped very grave, "and he is one hell of a footballer." The others were equally serious, all concurring except the scowling Winston Jones who considered himself nonpareil. "If he takes it into his head that doing the Paddy O'Rourke Talk Show is a point of principle, he'll do it. The F.A. will drop him from the squad. And our chances of winning –" he shrugged their non-existence. "If Jacky can't play, I don't think I will."

"I'm wiv you, Jim, boy!" Benny clapped the fair haired six footer's back. "Who else is?!" Joe Berrigan shook his head. David Lewis was frowning, Eddy Corelli troubled. Other Conservatives were vacillating, some negative.

"If the others will, I will," Jed Lennox declared.

Curly Greenhalgh addressed Benny and Jim: "I'd join you, lads, but I'm yellow."

"Jingo?" Benny queried.

The midfielder, head down, muttered: "If the others will, yeh." His gaze raised to hold the Cockney's: "I want to play i' World Cup, bad."

"Benny!" the interruption came from the physiotherapist in the dressing room doorway. "Miss Becky Serene is waiting for you."

CHAPTER 35

Jacky pulled on his tracksuit trousers; behind Britt Anderson on the college football pitch, the camera and props crew were packing away their gear, the extras leaving, Chicago's suburbs glowed up the dusk.

"You were superb, I knew you would be," she said.

"I haven't spoken to my sponsors yet."

"Chuck Bengtsson's in California on business, and Senator Velasquez is tied up in Washington. You'll see them both at the Anglo-American Trade Exhibition this Saturday. The Senator will be at the official opening ceremony with the Mayor of Chicago, the British Ambassador and Foreign Secretary. And since Chuck Bengtsson is a member of the Exhibition's organising committee and his associate companies are providing about a tenth of the exhibits, Chuck will certainly be there."

Jacky put on his tracksuit top. "How did you get mixed up in this, Britt?"

"I set it up."

"Why?"

"Because of you."

"For the money," he stated, "because it's a good business deal."

She smiled. "Do you believe that?"

"Yes."

Smiling, she gazed at him, saying nothing for some seconds. "I'll make love to you any time, anywhere, anyhow it pleases you, Jacky," her voice was quiet.

Lust and fear lurched, submission to her beauty, memory of their lovemaking. "Don't," his appeal was low.

"I like you. Want you. Too much," her eyes showed suffering.

"I love Mary, and our little girl."

Sadness, pain, friendly understanding were in her smile; her manner revealed acceptance and challenge: "So you'll tell her what I've just said."

"There's no need," he feared Mary's jealousy.

"You should tell her."

"No."

"Yes," she spoke quietly. "You should tell her."

CHAPTER 36

"Britt Anderson's a no-good cow," Becky Serene asserted; Benny Cawthorne, naked with her on his bed, rubbed his face from one breast to the other, kissing each, savouring her softness with his lips and teeth. "Going after a happily married man like that. And Jacky Day's a little bastard, having it off behind his wife's back."

"Nah," Benny disagreed. "Jecky ain't no bastard. He's a man of principle – that's the trouble. If the F.A. don't give way, goodbye World Cup."

"He ain't got no principles."

"I can't forget Joe Berrigan and the other gutless baggers!" Benny judged with his feelings. "Trelawney's alright – he's backed Wyckliffe from the first."

"Cheating on his wife and little girl," Becky continued.

"Jim Arrowood rang his dad for help, and his girl friend her great-grandma."

"All Jecky Day cares about is himself. Like you, you bagger! Oh Benny, Benny! Why do I always go falling for the wrong man?!"

"Don't fall for me, Beck." She hugged her smooth whiteness tightly to him. "I ain't worth it, angel."

"Don't I know it!"

He stroked her head and long black hair, nuzzling its freshness. "Gawd, you're lovely, dawling! you really are. I fancy you."

"Well, you've got me, ain't you? in your power for the next hour. I'm only a poor, hepless maiden. Here! What ' you fink you're doing!? Ooh, I like it! Do it again!"

Sprawled on his back on the bed, Benny mused: "I don't want to withdraw from the squad. But what can I do? We' got to support Jecky. He's right. The F.A. are using us to promote British Industry and stuff.

What's that got to do wiv football? So why can't Jecky do his programme? It ain't interfering wiv the game." Becky began using the lavatory, he called out: "Glamour girls like you shouldn't need to piss!" She emitted a long raspberry. "Christ! You'll blow a hole through the bladdy floor!" The toilet flushed. "What time you leaving for Las Vegas tomorrow?"

She came out of the bathroom drying her hands on her towel: "Three o'clock."

"You'll knock 'em dead."

"You fink so?"

"Wiv your face and figure? Cor!"

"Garn!" she flicked the towel at him, making him roll on his side.

"You'll do me an injury, girl!"

She sat on the bed and stroked his thigh. "I'll miss you, Ben," she said softly. "Can you remember when we was little kids? I was going to be a rich pop star, and you'd play for England."

"Yer. Now we ' done it. Back to London Town, World Champions – sort of fing my Uncle Ralph would've been glad about, poor old bagger."

"The F.A. might give way," she was sympathetic.

"Jecky's holding a Press Conference after training tomorrow to have it all out."

"I don't see why the fuss. He's got the publicity he wanted – so he don't need do the programme."

"That's not the point."

"He don't care how you and Jim Arrowood and the others feel! I fink he wants to get dropped from the team and sent back to England. Then he can be remembered as the Big Man of Principle the rest of his life."

Benny's contempt was total: "Don't talk daft! Women! – you don't understand a fing!"

"I understand he's two-timing his wife! I wonder how much they'll ask him about *that* at his Press conference!"

"You don't understand nuffing," Benny's disgust was flecked with doubt.

"I know that cow, Anderson! And he's got such a nice wife and lovely little girl. Men!"

CHAPTER 37

The People's Mirror man sipped skimmed milk for his ulcer. The Tory-Express reporter blew bubbles in his dry ginger for fun. The Daily Telegraphic freelance belletrist drank from a tumbler three quarters full of neat gin. The Chicago Tribunal and Chicago Star representatives imbibed iced tea spiked ninety per cent with bourbon. Three Canadian journalists and one from Detroit were taking turns at a bottle of Scotch. The New York Times sports writer had black coffee, the Times, white, the Manchester Guardian female reporter, orange juice. Other press people were swallowing beer and assorted beverages at comfortable speeds. Apart from the gulping and slurping, the only other sound was of the Tory-Mail reporter's aggressive: "Why do you have to be different?!" Why can't you simply accept management ruling like everybody else?!"

"Because the ruling is unfair," said Jacky. "Next question."

The Tory-Express man stopped blowing bubbles and called out: "Aren't you using your special position, Jacky, to try and blackmail English F.A. officialdom?"

"What special position? I haven't any special position. I ain't blackmailing anybody," Jacky retorted. "I'm a man trying to make a living, as I've explained these last few minutes," he glanced at Denzil Wyckliffe standing by the wall three yards to his left. "There's both a point of principle and money for me involved."

The People's Mirror man said: "The whole of the Labour Party supports you, Jacky. Public opinion polls show 70% in your favour, and The People's Mirror is backing you 100%!"

The Chicago Star sports columnist growled: "We'd like to know we're with you, Jack." His countrymen nodded approval. "We're pretty strong on the right to free speech and democracy in this country."

The New York Times reporter stood up, and concentrated on Jacky:

"The English sahccer authorities in London say they wish to avoid controversy and unwanted publicity by banning players from appearing on television programmes: why haven't they forbidden you this Press conference?"

"Our team manager can better answer that."

Wyckliffe said: "Jacky made his views known to The People's Mirror yesterday, and short of disciplining him – which causes bad blood and is entirely against my inclination – or dropping him from the team which I will not do, there was no point at all in stopping this meeting when he suggested holding it."

The Manchester Guardian reporter asked: "Are you in favour of this television ban?"

"No," Wyckliffe was firmly neutral in tone.

The Tory-Mail was aggressive: "Isn't your attitude disloyal to your superiors?"

"As England team manager, I'll carry out orders that are official policy and which I am not prepared to resign over. But I will not pretend I like those policies when I do not."

Several journalists expressed approval.

The Manchester Guardian columnist focussed decisively on the England Team Manager: "You personally would give Jacky Day permission to do this television programme?"

"Yes," Denzil Wyckliffe assented firmly.

"Then where's the problem?! the Detroit man called out. A theme repeated by others present.

The Times reporter stood up and voiced the opinion of the more enlightened among the British conservative Establishment: "In view of the immense publicity during the past twenty-four hours, Mr Wyckliffe, don't you think the F.A. might re-consider its original ruling and thus permit Mr Day to participate in the Paddy O'Rourke Talk Show?"

"It might also order his dismissal from the team if he defies its ruling."

CHAPTER 38

"Why didn't you tell me all this before now?" Mary was tense with anger.

"I didn't want to," Jacky said softly.

"You should have! That bitch! That damn scheming prostitute! I suppose you were considering taking her up on her offer?"

"Mary," Jacky reproached her.

She reacted instinctively: "I don't want you to see Britt Anderson again or have anything to do with her."

"Alright," Jacky agreed with finality.

"The dirty little cow!" the diminutive Mary was fierce. "Running after you like this, a married man with a little daughter! It shows clearly what she is," Mary walked up and down in the hotel room. "She must be crazy. What does she hope to gain?! You haven't encouraged her, have you? Have you, Jacky?" fear glimpsed through the appeal.

"No."

She was worried, uncertain, arms crossed underneath her breasts. "Then why is she doing this?! Oh, I wish I'd never tried to be so liberal and broadminded! Are you sure you haven't encouraged her?"

"I told you, Mary."

"Yes, but can I trust you, Jacky?" She realised: "I have to trust you, don't I? I'm frightened," she admitted.

Jacky walked to the phone: "I'll tell her I'm not coming tonight. Then I'll tell the sponsors I don't want to work with her or have anything to do with her at all in any way."

"Wait," Mary was decisive, though troubled.

"I'll explain why."

"She got you the contracts. They're legally binding. She'll have contracts, also."

"So? I don't have to do anything I don't want to."

She was calm: "Do the work with her, Jacky. Finish it."

"But you don't want me to."

"I was jealous. Still am. And frightened."

"Nothing to be frightened of."

"She's beautiful. And she wants you."

"You and Jessie mean more to me than she does, Mary."

CHAPTER 39

Jacky forced his attention from Britt Anderson's beauty to the slow-moving lights of a ship several miles out on twilit Lake Michigan. "Why are you interested in me? There's no sense in it, no future. What happened in London was a mistake and won't happen again."

Darkness blurred the water's ripples. He strained against her silence. Trees and bushes rustled. A car door slammed fifty yards away. Somebody began laughing, voices raised momentarily, words indistinct. Smell of night grass, leaves, and her perfume.

Britt Anderson's voice was quiet: "What happened in London was no mistake. You're too honest to lie about that." Jacky bit his lip, remembering her nakedness, the tight clutch of her vagina, the ecstasy and post-coital tranquillity and peace, aware of her beauty, her warmth, he lusted for her afresh, wishing to surrender, enjoy all she offered yet conscious of Mary and her importance to him, their life together, Jessie. "You're a good man, a faithful man who would never have bothered with me or any other woman if his wife had loved him with body and soul and filled his every need. Your present wife got you first. If I had had you first, no other woman would ever have had you. I would have done everything for you, for our happiness, everything. never consented to other women! Never!"

"I love Mary, and our little girl. We've got our life together. I shan't make love to you again, Britt."

Her eyes were wide; expression yearning: "You are the only man I've met that I both feel and judge I could live at peace and in harmony with for the rest of my life. That's why I want you."

"I'm married," his throat was dry.

"I'm yours any time you want me: anywhere: anyhow:" she spoke quietly, "because I trust you. Oh Jacky," she flicked away tears with her right forefinger, smiling, "I meet a man for the first time in my life I could be happy with, and he's married and refuses me."

"But you can have any man, you're so beautiful! you're rich, you've brains, you've everything! Apart from football, when I'm off the field, I'm nothing special at all!"

"To me you are," she retorted softly, smiling.

"I'm staggered. I mean, I am, Britt. If I were some tall, handsome he-man! But I'm not! If I weren't married –!" he broke off with a baffled, flattered laugh. "I would –. Well, I am, and my wife is good to me and for me. And I'm a bad husband for even talking to you like this!" he turned and walked purposefully away. "I'm going back to Mary and my little daughter right now!" Britt kept pace with him.

CHAPTER 40

From a cloudless sky, the four o'clock sun cooked the humidity quivering about the stadium's parched tiers. Stray urgent shouts from various England players touched the awareness of the sweat-soaked rest grouped training on the turf, probed the empty stands' shadows and floated diffuse unheeded echoes.

"The F.A. meeting in London should be ovver now," Curly Greenhalgh nodded Jed Lennox's header to Jingo Byrnes. "They won't let him do the programme," he forecast pessimistically.

"Brazil nine-two, and Italy four-nil yesterday," Dave Lewis's forehead punched to Jed Lennox who directed to Curly.

"Training matches against local sides," Jingo Byrnes belittled the victories.

"They must let him do the programme!" Jed Lennox burst forth.

"No 'must' about it," said Curly. "The F.A. won't give in."

"If we'd all stood together!" Jed Lennox was regretful.

"Joe Berrigan and you wouldn't turn your noses up at money, young Lewis," Curly panted.

"Nobody's asked me yet," Dave Lewis said.

"With eighteen kids and another on the way, Joe could do with the money," Jingo Byrnes grunted.

"Ridiculous!" Curly gasped. "Just 'cause the Pope says don't use contraceptives! The Pope wants 'em to breed so they can take over the world and make the rest of us do what he wants."

"You're talking bloody daft, Curly," Jed Lennox was scornful.

"I'm not! The religious people want power to rule ovver us!"

Tempers flared as arguments raged around the supremacy of one religion over another. Jingo Byrnes favoured aspects of Islam, particularly around sex, whilst Curly and Dave Lewis posed their objections firmly. Jed reminded Jingo that Dick Trelawney and Joe were fit to punch him last night. Curly gave his views on his sexual preferences for older teenagers.

"We'll tell your lawful wedded, Curly," Dave Lewis threatened.

"Bloody hell, don't do that!" the bald man was apprehensive. "She'll think I've got one!"

"Is your wife jealous, Curly?" Jingo wondered.

"Jealous?! You'd think I'd hordes of beautiful women after me to hear her talk! What about Winston's girlfriend, eh? The police chief's daughter from Mississippi."

"He wants to watch it with her," Jed Lennox was serious. "She's trouble."

"Winston is, you mean. Wyckliffe's had to tell him off several times already."

"I know," the coloured youth was worried.

"The F.A. should be contacting Wyckliffe with their decision any time now."

"And another ten!" Richard Trelawney grunted; he, Benny Cawthorne, Eddy Corelli and Sid Garner, hands clasped behind their heads, were doing quick sit-ups.

"I'm done! I'm done!" Eddy Corelli gasped in exhaustion.

"You will be if you don't get fit," said the shirtless Benny Cawthorne. "Fink of how the Brazilians and Argentineans are suffering right this minute, and those poor Poles and Chinamen, not to mention the Eyeties and Krauts," the muscles of his bare, lean stomach bunched big and hard as he worked.

"Ten more!" Richard Trelawney urged.

"You going out with your new girlfriend tonight, Benny?" Sid Garner gasped through his horse teeth.

"Nah, we're stopping in."

"Like Jacky," Eddy Corelli strained. "Is it true Mary's jealous of that blonde?"

"Perfect! Beautiful!" Wyckliffe hurried to place a fresh ball. Jacky ran as though he intended swerving the free kick round the row of dummy defenders between him and the twenty-five yard distant goal. Instead, he flicked deftly to Jim Arrowood, sprinted diagonally right and lobbed Jim's return hard over the penalty area where Winston Jones, dashing in, jump-headed sideways for Bobby Milburne to score.

"Lovely!" said Wyckliffe. "Superb, lads!" He wiped sweat from his forehead. Around the ground, the various groups worked at their allotted tasks.

"Mr Wyckliffe!" Near the entrance to the dressing-rooms tunnel, an American stadium employee was waving. "Telephone from London, England!"

"Relax," Jim Arrowood advised a tense Jacky. "With two dukes, five earls, seven viscounts, assorted barons, baronets and half Britain's richest and most powerful men pushing for you behind the scenes, you'll do your programme."

"The F.A. must stand firm," said Joe Berrigan, bold and provocative. He threw the ball at Jacky. "I hate socialism! Ban all socialist propaganda and socialists!"

"That Tennessee congressman Paddy O'Rourke has invited," said Jacky, and passed to Winston Jones, "is twice as reactionary and half as subtle as you are, Joe!"

"The ex-prostitute, his other guest, would convert you to Primitive Baptism, Joe!" Jim Arrowood inveigled, then raced to head to Bobby Milburne.

"I wouldn't mind facking her!" said Winston Jones. Bobby Milburne scored with a seemingly casual left foot flick so hard it spun from Joe Berrigan's grasp and bounced in off his right post. "Bit old, but beautiful tits!"

"Wyckliffe's too lenient with you," Joe Berrigan was stern. "You need teaching discipline – and morality."

"Fack off."

"When you catch VD or Aids, it'll serve you right. It'll be too late crying then!" Joe Berrigan slung to Jacky to continue set-pattern practice.

"God's punishment on the wicked," he levelled his arm and squinted along it at the Brixton lad.

"You don't," Jacky fed Jim Arrowood, "believe that rubbish, Joe!?"

"'Not rubbish!" Jim's lob struck Winston's skull. Bobby's right footer extracted a diving, one handed deflection from Berrigan which Jacky sprinted to retrieve. "If people obeyed God's laws, there wouldn't be any Aids or sexual disease!"

"Your turn, spaceman from another galaxy!" Jim Arrowood called. Bobby Milburne sprinted, zigzagged, and dashed curving to chip over the dummies to the burly target man, Jacky, defending, challenged: Jim crossed for Winston to score.

"The Yanks are bluidy crazy," Bobby Milburne muttered. He set up a fresh ball. Jim Arrowood chuckled irrepressibly at the teenager's disgust so richly revealed in finest Geordie. "What're you laugh'n at, Jim, man? Call'n me a bluidy spee-us-man!" His repeated disgust made the fair haired six footer laugh freely. Jacky, Winston Jones and Joe Berrigan were chuckling. Bobby grinned hesitantly. "Call'n me a spee-us-man, eh? What'll they bluidy think of next?"

Jim Arrowood called, friendly: "You're lucky not to have Richard's and my fan club, Bobby – all the homos parading with placards: 'Jim's dandy for me', 'I would if Arrowood'. Your bottom left corner," he called to Joe Berrigan; his twenty yarder tested the goalie's dive. Winston Jones sent one for Berrigan to leap right, Jacky for him to spring left. Bobby's right footer was so hard it spat from the perfectly positioned keeper's grasp.

The seventeen-year-old prepared to resume set-pattern practice.

Jim Arrowood said: "I'm surprised the coppers don't pull 'em in with slogans like they have."

They repeated Bobby's lob variant.

"'I love big Dick!' 'We love big Dick!' It's a bit near the bone, isn't it?"

"Homosexuality's a vicious sin!" Joe Berrigan threw savagely at Jacky who overhead-kicked for Bobby to recommence manoeuvres. "Unnatural! Full of disease and filth! They should ban them!"

"Castrate 'em!" Winston Jones grinned sadistically. "Kill 'em!" He scowled: "And all the Ku Klux Klan and Guardians of American Morality what keep shouting about me wiv white women!" he shot fiercely.

Joe Berrigan rolled upright with the ball. "They're right! Wyckliffe should ban you – and Cawthorne!"

"Wyckliffe's back," Jim Arrowood observed.

"For curiosity's sake, Jacky," the England Team Manager watched the thirty yard distant Winston Jones exchange rôles with Jim Arrowood, "would you have defied the ban?"

"What?" the stocky man, smiling, cocked his head with eyebrow raised, "and risked the good of the team?"

CHAPTER 41

On the England squad's lounge television screen, film snippet followed film snippet: Jacky scoring penalties; heading goals; sprinting, dribbling, combination passing, playmaking; setting up goalscoring chances for others; being kicked and charged, retaining his balance and momentum, dribbling round two defenders and dummying two more within three yards and lobbing over the goalkeeper to score from a seemingly impossible angle.

"Ladies and gentlemen," Paddy O'Rourke, the programme leader, announced, "our final guest for tonight, arguably the greatest sahccer player in the world, Mr John Day of Notting-haam Forest sahccer club and England! Give him a big hand, folks! Welcome to the show, Jack. Glad you finally made it."

"I'm pleased I could," said Jacky.

"You nearly didn't. After all the hullabaloo – like to comment on it?"

"I wanted the money."

The studio audience applauded enthusiastically, Paddy O'Rourke laughed. On Jacky's right, the ex-prostitute and the grey haired and leathery looking Tennessee congressman were smiling.

Paddy O'Rourke described Jacky's sponsors and the products the Englishman was advertising, and, turning to Jacky, rounded off: "So even a socialist is in'erested in money, huh?"

"You can't live without it," said Jacky.

The Tennessee congressman attacked at once, "You'd need to if we had socialism," evoking cheers, clapping and shouts of agreement from the studio audience. "It's a disease, socialism. We ain't got it in America, and, God willing, we never will have.

Though we've gotten enough creep'n' socialists in Washington and half the state legislatures throughout this country."

"It's a pity you haven't got socialists in power all over this country!" Jacky retorted. "Then the United States wouldn't have all the unnecessary slums, starvation, poverty, sick and uncared for people it has!"

Richard Trelawney winced. Beside him on the settee in Mary's and Jacky's suite, Jim Arrowood grinned aslant at Beth Langdale. Mary, intent on the programme, was in one armchair, Joyce Trelawney in the other, nursing the sleeping Jessica. "I hope he doesn't forget to mention our stand at the Exhibition." Joyce said placidly.

"Attaboy, Jecky!" Benny Cawthorne chortled.

"Rubbish!" Joe Berrigan sneered.

"Agreed," said David Lewis.

Half the England squad were delighted. Others were shaking their heads.

"You nivver did have much bloody sense, Joe!" Curly Greenhalgh derided. On the screen, the congressman was instancing the Soviet Union, its satellites, and other oligarchic bureaucratic non-democracies to support his arguments.

"None of those countries was socialist," Jacky opposed. "Some aspects were, and where they were, or are, they're very good!" The Tennessean growled denial. Jacky flowed on: "All those countries you name are poor ones that modelled their systems on Russia's, created by Stalin, one of the worst tyrants in the history of the world! In my country, and throughout Western Europe, socialism has shown its immense value for people and for the lasting good of humanity!"

Socialists and men and women of reformist views throughout the country were joyful with full approval. Reactionaries gnashed their teeth.

The ex-prostitute was speaking with warmth close to fanaticism about religion.

"She's not a bad looker, is she?" Curly Greenhalgh commented appreciatively. "Look at that figure, eh?!"

"She'd swallow you alive, Curly. You'd never get out again," Benny Cawthorne grinned.

"And if you did, we'd tell your wife," Dave Lewis said.

The television company's switchboard was busy receiving phone calls enunciating everything from ecstatic praise to vituperation. Plus six death threats: three screamed, two growled, and one very softly and concisely delivered. Four of the calls were successfully traced.

"The Bahbel is mah strength and mah consolation in mah hour of need," drawled the Southerner. "When Ah'm up there on Capitol Hill and all the evil forces of Yankee cussedness are conspiring ag'in' me to thwart mah just and rightful cause, the Good Book provides comfort and the will to fight on to victory."

"Amen," breathed the erstwhile whore reverently. "To those who believe in Him and His only begotten Son, the Lord Jesus Christ, they who truly repent of their sins and live in righteousness shall enter His kingdom and live forever in peace and joy everlasting that surpasses man's understanding!"

"As a good Catholic," said Paddy O'Rourke, crossing himself, "I can agree with that. Got any comments on the matter, Jack?"

Jacky hesitated a moment then decided to be frank: "In doing different tests, I've done psychological, too, met different psychologists and psychiatrists. And they all agree on one thing: Religions are emotional crutches that help people bear their fears and suffering and ignorance. If you feel you're all alone in the world – which we all are, ultimately –, it's a very fine consolation to think you've got a Friend who knows everything, is All-Powerful, Who loves you and Who guarantees you everlasting life in a wonderful, happy Paradise."

"He does," the former harlot evinced conviction.

The Southerner required certainty: "I ain't sure where you're headed, son."

Paddy O'Rourke was: "Are you an atheist?"

"Yes."

"I'm sorry to hear that," Richard Trelawney condemned.

"God is not mocked," Joe Berrigan stated. "Jacky Day will find that out when he dies. Hellfire is very real."

"Is that what awaits us Jews, Joe, for killing Christ and not being Christians?" David Lewis inquired.

"There is nothing to stop anyone from becoming a good Catholic and saving his soul from eternal damnation," Joe Berrigan was completely sure of himself.

Mary responded: "Religion is based on fear of death and on human sentiment and therefore can and does take any form which imagination gives it."

Richard Trelawney was emphatic: "God made everything, including science and scientists! He sent His Only Begotten Son, Jesus, to show us the Way, the Truth and the Light!"

"And who made God?"

"You two will never agree on religion," said Joyce.

"What a quaint eccent thet American hes, hesn't he?!" Beth Langdale was enthralled by the Tennessean, extolling his Christian fundamentalism with much emphasis on Satan roasting sinners; the ex-prostitute kept interrupting, protesting, adjusting his views to suit her own, yet generally was in agreement; Paddy O'Rourke expounded Roman Catholic dogma on the Virgin Birth and the Holy Mother of God.

"I don't think the Virgin Mary was a virgin," said Jacky. "She was a religious woman in a superstitious society, pregnant by a man, who – if the New Testament is accurate, which I believe it isn't – convinced herself her foetus was the most wonderful ever – her tribal god himself, the Jews' God in human form –, only God Himself was good enough to father Himself and beget her beautiful little baby. If any civilised woman today were to say her child was God Himself fathered by Himself, sensible people would recognise that she was joking, temporarily deluded, or totally off her head."

"And this is the guy you've gotten me contracts with?!" Chuck Bengtsson lowered his 6'5", 230 pounds onto the settee beside Britt Anderson.

"His honesty is refreshing," she retorted, "after all the lying and hypocrisy one hears every day."

"He'll certainly be news after tonight!"

Joe Berrigan's face was twisted with dislike and rejection. He absorbed the varied and conflicting reactions of his team-mates. His lips parted to voice contempt and insult. Then he shrugged: they were only Protestants anyway, atheists, a Jew, and Jingo Byrnes a Muslim lover, not worth arguing with.

Paddy O'Rourke spoke above his countrymen's outbursts and the audience hubbub: "What you just said gives deep offence to Christians the world over!"

"And to me in particular!" the reformed whore was passionate. "The Blessed Virgin was the perfect mother! the hope and gentle consolation for all us weak sinners here on Earth! She was womanhood undefiled! the Miracle of God's Love and Endless Goodness toward humanity!"

"You're gonna' fry in Hell, boy!" growled the Tennessean, "just like that other English guy, Charles Darwin, with his crazy ideas!"

"I didn't, and don't, want to hurt anyone's feelings, nor give offence," said Jacky. "But I said what I think and what I believe! And as to frying in Hell, I honestly believe there is no Hell, nor Heaven, nor any life except here and now. And the only Hell we have is the one we make ourselves, right on this Earth!"

"Oh he's magnificent, isn't he?!" Britt Anderson, eyes glistening, leant forward toward Jacky, hugging herself in proxy.

Chuck Bengtsson's innards churned, spuming jealousy that reason congealed. "You care for the guy," his tone held surprised comprehension.

"Too much!" Shrewdness checked spontaneity. "I never pretended otherwise."

Unheeded on the screen, Paddy O'Rourke lashed Protestant England about Catholic Ireland.

"I thought it was business," pain oozed through his wryness.

"I don't love you, Chuck," she was direct. "You know that. You're a wonderful man: big –," humour quirked sincerity, "handsome – virile –," Chuck Bengtsson, smiling sombrely, shrugged disavowal and acceptance and half turned away. The Tennesseean was championing

America, Christianity and Capitalism, the ex-harlot flittering arabesques and piquant curlicues of personal reminiscence and insight. "Friends? – Chuck? – Darling?"

"Nationalism is rubbish, a blight and curse on the world!" Jacky declared. "And particularly Irish nationalism!"

The England squad were cheering and laughing. "You tell 'em, boy!" said Benny Cawthorne.

"Nationalism is out of date. People should be trying to co-operate with one another instead of squabbling and falling out, hating each other, killing one another because of Nationalism! It's all stupidity! Boasting about National pride, our great Nation, how wonderful we are and how useless the others are, it's folly! Nationalism is a bane on mankind! Nationalism and Religion have led to more suffering and millions of deaths than anything else in the history of humanity!"

"We'll have to use your Jacky with discretion," Chuck Bengtsson was decided. "Counterbalance him so that he does not offend the wrong people."

"Not true religion!" Richard Trelawney denied passionately. "True religion is peace and harmony, respect for life, and glory in God's work!"

Paddy O'Rourke was vigorously venerating Patriotism, the Nation State, Ireland and Roman Catholicism.

"True religion?" Mary queried gently. "All the killing and persecution by Christian Churches, Muslim proselytising of Africa and Asia by armed force, Hindus slaughtering Muslims, Sikhs murdering Hindus. Every true religious believer has always cherished the true religion – his own," she finished dryly.

"Killing and persecution is not true religion!" Richard Trelawney was fervent. "Respect for life and reverence of God's Truth is true religion!"

The ex-prostitute touched fanaticism with each gust of emotion she swirled into speech. The Tennesseean chewed gum and flung out an occasional caustic comment.

At the television company's switchboard, a word for word repeat of the quietly spoken death threat on Jacky's life was received. Tracing it again proved unsuccessful.

"People believe all sorts of things," Jacky was earnest. "And they are all convinced they're right. And there are huge numbers who hold diametrically opposed beliefs. So somebody must be wrong."

"Only the Pope since 1873 is infallible," grinned Paddy O'Rourke, eliciting cheers from his co-religionists and causing the reformed whore to shake her head in firm denial and the congressman to look cynical.

Jacky went on: "What people need is good food, clothes, a place to live, help when they're sick to make them well, and healthy surroundings to live in so they needn't fall ill so often. They certainly do not need to fight and kill one another about ideas, most of which are daft anyway!"

"His religious and socialist ideas are," said Joe Berrigan. "Daft isn't the word for them – imbecility, that's atheism and socialism!"

"Millions have died fighting over those ideas, that's for sure," said David Lewis.

"Daft is the word for you, Joe!" Curly Greenhalgh attacked. "Up the Workers!"

On the screen, the panellists were flinging comments on religion, national and ideological conflicts, international terrorism. "I hope Jacky remembers to mention the Anglo-American Trade Exhibition," said Joyce Trelawney.

"Perhaps we can finish our last few minutes tonight on a lighter note, though just as serious. Our English guest is not merely a fiery speaker, but the world's number one sahccer player. And right now, the news of the hour is the World Cup sahccer Tournament about to begin here in the good old U.S. of A. What're your thoughts on your team's chances and the Tournament in general, Jack?"

"First, let's give the game I play its proper name. Football, Association Football, the correct name by which it is known and loved by hundreds of millions throughout the world."

The Irish-American explained, not unfriendly: "Sahccer is what we call it in this country, Jack."

"I know. It was a nickname given to it at English public schools where only the sons of the rich and privileged went, the English Conservative

Establishment, snobs who despised and sneered at the working man's game, football – footer –, my game, the world game. The sort who caused the Irish Potato Famine. They played rugby football – rugby – and, above all, cricket. Football was something to look down on, and is to this day – by them," Jacky's contempt for their contempt was clear. "The first formal rules of the game were drawn up by the English Football Association. The word soccer comes from as-soc-i-ation," Jacky's anglicised Italian pronunciation was doubly excruciating, emphasising as it did the sound SOC.

"Football in this coun'ry means something else," the Irish-American pointed out mildly.

"Sure does, and that's mah game," growled the Tennessean.

"Football is played with the foot and the ball," Jacky explained. "They're the most important components. Like baseball, where the base and the ball are. Football is not the right name for the American game: the most important things are the grid and the ball. It should properly be called gridball."

"I like it – gridballer," Britt Anderson nudged her elbow into her settee companion's side, correcting herself, "ex-gridballer."

The big multimillionaire grunted, smiling.

"Brazil, yes, they're a skilful team," said Jacky. And the Italians, and Argentina. The Germans, of course, are always good. This is the World Championship. The teams here are supposed to be the best in the world."

Paddy O'Rourke was critical, naming half a dozen countries not represented, and was ironical about the way England had qualified.

Jacky defended England's right to participate, and, in response to O'Rourke's prompting, analysed the England squad and its chances.

Joe Berrigan was categorical: "It was totally wrong and gutless of the F.A. to let him go on this programme! Preaching atheism and socialism! Attacking religion! Imbecility! Lock Jacky Day up, and everybody with views like his, and throw away the key!"

Other team-members did not agree and trenchantly told him so.

"Listen! Listen!" Benny Cawthorne urged.

"And with eighteen kids, all under twenty, and another on the way, our goalkeeper, Joe Berrigan, is in the market for every reputable way of making money that any businessman listening to this can put in his way. I will advise you, however, that he is a Roman Catholic and will not do anything against his beliefs."

Abashed but unrepentant, Joe Berrigan was grinning. His detractors, guffawing and irreverent, jibed at him.

"And that goes for the rest of our squad. We're professional athletes, out to earn money. Our playing careers are short, so naturally we want to make ourselves as financially secure as we can while we can because none of us knows what the future will bring when our footballing days are over."

Jubilant around their television screen, the English players watched Jacky speaking well of the excellent administrative arrangements and hospitality they had experienced in the States.

"Tomorrow afternoon, we shall all be at the Anglo-American Trade Exhibition here in Chicago, promoting British products and Anglo-American business co-operation. The British Ambassador and Foreign Secretary and the Mayor of Chicago will be there. We hope as many as possible of you will come, particularly businessmen and farmers with money to invest: British industry is showing the best it has to offer, that is, among the best in the world, so you will definitely not be wasting your time in paying a visit. And when you come, be sure to visit the West of England stand, with gen-u-ine English souvenirs imported direct from England by our skipper's wife, Mrs Joyce Trelawney."

Joyce's shriek and start of delight almost awakened the sleeping Jessica.

The voice in the television company switchboard operator's earphone was quiet, almost caressing: "Hallo, again. This is my third and final call." The telephonist recognised him and immediately began speaking non-stop, striving to prolong the contact; he ignored her. "I am going to kill Jacky Day. Yes, I have definitely decided upon that. Communist, socialist, whatever you like to call him, anti everything I have ever believed in and fought for. I'm going to kill him. You will not hear from me again until Jacky Day is dead."

CHAPTER 42

i

"Pleased to meet you, Mrs Day, Jacky." Chuck Bengtsson's huge paw clasped warm and gentle. Mary's gaze flickered from his Nordic features to Britt Anderson's white attire and blonde loveliness: a perfect match: why did she need to chase Jacky? "Plen'y of cops and security men about."

"The Foreign Secretary's and British Ambassador's visit," Britt Anderson gave the reason.

"No. They threatened to kill Jacky last night," said Mary.

Jacky dismissed the notion: "Nothing to worry about. It's happened before. The usual crackpot."

"Yeah," Chuck Bengtsson rumbled, "we do have a few of them in this coun'ry. I guess you have some in yours as well, though Britt has her own ideas on that."

Mary noted the big man's love for Britt Anderson and her easy acceptance of it. The knowledge removed some sharpness from her apprehension concerning her husband. Behind Britt Anderson, across the hall in the children's play section, Joyce Trelawney stood beside Jessica riding a mechanical rocking horse. Sunlight through the roof windows, policemen on the office-floor gallery round the hall walls.

I could smash the socialist bastard's head in, blow his face off! One bullet. Power floated; ecstasy of violence to come gushed saliva into his mouth.

"You should ban private ownership of guns," said Britt Anderson, "then you wouldn't have so many killings."

"Guns are part of the American tradition," Chuck Bengtsson disagreed. "As American as pumpkin pie, Thanksgiving and a man's Constitutional right to defend himself."

"I hate them," said Mary. "I'm afraid of Jacky getting shot."

"No risk of that here with all these police and security guards about," Jacky assured her.

Logic mixed with bloodlust: he needed the hall filled with people, the panic and tumult killing would bring. He could pick his time; the rifle was in place, his plans well made.

"I wish I were back home in England! I feel so safe there!" Mary noticed the big American's quirky smile that mixed opposition with sympathy: "I'm sorry," she was contrite. "I didn't mean to be rude. Really."

"It's understandable in the circumstances, Mrs Day," the multimillionaire appreciated.

Britt Anderson was businesslike: "Shall we do some filming before the dignitaries arrive?"

"As loyal subjects of the Queen, I guess you're longing for the honour of shak'n' the Foreign Secretary's hand and bowing low to the Briddish Ambassador?" the big American provoked, grinning.

"I can hardly wait," said Jacky.

ii

The hall was filling up. Around the edge of the monster combine-harvester Jacky and Mary stood close to, Jim Arrowood was in expert discussion with several weather beaten Mid-Western farmers about crops, agricultural machinery and farm management, his girlfriend quiet at his side. Benny Cawthorne, further down the aisle at the Rolls-Royce stand, was joking with the blonde, brunette and redhead models who were laughing. Across from Benny, Winston Jones and Jed Lennox were with three conservatively attired black businessmen. Twenty yards to Mary's and Jacky's left, Joe Berrigan, Eddy Corelli and David Lewis were talking to two tanned, well dressed and middle-aged types and a little, elderly man with a bald pate and big hooked nose. Other England squad members were scattered about, perusing various exhibits, conversing.

"She seems to know everybody," Mary said tartly. "Probably slept with them, too." Britt Anderson, smilingly at ease, was chatting with the attentive British Ambassador and lean, grey haired U.S. senator. The Foreign Secretary was slaying imaginary wildfowl with a double-barrelled shotgun. Chuck Bengtsson, in front of the English aristocrat, was holding other weapons for him to test. Chicago's mayor looked nervous. The numerous security men guarding the dignitaries flicked glances about, vigilant for danger.

Come out from behind that machine, you commie bastard, you fuck'n' red! Impatience and hate surged, longing to smash home the bullet and splatter bone and blood. One shot, one clear shot that's all I need.

"I've looked forward to meeting you, Jacky," the greyhaired American released his grip on Jacky's. "Britt told me a lot about you."

"And me about you, Gabe," Jacky answered the Senator; the British Ambassador flinched an eyebrow at Jacky's purposeful use of the American's forename diminutive; the Foreign Secretary looked ironic.

"She's quite a girl, aren't you, Britt?" said the Senator. Britt smiled neutrally.

"She's the best," Chuck Bengtsson came in strongly. "That's all we do business with, ain't it, Gabriel?"

"And in Jacky, you've got the best," said Britt.

"The very best," Mary superimposed.

Come out from behind there, you bastard! Just one shot, just one!

"Yo're a controversial mehn, Mr Day," the Foreign Secretary drawled and clipped, the left side of his face twisting a smile and a single mote from his hidden mountain of disdain.

"The whole of the Government to which you belong is controversial," Jacky retorted, "and I'm looking forward to the next General Election when your Party will be out of office."

Chuck Bengtsson guffawed; Britt Anderson bit her bottom lip and turned her head to conceal merriment.

"That's straight talk'n'," the Senator chuckled.

The Mayor of Chicago's smile was uneasy; the Ambassador's thin; the Foreign Secretary's amiable through years of skilful deceit. "We shall have to see, shan't we? I believe you were interested in the motorcars, Senator, Mr Mayor?"

Shit! I can't get the bastard! Too many big guys in the way! Get the hell out of there, you sons of bitches! One shot! Just one clear shot.

Startled by Mary's suddenly jerking her head to stare wide-eyed at Jessie in the children's play area, Jacky thrust his head and upper body forward to see round Chuck Bengtsson and Britt Anderson, the big security guard beside him twitched instinctively aside: the man's face disintegrated splattering blood, brain and bone: Jacky's dive knocked Britt and Mary to the floor; his lower body covered Britt's upper, he hugged Mary's head and torso under him, his right leg pulling the rest of her shielded.

Two fifths of a second later, Chuck Bengtsson was over Britt; the bodyguards were protecting the dignitaries, weapons out seeking the danger source.

A woman screamed, a man exclaimed, security men acted fast and logical. Tumult and panic began. The Mayor of Chicago was groaning in a shocked voice he had been shot.

Mary heaved struggling fiercely to rise: "Jessie!" Jacky held her pinned.

"She's alright. No danger there," Jacky kept his voice low and comforting. "Keep still. Keep still, Mary!" he bit out. "Let the guards do their job!"

CHAPTER 43

i

"It's alright, Mam, I tell you! There's nothing to worry about. It wasn't me the gunman was after. It wasn't!" Jacky quashed his mother's murmuring protest. The Foreign Secretary had been threatened, the Senator had been threatened, the Mayor of Chicago had been threatened." He over-rode her nascent objection: "It was the Mayor of Chicago who got shot, wasn't it? not me. There you are, you see. Now don't go getting worried about nothing. Yes, Mary's okay. Not a thing wrong with her, Mam," Mary emerged from Jessica's room and, pausing in the doorway, silently inquired whether she should take the phone, Jacky indicated yes, "and Jessie's alright. We're looking forward to our first match and we're going to win, of course. We'll do well in the World Cup, I feel it in my bones, Mam. Is everything alright at home? Good. Remember," he encouraged her, "you don't have anything to worry about here! You just concentrate on staying fit and getting fully recovered again. You'll keep your fingers crossed for us, won't you? That's the spirit. Good old Mam. Yes, here's Mary. You can have a word with her now. Goodbye, and take care."

ii

"The killer wanted you," Mary was tense.

"No, not me," Jacky derided the idea. "One of the politicians."

"You, Jacky! You!"

"Never!"

"Yes, you! Oh, I hate this, Jacky!" Her emotion became quiet resolution: "I've considered it carefully – Jessie and I are returning to England immediately."

"No," he opposed instinctively.

"You want Jessie hurt?!" She calmed herself, realising: "No – that's not fair. Remember, I did not wish to come to America in the first place. Now all this! Someone tried to kill you, Jacky, and will try again."

He was sceptical: "It wasn't me he was after, I tell you, Mary."

"It was you. And when he cannot kill you, he may try and kill Jessica and me! The F.B.I. security chief made that quite clear!"

"He was talking rubbish, Mary." Jacky's disbelief was total. "There's no danger to any of us."

"No danger?! – when some cunning, deranged murderer shatters a man's head with a bullet meant for you, kills two policemen and leaves a third shot in the chest and head and nobody knows who he is or where he is?!! Oh, come on, Jacky, talk sense!"

"Nobody is trying to kill me. I'm not important enough. It was one of the politicians he was after, not me!"

"The security people don't think so."

"They're simply not taking any chances."

"Yet you want your own little daughter and wife to!"

"Mary, please!" he appealed. "Here at the hotel, crawling with bodyguards, you're as safe as safe can be."

"And you expect us to remain confined in this hotel all day while you're out training?! No! No! No! We did not come to America for that! I did not expect any of this, Jacky! It's a madhouse, and I'm terrified!" She was firm: "I'm taking Jessie home to England where she definitely will be safe."

"Mary," he pleaded, "be reasonable. I want you and Jessie with me. Do you really think I would risk either of you if I thought there was any danger? All these security measures are precautions. Those crackpots who rang up the television station have nothing to do with this business."

"It was you the assassin was after! And being insane, by killing Jessie and me, he could injure you, the security people said so!"

"I don't believe it. He meant shooting one of the politicians, not me. And when that wounded policeman comes out of the anaesthetic, maybe he will be able to help identify the killer and prove it definitely, then you can relax."

"*If* he comes out of the anaesthetic! If he can talk when he comes out of the anaesthetic! If his brain hasn't been destroyed beyond repair by that bullet which smashed into it! Jessie's not going to be murdered like that poor bodyguard. We're returning to England this evening."

"Don't, Mary," he begged. "Or if you really have set your mind on leaving, stay in the States, or go visit that old school friend of yours in Toronto. You'll be safe enough in Canada, surely, till this has blown over, then you can come back."

She clutched herself to him: "Oh Jacky! Jacky! We'll never be completely safe anywhere in North America!" Her frightened wide eyes stared into his: "You're in danger! We all are! And the wisest thing is for me to take Jessie to safety so they can concentrate on guarding you."

"I don't want you to leave, Mary."

"We're going," she was determined. She relaxed into a tight smile: "The one good thing about all this is that you won't be doing any more filming or have chance for any more cosy tête à têtes with Britt Anderson."

CHAPTER 44

The heavy maroon drape's cool velvet against her nudity gratified Britt's senses, titillated frail, vague yearnings of lust, freedom, and self-effacing affection, while through the venetian blinds her imagination twisted the darkness and mansion grounds foliage into assassins tensed to kill.

"Come back to bed, Britt. There's no one out there. Nobody knows I'm here, except the security people. I'll be the first to know of any new developments, believe me. They'll get that guy, Wolf Wehrman, soon."

"But they don't know it is Wolf Wehrman!"

"Ex-Chicago cop, ex-security guard who'd worked that exhibition hall so many times he knew it better'n the back of his hand. Nazi homicidal maniac on the run from a top security institution out in California these last six months."

"But the TV switchboard operator couldn't identify his voice – not for sure!"

"He probably wasn't the one who rang. You're still scared it was your Jacky he wanted to kill, huh?" resigned acceptance was amusement.

"Yes. And now his wife's run out on him, taking their daughter with her."

"Reasonable. They're out of harm's way over there in England."

"She deserted him! I would never have done that! Never!"

"He probably wants it."

"No! He didn't! He said so when I rang him. No more filming, extra tight security. Chuck Bengtsson wants me to go to Montreal with him tomorrow. I could get contracts for Jacky."

"It could take your mind off things here. You really are a beautiful girl, Britt, naked in the twilight by that window, long blonde wavy hair tumbling about slender shoulders, your wonderful breasts, long legs and graceful curves; like some legendary lovely princess from a Nordic saga."

She grinned at the sparse, elderly man sat up in the double bed, his seamed brown face and pale blue pyjamas a contrast against the bed linen's whiteness. "Senator Velasquez, what would your faithful Catholic voters do if they could see and hear you now?"

"Be jealous, or wish me good luck."

"And the bishop and the cardinals, and the Pope you went to see in Rome last year?"

"They'd understand. Holy Mother Church has the institution of confession and forgiveness of sins, remember," he held out his right hand for her to join him. "Besides, I'm a widower, sixty-three and impotent – no good now to any woman in bed." Her small soft hand squeezed his in sympathy. "And you're a beautiful little fairy princess who reminds me of my daughters when they were small and trusted me, pure and clean."

"You're a good man, Gabe."

"Tell that to my enemies, including the guy who took that potshot at me."

"It was Jacky he was trying for."

"Sure," the lean grey haired man was at ease. "The Mayor of Chicago is positive *he* was the target, and the Briddish Foreign Secretary thinks he was. You didn't tell me your Jacky had had a spot of bother with some Chinese tongmen in London, and paid out £20,000 on a bet his brother welched on." He noted her raised eyebrow and little smile: "You knew, huh? I guess you love the guy?"

"I'd be better for him than his wife."

"I thought he was happily married."

"I know things you don't."

"What's so special about the guy?"

Britt gave a little head shake, not wanting to discuss Jacky further.

He persisted: "You've got brains, you've got money, you've got exceptional beauty. You can have any man you want. I know I'm a lucky old fogey being here like this."

She caressed his hair and leant to kiss his cheek. "You're a friend, Gabe. I know it gives you pleasure seeing me, having me near. And I like you holding me close and stroking my head: it's a bit weird but it reminds me of when I was a very little girl with my daddy."

"What about Jacky Day's little girl, if you take her daddy away from her mommy?"

She pulled back, stiffening. "I would be her mummy."

"Sure you would, and her real mommy and the news media wouldn't say a word. And what if he left you – as you want him to leave his wife – for another woman?"

"Never," she sat up straight and proud. "I'd do everything for him – anything."

The Senator, amiable, patted her hand: "Not that any guy in his right mind would ever leave you. I wouldn't, not at his age. Not at any age for that matter. It's more likely you'd leave him."

She comprehended: "You're a crafty old man, aren't you? – playing the Devil's Advocate."

"That's what friends are for. 'Want to talk about Jacky? Maybe I can help."

"Nobody can help. It's between us two. Thanks anyway, Gabe. I shall go to Montreal tomorrow."

"Me, Washington. Back to the grime and slime, and the action – if that Nazi doesn't hit me first."

"How can you joke about it?! It's Jacky he's after. If only that policeman would come out of his coma and describe the killer! then we'd know for sure! Maybe the man they're hunting isn't the man!"

CHAPTER 45

As the second ringing signal stopped, he hung up and dialled again.

"Hallo, lover," the androgynous voice lilted, "I've been waiting for you to ring. 'Coming home soon? I miss you so much, you gorgeous man."

"I never left. I told you that, before I went out to buy the groceries."

"I know you did, honey. How could you leave?! How could I let you leave? You never left. Except like now to buy some groceries, and perhaps some other goodies here in little old Los Angeles."

"I may be an hour or two delayed. But you get my skins and studs and white stetson out: they're going to be seen around the neighbourhood tonight, and tomorrow night and every night, right?"

"Right. You're so sexy in leather and steel."

"And maybe we'll take in a couple of parties in Hollywood I heard about, with some of your actor friends – and your fat faggot producer." Across the street, a man removed a Chicago Tribunal from a news-stand without paying, and a train rumbled by on the Loop.

"Don't make me jealous, sweetheart!" the protest was ultra- feminine.

"Just make sure my stetson's white and my studs gleam."

Jukebox glare, men's voices laughing and shouting, bar sounds: "Yah?"

"Heil, mein lieber Junge!"

"Heil! Shi-it! I can't hear myself speak! Just a minute, huh?" The phone's clattering down crackled the receiver. "Shut that fuck'n' door!" The background noises in the receiver diminished. Silence.

A train rocked by on the Loop.

"Heil! Wie geht's!"

"Pretty good. Can we talk?"

"We're clean. Go ahead."

"Start hitting the black shit – now!"

"You're ready?"

"I'm ready. Hit 'em as planned! Untermensch!"

"Right on."

"But leave that fuck'n' Jew commie bastard son-of-a-bitch till I give you the high sign. Then," Wolf Wehrman's voice was low, its hatred pulsing, "hit him!! hit him!!!"

CHAPTER 46

"We shall get him," the F.B.I. man assured the three Englishmen. "When, Mr Vanderskoon?" Wyckliffe, without taking his gaze from the American's face, put the security arrangements folder down on his office table.

"Fast. He's had all the breaks so far. We missed him by no more than fifteen minutes last night at that ex-Nazi's where he's been staying."

"But is he the one who threatened Jacky?"

"We don't know, gen'lemen. I wish we did. All we can do is play it by the book and give you maximum security cover. The President's taking a personal interest in this. Believe me, we're doing everything humanly possible."

"I believe you," said Wyckliffe; Richard Trelawney nodded.

"I still don't think he was after me," said Jacky. "Everything points to the Mayor of Chicago."

"We're tak'n' no chances."

"It's bad, keeping the squad penned in all day when they're not training," Wyckliffe stated.

"We've advised all the other teams to do the same," said the F.B.I. man "Some squads have had their people locked up from the beginning. The Brazilians and Argentineans and Italians, for example."

"Is it true a death threat was made this morning against Karl-Dieter Hoffman and the German team?" Richard Trelawney asked.

"It's true."

Jacky said: "Hoffman can't help it if his grandfather murdered thirty thousand Jews during the Second World War. He wasn't even born then, nor any of the rest of the German lads."

"The United States is a democracy," the American explained. "We can't stop people demonstrating. Like other countries, we've got our share of weirdoes and crazies. More'n our fair share, I sometimes think."

"We'll follow your instructions to the letter, Mr Vanderskoon," said Wyckliffe, "and hope with all our hearts that you get that killer as quickly as possible."

CHAPTER 47

Through the thin pale curtains, across the forecourt, above the entrance to the main building, the neon sign MOTEL flowed from blue to white: beside it, the smaller word VACANCIES glowed bright green; only two of the five visible guestroom windows shone. Sound of occasional traffic whooshed past on the road eighty yards away. Low burble of pop music from the radio. Faint smell of pinewood. Fresh clean pillow.

The news signal brought him alert. "And here is all the latest news of the hour brought to you on the hour every hour by Radio VKNG from downtown Minneapolis! Ten people died after a fire bomb explosion destroyed an N.A.A.C.P. locale in Los Angeles just after four o'clock this afternoon. The recently retired head of Californian Ronald Reagan Hospital was found brutally tortured and shot to death at his home in Santa Monica tonight." The man on the bed smiled, closed his eyes and breathed in his deep enjoyment as the newscaster talked of swastikas and Stars of David carved in the corpse's flesh.

"The hunt for the man who wounded Chicago's mayor and slew a Secret Service bodyguard last Saturday continues. The suspected killer's car was identified in Indianapolis, Indiana, at three o'clock this afternoon. The automobile was sold yesterday in Gary, Indiana, by a white Caucasian male who police think could be the man they are look'n' for. West German World Cup officials are taking seriously death threats uttered by a presumed Jewish extremist against their star player, Karl-Dieter Hoffman. Local St Paul beauty queen lands lead in planned Hollywood epic. These are the headlines. Further news in detail after this message from Shidy's Little Wonder Worker, the pill that guarantees –"

Eyes closed, smiling, he savoured the incinerated bodies, the mutilation and agony, the murder in Santa Monica, recalled the ecstasy of power and hate when killing the Secret Service man, then the policemen.

Visioning Jacky Day, frustration spiralled searingly, then transformed into purposeful sharp sequences of Soldier Field Stadium.

He would kill the little communist son-of-a-bitch on television in the middle of the England-Poland game. Then the billions of communist-socialist foreigners bleeding America dry would know he had seen through their conspiracy, through their fellow-travellers, pinkos and reds rotting America from within, planning to take over the world.

Sharp, clear images flitted of Soldier Field's exits and entrances, possible shot angles, hiding places. He let them drift and blur – no hurry. Alone out there in the woods the next few days, he would work out the details.

"And that was the news from Radio VKNG, Minneapolis! Lie back and enjoy mood music from now till dawn on your friendly station, VKNG, Minneapolis."

Across the forecourt, a guestroom window went dark. The MOTEL sign tendrilled blue into white, the green VACANCIES gleamed at the universe.

CHAPTER 48

The F.B.I. man said: "We think Wehrman's in California. The judge this morning in San Bernadino, cut with swastikas and Stars of David, sentenced him. Ballistics show the murder weapon is the same one used to kill the former head of the Ronald Reagan Hospital he escaped from six months ago."

"Can we relax security measures? – let the players get out and about a bit?"

"Sorry, Mr Wyckliffe. We can't allow that. We daren't take any risks. The President wouldn't want it, and you wouldn't want it."

"No, of course not."

"Speak'n' as an individual on behalf of ordinary Americans, I'm real sorry it had to turn out this way, Mr Wyckliffe. All we American sahccer fans were look'n' forward to the United States staging the best World Cup Tournament ever, and showing all our visitors and the world that we were real glad to have you all here."

Wyckliffe was smiling: "We know that, Mr Vanderskoon. We on the squad appreciate everything you're doing for us, the enormous effort you're putting in to protect us."

The F.B.I. man was grimly certain: "We're going to get this nut. There's no way he can hide. The President's given it maximum priority, and that's a lot of resources! The heat's on and the rats are running: the Mob's hurting, and it doesn't like that." Realising the Englishman might not understand his terminology, he clarified: "We're gett'n' co-operation from the criminal underworld like you wouldn't believe, Mr Wyckliffe."

"Just so long as you capture him. The one good thing about this is that Jacky thinks it's a fuss about nothing. He's convinced the assassin was trying to kill one of the politicians, most probably the Mayor."

"Could be. But we're tak'n' no chances. Your Foreign Secretary is back in England, the Senator flew off to a conference in Geneva, Switzerland, this morning; which leaves us only the Mayor and Jacky to worry about. We're gonna do a prime job guarding both."

CHAPTER 49

"Fack 'em!" Winston Jones was scowling viciously. "Fack 'em!!" he kicked the wall savagely, splintering the woodwork, which brought instant protests and reproaches from the other six English footballers playing cards and drinking beer in his and Jed Lennox's room. "Arseholes to 'em! I don't give a shit about the bastards! Keeping us locked in here all the time! I need a facking bird to screw or I'll go facking bonkers!"

"You are fucking bonkers," said Curly Greenhalgh, "kicking that wall like that, you crazy bastard!"

Winston glared at the bald Mancunian, instinctively preparing to punch him in the mouth, then realised the sense of his criticism. "Well, it's alright for you lot, you don't need it like me." Protests came from five of the six. "Jed's got his bird in the reception he's sticking it to every night. Cawthorne's always got crumpet waiting for him after dinner. And Jim Arrowood and Trelawney are alright wiv their women. I need it! I need a facking woman!!" His kick splintered the wall further, and occasioned additional outcries; Jed Lennox pulled him away and pushed him backwards to trip sprawling onto his bed.

"Be bloody glad you're locked up in here safe!" Curly Greenhalgh told him. "The Ku Klux Klan and that Mississippi bint's cousin she's so scared of can't gerr at you in here."

"Fack him! I don't give a shit about all them bastards! She'd no need to be frightened of them. She could come here."

David Lewis told Winston quietly: "You, Jed, and me, a Jew are better off in here than outside with a Nazi murderer running loose."

Winston retorted: "He's in California near Los Angeles, ain' he? Potted another black today. He's got the coppers snookered, ain' he?"

"You don't want to joke about it," Eddy Corelli admonished him.

"I don't give a rat's fart. They're all nutters. All I want is my bird here."

"You reckon he was after Jacky?" Eddy Corelli wondered.

"No," said Dave Lewis. "But when one madman starts, it gives the others ideas."

"Jacky's taking it bloody calmly, I must say," said Curly Greenhalgh. "If a nutcase had threatened to kill me and just missed blowing my head off, I'd be shitting razor blades!"

Jingo Byrnes said: "He's worried about Mary, and that blonde."

"I'd like to fack her – the blonde," Winston Jones specified against Jed Lennox's frown. "Not that I'd say no to Mrs Jecky Day, but she ain't my type, and she ain't here, is she?"

Sid Garner judged him an animal; the others concurred.

Curly Greenhalgh wondered: "How do you mean, Jingo?"

"He never thought that bloke Wehrman was trying to kill him. Now it's pretty certain Wehrman's in California, Jacky's not bothered about ought else except his missis in England, and that blonde here."

Curly Greenhalgh was serious: "We all know Mary's jealous, but she's no reason to be." He suddenly became genuinely curious: "Has she?"

"'Course she has!" scoffed Winston Jones. "Jecky Day's been screwing that blonde somefink rotten! If he ain't, he's a cant! I know I would if I had the chance! I'd do it right now if she was here! Oh Gawd!" he groaned, "just talking about it," he crossed his thighs to conceal his erection. "What I fink we ought to do is slip the hotel porter a few quid and get some whores in here. Who's in favour?"

"Wyckliffe would be against it," Curly gave warning; Jed Lennox nodded.

"Fack Wyckliffe! Just because he's too old to get the bagger up! All he finks about is training and football."

"That's what we're here for," Jed Lennox was serious.

Eddy Corelli said: "I'll be glad when it starts."

Nobody spoke, all were thinking of the World Cup tournament, each preoccupied with his private aspirations and fears. Except Winston who moaned: "Oh facking hell! I've a good mind to break out of here somehow and get a taxi over to that bird's!"

Jed Lennox reacted immediately: "Don't even bloody think on it! You'd get sent hom' straight away."

Winston answered, sulkily defiant: "I don't give a shit."

Jed was certain: "You do. And you know you do. So don't be bloody silly."

Winston, scowling, turned away, and walked to stand near the window.

Curly Greenhalgh was frank: "When it comes to getting picked, we've no mates. We all want to play."

"Win." Jingo Byrnes's correction, so quietly spoken, contained such dedication that they all looked at him. He sketched a smile. Zealous. Introspective.

CHAPTER 50

"But it's safe now!" Jacky's bed was perfectly made, pillows crisply white, men's voices passed laughing at the end of the hotel corridor, ten yards from his and Benny Cawthorne's room door. "The maniac who tried to kill the mayor is in Los Angeles, two thousand miles from here! The police will get him soon. He's not after me. Never was. There's no danger, Mary. I want you with me. I miss you."

"Oh, Jacky."

"You and Jessie can catch a plane tomorrow afternoon and be with me tomorrow night."

She began in monotone: "We're not coming, Jacky. Jessie's safe here." She grew passionate: "And I wish to God you were, too!"

He spoke soothingly: "Keep calm, Mary. How is Jessie?"

"Playing."

"And my mother?"

"Worried sick. What do you expect? We all are! I can't understand you, Jacky!"

Before she could continue, he asked: "And Harry? How's he getting on in his new job?"

Her voice lightened: "Fine. He likes it, and his girlfriend and their flat in Nottingham. Jacky," remembering, she was serious, "on the news this morning, a Chinese drug dealer was found murdered in a house in the Elephant and Castle in London."

"So?"

"Well.."

He told her to forget it, it was nothing to do with them. "When they've got this madman who shot the Mayor of Chicago – which they must do any day now – will you join me then?"

"No."

He sighed her name.

She was jealously curious: "You're not seeing Britt Anderson, are you?"

"She's in Quebec getting contracts for me."

"I don't want you to see her! have anything to do with her!"

"Mary," he pleaded.

"I wish! – I wish! – " She regained control and said wryly: "It's a mess, isn't it?"

"Fly back, Mary," he coaxed.

"No," she said firmly. "Jessie's crying. I must go."

CHAPTER 51

i

"Twenty-five burned to death in that coloured nightclub bombing last night, thirty more seriously ill in hospital, five shot and killed trying to escape!" Wyckliffe's horror was plain.

The F.B.I. man said bitterly: "What bugs me is they not only let the guy escape after the shoot'n', but they let the Press find out they'd gotten his faggot boyfriend, God damn it!"

"Maybe this actor is telling the truth, Howard. Maybe Wehrman never was at his apartment."

"With his fingerprints and gear all over the place?"

"These past ten days, I mean. Maybe this actor liked wearing other people's things, doing impersonations. Maybe he's out after publicity. Maybe –"

"Sure," said the American.

"Well, at least Wehrman can't bother us in Chicago if he's in Los Angeles. We can get on with our training."

"I guess you'll tape the opening match this afternoon for viewing later."

"We're taping all the matches."

ii

"Jacky?"

He sucked in a deep breath to steady his respiration after running up two flights of stairs from the television lounge. "Britt!"

"You now have some very lucrative contracts in Canada!"

"Wonderful! Have you just got back?"

"Ten minutes before the Brazil game – they were magnificent, weren't they?! Did you see all those police and bodyguards protecting the governor of California!? That maniac Wehrman certainly has frightened everybody! Another three victims of the Los Angeles nightclub bombing died this afternoon. At least Wehrman's no longer after you."

"He never was."

"I wish you were with me, darling," she murmured. Jacky, embarrassed, blushing, turned his head away, receiver still to his ear. The whiteness of the pillows and sheet tops gave neutral reception. "I'm all alone in a secluded mansion, tranquil surroundings, far from prying eyes and gossip. The F.B.I. are probably recording this. Let them. I need to see you, Jacky, and talk over the new contracts. Lots and lots of money!"

"Tomorrow. After training. I'll tell the security people."

CHAPTER 52

A prowl car howled whewing by in the fast lane. He judged its speed in the high nineties. Traffic normal on Lakeshore Drive for Sunday night. Downtown Chicago's skyscrapers ahead. Michigan's water with boats miles out.

He eased back in the driving seat, slowing the car. Everything was ready now he had fixed the power and telephone cables.

First the smokebombs would go, then the incendiaries.

Savagery lusted as he imagined the third and final series of explosions about Soldier Field Stadium, tossing blood-spraying shattered bodies whirling in the air: the screams, the agony, the terror.

At that moment, he would kill Jacky Day.

He sucked in a deep breath, and exhaled, smiling.

The country and western music faded suddenly: the disc jockey announced a flash from the newsroom.

"After a shoot-out in Los Angeles a short while ago which left two wounded and one bystander dead, a man believed responsible for the city's firebomb slayings was arrested by F.B.I. agents. The man is now undergoing surgery for bullet wounds in his right lung and both legs. For further details – our man on the spot."

The fucking, stupid, son-of-a-bitch bought it! He bought it! Scowling, teeth clenched, Wehrman deliberately kept the automobile at steady speed.

He would not talk. Not that bastard. They chopped him in pieces, he would not say a thing.

The Feds would still think he was in L.A. They all would.

Till tomorrow night.

Till he blew the head off that stinking little commie bastard.

CHAPTER 53

i

"And you think he could be in Chicago," said Wyckliffe.

"Denzil, he could be anywhere," the F.B.I. man answered.

"For a madman he's doing damn well!"

"The craziest guys are often the smartest. This guy was a cop, a good cop – once. He also learned plenty at that security job."

"And he's in Chicago planning to murder Jacky Day."

"Possibly. We ' been putting a lot of pressure on a lot of people in a lot of places out on the Coast look'n' for him. After what's happened there tonight, we've gone off the defensive onto the offensive here in Chicago. The Mayor of Chicago wants him. The President wants him. We all want him. And, Denzil, if he's here, by God we're gonna get him!"

ii

"You see – they are good contracts," Britt smiled.

"Yes," Jacky agreed. "Clear them with my financial adviser tomorrow and I'll sign everything."

"The proverbial canny Scot."

"Och ay. He's done well by me. I owe a lot to him, and to Jim Arrowood's dad. And Mary."

Britt's indulgent smile disappeared: "I would never run away and leave you in danger like she has done."

"I'm not in danger."

"While that killer's loose, yes."

"No."

Her left hand covered his right, palm down on the table. Contact shocked his emotions, memories of their intimacy in London, Mary's jealousy: fear of scandal – he glanced around the reading room; three England players were reading newspapers, another was penning a letter in the brightness of the writing table lamp nearest the door almost diagonally opposite where he and Britt sat in the room's inmost corner. The soft warmth of her touch triggered lust. He did not want to wound her by withdrawing his hand. Besides, he liked the contact. And why shouldn't Britt put her hand on his to show fondness? It was innocent, hurt no one. He felt guilty, but also at ease.

She consoled apprehension: "They're guarding you well, anyway."

"Too well. Some of the lads are very on edge at being confined all the time," he turned his palm to clasp hers gently.

"You?"

He withdrew his hand. "Me too. But I train extra hard to work it off. In the hotel gym, like some of the other players: Jingo Byrnes, Jim, young Bobby and Jedder, and Benny Cawthorne doing his bouts of one arm press-ups and Kung Fu. Everybody's looking forward to tomorrow's game."

"I almost wish you weren't playing. With that killer loose."

"You're as bad as Mary."

She spoke before he could expound: "Except I wouldn't leave you. He'd have to kill me first."

"Mary was frightened for Jessie."

"She left you in danger."

"I'm in no danger."

"In here, no."

"Not anywhere."

"I don't believe a woman has a right to own a man all his life merely because she met him first. It's a kind of moral and physical slavery."

"Mary's a good wife to me. I don't want you talking like this, Britt."

"I'd be perfect for you, do anything and everything, have your children – they'd be beautiful children."

He put in: "So is Jessie."

She continued quietly: "I'd do anything, everything, go anywhere, everywhere, with you, for you."

Jacky stared, troubled, at her serene seriousness. Completely free of make-up and jewelry, her hair pulled to her skull in a tight bun at her nape, wearing a long armed, high necked severely cut navy-blue dress, she had the purity of a two-year old girl encapsuled in exquisite womanliness.

He lusted after her. Mary's image sprang guilt. "You flatter me, Britt," he kept his voice steady, using memories of his wife to try and stop his desire.

"I could live with you," she said gently, "be at peace with you."

"I'm married," he countered. "Mary says Chuck Bengtsson's in love with you, that you make an ideal couple, that you're sleeping with him."

"Does that make you jealous?"

"No," he rejected the idea instinctively, then showed doubt instantly, "well – it's none of my business, is it?"

"Yes – if you want."

He stared into her quiet eyes, not knowing what to say. Reason dictated: "No," he replied. "it's your business." His tone changed: "Britt, some of the lads asked me if you'd act for them, try and get them business contracts."

"I can probably arrange some modelling for you, Gerald," Britt critically considered the good looking, broad shouldered coloured youth.

"And Curly," Eddy Corelli, grinning, put in, patting Greenhalgh's bald pate, "can advertise hair tonic."

"You cheeky bugger!" the bald man grunted amidst the mirth, then embarrassed at swearing with ladies present excused himself: "Oh, I'm sorry! I forgot!"

Britt was serious: "We could fix something up like that, Colin, if you're interested?"

"Money!" said Eddy Corelli, nudging the bald man hard in the ribs.

With a little smile, Dave Lewis was provocative: "What would your wife say, Curly?"

"Money!" exclaimed the Mancunian, eyes wide and gleaming. "Fix me up, if you can, love! It'll not make my hair grow. I wish it would."

"David, I could try to get you something, using the Jewish angle. If you don't mind?"

Dave Lewis said he did not. Eddy Corelli said that his ancestors came from Italy. Britt told him she would do her best. "They call you the spaceman from another galaxy, Bobby," she began.

The young Tynesider, staring at his feet, muttered in broad Geordie: "They're crazy, man." Even in his low mumble, the disgust was thorough: "Calling me a bluddy spee-us-man!" Eddy Corelli, smiling as widely and sympathetically as the other group members, clapped his two-year younger team-mate on the shoulder: "You'll show 'em tomorrow, Bobby!" The six players in the group were suddenly purposeful. "We all shall." Nods and mutters of agreement.

"What worries me is that nutter," Curly Greenhalgh's concern was clear.

Everyone looked automatically at Jacky who said: "It's not me he's after! I merely happened to be there when he shot the Mayor." Since they all wished his analysis to be correct, no one disagreed.

Eddy Corelli said: "The place is crawling with nutcases, isn't it? I wish it weren't. I would like to go out and have a look at the town and see the sights."

"We're safe in here," said Dave Lewis. "Another anti-Semite rang up and threatened me tonight."

"And the Ku Klux Klan are after Winston," Eddy Corelli noted.

Jed's girlfriend said: "They're dangerous. Those warnings about him and that white girl from Mississippi are serious."

"I can't make him understand it, though," said Jed.

"Her family are bad trouble," said Jed's girlfriend.

"She hasn't been to see him, anyway," said Eddy Corelli.

"Too scared. Her family's looking for her," Jed commented.

"I wish they would find her and take her back down there among their other Southern belles," his girlfriend said. "She's the sort of white woman blacks get killed for."

"Not Winston," Curly Greenhalgh asserted. "I can't see him caring enough about anybody to get killed for 'em, can you?"

"Denzil won't give him the chance. He's keeping uz too well locked up," said Jacky.

"I'll bet old Wyckliffe's down there with his legmen analysing the Brazilians and the Eye-ties and the Jerries and the rest," Curly said.

Britt marvelled: "The Brazilians were brilliant last night! – and the Italians very competent, I thought. But not like the Brazilians – they were fantastic!"

The players were smiling at her enthusiasm. "She hasn't seen us yet, has she?" said Curly. "We're great, we're wonder-workers, we eat the competent for breakfast, and the fantastic for dinner, tea and supper, don't we, lads?!"

CHAPTER 54

Fear was exaltation, abandonment to death: his .38 Police Special levelled steady on the chair-blocked doorway which seemed to jerk and sway in the twilight. In the room to his left, groans from the salesman and his woman, creak of their bed. To his right, the whine of the wakened child, the murmur of its mother. Behind and above him to his left, through the venetian blind window, no sound from the motel parking lot.

He laid his weapon on the floor beside his mattress. His watch glowed 2 a.m. He eased down to rest comfortable on the pillow. If the cops had been told, they would have been here by now.

No reason the night clerk should know him. His hair was dyed brown, cut short with sideburns. His clothes, ordinary. But when he had taken the glasses off to rub his ear, the guy had looked at him as if he recognised him.

The Mob was helping the cops. His contacts had told him that.

After tomorrow – no way would they find him! when he had blown that little fuck'n' son-of-a-bitch commie's brains out in front of the whole world, he'd be long gone – if those chicken shits in New York and Washington had balls enough to follow the plans he had sent them.

He listened afresh. Only his breathing, the constant ringing in his head, the furtive clamour of his neighbours. He peered through the venetian blind at the empty concrete between his wing and its shabby counterpart. For a moment, the grimy grey appeared to swirl and seethe sucking the shadowy wall opposite and himself into a mawlike corrosive morass as endless as terror in infinite pain.

He jerked back, eyelids squeezing, twisting to grab his gun and kill his anguish. Sweating, gasping, he scrutinised the gloom, each sense alert to its implacable, ineffable, invisible monster.

His Old Man was weak. Had talked. Never killed his enemies. The Old Man had never made him shed one tear no matter how hard he flogged. Hatred for his father brought bloodtaste, a huge roaring in his skull. Kill the Communists and Jews!! They cause all life's evil!! His father had known! He had respected his father although he had been weak and died and never done a thing about the Reds and Jews running the country, the blacks trashing the world and stinking the air by breathing.

Tomorrow he would kill that commie, Jacky Day! Only with blood did they understand.

He relaxed.

The motel corridors were too narrow, the cover too bad for an effective assault. The concrete outside provided no protection for attackers. Try counting on surprise and rushing him? Negative. He would fight, and cops and innocent people would die because the motel walls could not stop bullets. Evacuate the guests? – that would alert him. No, if they had been going to rush him, they would have done it already. He was safe till morning.

I'll leave simultaneous with the woman and kid. Use them as hostages, if necessary.

On the wall above the motel desk clerk were three aerial photos of Chicago. The clerk took the room key from the ringless white woman pouting kisses at her slant-eyed sallow babe in arms. Damn kid had not stopped crying since dawn, now look at it, laughing its face off. He would be laughing himself, too, tonight.

Excitement curled.

Power.

He looked at the lobby: cream walls, hung at yard intervals with two by one-foot colour photos of Chicago. That coffee smell was good. He would stop and eat some breakfast some place. A fattish man in a blue suit sat reading the Chicago Tribunal near the corridor leading to the left wing guestrooms in one of which a radio was playing rock and roll music, loud enough to hear but not too loudly.

He gave the clerk his room key and, carrying his grey canvas zip-suitcase, followed the young family out into the early morning sunlight that made him blink. The air was warm; oil and fume stained. Light flashed off a car window on the parking lot boundary to his left, gleamed off others. The rock and roll he had heard inside was also playing to his right from a white Thunderbird with smoked glass windows and its doors open, two men changing a wheel. Automobiles and trucks were slanting by on the road. Office buildings. Apartment houses. A blue sky. Cloudless.

"Freeze, Mister!"

The fattish, middle-aged man's face erupted blood, smashed flesh and bone; his own shot tore through Wehrman's left triceps as the killer dived right.

From around the motel parking lot and guest room windows, so many bullets thwacked into the leaping figure that he swung and paused in mid-air. Twenty blew his head to fragments; eleven in his throat and neck all but decapitated him to jet blood spraying freely about. The carcass twitched and jerked as quick metal continued to break bones and wrench and tear it into a sodden, stinking mass.

Weapons mostly empty, the firing ceased.

The baby was screaming; its parent stared in terrified revulsion at the twenty-yard distant dead man.

Rock and roll wafted thinly about the parking lot.

"Well, the Mayor can watch his sahccer match in peace this afternoon," the Chicago police captain spoke.

"After what's happened in Los Angeles and here," said his F.B.I. equivalent, "I'm not so sure."

CHAPTER 55

"The Mayor of Chicago won't be at Soldier Field for the match. His people have advised against it." Howard Vanderskoon paused; Wyckliffe eyed him steadily. The F.B.I. man's worry, though restrained, was obvious: "They're right. We can't say for certain there isn't somebody out there planning to kill him, or Jacky."

Wyckliffe said: "I can't see anybody beating your security measures, Howard."

"No matter how good your security is, there's always a way through it. Denzil, I want you to keep Jacky away from Soldier Field today."

"No!" the Englishman reacted forcefully, then became hesitant: "I mean – well – look – Howard." He prepared to give reasons, then reiterated firmly: "No."

"We think he planted bombs and rifles, destructive diversions somewhere. We need time to search and follow up leads."

"I'm playing Jacky. The madman's dead. The security precautions you've taken are unbreachable. I'm playing him."

"If you give us till Saturday, the Argentina game –"

Wyckliffe, decided, shook his head: "No."

"We'd have time to check and double-check," Vanderskoon appealed, "thoroughly investigate every possibility."

"No," the England Manager stayed firm.

The F.B.I. man condemned his attitude: "It's a man's life, Denzil."

"No, it is not. The killer you were chasing is dead. Whether he should have been captured instead of shot is a different matter. But he's dead – and the danger from him is gone." He over-rode the F.B.I. official's attempt to interrupt: "Your police work and security coverage have been superb. You're satisfied you've done everything imaginable to protect Jacky and the rest of us today?"

"Yes, except I don't want you to play Jacky. If that guy has accomplices out there like he had in L.A., they could be waiting to kill Jacky today. Five bombs and three sniper rifles were marked out on the plans found at that firebomb killer's. Bombs triggered by short wave radio transmitter – like the one found in the motel car park here this morning."

"Why didn't they explode the bombs and use the rifles on Saturday at the Brazil-Belgium game?" Wyckliffe wondered.

"I don't know," Vanderskoon was baffled. "I just don't know. These guys are crazy. And when you're deal'n' with madmen–," he shrugged his helplessness. He spoke shrewdly: "All I know is that if this guy we got this morning has helpers, we could be in bad trouble, and that's why the Mayor's not going to be at the match, and I don't want Jacky there either."

"You've not found any evidence to suggest he has helpers, have you?"

"No. But in Los Angeles he had, so why not here?"

Wyckliffe moved away, frowning.

Vanderskoon watched for several seconds then persuaded him softly: "Don't pick Jacky today. Save him till Saturday. Give us this week."

The England Manager turned toward him: "No," Wyckliffe's face showed stress. "If the killer had been loose, if you were certain he had accomplices who were planning to murder Jacky, yes, I probably would. Neither is the case. We're going to rely on your security measures."

CHAPTER 56

i

Smoke puthered up from the turbulent, screaming bellowing crowd under the huge Grecian pillars at the top left of Soldier Field stadium.

Wyckliffe's gaze sprang from Jingo Byrnes contesting possession in the centre circle with two red-kitted Poles: "Crack! Crack! Crack!" the sharp, small explosions slashed certainty of Jacky's death through his terror. With endless desolation, horror and self-recrimination, Wyckliffe focussed on his white-shirted, blue-shorted players, seeking the staggering mortally wounded man.

Jacky beat the midfielder to the ball by half a stride, jinked right went left round a second red shirt: his fifteen yard sprint took him to the penalty area corner, only the left back between him and the goal.

The England Manager's fear, crashed through with exultation and relief, shuddered gradually receding into basic anxiety and strain. Replay of the goal on the electronic screen: Jacky approaching the defender, swaying left going right and chipping over the outward rushing goalkeeper. Time on the clock, eighteen minutes.

Up near the Grecian pillars, immediately above the smoke-reeked area, police were flogging frenetically with billy clubs at some of the crowd waving Union Jacks.

ii

"Okay, lads!" Wyckliffe's raised voice stopped conversation; the physiotherapist continued massaging Richard Trelawney's right leg, his assistant worked on Jed Lennox's left thigh, the team doctor was bandaging Dave Lewis's left ankle; players stood about the dressing room towelling down, changing into fresh kit, drinking their salts and vitamin concoction. "Not much to say, except keep it up, you're doing a fine job – especially you, Colin," he singled out the bald Mancunian who, smiling pleasure, pride and embarrassment, ducked his head to his beaker. "Any comments –ideas – anybody?" Wyckliffe peered around.

"Yer," growled Benny Cawthorne, and drank a mouthful, "what ' we gonna do about that centre forward? He's bladdy near crippled these lads here," the Cockney jerked his head at his fellow defenders. "That bladdy ref's blind! He don't see a fing. He don't even look at his linesmen, and they're waving like hell!" Nods and agreement from other players. "Look at poor old Jed's thigh here, facking studmarks all over him! I'll tell you one fing, that bagger had better not try it on me!"

The England Manager was calm. "Anybody any comments? No? Right, lads – play sensibly and keep out of trouble. That's all."

Hubbub resumed. Wyckliffe talked earnestly with the doctor and Dave Lewis.

Winston Jones, scowling, muttered to Jed Lennox: "Facking Greenhalgh, eh? I'm better'n that bastard! Facking making me sit on the facking bench all the facking time, and keeping us locked up in the facking hotel! No facking crumpet, no facking game! If I'd've been playing, I'd've had a facking dozen by now!"

iii

"Oh, no!" Wyckliffe groaned. Dave Lewis, kicked hard on his left ankle, hopped, staggered and fell. The African referee, waving aside English players' protests for him to send off the offender, grew suddenly angry, his hand darted toward his breast pocket and notebook: Richard Trelawney, arms widespread, drove his protesting team-mates away from the official and avoided an England booking.

"Eddy Corelli stays back in defence, Bobby midfield," Wyckliffe instructed. "Good luck, Winston."

Winston's thirty yard right footer smacked the angle of bar and post and spinning and gyrating zoomed high over the penalty area. Jim Arrowood, elbowed between two Poles, outjumped them and deflected the crazily whirling leather inwards. Jacky's quick precise stab killed its spin to cross three yards through an eighteen-inch gap of converging defenders: Bobby Milburne scored.

In his Working Men's Club in Newcastle, amid the laughing shouts and cheers of the packed bar room, Bob Milburne senior's normally hard countenance relaxed into a near smile; he rubbed his chin with his right thumb and his left hand dropped to his side to scratch his whippet's head.

A smoke bomb twirled through the air at the other side of the stadium; fireworks were banging in the air; Wyckliffe cringed at each explosion, fear darting, gaze flicking to Jacky, other England men.

Police were clubbing purposefully among the England supporters. Plainclothes security men about the gangways were talking into two-way radios. Howard Vanderskoon, invisible at work.

Maybe he should pull Jacky off. With a two-nil lead and nineteen minutes left. No! There was no danger. If anything had been going to happen, it would already.

Wyckliffe repressed objections, fear, wiped away sweat; sun in the seventies, humidity high.

Substituting Jacky was neither fair nor sensible.

He registered the game ceaselessly: the Poles' superb teamwork, tight defensive play, no miskicks, no wrong passes. His own men's skill.

The burly centre forward and Richard Trelawney crunched shoulder against shoulder, knocking each other staggering. The Pole was not a dirty player. Hard and rough, a trier, not vicious.

Jacky backheeled to Jingo Byrnes in England's centre circle, Jingo sidefooted to Bobby Milburne; Jacky, sprinting diagonally left, drew two defenders across to counter him. Jingo Byrnes, a Pole plunging to tackle, caressed Bobby's return right, feinted infield deceiving a second Pole, continued right and kicked hard towards the distant penalty area's near corner.

Dan Arrowood exhaled with a whoosh, eased his eighteen stones back into his armchair, and stretched long legs out along the brown sitting room carpet at the television set. Through the window, Lincolnshire June crops alternated with livestock grazing meadowland. "Our Jim's scored," he called to his wife making tea down the flagstoned corridor in their farmhouse kitchen. "A magnificent pass from Jingo Byrnes."

"That horrible man! They should have kept him in prison!"

The Polish centre forward was squirming on the turf; the referee was holding up a yellow card; Benny Cawthorne, snarling, inimical, was twisted round, savagely indicating studmarks oozing blood from the back of his left thigh. Richard Trelawney and Jed Lennox were diverting his rage from the African and centre forward.

"Not too bad, is it, Benny?" Wyckliffe, anxious, wished; the physiotherapist and team doctor worked on the injury.

The Cockney raged where he lay near the touchline: "Another few inches and he'd have smashed my facking kneecap! The cant! The facking bastard! Shows me a facking card and he don't do a fing to that bastard!"

Wyckliffe looked inquiringly at the doctor who nodded, unworried. The England Manager clapped the East Ender friendly on the shoulder and ordered him carried inside on a stretcher.

iv

"Congratulations, Denzil," the F.B.I. man said. The England Manager thanked him. From the other side of the dressing room door, the players' laughter, shouts and conversation reached through; smell of sweat and embrocation. "We got three men who tried to bring in rifles, eleven were carrying handguns, three hundred and forty-six had knives, knuckledusters and various other weapons." Vanderskoon went on to detail the different ways people had tried to breach security: most were simple, some ingenious, all were dangerous, a few deadly. "We're going to have to maintain maximum security throughout the whole series, Denzil. I was hoping we might be able to ease up a little. But with the President's insisting personally on the phone to me before the game that nothing's got to happen to you guys, there's only one way we can insure that for certain."

"I was hoping things could relax," said Wyckliffe. "It's no joke for the lads being locked up like a lot of luxury convicts."

"You won, anyway. Jacky's okay. We' got a week to do some hunt'n', run down Nazi madmen and any others, before the Argentina game."

"That's the big one," Wyckliffe was serious. "Argentina are potential champions. We've got to be able to beat them if we're going to win this tournament."

CHAPTER 57

"But the killer's dead, Mary!" Jacky's frustration approached angry despair.

"It's too dangerous! I'm frightened!"

"It's not dangerous," he gentled her.

"It is! I'm not risking Jessie's life, Jacky!"

"You won't be. I *need* you, Mary," his desperation was clear. "I want to make love to you," he told her frankly. "I'm going crazy here on my own."

She did not soften: "You'll have to put up with it."

"Damn it!" Resignation tinged bitterness. "It's obvious you don't miss me."

"That's unfair, Jacky! More than anything else, I want this World Cup over and you safely home with us. I'm frightened, Jacky," she admitted.

"You don't have to be, Mary!" he was exasperated. "The madman is dead! I want you here with me, darling, to hold and make love to," he cajoled.

She said, rather hard: "You'll have to do what all the other men do when they want a woman and can't have one – use your hand."

He scowled at the empty room's cream walls and sterile utilities. "Beautiful, isn't it? That's the attitude that sends men looking for other women. "

"I didn't mean that, Jacky!" she appealed. Her emotions became warning jealousy: "I don't want you going with Britt Anderson, nor any other woman. If you do –." Her hardness broke: "Oh Jacky! What's happening?!" she was frightened. "We mustn't quarrel." She appealed in a tiny voice: "Jacky."

"It's alright," he said, though he knew it was not.

"I don't want you to go with Britt Anderson, meet her, have anything to do with her!"

He spoke neutrally: "She's got me some very profitable contracts. I have to meet her for business purposes."

She was vindictive: "Damn her! Damn the bitch!"

"That's not doing any use, Mary," he said levelly. "Have you any news to report from England?"

"No – yes, there's been another Chinese killed in London."

He told her to forget it.

"And your mother wants you to phone her. She's worried about all the things they're writing in the papers about you."

"I'll ring. I wish you'd take a plane out here tomorrow, Mary."

"No."

"Okay," he almost succeeded in concealing his disappointment and resultant abruptness. "Take care of yourself and little Jessie," his order was a plea of much warmth and tenderness.

"Yes, Mam, he was the killer, definitely, and he *is* dead, and you need NOT worry, I am safe."

His mother's tremulous voice revealed her frailty: "On the television, they said the police and those people guarding you – what do you call them? F.B.Y. or something, Secret something – they said on TV they were looking for others, and there are still people trying to get at you to shoot you," she was near tears.

Jacky was brisk and encouraging: "Rubbish, Mam. We're safe as the Rock of Gibraltar here. The only way they could get at uz is if they dropped a hydrogen bomb on uz, and then the Yanks would catch it before it hit the ground, they're looking after uz so well."

His mother believed him and in her quiet voice asked: "What about Mary and your little girl then?"

"I wish they were here with me. But she won't come back."

"She's safer here, Jacky."

He changed the subject: "How are you then, Mam?"

"I had a bit of a blackout this morning," she said in her slow, hesitantly careful voice. He controlled his concern; these things happened to her; they were part of her illness. "I worry about you, Jacky."

"Don't. You mustn't, Mam. There's no need. Just you take care of yourself and take it easy, and don't worry about me."

"Is your head alright now? And they're giving you good food, and the water's alright, is it?"

"No problems," Jacky lied cheerfully. "We won today, and nobody's too badly hurt except Dave Lewis who got kicked on his ankle, and Benny Cawthorne who's as tough as an old boot and will be alright for our next game on Saturday."

"They say terrible things about you in America, I've been reading the newspapers, the girl has."

"Most of it's rubbish they write, Mam," he scoffed cheerily.

"They were saying you were Satan's servant on Earth, and you would rot in Hell, and all things like that. Awful," she was upset.

"Forget it, Mam," he spoke lightly and firmly. "They're idiots. Don't bother about them."

"It worries me," she grieved. "On television, they had this big fat man, from Texas, I think. A preacher. And other preachers, and– and– church, and– and– religious people, and– and– they all attacked you for what you said on that American television programme. And there was a big millionaire, and– and businessmen, they said you were dangerous and shouldn't have been let in America. And a lot of our newspapers keep on criticising you for it, and on the television as well. I wish you wouldn't speak out like you do, Jacky."

"Has anybody criticised my footballing skills, though, Mam?"

"No."

"That's all that matters, Mam," he assured her with firm good humour. "It's for my football I'll be judged, not my politics nor ideas nor anything else. There are lots of smarter, cleverer, more knowledgeable blokes about than I am, better in every way than me – but not at football. There, I can hold my own with any on 'em. And *that's* where they'll judge me, ultimately, Mother. As to the rest, don't listen to it or pay it attention – it's rubbish, and rubbish isn't worth bothering about. Fools and big mouths and big heads will do anything and say anything to get attention and prove in their own estimation what wonderful people they are. Forget 'em, Mam."

"I can't help but worry," she said weakly.

"Don't. I can look after myself a lot better than you can. All you have to do is get better. Now, you'll try, won't you?" he urged with brisk good humour.

"Yes."

"Right-o, Mam, I'll say goodbye for the time being. It's pretty late here. And tomorrow is another day."

CHAPTER 58

"Aw, facking hell!" Winston Jones in his fury kicked the chair so hard it flew several yards to the centre of his and Jed Lennox's room while the splintered leg whacked against the wall to drop into a flower vase.

"You daft bugger!" said Jed. "What do you think you're doing, smashing the bloody place up? You got one bollocking the other day for kicking the wall and damaging it, now you're going to gerr another."

Winston was scowling, unheeding. "Facking cants, locking us up in this facking place like this! That bladdy stupid Louella! She's got nuffink to be frightened of! Fancy finking her cousin's going to kidnap her off the street and take her back to Mississippi or wherever the hell she says he's going to take her, and lock her up in a cellar in a house in the backwoods somewhere and make her marry him and give her five kids! Facking ridiculous, ain't it?! People don't do that kind of fing. It's too facking stupid, ain' it?"

Jed was serious: "I'm not so sure. She knows better than we do: she comes from there. The Ku Klux Klan are bloody dangerous, mate. They'd murder you and bury you in some lonely spot and no bugger'd ever find you."

"Don't you start being a cant!"

"It's right. My grandad knowed a bloke from Jamaica who'd been down there in the 1930s. They'd chuck petrol ovver a coloured man and burn him, or hang him, or bloody shoot him. They would," Jed was serious. "Not on'y that, I seed a television programme about it, a couple of years ago. All a white woman had to do was accuse some poor bugger of h'ving done summat to her, and they'd tek the poor sod and chop his balls off, then burn him."

"Garn."

"It's right."

"Well that was then, wasn't it? I don't give a fart about all that. Since the stupid bitch won't come over here 'cause she's in hiding, I've got to get out and visit her, ain' I?"

"Forget it. There could be some moore on them bloody nutter Nazi buggers out there waiting to put a bullet in you. Or the Ku Klux Klan. Or some other bloody madman. They're not keeping uz locked up for nowt, you know."

Winston was indignant: "It's alright for you baggers what's getting your end in, ain' it?! But I'm not, and I facking want to! The hotel management's very bladdy moral, and all the rest of the cants. It's not doing me any good – I can't get a screw! I' got to get out o' this place, and I fink I've found a way to do it."

"How?"

"That geezer what works in the kitchen and what takes the empty plates off the tables."

"Looks a lot like you – Christ! Go on, Winston. Finish it."

"You're not finking of telling on me, are you?! 'Cause if you facking are!!"

Jed said slowly: "Goo on."

"Well, I thought – you'll not facking tell, will you?"

"No. Go on."

"It's like this, you see. They can't tell one black from another anyway. And he's got this yellow and purple jacket, ain' he? and sunglasses and baseball cap, what I told him I liked. I could buy them off of him, couldn't I?"

"Yeh, but –"

"They work shifts and change wiv one another. They get off at nine-thirty. I could walk out in his clothes, couln' I?

"It wouldn't work. They'd spot you. And how are you going to get back in again if you did gerr out? They've all got identity cards they've got to show when they come in."

"He could forget his in his jacket, couldn' he? when he sells it me. If I give him a hundred bucks. It's worth it for a night wiv Louella."

"Too risky. Besides, he could get into trouble as well as you."

"Arseholes! He told us he was finking about going to New York, din' he? It's not his fault if I walk out through the kitchen and he goes out through the front. As far as I can see, there's no risk at all. I walk in next morning wiv the kitchen lads at quart' to six. If the security guards ask questions, I show 'em his identity card and make sure they don't get a good look at me. They don't know this guy all that well, do they? Then I'm back here and laughing."

"No, Winston, for Christ's sake, don't do it! It would bugger up your chances with the England team if they caught you."

"Nah, they won't catch me. White men don't recognise blacks if they're wearing the same clothes and they're about the same build. Gawd, the times I've got away wiv swapping clothes in London!"

"Don't do it, Winston. Don't even think of it."

"You said you wouldn't tell on me, right? Right? You promised you wouldn't! Right?! Right?!"

"Yes," said Jed, "I promised, and I wish I bloody hadn't now. They're not keeping uz locked up in here for nowt, I've telled you! There are mad, crazy bastards out there who'll shoot you! That bugger as nearly got Jacky Day at the Trade Exhibition was firing real bullets that kill you, you bloody fool!"

"He's dead, ain' he? Nah, there's no danger to me. I'm getting out o' this place when I get that guy's gear – if you don't go opening your big mouth."

CHAPTER 59

Denzil Wyckliffe was frowning, strained: "So you think there could still be attacks made on us?"

"I'm sorry, Denzil, I really am," said Howard Vanderskoon.

Wyckliffe, preoccupied, sat down. "Imagine all those bombs going off at Soldier Field among that crowd, eh? Christ, Howard, oh Christ. And the rifles. If Jacky had been killed –. Can you be sure you haven't missed anything?"

The F.B.I. man replied crisply: "We've triple-checked that stadium with every device and technique known to man. It's clean: no bombs nor weapons there now. Nobody was shot at the Poland game, the bombs did not go off. Everything points to the guy they blasted at that motel being a loner."

"Can you be sure?"

"No. But we're giv'n' it everything we' got to be as sure of all the facts as we can and follow up every lead and take every precaution. We're checking up on every known Nazi in the United States and Canada."

"And the unknown?"

The American shrugged defeat: "There you ' got us. He was a faggot. And among the faggots, you get some mean, mad, bad, bastards like that firebomber buddy of his we picked up in L.A. He could have a dozen guys like that around Chicago, or he could have none. We' just got to play it safe. Hell, Denzil, out there we' got every kind of nut imaginable! Chicago's swarmin' with 'em. We know the Klan are there because of Jones and the white girl from Mississippi. We don't believe the I.R.A. are there because of what Jacky said about Irish nationalism on the Paddy O'Rourke Talk Show, but we are not ruling the possibility out. We ' got that crazy dame who rings up at one in the mornin' every mornin' sayin' she's gonna castrate Joe Berrigan to stop him fathering any more children. We' got fey guys ringing after dates with Dick Trelawney, Jim Arrowood and Benny Cawthorne, with Winston Jones and Jed Lennox thrown in occasionally for variety. Then we get little girls wanting to talk to Jingo Byrnes. We get bomb threats from Argentineans not satisfied with Briddish action over the Falklands. And then we' got the religious cranks and assorted nuts. My, oh my!" the American concluded, raising his eyebrows, smiling and shaking his head in resignation.

Wyckliffe sighed. "I wish we could escape for an hour or two and be free to relax. Jacky asked me this morning if he could get out and do some filming, be on his own for a while."

The F.B.I. man was alert: "You said no, I hope?"

CHAPTER 60

Lust surged and swung in Winston Jones's head, his erection was thick between his left thigh and trouser leg. He jabbed his finger against the doorbell. Noise from the party on the second floor mingled with that from the one on the first. Smell of hamburger cooking. Drunken voices and laughter billowing up from the stairway.

"Who is it?" the girl-woman voice was anxious.

"Who do you fink it is, dawling? Father Christmas! Come on! Open up!"

Bolts and chains rattled, then he was in the room watching her re-bolt and re-chain. "You did it! You did it!" With her wavy blonde hair curling about her shoulders, her big blue eyes, and pretty little girl face, she was so much a baby doll that a sophisticated observer would have sneered amusement.

"Course I did. Nuffink to it. Easy."

Her wide-eyed lust concentrated on his rigid sexual member, his on her curves. Then they were kissing, hugging and fondling. "Take it off! Strip me! Fuck me! Do it to me!" she gasped as he thrust his hand down her dress front. With one big yuck, Winston had her naked to her white high heeled shoes, and was hopping about round the room trying to prevent himself from toppling over as he struggled to get his trousers off.

Preoccupied with lust, vaginal fluid copiously flowing, she stood with legs astride, back to the bottom of the bed, intent on his big prick and muscular black thighs and rear.

Winston was in her, driving away, she was gasping, moaning, quivering, rigid.

On the ninety-seventh second after entry into her tightly clutching vagina, he threw his head back, muscles taut, reached the first of his final long strokes to hurl forth semen and create ecstasy.

"I ain't even had time to take m' facking coat and shirt and socks orf," he muttered, kissing and biting her throat and neck. His penis was still hard inside her, his excitement eager; but his nineteen year-old's fierce lust was temporarily tamed. He was content to enjoy the calmer sensuality of contact with a soft, good-smelling woman's body.

"Aw, Winston, you're so won'erful," she breathed, "but you came too quick, honeh."

"What the facking hell do you expect awfter I've been saving it up all this time?!" he said indignantly. "I'll get my coat and shirt off to it in a minute, and m' socks, then I'll show you."

Wellbeing, languor, warmth that rippled and circled pleasure at every movement of the two- inch thick black cock inside her: she moaned a little sigh of pleasure, and, picturing her Daddeh's rage and shame at her screwing a black man. She savoured her defiance, shuddering and thrusting her small pink, cunt to engulf and accept sweetness and desecration.

Winston pressed her splayed, doubled back legs down to her shoulders, supporting himself as he screwed and twisted varying speed, direction and depth, bringing himself towards climax then slowing to prolong the pleasure and enjoy the white girl with big, blue eyes and half open mouth who alternately smiled relaxed pleasure and contorted wincing delight.

"You're a hot little bagger, ain' you?" he praised her. "You've got a smashing pair of tits, and a lovely little figure. You do it beautiful."

"Why, theng you, Winston. Ah told you Ah lahked it. Ain't you gonna do it again to me now?"

"Facking hell! What do you fink I am?! Some kind of facking animal or somefink?!"

"Beaudiful," she smiled fatly, and, her left side against his, stroked his belly with her right palm, pulled his limp penis and cupped his scrotum.

"You'll just have to wait, won't you, dawling? till I can get it up again."

"Maybe Ah kin help you, honeh." Her lips plucked his right nipple, then kissed purposefully down his belly to nibble and suck his penis.

"It's no good, Louella," he told her definitely. "You'll have to wait till I feel like it. It'll not take all that long."

They lay side by side.

"Ah'm frahtened that B'lly Joe'll fahnd us here together, Winston. He's dangerous."

"Fack him! You're nineteen years old. You can do what you like."

"You don' un'erstand mah family and you don' understand Messesseppeh and the South, Winston. Mah daddeh's got powerful friends heah in Chicago, both in the po-lice and in the Mob. Nobody's gonna go askin' too many questions if anytheng happens to me, if you see what Ah mean."

"If anyfink happens to me, they are!"

"B'lly Joe don' care about that. He killed a couple of black men down in Louisiana, Ah reckon, on account of me," the Brixton youth sat up wide-eyed glancing from door to window, alert to threat, attentive to every sound, alarmed yet reassured by the noise from the parties, "and another, Ah think, in Arkansas."

"Why din' you tell me this before?"

"It's not the sort of theng you tell people till you know them better, Winston, darling. You ain' scared, are you, honeh? Ah told you *Ah* was. Ah *told* you, " she spoke earnestly.

"Right. You did." He relaxed. "What the hell? He ain' gonna find us here. We're alright."

"He's found me befoah. He's real good at finding me, I'll grant him that, even though he ain't much good at anytheng else."

"Screwing you, you mean?"

"Aw, Ah'd never let B'lly Joe touch me! Never! He knows that. That's why he keeps running after me," she paused with a tiny, puzzled frown, "Ah guess."

"And your father and your mother and your family? What do they say? Why can't they let you live your own life? You're nineteen, for Christ's sake!"

"Mah Momma thinks Ah should be a lady, and mah daddeh," she said bitterly, "thanks Ah'm still a little girl. And they both want me to marry B'lly Joe which Ah ain't," she began shaking her head in firm determination, "gonna do, not in a million, years!"

Winston rolled onto his right side, and grasped her right breast with his left hand, his face nuzzled her other breast: "Forget 'em, right?"

"Raht," she agreed, and stroked his back, and breathed deep enjoyment, put her head back, closing her eyes. "Ah could go to London, England. They'd never fahnd me there." She wondered if he had heard her: "Honeh?"

"What?"

"Would you help me in London, England, if I went?"

"Yer. Sure," he continued rubbing his face against her, kissing her throat and neck.

"How would Ah find you, honeh? Your address and phone number."

"You could send a letter to me at the Arsenal Football Club, couldn' you?"

"Yes, Ah could. Ah never thought of that, honeh. You're hard again, you beautiful theng." She was suddenly apprehensive: "You ain't got troubles with your famileh, Winston?"

"I ain't got no family. Only an aunt, and the less I see of her, the better."

"Your parents?"

"Dead. Forget all that stuff. Let's get on wiv it."

"Ah lahk to watch it going in and out. Aw, that feels so good! Mmmm."

In the mirror, Winston watched his image stood gliding into her from behind where she bent stiff-legged supported by her forearms on the bed, head stretched back, eyes closed, smiling.

Astride him, she quivered and twisted, face contorted, appreciating the hard blackness gleaming against her vulva's pink rubbing her clitoris, deep and tight inside her, inciting her to orgasm.

"Honeh, you are beautiful!" she murmured, frictioning her face against his genitals, inhaling his musk. She kissed and sucked his penis. "A stud. A real stud."

Sated, totally cleaned of lust, he lay atop her. "That's it for tonight, girl. I've got to get a couple of hours' sleep now, then get back to the hotel. I've a hard day's training tomorrow."

ii

The loud knocking brought them fully conscious to stare at the door through the night's shadow; noise continued from the parties.

"Who is it?"

"It's me, Louella."

"It's B'lly Joe," she whispered into her bedmate's ear. Winston was out of bed reaching for his underpants. "Go away, B'lly Joe! Ah don' want one single theng to do with you!"

"Open the door, Louella, 'cause yew know Ah'm coming in."

"No, you ain't! Go away!"

He was suspicious: "Yew got a black in there with yew?"

"You go away from here, B'lly Joe, and leave me in peace!"

"Aw, de-amn!" he decided, disgusted and growing angry, "yew have got a black!" He charged the door, the lock and bolts partly gave. Winston Jones had his shirt on. "Ah ' seen him!" The next charge burst into the room. Winston was fully dressed in yellow and purple jacket and black baseball cap. "Hold it raht there. This Colt .45'll blow your guts out, boy!" The staring wildness in the good looking intruder's face enhanced the threat.

Winston, hands up, eyes as wide as the tall white man's, only his with fright, declared fervently that he was not moving.

"Shut up!" the newcomer ordered, and turned to complain: "Louella, yew ain't nuthin' but a little slut. But Ah loves yew anyways. Git some clothes on while Ah attend to this black." His left hand clicked a flick-knife gleaming in the lamplight. "Ah'm a-gonna cut your cock off of yew, yew piece of shit. Yew ain't gonna mol-est no more white girls!"

Louella leapt at him, scratching his face, knocking the revolver exploding from his hand.

Winston sensed the suck of a bullet passing his right ear.

His departure from the room was abnormally swift. Down the stairs five at a time, his passage along the ill-lit empty street during the following few seconds merited him the title of fastest man in America. Rounding the street corner into the alleyway leading to the main thoroughfare, a police patrol car parked sideways blocked his way. Unable to halt, he accelerated to maximum and soared over it.

"Cher-rist!" exclaimed the patrolman by the car. "Stop! or I'll shoot!"

"He's clean," the second patrolman completed his search for weapons.

"Of couse I am! This bladdy guy back there was awfter me wiv a gun!"

"Nobody here in this room." Sound of the continuing parties thudded up from below. "There's something fishy about this guy. He talks kind of funny like some television movie from England. I ain't sure you didn't rob that liquor store, boy. We're taking you back to the station."

CHAPTER 61

i

Wyckliffe regarded the youth grimly: "You've hit the World headlines, you've made a laughing stock of the American Secret Service by betraying the trust and confidence they had every right to expect of us, men," Wyckliffe's hard tone suddenly roared into controlled rage, "who are risking *their lives* for you, for *all* of us!! Do you understand that, boy?! Risking *their lives*! Winston hung his head low, scowling resentment and habitual bitterness at being shouted at, but mostly he was ashamed, fighting off disappointment which edged into insupportable despair at what must inevitably come: being sent back to London in disgrace, never more to play for England. Wyckliffe turned his head aside, breathed in deeply and regained full control. His attitude was hard: "Do you understand that?"

Winston's head went even lower: "Yer," he muttered.

"The pressures on me to send you back home, kick you off the squad for good – well, you know what they are! Is there any reason why I shouldn't? Is there?"

Winston Jones, in despair, did not speak.

"Answer!!"

The younger man's choked voice was barely audible: "No."

"No, there's none." Wyckliffe, frowning, head bent, left hand grasping right wrist behind his back, began breathing hard; then he relaxed, though stayed firm. "What have you got to say for yourself?"

Winston's head stayed down: "Nuffink," his voice was low.

"You'd betray other people again, given the chance, would you?"

Winston Jones shook his head at the ground: "No, I wouldn't," he murmured.

Wyckliffe's voice lightened: "Do I have your word on that?"

Beginning to hope, Winston Jones raised his head long enough to look at the England Manager: "Yer."

"Then keep it," said Wyckliffe, and Winston, drawing in a deep breath of enormous relief lifted his head. "I'm not sending you home. What punishment should you have?"

"I d'n' know."

"Work hard. Be a loyal team-mate. And keep your word." Wyckliffe was relaxed: "Now join the others." He gestured with a nod and a wave of his right hand and forefinger at the door: "Go on."

Winston Jones, incredulous, lightheaded with relief, needed no second telling.

ii

"We've got to give the boys some relaxation, Howard," Wyckliffe was earnest. "Surely, it must be possible in some way?"

"Not without weakening security, and we don't want to do that yet," said the F.B.I. man. "We can't swear that guy shot on Monday was a loner here in Chicagoland. Things point that way. But we can't be sure. Now we've got the Klan involved with Winston Jones, though I don't think we're going to have too much trouble with that one, since his little lady love is on her way back to Mississippi."

"Let's hope to God she stays there! Though this business with her and Winston Jones definitely does show we must do something to dispel our prison camp siege atmosphere."

CHAPTER 62

"Panther Rodriguez eat your heart out!" Curly Greenhalgh chortled, and wiped sweat from his eyelids. Joe Berrigan, panting, rose on one knee, Jim Arrowood refrained from scoring into the empty goal. Beth Langdale, nursing a water bottle in the shade, clapped; Jim waved acknowledgement.

"Okay, Panther Rodriguez is the best," Joe Berrigan admitted. "Probably the finest goalie ever. He's half Argentina's team."

"And Miguel Araujo and Pedro D'Elia the other half," said Curly.

Jim Arrowood objected: "Argentina are better than a goalie and two players. Out of their last ten games, won eight, and drawn two and those against Brazil and Italy. They have to be good."

"Thanks to Rodriguez," said Joe Berrigan.

"I'm better than D'Elia – watch this!" said Curly, and began his solo attack. Joe Berrigan dived the wrong way but succeeded in toecap parrying the bald man's attempt.

"Maybe not D'Elia, but perhaps Winston on an off day," Jim Arrowood grinned. Curly laughed. Joe Berrigan was austere. Seventy yards away, Winston in lemon yellow strip was passionately kissing a similarly clad coloured actress.

"It's immoral," Joe Berrigan gave judgement. "Wyckliffe's little better than a pimp, him and that blonde madame," his contempt and disdain were barely controlled, he glanced towards Britt Anderson conversing with Jacky Day in the far stand. At the other goal, Jingo Byrnes scored a penalty past the reserve keeper.

"I reckon you're jealous, Joe, 'cause you're not getting any," Curly Greenhalgh taunted.

"The F.A. should stop it!" Joe Berrigan's anger flared. "It's wrong! Totally wrong!" He glared at the film unit working with Winston, the black model, two white actresses and other England team members. "Wyckliffe is far too lenient! He should have kicked Jones off the squad for ever! He should never have let Jacky Day do those TV programmes! – speaking like that about God and the Virgin Mary!" He rushed from the goal area towards Arrowood spurting at him beyond the eighteen-yard line. Arrowood swayed left went right and lifted the ball over the sideways diving arm-leg-waving goalkeeper. Beth Langdale clapped anew.

Blonde hair effulgent under pink and white, broad-brimmed lace hat. Perfectly proportioned unblemished womanhood in pure white, sleeveless dress. Beauty so ethereal that awe glittered crystallised in Jacky's gladness. Britt exhaled deeply and turned again to him from momentarily regarding Jingo Byrnes's relentless penalty scoring. Her perfume and reality caressed his lust lunging for satiation. He clasped her upper right arm, voluptuous in its smoothness.

His arousal excited her: "We can go inside and find a room somewhere," she smiled, yielding, happy, desiring a quick consummation. His grip held her from rising, his contorted features revealed conflict and pain.

Mary's jealous antagonism rived and lacerated his yearning, her angry anguished tears gushed acid on his libido, yet still he wanted Britt. Mary was not there! He *needed* the soft luxury of a woman to engulf with her hurtlessness the wild fury of his being and transform into ecstasy the huge passion wrenching and rending him from frustration to despair.

Mary with Jessie in her arms, both sobbing. Mary screaming jealous hatred, reviling him, endlessly unforgiving, limitlessly rejecting him, their loving trusting marriage irreparably destroyed.

Jacky jerked spasmodically away from Britt to slash his perception at the quavering stadium, bound in sunlight and shadows. No relief there! Only torrid barrenness. And beyond its edifice, enemies and suffering, his abasement, his death. Mary meant affection, tenderness, consolation, security, home – Britt Anderson, physical beauty and temporary assuaging of passing desire.

Britt leant forward, palms on Jacky's left thigh, noting his quick then deep inhalation: "What is it, Jacky, darling?" she asked softly, wholly his.

"Mary."

"You're with me," she murmured gently. "She left you. She's three thousand miles away."

His fists clenched on the seat top in front of him, he stared at the shimmering cloudless blue. Resentment at Mary commingled with lust and guilt.

"You're always beefing, Joe!" said Curly Greenhalgh. Joe Berrigan, smiling at finally thwarting an Arrowood endeavour, climbed upright. Jim curved running to drink from Beth Langdale's water bottle. "Denzil does what he does for the good of the team. Are you against the cabaret-party he's fixed up for us on Sunday?" Curly challenged.

"No," the Liverpudlian admitted reluctantly.

"Hurray for Joe!" Jim Arrowood's shout alleviated Berrigan's dourness.

"It's a good idea – helps take our minds off being locked up," the keeper tossed his ball after Arrowood and walked goalwards. "It should be entertaining – top local variety artistes."

"And Becky Serene flying in special from Las Vegas to top the bill!" Curly exulted.

Joe Berrigan's distaste was as marked as his cynicism: "And you know *what* she's coming for, don't you?"

Suppose Mary did not love him? – endured him only for his wealth. Shock numbed Jacky isolated, chasmed reality disintegrating and volatising into terror. She had changed after Jessie's birth, not wanted him as before, put Jessie first. Maybe he had never been first with her as she with him.

"Are you alright, Jacky?" Britt's compassionate concern was strong and gentle.

He registered his name, her tone: his head turned jerkily, mumbling a response, expression puzzled, eyes unfocussed.

"Jacky, darling," she consoled his suffering. "You're safe," she stroked his arm. "No one can hurt you. I won't let them."

Her gentleness and beauty relaxed him.

Mary!

Torment twisted him afresh: he gazed frenziedly at the sky rimming the far stand.

"You're frightened, aren't you?" she discerned.

"Yes," he admitted. She squeezed his hand sympathetically. Her softness soothed his turmoil into countering his guilt. "I try to concentrate on football and forget everything else – Mary and Jessie's not being here, that there might be madmen trying to kill me," he writhed in fear. "All the poison pen people and religious and other fanatics who hate me for telling the truth. The news media out to kick my head in like that Italian did," his right hand instinctively covered his glowering, contorted countenance. "I worry about everything – the Argentina game, the World Cup." He confronted her, his left hand's clenching on hers inflicted pain: "I want you!! Yes, I want you!! Your beauty, everything else about you! But I'm married, Britt," he turned away, tortured, staring across the stadium, seeing scarcely noting. Jingo Byrnes scored another penalty: its sound arrived thickly. "If I were a Muslim, we were all Muslims, I could have two wives! But we're not, and I can't. Mary would not have it."

She spoke quietly: "I would."

Jacky looked at her, then away around the seats and turf, to the sky where a helicopter was whirling some miles away, distinct and tiny. "I wish I were free. From all the worries and pressures. Somewhere – anywhere – I could relax, be myself, away from it all, at peace."

Jim Arrowood and Beth Langdale, hand in hand, followed by Curly Greenhalgh and Joe Berrigan were leaving the field. Winston Jones and his team-mate co-actors were trotting towards the dressing room tunnel. Jingo Byrnes, dedicated as ever, worked on.

"It's peaceful where I live at the moment," Britt murmured. "Big secluded grounds with bushes and trees and flowers and shaded grass, and a swimming pool, a quiet mansion with cool rooms and stillness, the only sound, birds singing. You could sit in the garden, swim in the pool, doze in the shade, read a book or a newspaper, listen to music. You could be alone. Or I could be with you. On your terms. As you wished."

Denzil Wyckliffe, followed by several England players fresh and cool from their post-training shower, emerged from the dressing room tunnel.

Jacky stood up. "Are you coming to our cabaret on Sunday?"

CHAPTER 63

i

"Oh shit! Oh facking hell!" Benny Cawthorne kicked the ball out of the goal. Joe Berrigan was having his injured shoulder examined. Miguel Araujo, caught near the centre touchline, was hidden under all ten of his ecstatic team-mates.

In Hull, an old, bald negro town bus-driver was miserable in front of his television set as he watched the Argentine master dribbler wrong foot his grandson.

ii

Wyckliffe helped tend to his men's needs, fetching and carrying, exchanging earnest words about knocks and bruises, circulating, noting complaints, observations, ideas. Everyone accommodated, he claimed attention: "Okay, lads! The X-rays on Joe show nothing broken, so with any luck, he'll be fully fit in a few days. Right, the job in hand: I've counted five half-chances where we might have scored. They've had three, and one good 'n."

Jim Arrowood, wearing only shorts, towelling down with one hand while holding a mug of sports-drink in the other, said: "That goalie's got the right name, Panther. I should've knocked that one in from twenty yards. How he got to it, I d'n' know."

"Same wi' me," Bobby Milburne mumbled.

Jed Lennox was miserable: "That bloody Araujo." He rubbed his forehead, upset. "I've a hell of a job wi' him. He's Jacky's class."

"Keep up the good work, Gerald," Wycliffe encouraged him. "We knew what he was, him and D'Elia – well done, Benny," he congratulated the Cockney for neutralising the Argentine genius. "We knew it was going to be difficult, but you're managing him, Gerald, and that's all we need. That goalie is superb. But he's got," Wyckliffe was serious, holding up his left forefinger, "one fault – when they attack, he comes right out and, I think, a few yards off his line. So if any of you big kickers," his gaze went from Jim Arrowood to Jingo Byrnes, Bobby and Winston, "get a chance to drop a fast one over him from fifty or sixty yards, grab it! That applies to everybody. I don't need to remind you to have a shy at every half-chance from thirty, thirty-five yards you can. Okay, they've got a tight defence: Sanchez the Indian left back isn't fast enough to outrun either of you lads," his gaze took in Arrowood and Winston, then included Bobby and Jacky. "He's good, he's clever, he's not coming out of position. But if you *can* get him out of position –. And remember, you're better in the air than they are. One of those five half chances I talked about came from Winston's header. We've only had one long throw-in deep in their half. You know the moves, you've practised them so that you can do them in your sleep – let's see 'em."

Argentina were trying to slow the game down, England to keep it fast. No miskicks, no wrong passing, flawless ball control. South American willingness to solo run and dribble, quick, hard, skilful; neat short pattern play varied with long looping crossfield and upfield passes with occasional preference for the extra difficulty of keeping the ball off the ground rather than on it. England, direct, hard in the tackle, dribbling only when forced, holding the ball on the turf except when creating heading situations, using whatever kind of pass was required to pressure the opposition.

Araujo rounded Jed who stabbed the ball off course, forcing the Argentinean to lose full control: Richard Trelawney moved and blocked off view of the goal; Araujo passed back inside to near the penalty spot where D'Elia struck an instant before Benny Cawthorne: the ball looped and twisted, and England's goalkeeper palmed it with difficulty over the bar.

Jingo Byrnes first-timed from Richard Trelawney's header off the Argentine corner. Jacky, near the right of the England penalty box and facing his own goal, went down in an overhead kick which caught everyone except Jim Arrowood by surprise.

The Indian, Sanchez, visage vellicating, teeth gritted, sprinted to defend, knowing he was too late.

Jim Arrowood curved the ball wide of the out-rushing Panther Rodriguez, then flung back his head in anguished disgust as the South American demonstrated why he was Number One in the world with a phenomenal leap which thrust his fingers at the leather and deflected it so that its subsequent twenty-yard flight ended by smacking the far goalpost and not the back of the net.

Curly Greenhalgh, hurtling in to meet the rebound, collided solidly with the Argentine right back.

Oh please, God, the bald Mancunian thought as they put him on a stretcher and his right leg surged pain, please don't let it be bad.

Winston Jones did not feel his shirt rip from his back as he outjumped two grasping, jostling defenders and back-headed high into the penalty area.

Bobby Milburne sprinted five yards and soared upwards, also backheading.

Mrs Arrowood, knitting in her bay window alcove's Lincolnshire evening sunlight, saw her husband lean forward in his armchair. "What do you think, dear?" She held up the three-quarter finished white sweater.

"What? Yes. Very nice. Damn me if that goalie didn't nearly get his hand to that one also!" He settled back in his chair. "Our Jim's just scored," engrossed in the screen, he informed her as an afterthought.

For the next ten minutes, Argentina tried to overwhelm England. But with Jacky, Jingo Byrnes and Bobby Milburne controlling midfield, the South Americans were forced to defend and rely on counter-attacks.

Winston Jones hit the crossbar from twenty yards and sent the ball thirty up in the air. Jim Arrowood compelled Panther Rodriguez to three full-length saves. Bobby Milburne had a twenty-five yard left footer tipped round the post.

Jingo Byrnes's power shot from Jed Lennox's pass was plucked down and casually bounced one handed. Three quick paces and a huge kick over midfield probed England's weakness on the left as Jed Lennox sprinted vainly to regain his defensive position.

Benny Cawthorne was impassive: the Russian referee booked his particulars. Behind the official, Araujo, grimacing theatrically, alternately shaking his supposedly injured leg and limping exaggeratedly, was totally unhurt. D'Elia positioned for the free kick a yard outside England's penalty area. Jacky Day was speaking urgently to a grim-faced Richard Trelawney who was nodding assent. The red card came out; the Cockney stayed impassive.

D'Elia's swervekick was hard – and a goal.

"Jacky Day is going to mark Araujo! Is that wise?! Can he hold him?! Is he capable of playing defensively at this brilliant South American's level?!" the television commentator's excited anxiety cut through Pete Gregg's and many another viewer's gloom at England being a goal down with only ten men and twelve minutes left to play.

"You stupid, ignorant bugger!" the beefy Trenton farmer growled at his screen. "Jacky started his career as an attackin' halfback, you bloody fool!"

His wife said; "I wish you wouldn't swear like that, Peter. It's not good for the children."

"They're not here. Anyway, these stupid bastards like him," Pete Gregg pointed at the screen, "gerr on my tits! He's like a bloody old woman! knows nowt about football!"

"Jacky Day's mother wasn't very well tonight when I called in on my way home."

Pete Gregg, serious, looked at her: "She seemed okay this morning. I'll go down again after the match and have a word. It's latish, but the lads'll be there. I promised Jacky I'd keep an eye on things for him."

The Day-Araujo duels were brief: duets of grace and swiftness. After his fifth failure, the Argentinean changed positions, wandering crossfield: Jacky stayed close.

Jed Lennox contained D'Elia.

Argentina stressed England. Richard Trelawney headed off the goal-line. Eddy Corelli was winded when preventing an otherwise goal with his solar plexus. Joe Berrigan's substitute saved nine times in five minutes.

Jacky's quickness in the goalmouth won him possession. He dummied two Argentineans right, a third left and sprinted right. The Argentine half was empty save for Panther Rodriguez well out of his goal. Winston Jones was unmarked.

"Take yer time! Over the goalie!" Jingo Byrnes shouted urgently.

Winston, several yards inside England's half, sighted carefully and looped hard: Rodriguez was dashing goalwards.

The ball took ground six inches behind the goal-line in the exact middle of the goal.

"Yew kin cheer! But yew ain't a-gonna see that black ag'in!!"

Louella's face and mouth tightened, her nostrils flared and her chin went up; she stayed silent, ignoring her father in his police chief's uniform, her mother and her younger brothers.

iii

Howard Vanderskoon picked up the phone and said his name. Below him, through the window glass, around Soldier Field Stadium, cleaners were busy sweeping and stabbing up rubbish left by the departed crowd. In the field's centre circle, a trash collector pulling his handcart jabbed twice at a white object before spearing it.

"The firebomb guy in L.A's talk'n', Howard."

Vanderskoon became alert. "The bottom line?"

"Is that the guy who shot the Mayor of Chicago was a loner."

CHAPTER 64

Mary's eyelids fluttered against the sharp sunlight's dazzle off the white newspaper around the caption, CABARET FOR ENGLAND, above a large photo of Becky Serene and a smaller one of Britt Anderson. She controlled her jealousy. Headlines of the other Sundays strewn about the coffee table and settee pierced and cowered her with their contents: "NAZI MADMEN planned deaths of Jacky Day and Jewish Governor of California." "KILLER CONFESSES: 'We were loners'." "CALIFORNIA GOVERNOR DEATH PLOT." "L.A. BOMBER BRAGS 'We were loners' – but were they?"

Arms pressed to her sides, left hand cupping the telephone receiver, right hand clasping its microphone, Mary shivered and turned glancing fear-eyed around the sunny room and out to the tranquil lawn and countryside: "Even safe at home with Jessie, I'm frightened, Jacky," she spoke.

Her husband's voice was thin and metallic in the telephone earpiece: "Come back here, Mary. We're well protected."

"We're not coming."

"I miss you. There's no danger, Mary. The madman is dead. I've got a personal bodyguard twenty-four hours a day. I'm going crazy on my own. I *need* you, Mary!"

"Jessie needs me, also. Her welfare comes first. It's only for a little while, Jacky." Staring at Britt Anderson, she repressed jealousy. "You'll be home soon."

"But I *need you* with me *now*."

Moving her attention from the firebombed Chinese restaurant in the Sunday People's Mirror, Mary was calm: "How long are you going to be in Chicago?"

"Wednesday. Then after the China game, we'll fly to New York. Unless Poland and we lose to China," his tenseness broke with a chuckle at the improbability.

"The earliest I could get would be Monday night," she explained patiently, her tone revealing her total opposition and his unreasonableness. "Worn out from rushing around and travelling, and with poor little Jessie exhausted." Thus he was cruel. "We're no sooner in Chicago than we must fly off to New York." Heedless of others. She remembered: "Oh! – Rob Jarvis dropped in this morning," her gaze was on the CABARET FOR ENGLAND article and its brief but ill-willed reference to Jacky and Britt Anderson. "He brought several projects you might find interesting. He'll have them with him to New York. Can you get Rob two tickets for your last game there, Jacky, and for any subsequent England matches?" She focussed on the Sunday People's Mirror photo of the fire-gutted building.

"I'll try."

"Jacky, the Chinese gang war's moving north. They bombed a restaurant in Leicester late last night." She eyed Britt Anderson afresh. "Harry's worried, so am I – you don't need to admonish us – we know we needn't be!" Staring at the blonde woman, her jealousy seethed almost into malice. "Harry was here an hour ago. He's gone over to your mother's. Your sister Joanna and her family are motoring up to her mother-in-law's in Lincoln, so doubtless Joanna will be visiting your mother as well. Your mother seems to be improving, Jacky. She asked me to tell you not to keep ringing her every day, it costs so much money!" They laughed. She forced herself to observe the resplendent rusticity outside; she spoke lightly: "Jacky – you're having a cabaret tonight. Why didn't you tell me?"

His pause was minimal: "I didn't think."

Reason lost: "Because you'd invited Britt Anderson, hadn't you?!"

"No!" he protested, defensive.

"Keep away from her!! I don't want you having anything to do with her!! – not even talking to her!!"

"But – "

"No!! Stay away from her!! Promise!! Promise!!"

CHAPTER 65

Right thigh between Benny Cawthorne's legs, nude together on her doublebed, Becky Serene said: "Your mate Jecky's fallen out wiv the blonde bitch, has he?" She plucked a hair from his chest; he rumbled a curse at her avid face.

"Nah. It's Mary. She's jealous. That's why he went to bed early after your last number, the poor li'l' bagger. He's been under a hell of a lot of pressure. It's a wonder he don't blow apart wiv it. He's jumpy at everyfing. Somefink's got to give, the way he's been since yesterday."

"If I were Mary, I wouldn't leave him here alone wiv that maneater around after him. He's a man, and they ain't to be trusted, none of you baggers! You're all faithless. Not one of you's dependable. She's after him for what she can get out of him, just like she's done wiv every other man she's ever had anyfing to do wiv."

"What 'you talking abaht?" Benny was sceptical. "You don't know nuffink about her."

"They do in Las Vegas. The Mafia know a lot about a lot of people, especially when they sleep regular wiv senators and millionaires like that Chack Bengtsson whose bladdy great house she's staying at rent free. And others."

"What others?"

"All the top businessmen and bigshots she's slept wiv to clinch business deals. She's got her head screwed on all right. She's gonna feather her own nest and use everybody and everyfink she can get her hands on or her legs round. Behind that pretty li'l' face of hers and blonde hair, she's a right li'l' tart!"

Benny was grinning slightly: "I didn't fink you was jealous of her, darling."

"Jealous of her? Nah. You' been screwing her, have you, you bastard? It wouldn't surprise me. Nuffink you do would surprise me." He grinned up at her. She put her hands round his neck, her thumbs on his throat, and said in a trembling, yearning, submissive voice: "I ought to strangle you, you rotten man!"

"What have I done to you nah?"

She swung suddenly off him and the bed, catching up her yellow silk dressing gown. Sprawled relaxed, he watched her cross the room putting on the garment. She stood with her back to him and face to the wall, and asked in a small voice: "Will you marry me, Benny?"

"You're too good for me, Becky, love."

She turned, and, with longing face, said: "I'm not."

"You are. Much too good for the likes of me."

"I'm pregnant, Benny."

He made casual conversation: "You're going to have the abortion in Las Vegas, are you?"

"You bastard!! You bastard!!" She snatched a vase full of pink roses from the sideboard and threw it at him. He twisted deftly aside and onto his feet. "You pig!! You bladdy bastard!!" She threw three more vases at him, strewing the room with water and multicoloured wreckage.

He dodged about, protesting: "What's all this then?! What have I done?!"

She was crying big tears: "It's yours, and you want me to kill it! You swine! You rotten swine!"

"I don't," he was aggrieved. "You can have it if you like." In fury, she flung a big metal pot of lupins at him; he avoided the vase but not its contents. She kept throwing till there was nothing left while he danced and hopped around, pleading and cursing and pulling rose stems from his feet.

"I'll sue you," she said bitterly. "I'm going to have the baby."

"Have it, then," he placated her.

"I want to marry you, you bagger!"

"Have a bit of sense, girl! Me?! Married?! I'd be the worst bladdy husband any woman'd have nightmares abaht!"

"The baby's got to have a father."

"Alright, I'm the father, then! I'll pay to it."

She howled: "You bastard!!!" and looked frenziedly about for something heavy to hit him with. She picked up a chair, but it was too heavy for her to wield easily. He caught and held it.

"Here, here! You'll do yourself an injury, darling!" She kicked him and he let her because her slippers were soft and did not hurt him. He held her wrists when she tried to scratch his face; and pulled her close and locked her helpless when she tried to knee his groin.

She went limp, sobbing, with big tears: "You're hurting me!" He let her go and she promptly attacked him, so he locked her again.

"What can I do?" he was perplexed. "What can I say? You know what I am. I'm no good for women! I've always said that, ain't I? You know what I want you for! I've never made no secret of it, Beck, love," he took all the blame. "I'm a swine. I'm utterly unreliable wiv women, I've always said."

"I thought – what's it matter what I thought?! – I thought, you're twenty-six, Benny. We get on well together. I love you," she whimpered. "You'd make a good father. Fink how you would like a li'l' boy of your own to teach football, and wiv a li'l' girl, she'd look up to you and you could tell her stories – you'd be good at that, you sod!" She continued tearful: "You ought to settle down, Benny, you did, and I'd make you a good wife, I would."

"Yer, and wiv me running after all the women! And what about your career? This big Hollywood movie you're gonna do?"

"I don't care about my career," the tears were large, "I love you. I want to settle down and live wiv you."

"Jesus!" he released her, and caught up his underpants and trousers.

"Benny," she whimpered in a very tiny voice.

His dressing continued at speed, he had his socks and shoes on: "You ain't catching me like that, Becky!"

Her tears were going, her anger returning: "You bastard!"

"I am! I am! I agree!" he was buttoning his shirt.

"You bagger! Run away! Go on! That's all men ever do! You use women, then leave us to it to try and clean up your shit!" Anger flayed through her tears: "You're faithless, no-good bastards, the lot o' you! Not one of you's to be trusted! Not one! I thought you loved me," her voice was breaking, "and all that other talk was just your way!" She could hardly speak for sobbing. "I thought you really cared about me, Benny, really liked me for myself."

"I do! – that's why I won't marry you, Becky, because I am no good."

"You're not," she whimpered, "you can be so nice and gentle and considerate. You've got to grow up some time, Benny. You can't go on being a little boy for ever, playing football and Kung Fu and all the rest of it."

"I don't want to get married," he told her, and her sobs increased. "Aw, come on, girl, if I was finking of getting married, I'd fink of you first. But I ain't finking of getting married."

In a low voice, tears flowing, she said: "Go on, you rotten animal. Leave me alone. Get aht! Go on!! Clear off back to Jecky Day, and teach him to treat his wife better than you've treated me!!"

CHAPTER 66

The eight o'clock sun danced motes over the unmade beds. The call signal rang and rang at his home in England. One minute went. She could not have gone out. Mary must be there. She knew he was going to ring.

Two minutes. She could not have gone out!

Three. She must have.

After five minutes, Jacky put down the phone, sucked in several breaths fast through his mouth, then one long one, trying to maintain control. What to do?

"Your mother's sleeping. Is it –?"

"No!" Jacky interrupted the girl. Whatever you do, don't wake her up! 'Everything alright there?"

"Yes. The doctor's been this morning. They talked about you. Your mam was pleased when they all wrote so well about you in the papers yesterday."

"Give her my regards when she wakes up, and tell her that all I rang for was to see if she was okay."

"You're bladdy jumpy, Jecky!" Benny Cawthorne commented as the England players boarded the coach to their training session.

"Yes," his tone was curt. Frowning, he turned his back on the Cockney, avoiding all contact with those about him.

"I've got to get away, Denzil! have peace and quiet on my own! relax."

"I've noticed that all day."

"Clean away from the team, this hotel, everything!"

"All right," Wyckliffe consented. Jacky's tension eased. "Where were you thinking of going?"

"I don't want to say."

"I have to know, your bodyguard will as well, and the security people."

"Oh Christ!" Jacky jerked turning aside. "I wanted to get away!!"

"You can. We can make it discreet."

Jacky looked down, hesitant, shy, afraid of the other's reaction yet wild inside, and determined: "Chuck Bengtsson's place. It's quiet and beautiful and out of the way, I've been told. Just what I need. Freedom from pressure. Somewhere to unwind."

CHAPTER 67

i

Utter relaxation. As if his every muscle were smiling, resting, absorbing ease, storing what he knew would become vitality. It was hot here in the tree's shadows; the pool was only ten yards away – in the sunlight, but kept constantly cool, Britt said.

Jacky's eyelids flickered, his descent to sleep floating upwards. Through his lashes, over his forearm where he lay on his belly: his yellow terrycloth towel groundsheet; grass; bushes; another tree in whose shade Britt Anderson, wearing a small-check pink and white gingham frock, sat reading in a deckchair. Beside the chair, a portable radio with earphones, and a big tan briefcase.

Against the darkness of his closed eyes, myriads of camel legs hastening across a hinted desert. A bird chirruping. Sound of his breathing. Body in wellbeing, consciousness drifting down, down..

Home and its countryside. Mary and Jessie in the kitchen in sunlight. No, it was night time in England. Six hours ahead. Mary should have stayed with him. Wellbeing and near sleep encompassed and permeated her image, Jessie asleep in bed, the Chicago killer hazy in the shadows – but he was dead. Mary had her reasons for going home. She would be at her mother's.. Somewhere..

His mother. In the front room on her bed overlooking Trenton village and the valley's peaceful summer. She was ill; they were doing everything they could, though. He had paid. He would pay. His mother smiling at him. Worrying. Worrying about him. Her headaches, her 'do's. His head, the Italian, Angelo, kicking him. His Secret Service bodyguard protecting him, guarding Chuck Bengtsson's mansion and gardens.

The Italians were a good side, difficult to beat. But England's new team under Wyckliffe was better than the one that had lost in Rome.

The Germans, dangerous, but had England's pre-Wyckliffe problems – diminishment by age and injuries.

The Brazilians. Brilliant. Would be waiting for England in the Final, or possibly Argentina. Or Uruguay.

It didn't matter who got through, didn't matter.

Wellbeing dulled worry's sharpness before it emerged.

The Final. Himself holding up the Cup to the cheering crowd. Joy! Triumph!

An assassin sighting along his rifle, squeezing the trigger: Secret Service bodyguards drifted..

The F.A. Cup at Wembley. He had loved that victory.

The European Champions Cup in Paris when he had scored the penalty which had beaten Juventus.

Penalty taker.

He had never missed a penalty yet; his memory, lazily rapid, sequenced several. You should never miss penalties. Jingo Byrnes had not either. Curly was a pretty fair penalty taker. Jim.

The City Ground, Nottingham.

League Champions. Not the glamour. A hard season of many won games.

Wyckliffe had put together a winning team.

Jim Arrowood's scoring from his through pass; himself scoring, young Bobby, Winston Jones, Jingo, other England players.

Zest for life at each stride, breath, feeling, thought. Winning the World Cup in Philadelphia!!!

Excitement surged him awake so fast it snatched him into sitting upright.

Britt Anderson looked across smiling from her book. "You awake?"

"Yes. What are you reading?"

She turned the book towards him; realising he was too far away to see, she explained: "Japanese. Studying, you know." Her right hand plucked up the earphones hung across the radio. "I've been learning it a few months. Cassette language courses. Ideal for easy learning. It's Chinese and Japanese at the moment. I'm fairly proficient in Arabic now. Business – and pleasure."

"Britt. Is it true you've made love to men to clinch business deals?"

"Did Benny tell you that?"

"Have you?"

She gazed at him solemnly over the intervening six yards. Worry stressed her face, her eyes flicked aside and down, then came back at his. "Yes," she admitted quietly.

He looked away. Disappointment that was jealousy surged at him; he knew it was unreasonable; she could do what she liked; he was a married man with a little daughter.

"In the beginning," she explained levelly, "I was poor and alone. Had all my personal and family trials and tribulations. Had only myself to rely on, and was determined to be rich and independent of everyone. I was beautiful and men wanted me. I used that to profit myself."

"As a whore," Jacky's disillusion required facts.

"No," she replied levelly. "But, yes, if you like, as a whore. I never took money for a quick screw or a night in bed. It was part of something else. Yes, I made money. But I never degraded myself in my own eyes. Not any more than the men did in theirs. They were all clean, healthy, respectable businessmen whom I slept with in order to gain profitable contracts. All seven of them." She saw his disgust and defeat: "You're shocked."

His gaze lifted from the grass to her: "Yes."

"Sex didn't mean so much. It meant more to them than to me. I took part in a soft porn movie, too. I'll tell you everything. Better to know it from me than from someone else. I was seventeen, and I wore a chestnut wig and tinted my pubic hair. I got two thousand pounds cash which I invested in shares that quadrupled inside a year. I sold them at the top of the market, and put all my money into three small companies. Within six months, one had doubled, one had quadrupled, and the other quintupled. I knew the right people, you see. And I didn't need to sleep with them: I didn't want to. I made love only to those I chose, and I did not pick very many, Jacky, because I was interested in making money, not sex, unlike my parents. And my old Nazi grandfather, the bank director in Strasbourg, approved, and I used him as a sounding-board and told him only what I wanted him to know."

"Used him," said Jacky.

"Yes."

"Like you're using me with these contracts, and the rest of the lads."

"I don't need that money, Jacky. I am a rich woman. I knew of you through Benny. His mother's German, like mine. Football doesn't interest me so much. Benny's a crook or the nearest thing, and a tough guy, a local Cockney celebrity whom I rather like. During all that by-election publicity, he spoke well of you. I saw the programme you did for Swedish television. You intrigued me. So I accepted when he asked me if I were interested in being your escort that night. Remember the sex show?" Jacky nodded. She asked, whimsical: "Morality?"

He grinned ashamedly and dipped his head, to look up at once: "Alright. I shouldn't throw stones. Oh God!" he sniffed with a tormented, resigned smile, "who am I to throw stones?! I slept with you, and I am here." His upper body twisted aside, face contorting, frightened of Mary's jealousy yet not regretting being with Britt Anderson in spite of her revelations.

"You liked it, I loved it. So where's the harm?" she reasoned, serious. "Morality: rules formed out of forces moulding you from babyhood on – and your inclinations," she breathed a chuckle of conflicting emotions. "The Christian Churches' history and heritage of superstition, bigotry, oppression, ignorance and exploitation. Roman Catholics kneeling submissive in their hundreds of millions to old virgin bachelors who, under impressive garb and ceremonies are mainly and mostly intent on preserving and extending their own power. Orthodox Christians with their reactionary ways and ultra-conservatism. All the other Churches and sects with their myriad moralities that have ever been or are, with their double standards or triple standards or whatever standards where men may do what women may not, where this group can do what that cannot, where the rich and the privileged are given licence and admiration while the poor – opprobrium, punishment and death. Especially in the Muslim world. Where women are acknowledged as inferior to men and treated accordingly. In different Muslim countries, they mutilate women with female circumcision which repulsive practice is not even sanctioned by the Koran. Male circumcision isn't mentioned in the Koran, for that matter. Have you ever read the Koran, Jacky?"

"No."

"I have. All one hundred and fourteen suras of it. In the original Arabic. Plus many learned commentaries on it by many learned men.

God Himself speaking word for word via the Angel Gabriel in visions to His prophet, Mohammed. I've seen in various countries the public executioners going crazy with bloodlust – her face showed horror. "And the public floggings; and men with their hands and feet cut off for stealing! All the horrible folly of feudal barbarism! She calmed: "Morality. India: with its unjust Hindu caste system and all its unfair ways and doings. Japan: feudalism modernised, where women are definitely second class citizens. You can go through the world: Indonesia, China, Tibet, Burma, etcetera, Africa, Latin America, all the nationalities and tribes and groups of people that are or have ever been: all the religions and cults that are or have ever been – each with its different moral codes and different moral ways and different moral practices! Morality. Morality–" noticing Jacky's fascinated stare at her sardonic single-mindedness, she laughed prettily, holding the left half of her bottom lip between her teeth, and shrugging and wriggling and tossing her head. "I'm on my moral high horse, thanks to you, and my father, damn him!" Her gaiety vanished and she was serious: "No, not 'damn him.' You're like him at his best, Jacky. But you don't look like him, he's tall and blond – or used to be when I was a little girl. I look like him."

"He must be very handsome," said Jacky. "Not like me."

She studied him critically, unsmilingly: "You look like – a man."

"Well, I'm not a woman," said Jacky, and they laughed.

She relaxed back in her deckchair, and murmured: "It's beautiful here." Sun glinted off the blue sky reflected in the water and gleamed on the white tiles edging the pool. The thick, short grass's greenness evidenced liberal and regular watering. Maple trees, white oak, and birch shaded the grounds. Rhododendron bushes splashed red. Honeysuckle teased the air, and rose bushes shone fresh with their yellows, reds, pinks and whites. A big rockery was bright with almost every flower colour.

Britt spoke lazily: "In Japan, they have miniature gardens, dwarf shrubs and trees. In Ancient China, they had exquisite demesnes. Imagine living in one of those bygone dynasties. A high lady or lord, emperor or empress, in cool gardens with beautiful statues, wearing silk robes, surrounded by exquisite jade carvings and pottery and works of art."

Jacky, eyes closed, unmoving, said: "While millions of starving coolies worked their guts out and died like flies. I like it better here."

Britt, smiling, regarded his breathing belly and chest, his lightly tanned smooth body in minuscule dark blue swimming trunks. She wanted to go across, lie beside him, stroke him, and make love to him gently. But he had come for relaxation and peace.

"It's hot," he said, not opening his eyes nor moving. "I think I'll go for a swim." He was on his feet before he noticed her mild observation. "Coming?"

"Well, err, well," she gave a tiny, abashed smile, "I've only got this swimming cap," she picked up the yellow headpiece from behind her radio. "I don't have a costume. I don't normally need one here."

"You don't now," he said, and, shy at his boldness, dived into the water.

Her nudity overawed him: tucking her wavy blonde mane under the cap accentuated the size and beauty of her breasts, her ribcage and small waist, the curve of her hips. Her wide smooth belly with its fair beard. Her long legs, slender arms. Small hands. Small feet.

Blushing over staring, he lifted his feet and submerged.

"That was refreshing." Britt climbed out of the pool, conscious of his attention. She pulled off her swimming cap and shook her hair loose, bending with legs apart swaying and twisting her head and body, smiling at him through her tresses, artful in innocence. "I think I'd like a long drink and something to eat."

"Me, too." He lusted for her.

ii

"Look, I'm tired!" Mary Day's exasperation was clear. "I've been travelling for twenty hours! I've got a little girl asleep in my arms! I don't want to stand at this reception desk all night arguing! If you can't find my husband, and you can't give me a room, fetch the hotel manager and Mr Denzil Wyckliffe, the England team manager! and if you can't reach them," she turned from the reception clerk to the burly Secret Serviceman beside her, "contact your boss, Howard Vanderskoon: he, at least, will know where Jacky is at this minute and be able to tell him his wife and daughter have arrived, and are here waiting for him!"

Wyckliffe said: "You can have my room, Mary. I'll move in with somebody." He addressed the hotel manager: "You can fix up a cot for the little girl? Wonderful. Can you do it now? Thank you." Mary fussed tinily with the sleeping child beside her on Denzil Wyckliffe's office settee; the hotelier departed.

She was determined: "Where is he, Denzil?"

"I don't know exactly, Mary."

"You must know!" The child stirred. Mary continued softly: "He's under twenty-four hours a day surveillance with a personal bodyguard. He told me himself."

"I don't know where he is exactly at the moment," Wyckliffe said seriously, "and that's the truth."

"Is he with some woman?" Mary asked tightly. "Britt Anderson, for example. And you're covering for him."

Wyckliffe was under pressure: "Let me explain, Mary. No – please, Mary!" he raised his voice, interrupting her as she stiffened to protest; Jessica twisted, and rubbed her face, almost waking up. They stayed motionless and silent, watching the little girl settle back into sleep. Wyckliffe resumed softly: "Security restrictions have been eased since yesterday. All the squad have gone out to different places, making use of their first opportunity to get away from this hotel."

Her suspicions were allayed, not removed: "And Jacky went with them."

"In a way, yes."

Her suspicions were back: "What do you mean?"

"I mean that Jacky's been under a lot of pressure. An awful lot of pressure. A terrible amount of pressure!" he saw her face smooth. "Being at this hotel, under constant threat of death all this time and with all the demands made on him by the news media, public opinion, everything else – not least your leaving him." Mary bit her bottom lip, frowning and looking away, uncomfortable. "He was so tensed up, he came to me early tonight and said he was going crazy – and I could see he was. He had to get away from the hotel, the squad, football, everything – and relax. Somewhere quiet and peaceful, away from it all."

"Yes, he is like that sometimes," she understood and was calm. "Where did he go?"

"That's it." Wyckliffe gave a worried, excusing chuckle and gestured frankness. "He had to get away from everything – me included."

She regarded him, not sure whether to believe him or not. Wyckliffe looked her straight in the eyes and said quietly: "I can go to the security people and send a message to him telling him you're here. That might be the best thing. On the other hand, it might not."

She smiled, tired: "He might not be able to relax any more, you mean?"

Wyckliffe nodded, smiling: "If you got a good night's sleep, and met him tomorrow refreshed, it would be a pleasant surprise for him. But I can and will pass a message to him straight away, if you want."

And warn him I'm here, Mary thought, protecting your star player. Maybe he was telling the truth. She yearned for that.

"Are Joyce and Richard, Jim Arrowood and Beth, out, too?"

"Yes. Shall I get a message to Jacky?"

"No," she said, and Wyckliffe, relieved, smiled, and began talking of practical arrangements for her and her daughter's wellbeing.

She would ring Britt Anderson herself.

iii

"It's peaceful here," said Jacky, "cool, and so quiet."

"Those walls are eighteen inches thick, solid stone. They keep out the heat; the cold; unwanted sounds. It's built solid, all fourteen rooms of it. 1925. A rich banker."

"Did you help Chuck Bengtsson decorate?"

Oil paintings of different shapes, sizes, motifs and schools hung on the cream walls of the hundred square yard rectangular room with ample windows at each short side. Golden brown curtains. Medium and pale brown oak and teak and white birchwood furniture blended tastefully with the oriental carpets covering the polished parquet floor. Bookcases.

"I advised him on some of the paintings," Britt indicated them, "and some of his other expensive bric à brac. He's not much interested in art. It's an investment for him."

"Do you sleep with him?"

"Yes. But I shan't after tonight."

"Why not?"

She turned and her breasts were against his chest and her belly against his, her hands clasped at the base of his spine. Her blue eyes with their violet rims and unmarked whites were six inches opposite and level with his own. "Hold me, Jacky," her appeal was soft, her body warm, smelling of flowers, dispersing his resolve to enjoy sympathetic tranquillity without sex.

Mary was in England. Why had she not come? He had <u>needed</u> her.

Britt was so gentle and beautiful.

Physical excitement from copulation poured eager pleasure, joy at doing what he yearned for, relief that laughed and gratified with each thrust and clutch inside her.

She was so lovely, so feminine, with her smooth skin, breasts and roused nipples; her pretty face and slender softness yearned at him, delighted undemandingly, accepted and gave because he was what he was.

He climaxed fast and exquisitely.

Mary was in England. She should have come. With Britt's softness against him, caressing him slowly and so very soothingly, remorse was an intellectual exercise. He had hurt no one. He was glad he had made love to Britt, was with her now. Pleasure in her beauty, hunger for sex chuckled in his mind. And a determined carelessness that was freedom.

He took his time, positioning contact with her clitoris at each stroke, enjoying her tiny staccato whimpering pleasure so near pain, edging suckling's smiles from grimaces. Innocent, yielding, defenceless, hurtless: mature woman in the tight suck and rhythm of her body; her arms and legs urged and caressed, her breasts were soft against his face, nipples ready for his mouth, lips at his neck and shoulders smooth and thick on his, tongue pliant to his.

He lay on his back, drained of desire, at peace, relaxing, soothed yet mildly stimulated by her right hand slowly stroking his belly and thighs.

She kissed his left nipple, her right hand covered and her fingers caressed his genitals. "Twice," she murmured, smiling to his eyes, her lips pouted a kiss at him, his nipple at their corners.

"I needed it." He stroked her shoulder. "You're beautiful, Britt."

"I want you for ever," she sat up beside him looking down into his face. "I want five babies by you and to live with you and go with you and share with you all my life."

"I'm married," he said. "But if I hadn't been married. Oh God! I would!! Oh yes! I would!!"

"Do it," she urged.

"Mary," he said. "And Jessie."

"They don't own you! Nobody owns anybody! I'd be better for you than she ever was, ever could be, I'd do anything for you, go anywhere with you, never let you down."

"Never?" he quipped wrily.

"Never."

"That's what I said about Mary."

"You haven't let her down – she let you down, running away and leaving you when you needed her most." He felt Britt was right, though he knew all the reasons why she was not. "She married you at the start of your career and she knew she was onto a good thing. She's had everything out of you a woman could possibly want." He knew that was true, yet –. "So long as you've done what she's wanted, everything's fine. But *your* wishes, your aspirations for yourself, your dreams have had to take a second place or no place at all." Old quick and hidden grievances came flickering. "You could never leave the Nottingham area because she didn't want it, was studying, having a baby, it would upset the baby, etcetera, etcetera. But she never put *you* first, did she? To live abroad for a year, or two years or a few. To play in Italy or Spain or Germany or somewhere else, wherever took your fancy." He had resented that dismissal by Mary of his hopes, his longing for the freshness and excitement of new experiences in other cultures and surroundings. "She's used you. She caught you young and innocent when you had no experience of life – and she's profited from it. If you had met us both together for the first time and known us both together for the first time, which of us would you have chosen?"

Jacky turned his head aside. "I didn't though, did I?"

"Would you have chosen her?" she wanted an answer.

"I don't know: you're so beautiful. But Mary is.. Mary. And we've had our life together. And Jessie. I like my little girl. I don't feel guilty about being here with you, Britt. I'm going to have to pay for it. I don't care." Her thigh was smooth under his palm, her beauty peerless. "You're so lovely. Why haven't you married?"

Her gaze left his, features hinting misery and pain. "My parents, a bad marriage, with me in the middle. I wanted them to be happy together and love me. Yet when they broke up, it was beneficial. My dad wanted social justice and to be rich. He hadn't the education, the money," she paused, then admitted, "nor the courage. To break out on his own, be independent, think out what he wanted, how to get it, build up to it. Dreams," gentle longing mixed with bitterness, "big plans, ifs and maybes and might-have-beens and could-bes never came to anything because he daren't. He worked for that Norwegian-owned trading company all his life and still does. Dreaming of the big shows he would star in which he knew he never would. And my mother throwing it all in his face. Each with their lovers, and their constant rows and bickering, and me always in the middle. I vowed I would never have that when I grew up. And I haven't."

"You've never met any man to suit you?"

"You." They gazed seriously at each other for some seconds.

"Chuck Bengtsson? He's big, handsome, rich, not married. I would have thought he would have suited you."

"Chuck's a friend, that's all. He loves me. I don't love him. He knows how it is."

"What about other men in your life? Your past?"

"I haven't had any. Different boyfriends, men – lived with three, on occasion. I ended it each time because I felt nothing. I'm not a passionate woman."

"You could have fooled me."

She smiled into his grin, and ran her right palm down his front to cover his genitals. Twisted to bend, and suck his penis to erection, kiss and pluck it with thick lips. Knelt astride him and engulfed him in her tight smooth vagina, shaking her blonde mane, arching her breasts and pouting kisses at his bright-eyed interest. Then was hesitant and anxious: "Do you like me doing this?"

"Yeh. It's a lazy man's way of enjoying life." Smiling, she lay along his front. "I didn't know I was so potent." He realised: "We never took the phone off the hook!" Then remembered: "The guards will answer it. Otherwise, it always rings when you least want it."

"The one in this room is direct. The number's known to very few people. Chuck had it changed the day I moved in."

iv

"No, I don't know Britt Anderson's number, Mary," said Jim Arrowood. His girlfriend stayed silent. Richard Trelawney did not know either, nor Joyce Trelawney.

"Then," said Mary, "one of those others she's representing will have it. I want it. I want to ring her now. Tonight."

Jim Arrowood was ill at ease and told her to leave it till the morrow.

She was hard at him, suspicious: "You do know, don't you?! You don't want me to ring her because Jacky's there!"

The fairhaired man turned away, frowning, troubled: "No, I've told you, Mary, I don't know."

"Then I'll find out myself!" She started away, then stopped, addressing them with bitter insight: "But of course the others won't tell me either, will they?! You'll all be in it together!"

Joyce Trelawney said: "That's not fair, Mary. Richard," she ordered, "go get the number for her off one of those boys or Curly Greenhalgh." The England captain was perplexed till his wife's reasoning persuaded him: "She has a moral right to know – if Jacky were here, he would give it to her himself."

v

Jacky lay on his back, Britt, right leg between his, halfway across him face against his shoulder. He stroked her back's smoothness. "I don't know what I'll tell Mary," he murmured. "I don't even know if I should tell her." He was silent for some moments; she drowsed, content and alert. "I don't know what I'll do." His breathing was even, contact with her warm softness soothing; more seconds passed. Considering polygamy, he sniffed wry resignation, then, remembering Jingo Byrnes, asked: "Is it true, when he was in his fifties, Mohammed's last favourite wife was a little girl of ten or eleven?"

"Yes," she mumbled against his skin.

"I don't know if I could manage more than one wife. It wouldn't work."

"I'll take what you can spare me," her lips murmured at his neck, she raised her head to look directly down into his eyes, "though I don't really wish to share you with anyone. I want all of you. To be a housewife with five children who come running: 'Mummy! Mummy!' Breastfeed them all."

"'Could ruin your figure. It hasn't Mary's, though. She's got a good figure."

"Better than mine?"

"Different. She's – well, she's Mary. I wish – ."

"What?"

"I don't want to hurt anyone. Didn't. Don't." The phone's ringing startled him. She stayed unmoving, looking down into his eyes. "Aren't you going to answer it?"

"No. It's not important. You have beautiful eyes, Jacky. Grey-blue."

"You should answer it." She stood up, and momentarily overawed him afresh with her symmetrical curves and loveliness undulating to accept the call.

"Hello, Britt. This is Mary Day."

"Who? Mary –?"

"Day. Mary Day. Could I speak to Jacky, please?"

"Mary Day! Hello! How did you get this number in England?! It's not even listed in the local book here!"

Mary told her, and repeated her request.

Britt chuckled lightly and asked with ambiguous humorous astonishment: "Are you sure Jacky is here?"

"No. Is he?" Britt looked into Jacky's eyes. He took the receiver.

"Hello, Mary."

"Have you slept with her?"

"Yes."

"Then I'm going back to England tomorrow." She hung up.

Britt said quietly: "She has chosen. Let her go." Jacky stared at her, the shock of Mary's return and the coming emotional explosions balancing against his pleasure in Britt's beauty and thoughts of the future regarding Britt. "Stay here with me," she appealed. "Don't leave me."

"There's going to be a row," he said. "It will be worse if I stay. I'm going back to the hotel. It will give us all time to think." He smiled into her anxiety, reaching to stroke her hair and cheek, shoulders, breasts, her protruding nipples. "I don't regret making love to you, Britt. It was beautiful."

vi

His careful steady knocking on the hotel room door was loud in the empty corridor. "Mary! Open up, it's me."

"Go away. You'll wake Jessie up."

"Let me in, Mary."

"After being with that whore?! Never! Go on! Clear off! I'll see you tomorrow – when I've had some sleep."

CHAPTER 68

i

Mary spoke first: "You broke your word." Noise of people going by in the corridor outside Jacky's room. As he prepared to respond, she overrode him: "You gave your promise not to have anything to do with her again."

"I couldn't help it."

Her fury hurled forth: "Couldn't help it?! You liar!! Liar!!! I'm three thousand miles away in England worrying myself sick about you, and you take the first chance you get to go with that whore!!"

"I was lonely," he excused himself, defensive and miserable.

"And do you think I wasn't?! looking after little Jessie on my own there! Worrying about you! Worrying!!" she snorted her disgust. Her rage returned: "While you were playing around with that bitch!!"

"No! It's not like that."

"What is it like then?"

"It's – well – I was lonely," it showed in his voice and face.

She did not weaken: "And don't you think I didn't get lonely too?!" Her mood included the emotions she mentioned: "I was terrified, uncertain, worried and worrying about anything and everything, all sorts of things, while you," her anger flared, "were playing around behind my back!!"

"No!"

"Yes!! Like every cheap little worthless man I've ever heard of!!"

"It's not true!" Jacky protested low-voiced and defensive. "I was lonely, Mary, and desperate, going off my head cooped up in this place all the time! I needed – I needed –" he turned aside in anguished frustration, "I needed you, Mary! I begged you to come back!"

"To danger with little Jessie and mad murderers running about all over the place to kill us or kidnap us and torture us to death?! You're selfish!! Egocentric through and through, Jacky Day!! You didn't care what might happen to us!! what hell I've been going through!!"

"No –"

She flowed on: "Taking care of little Jessie!! Trying not to let my fear show!! To be sweet and kind and gentle, a loving understanding mother while father's playing around with a whore!!!" She was resolute: "I'm going to see that blonde bitch and have it out with her once and for all. I'm not putting up with this, Jacky. She can stay away from you from now on and you from her."

"It's not like you think. She's not a whore."

"She's a whore alright! Going out with you to sex shows, sleeping with you though she knew you were a married man with a little daughter! Then using you for all you're worth to make money out of you with these business contracts."

"That's not true! She's not interested in money."

Mary was indignantly amazed: "Not intere –!! You fool!! That's all she's interested in! That and all the mischief and harm she can cause for her own diversion! She's not interested in you! – any more than she's interested in all the other men she's ever had anything to do with! She *uses* men! Can't you see that?! Are you blind?! But of course you are. You're a man. You can't see any further than your lust where pretty women with good figures and legs open and ready for you are concerned!!"

"Britt's not like that. She likes me for myself. She doesn't need any money she can get through me. She's rich already."

"And how do you think she got rich?! By telling other men exactly what she's told you! You cretin!! I'm going to tell that bitch exactly where she gets off! She's unscrupulous, cunning and doesn't give a damn about you or anybody else, nor how many people get hurt, nor lives wrecked nor damage caused!!"

"You're unfair, Mary. Blame me, not her."

"I do blame you! And I blame myself."

"If I'd said no and done nothing, it wouldn't have been like this. I went with her because I liked her, because I wanted her; she appealed to me and still does!"

"You bastard!!" Jealousy became terror: "Oh Jacky! You mean you're going to leave me?"

Much shaken, irresolute, he stammered instinctively: "No – I – I – Mary – "

Strong, jealous, angry, she said: "You mean you want to have your cake and eat it?! Is that it? Have me and your home and family life while running around with that bitch on the side? Well it's not coming off! I won't have it!" Fear entered: "You haven't been with others behind my back, have you? No," reason re-asserted itself, "you couldn't have." Fear returned: "Could you?! Did you?! Those times you were late, couldn't get home?"

"I've never been with any women except you and Britt."

"Oh Jacky! What's happening?! I don't want our marriage to break up!"

" I don't either. But I do like her."

"You fool! She's using you! The sooner I see her the better. What a mess! It's me or her, Jacky! You can't have both."

"I like her."

"And you'd wreck our marriage for her?"

"I didn't say that."

"It's me or her."

"Aw, Mary," he turned aside.

"Choose."

"It's not as simple as that."

"It is."

"It's not been perfect between us, Mary."

"No – but good."

"I've had to do a lot of things I haven't wanted."

"Haven't I?"

"I'm not saying it's all your fault, I'm saying – trying – to say – how it is. I wanted – aw, lots of things! I wanted to play abroad," his yearning showed.

She was adamant, the subject closed: "We've been through all that."

His face and manner revealed hurt: "But I wanted, you see! I wanted! I know you had all the reasons, and I know they made sense! But still –."

"Well then," she was complacent, yet wary.

"I wanted!! you see. I wanted!!"

"But –"

His pain was clear: "No!! I wanted!! And I had to swallow it down and give way to you! You were right, and it made sense buying the farmhouse and fields and you getting your degrees and having Jessie and staying in one place to bring her up! But still –! " His features contorted with the pressure of being true to his emotions and the facts. "I know –" his left hand covered his face and he shook his head, "it's – it's – lots of things, Mary. Big things, little things, I wanted, but I had to swallow them down or forget about them or not even think about them because they could never lead anywhere."

"It's been the same for me," she defended herself.

He was under terrible pressure, desperate in his low appeal for understanding: "I'm not blaming you, Mary!"

She said with insight: "She's promised you perfection, has she? Complete satisfaction and fulfilment of your every want and need. The bitch! Oh yes. I know her alright. Promises are cheap, keeping them another matter! You'd find that out quick enough with her. But I'm not going to let her do it to us, Jacky!!" she was emotional. "I'm going to stop her!!"

The door opened quickly and Benny Cawthorne paced blithely in, leaving his key in the lock; a chambermaid was changing bed linen in the open room across the corridor; Curly Greenhalgh and Jingo Byrnes, passing, glanced in. "'Stop!' Did I hear the word 'Stop!'? Don't stop for me! You never do stop though, do you, Jecky?!" he picked up his watch from his bedside table. "Wiv all these beautiful women, eh, Mary?" he smiled friendship at her. Then remembered: "Britt Anderson is on the reception phone, Jecky."

Striking the Cockney's cheek full force, Mary exclaimed: "You –" his instinctive leg sweep and thrusting hand sent her sprawling, Jacky left-jabbed Benny's eye and his right sank with all his weight into the Cockney's solar plexus, his quickness parried the other's leg counter, "bastard!!!" Mary struggled up from the bed, intent on kicking the doubled-up, prone

Cawthorne, Jacky prevented her. "You pig!! You rotten – !!" she shrieked at the barely conscious Cockney. "You're the cause of his meeting that whore! encouraging him! throwing it in my face!!" she struggled and kicked wildly, but Jacky held her.

Benny crawled away, pulling himself upright with the help of furniture, wheezing "Jee-eesus! Facking hell!" He noticed Joe Berrigan and two chambermaids in the doorway and behind them, various England squad members. "Get out of it," he gasped at them. "A friendly discussion. Close that door!"

"Don't bother!" Mary was motionless. "Let go. Let go, I said!! It's alright. I won't touch that guttersnipe. And don't bother about answering that whore's telephone call at the reception desk – *I'll* do it."

ii

Journalists jostled around Jacky, shouting their questions, photographers wove patterns with their cameras trying to get a good shot: "Has Mary left you?!" "Have you and your wife broken up?!" "Did you spend last night with Britt Anderson?" "Did you give Benny Cawthorne his black eye?!" "Is Mary taking Jessie back to England today?!" "Are you thinking of marrying Britt Anderson ?!"

Denzil Wycklifffe pushed through the throng: "Break it up! Come on! Break it up!" He accidentally knocked in passing the Daily Telegraphic journalist's right elbow and nearly choked the Old Etonian in the gin the D.T's man was swallowing from his hipflask.

The Tory-Mail man shouted: "How does this scandal reflect on your position as team manager?!" The Tory-Express asked: "Doesn't this question your competence to lead England?!" The Tory-Sun called out: "Did you know about Jacky's relationship with a beautiful blonde not his wife?! Similar queries flung and hacked.

The England Team Manager spoke loudly: "That's enough! We have a morning training session to get on with! Out of the way, everybody! Out of the way, please!"

iii

"Keep away from Jacky!" Mary ordered.

"You don't own him," said Britt.

"He's my husband and the father of my child and if you think I'm going to let you take him off us and mess up all our lives, you're wrong!"

"You don't own him, you don't own me, and you don't tell me what to do! You were lucky – you saw him first. But you didn't love him enough to keep him, did you?"

"Don't talk about love! You don't know the meaning of the word! You're after his money and what you can get out of him, exactly as you've done with Chuck Bengtsson, that senator, and every other man you've had anything to do with!" Mary pointed at the mansion behind the blonde then gestured at its grounds around them. "You don't pay a penny piece for all this, do you?! Rent free as thanks for fucking Chuck Bengtsson!"

"Such language."

"Don't play the lady with me, Britt Anderson! You're a high class prostitute who picks her clients with a view to how much she can get out of them. Well, you've got your contracts with Jacky and you've made your money, but you're not having Jacky!"

"Says his slave owner who's lived off his back all these years, and used him as her meal ticket!"

"You know more about that than I do!" Mary's peering eyes and head indicated the building and vicinity. "You have the experience."

"Not of marital vice masquerading as virtue, convention as corruption eating a man alive from within year by year as you have with Jacky."

"On vice and corruption, you're the authority, not I."

"Who kept you in comfort while you took your degrees? Jacky! Who's had everything she ever wanted off him simply by taking it?! You!"

"I'm his wife."

Britt's laugh was a battle cry. "As if that explains everything!! All the big and little disappointments and defeats you've caused him over the years! The hurt and suffering he's had to hide because he daren't let it show because of you!"

"Jacky tells me everything!"

"And you don't listen! didn't! haven't! I would! do! shall!"

"You won't! Because you're not seeing him again. He's not having anything more to do with you!"

"He'll decide that! not you! And I shall too!"

"We'll see!"

"Yes, we'll see!"

"You think you could live with Jacky every day forever?! You?! You'd tear him to pieces! You're as hard as nails! You might manage it for a month or two, till the novelty wears off! You couldn't stand the humdrummity of cleaning a house, cooking, seeing that everything functioned perfectly for a man who spends his life travelling, playing football, training, training, training, for ever bettering his footballing skills as Jacky does!"

"Oh yes! And having his children too!"

"Never! You'd betray him with every man who took your fancy and strip him of everything he had! ruin him! and when you'd finished, leave him or throw him out, utterly destroyed! You're ruthless, cold, heartless! But you're not having Jacky to claw to death!"

"'Claw to death'?! That's all you've ever done all your married life! Ruthless?! cold?! heartless?! – you've stopped him at every inch of his way whenever he's tried to do anything *you* didn't like."

"He said that?"

"He didn't have to! But he did say it – it was there in every word he spoke, for anyone who was listening to hear it, how you organised his life to suit *you* and not caring a damn about him when it came to a straight choice of what you wanted and what he wanted! Your whole life has been one long sequence of what *you* wanted, *you* decided!"

Mary was defensive for the first time: "That's not true."

"Then why does he still dream of playing football in Germany and Italy or elsewhere?! Why did he sleep with me?! If he'd been mine as long as yours, he'd never need to look at another woman, never want! They'd have had to have killed me before they'd got me away from him when that murderer was after him, if I'd been his wife!"

"You were in Quebec busy making money and sleeping with Chuck Bengtsson!"

"Money's nothing if I had Jacky!"

"So you haven't got him?" Mary realised. Britt half-turned away.

iv

Wyckliffe was friendly: "How are you feeling?"

"Okay," said Jacky. "No. Worried."

"As to your private life, that's private," said Wyckliffe. "All I'm interested in is your game," he wanted to know.

"That'll be alright," Jacky assured him.

"The F.A. have been at me over you. The business with Britt Anderson, Mary and the episode this morning with Benny Cawthorne are making the headlines. I am, too, for not disciplining you. I just want you to know I'll support you."

"Thanks."

"If you need any help, let me know straight away."

"My mother will be worrying. She always does when the Tory news media attack me."

v

The Northwestern University stadium office's walls were pale green, hung with charts, lined with dark green metal filing cabinets; muscles rippled in his right forearm holding the phone.

Jacky listened to Britt summarising her clash that morning: Mary would never willingly relinquish Jacky. Britt understood everything, would always be there when he needed her, sketched dreams of their future domesticity together where he heard both yearning little girl and maternal woman.

Smell of sweat and liniment from outside, voices talking, laughing; the muscles of his legs neat in their football gear.

Lulled by her voice and the unreality of reality, his judgement floated, almost detached, almost impartial: all would be well, no need to worry: convention required his ending with Britt, yet he would not because he liked her, and a complete and sudden rift would be wrong and the worst.

"I'm truly sorry about all this uproar and scandal, Jacky."

"So am I." He took responsibility: "It's my fault."

"Mine, too. I don't tell them anything. I shan't. Ever." She analysed and reasoned, emotion nearly constrained: the present time would go, the World Cup competition end, they would be back in England, she would safeguard his interests, be discreet, always be there when needed.

Confused as to what to do, Jacky was honest: her beauty had overawed him, still did, he told her, her feelings toward him flattered him, made him both proud and frightened, given a fair chance together, they might have made a good couple.

"But I have Mary – and Jessie – and she's jealous. And then I've got the World Cup, and all the people after me, and at me, and on me, everything around me. It'll definitely be upsetting my mother. She's been badly, I told you."

She freed him quietly and completely: "No demands, Jacky: – I'm here, there, wherever, whenever you need me."

"You deserve better than this, lass," he was humbled and troubled. Along the passage, several England squad members were calling for him to be fetched, training was starting.

"I'll see your interests are looked after," she reiterated, her voice held longing, and wistful acceptance.

vi

The sun splashed its 87°F in 82H sweat sliming Jacky doing press-ups in unison with Colin Greenhalgh to his left and Jed Lennox and Benny Cawthorne to his right.

Mary would attack him and nag him: he was not looking forward to it, but he could stand it; he deserved it – he had given her his word and broken it. He was not God, he was not made of steel, he was fallible, he would be a good and dutiful husband now that she was here, with her woman's body to make love to and her support and friendship. Britt Anderson's vision enticed, but she was not the present. The killer was dead. Mary had come back. In spite of everything. It would all sort itself out fairly well eventually. The Tory Press and rightwingers were after him like the rabid frothing-at-the-mouth hyenas they were – he grinned at his overstatement, knowing it was a phrase of his socialist father's, became aware of his panting and plenteous sweat, the grass blades and soil and Curly Greenhalgh gasping: "Forty-one, forty-two –"

But the Tory Press, news media and rightwingers in general WERE always after him, WERE servants and arselickers of the multimillionaire Big Rich and conservative Establishment who despised football anyway as typically working class and therefore, in private, and sometimes in public, to be belittled and sneered at.

""Forty-nine, fifty, phew! Bloody Christ!" all four came to their feet, "it's hot!"

"It's lovely weather, Curly!" replied Benny. "Just right for a day at the seaside!" All four continued their exercises.

Jed Lennox gasped: "Wheere's the ice cream man then?!"

"He's coming over there, look!" the Cockney panted, moving in rhythm with the others: Wyckliffe was crossing the turf towards them from the tunnel.

"You want to ask him for some for your black eye!" said Curly. "It's a right bloody mess!"

"It'll be alright tomorrah!"

"I'm sorry, Ben!" Jacky squeezed out.

"Serves me right for walking into a family row and not ducking! Wyckliffe's beckoning you!"

"I've just had a phone call from your brother, Harry," Wyckliffe was very serious.

"What?"

"I've got bad news." Wyckliffe paused. His voice was gentle: "Your mother passed away half an hour ago."

Jacky kept it surface, repressing the lurch inside: "Oh? Well, she'd been ill. We expected it could happen. What was it? Another stroke?"

"Yes."

Realisation, like an earthquake chunking and crunching a granite plateau, smashed then splintered convention: he would never see her again, never. Never. He moaned, and his head writhed in dulled, fought-and-lost-against agony. He ran for the exit, groaning, sobbing tears not wanting to come, conscious that his reaction was futile, would change nothing, yet unable to control the inexorable, huge pressures within him.

He reached the stand's shadows, stopped and leant against the wall with his head bent against his left forearm, sobbing almost drily, his horror and suffering too vast to find easy escape in copious tears and sound.

In the sunlight, against the green grass, blue sky, the whiteness of the open seating and the stands' shaded darkness, one by one, on receiving the news, the England squad stopped training to stand and stare at the white-shirted bowed figure of their colleague in the tunnel exit.

CHAPTER 69

That little, brick building with its red-tiled roof with lilac bushes and long grass tangling about it was the morgue. In it, his mother.

Not wanting to go in, Jacky turned away. His dull heavy near-total repression of feeling was scarcely scratched and pecked at by present awareness and conscious thought. Sparrows were chirping. A blackbird was singing on the bough above the bramble thicket ten yards ahead slightly off to his left. A summer wilderness of grass and dog-daisies. Honeysuckle. That was a yew tree. And that was an oak. The barkless tree, gaunt against the blue with its three white fluffy clouds, was an elm. Dead.

Like his mam.

A yellowhammer flitted swooping and swift from left to right and out of sight. A chaffinch sang pink-pink, pink-pink.

His mother was dead.

He could not believe it. She was at home somewhere. And he would go back to America and play in the World Cup as he had told Wyckliffe. They had beaten China four-nil without him. Jingo Byrnes was world class. Old Jingo. Curly had missed a penalty. You should never miss penalties. The Italians were through to the quarter-finals, too. It would be them or the Germans in the semi. He preferred the Germans: Angelo had kicked his head.

"My mam's dead," he said aloud. He could not believe it, but he knew she was and nothing seemed or was important beside that: the World Cup, the Mary/Britt situation; Britt was in Sheffield waiting for him to ring – there if he needed her, wanted her –, and Mary, she never talked about Britt and him, did not know Britt had flown to England by private jet. He would not call Britt, had told her so; she had said she would be there anyway whenever wherever he needed her.

And Mary – she never mentioned Britt –, she was kind. Protected Jessie from his grief.

Everybody blamed him for the shock and stress that had killed his mother. His sister, Joanna, his brothers. No, Harry did not. Nor did others. He had not killed her – she had been a sick woman who could have died at any time for any reason, the doctor said, Mary said, he himself knew.

"You can go in behind the glass panelling," the woman mortuary attendant said softly, "if you want to stand beside her."

Jacky shook his head: he could see all he did not wish: it was his mother lying under that white sheet four yards away, no doubt of that. The skin at the back of his skull etched revulsion, his body seemed light and insubstantial, fear an endlessness of death, longing to save her, knowing yet not accepting that she was dead. Memory of her alive so short a time before, of her laughing and healthy when younger, her kindness and affection for him.

Emotion came huge and sudden.

"Are you alright?" the woman murmured concerned, and pulled the cord that closed the curtains behind the glass.

Head twisted aside, Jacky nodded, choking down sorrow and squeezing eyelids together, unsuccessful against tears. The woman spoke platitudes about death, evidencing her own mother's two years previously. Jacky nodded and murmured, conventional.

Yet what were her words and attitudes or those of any of them to him? His mother was dead. Dead. Nothing would bring her back. Nothing. Nothing meant anything beside that.

CHAPTER 70

"You killed her! you whore-mongering little bastard!" Jacky stared beyond his sister's head through the window overlooking the Trent valley. His two youngest brothers were to his left near the fireplace, Joanna's husband near the door, Harry near the fireplace. "Mary's the best wife a man could have and you betrayed her, whored behind her back, didn't give a damn about her or your daughter or the suffering you'd give to others when the scandal broke!" She howled her grief: "You *knew* how ill Mother was!! You KNEW!! You killed her!!"

"No!" Harry said sharply. "She could have died at any time, we all knew."

Joanna was intent on Jacky: "You're satisfied now?!! You got what you wanted?!!" Her husband muttered her name reprovingly and was ignored. "All she wanted was peace and quiet," Joanna's voice broke. She attacked through her sobs. "She *needed* rest to get better. She told me she'd asked you again and again not to get involved in politics, television shows, controversies, because it upset and worried her so! But you didn't care! You wouldn't listen! You never have! All your life!" She was controlled and sincere in her spite. "Even when you were a baby and a boy, you had to have everything *your* way! Selfish to the core! She humoured you because you were a boy, while I had to look after all of *you*," she rounded on her brothers, "and do all the housework and stop in because I was a girl and girls had to do those things! I hated it! Hated it!!! And Johnner spoiled you, and pampered you because you were a boy and played football! I hate football!! It's the stupidest, worst, most boring game ever invented!! A lot of ignorant morons kicking a ball about watched by cretins!! A useless activity, utterly pointless!! And they pay millions and give illiterate halfwit clods huge sums for that?! It's monstrous! They shouldn't get a penny piece! Wasting lives and time on that! It's something to be ashamed of, not proud! Who are *you* to get up and go on television and pontificate and lay down the law as if you were God Almighty? just because you're good at kicking a stupid football about! It's sickening! having to put up with your going around spouting Johnner's worthless old socialist propaganda and rubbish!"

"It's not rubbish," said Harry.

"It is! All of it! If he had treated my mother better and properly, she wouldn't have been so ill," she choked in sorrow, but let rage pull her through. "He had to be the Big Man, always the Big Man, never listened to anybody! He always knew best did Johnner! Oh yes, he told them, the Big Man –," in a gruff, hate-edged imitation of their dead father, she quoted: "So I asked them for my cards and money!' But he didn't think of his family at home in poverty going short and my mother having to go out and char and work on the land to earn enough to buy her kids clothes and see there was enough to eat because the Big Man was out of a job again!" She sneered: "His socialist rubbish, campaigning for the Labour Party and the nationalised, state-owned paradise! He was always boasting how clever he was, and yet he spent all his life as a penniless labourer! If he were *so* good and *so* intelligent, why didn't he use his brains to make something better of himself?! study, get a good job, make a success of himself instead of wasting his money killing himself smoking eighty fags a day while my mother did not even have a respectable dress, apart from that little old green one she had for best all the time I was a little girl, and his kids barely had rags enough to be decent in!! He made her old before her time, and you," she stared her hate at Jacky, "killed her."

"No!" said Harry fierily. "He didn't! And stop saying he did – or clear off back to Wales!"

His brother-in-law protested warningly: "Now then!"

"And you and all!" Harry told him. "Jacky's had enough trouble and problems without you buggers getting at him!"

Joanna was intransigent: "He killed her." The two youngest brothers, both near tears, made agreeing sounds.

"No!" Harry was equally intransigent.

"Let her speak, if it makes her feel better," said Jacky in a low voice. "Let them all say what they want," his head was bent, his left hand pressed unavailingly kneading his forehead against sorrow.

His sister was relentless: "You go out training kicking your football as if nothing had happened!"

"There's nothing else I can do," Jacky said dully.

"You'll go back to America and play in your stupid World Cup as if nothing's happened! while my mother's – my mother's – " she choked on tears.

"I don't want to," said Jacky dully. "I don't want to do anything." The heaviness that was death, life's inevitable, ultimate futility, numbed all feeling: he saw but did not notice the valley's beauty in the warm sunlight; his sister's husband was comforting her; his two youngest brothers were crying; Harry's head was bent, face suffering, shoulders moving from side to side. "Nothing's important any more."

CHAPTER 71

i

"Will you go back to America?" his mother's cousin asked.

"No," Jacky told her. "Not now."

"I haven't met your wife."

"She's at her mother's with our little girl." Jacky excused himself and went to stand and look down at his mother in the coffin. Her hand was hard and cold from the mortuary freezer, her face a mask, lifeless. His sister was crying silently against her husband's shoulder in the far corner by the bay window, Harry was talking to cousins by the empty fireplace. The room was crowded with relatives he had not seen since a child.

On the pathway outside, smoking cigarettes and chatting, the Danethorpe Co-operative Society undertakers. People on the roadside, many with cameras. Journalists.

Let them all come, do their worst, it did not matter any more what they did. She was gone.

His head was light, he felt dizzy, as though huge empty bubbles were rising up from his deadness. The day was dull, the trees dark green, the grass and countryside lush. Here and there through the clouds, pale blueness. Smoke from chimneys in the village. A little breeze. To feel was agony. So he did not feel.

ii

In the church, emotion choked his throat, but he concentrated on the hymns and let his tears fall as they might.

Along the gravel path from the church to the waiting cars, he listened to the crunch of his and others' footsteps and smelled the freshness of the air and saw the people outside the churchyard railings, many taking photographs.

In the cemetery, he noticed the different greens of grass and bushes and trees, the flowers at various graves, the wind rippling them and the vicar's white and black robes. Grey sky. A few drops of rain. The pile of earth marked the waiting tomb.

He did not listen to the parson's words. In that pale brown wood, with its nailed-down lid engraved ELSPETH DAY NEE BARKER, AGED 56 was his mother. She was there! He would never see her again! Never!

He cried, doubled over, rocking in the agony of loss, emotion urging him to leap into the grave, tear open the coffin, bring her back to life! Yet he knew she was dead, such an act unavailing. Others were crying. Their grief meant nothing to him: his own sorrow and life's endless loneliness and futility were too much to bear.

iii

Mary stared at Harry's immobile features, hazy in her girlhood bedroom's gloom. "Billy Woo will be safe in Nottingham. If he stays in London, Lee Kwang Yoo will probably kill him," Harry's voice was monotone.

Mary twisted round on her chair bending double over her writing table and lecture notes, hiding her visage in her hands: "Horrible! Horrible!" Realising, she jerked to face him: "You're in danger! They'll come for you, Harry!"

Emotionless, he shook his head: "Internal Chinese matter – they told him my debt to Lee Kwang Yoo was settled, his wasn't. Then they started on him. Lucky the police arrived."

Mary shuddered: "A broken arm! Poor boy!" Through the bedroom floorboards, her father's impassioned despair at a goal in the England match sat her upright, attentive to the adjacent bedroom where Jessica lay asleep; she stamped to warn those below about the noise.

"My fault," Harry tonelessly accepted responsibility. "That's why I must help him. Lee Kwang Yoo will never know."

Fear at death's certainty drove Jacky sprinting, maintaining perfect ball control, across the meadow toward the thirty-yard distant white blob, his other football. Memories of his mother's corpse in her coffin. Horror and sorrow.

He left footed a swerving sixty yarder at the five barred gate into the next field, and dribbled his second ball, zigzagging and feinting, unconscious of his lead-weighted training jacket, his sweating, his harsh breath. She was gone. Forever! Forever!

He cried wheezingly, concentrating on quick precise dribbling to maintain his sanity and guide his torment.

His sister's hatred halted him motionless, for some seconds vitiating and estranging for him the carmine and aureate sunset, its sheen on the Trent, the tranquil gloaming.

Harry was right: Joanna blamed him for her own guilt and shortcomings.

"I did cause Else's death," Jacky told the grassland and river, "but she was ill. She could have had that fatal stroke at any time." The admission was a conviction absolving him of guilt but not grief. Memories of his mother a few weeks previously caused tears without his realising it. Three quarters of a mile away, across the next field, someone was jogging along the river-bank.

Terror of death.

She was not dead.

But she was.

His sister and youngest brothers judged him guilty.

The Tory Press and news media, also: their condolences merely added venom to their criticism. Mary did not. Britt did not, waiting for him in Sheffield, for a message he would not send, had told her he could not send.

Harry defended him. Was that because he had helped Harry with the Chinese? No. Harry understood their mother's illness.

Jacky stared across the river noting the dim light. What did it matter what anyone thought? It did not. What did anything matter? The Chinese, their gang war. Trivial, all meaningless, nothing meant much with Else gone.

He lunged to sprint swaying and curving, jinking, ball under control, sobbing, recalling his mother in younger days, smiling, laughing, glad, taking him for walks as a little boy on Sunday afternoons across these fields, racing him, chasing him, being chased by him. Oh Mam! Mam! pain tore out tears as he ran.

Approaching the field gate, he lofted toward an eighty-yard distant cattle trough, and sprinted full speed to vault the gate and flick his other football up and ran fast with it kicking it alternately with left foot then right not letting it strike the ground.

He halted abruptly, lowered the leather inert on his right foot to the grass. Why bother with this? It was meaningless. He had begun with football because of his dad. Johnner was dead. His mother, too.

Fear and grief made him stare, head twisting, face contorting, at the fields with their bushy trees and high hedges, the dusky sky, refulgent west and river. The approaching runner trotted nearer.

What did football matter? Nothing. He had played it for his dad and because he was good at it, liked the feeling of accomplishment and purpose it gave, the cheers and glory, and later, the money and fame. It meant nothing beside Else's mortality.

To go back to America, do his best, be attacked and publicised, he did not want it any more. Only safety, security from hurt.

Mary never spoke about Britt; she held that against him; but otherwise gave him every sympathy. Britt wanted him, flying all the way back to wait, anonymous in Sheffield.

It was a mixed-up mess with everybody hurt and nobody happy except the scandalmongers and muckraking journalists who had killed his mother with their troublemaking.

He bent double, forearms in front of his face, hands over his head, ineffectively shielding against the agony of her being gone, his terror at his own inevitable annihilation and the knowledge that he had given his enemies their occasion and was therefore the most culpable.

Everyone hated him.

Yet that was not so. Among the representatives from every family in the village who had been in the church had been most of his old Trenton F.C. boyhood team-mates, including Pete Gregg, who had kept an eye on things for him and looked after his mother's interests, the runner coming across the field towards him.

I don't want Jacky to return to America! Mary gazed unseeing at her lecture jottings. Wehrman is dead but those Vietnam veteran friends of his the F.B.I. knows Wehrman wrote to are not! They'll kill Jacky if he returns! But he won't. He says he won't!

Mary regarded the twilit garden, hating Britt Anderson, wanting to scratch her face, bite and beat her, destroy her beauty, kill her, imagining a Nazi assassin's bullet striking the blonde woman instead of Jacky.

Blood red and death purple, gold wealth and mood indigo, symbols for your civilised savage, Mary, objective, judged the sunset.

And now this Chinese gangster business resurrects itself, oozing fresh distress.

Logic checked her apprehension: Harry and Jacky were safe, the Chinese boy had said so – he knew his people.

From below, muted hubbub from the game, and praise for Jingo Byrnes. No sound from Jessie's room.

I hope England lose, she thought. Guilt at disloyalty strove vainly with honesty. Defeat meant Jacky would be safe, would abolish the choice to return or stay. Would secure him from Britt Anderson. Mary's relief mingled with regret at England's impending failure.

She could work undisturbed at Bio Veracity. Jacky could heal his grief in peace. Look after little Jessica. If only she could become pregnant again! Preferably a boy. For Jacky, a son. For Jessie, a companion. It would bond them together. Totally shut out Britt Anderson. Compensate Jacky for losing his mother. Poor old Else.

Memories came, and, with them, sorrow. Mary closed her eyes, tears spurting.

"Jim's scored!" tensed her alert.

"Are y' alright, boy?"

"Ye'. I'd've thought you'd've been watching the match. It's on now, i'nt it?"

"M' missis was talking to y' sister and brothers. So I thought I'd come down and join you. It's gerrin' dark. Y' can bre'k a leg easy as owt here – too many bloody potholes and ruts about in these here marshes."

"It didn't matter. Nothing does much now."

Pete Gregg was serious, voice low: "I know how you feel, boy. I've been through it m'sen wi' my own mam. Nothin' anybody can say can help. But you've only got friends around here, boy, you know that." Jacky began to cry. With his bowed head, a small figure beside the 6'2", 16 stone Gregg, both tiny in the fifty acre field under the blue-black sky. The farmer went on quietly: "It's not the same for y' mother as with y' father because he nivver meant as much to you."

"It was my fault she died!" Jacky had trouble articulating.

"It wasn't! It w' nobody's. She was a sick woman, y' mam. A good sort. One o' the best." Jacky cried freely. "Everybody 'round here knows that, Jacky. And as to all that shit they write and talk about some girlfriend you've had besides Mary, your mam would have stuck up for you again' 'em all, you know she would, like she al'ays did. She wouldn't ha' blamed y', not her! Christ, boy, if my missis found out how many women I've had on the sly this past ten year –!"

Jacky grinned through his tears at the burly farmer's delivery.

"Ay," said Gregg, "and if you think of all the other married men who've fancied a bit of variety –."

"It's not like that."

"Well, the point is, nobody's perfect, and nobody's blamin' you. Your mam wouldn't, that's for sure. And she wouldn't have let anybody be nasty about you or pull you to pieces unanswered while she was around." Jacky was smiling, blinking away tears. "She was proud on all you lot, all her kids. Especially you and Harry. But all on you. Iv'ry one. She didn't know owt about football, though, y' mam."

Jacky grinned, tears ceased: "She wasn't interested."

"She didn't care whether you won or lost. You were still her son."

"Yih."

Side by side, they stood looking west over the river and countryside engloomed save for the vanished sun's glow.

"Brazil are good. They look like finishing up in the Final. Zezinho, Barboza the Bomber, Vivi," the big farmer was smiling, "Pedro Maluf, Lopez," chuckling, he relished the un-English names, "Chico and Lulu and Dudu. And the Black Bludgeon," he was serious, "he's a rough bugger is that Paolo Souza. He's gotten away wi' some very bad fouls the ref. hasn't seen or else let the other team play on because they had the advantage. He's in Angelo's class is that bastard, when it comes to dirty tricks and putting the boot in. How's your head, boy? I've noticed you've fought shy of heading the ball or gerring bashed on her."

"It's alright."

The big man declared: "The Italians are good – you can't take that off of 'em. But, oh, they do get on my tits! Waggin' their bloody arms about and arguing o'er nowt! And rollin' in agony on the bloody ground when they haven't even been touched! And all the dirty tricks they've got! Angelo's the worst, but some o' them other buggers aren't far behind him – Villotti the villain and Sindona the sinner, and Renato Calvi, and Pietro Gelli, that bloody big girl! That's what they remind me on, the lot on 'em, a load of big girls! wavin' their bloody arms about, and screamin' and yawpin', and stickin' their chins and their arses out and putting their hands on their hips, like a lot of bloody women!" Jacky, though numb inside, was smiling at the big man's disgust and vehemence. Pete Gregg noticed. He softened: "Well, they do. Mind you, they can play football. Bloody skilful players! But, oh, the bastards do get on my tits with all that fuckin' about! When are you off back? Tomorrow afternoon?"

"I'm not off back."

"You're not?! Well," the burly farmer became quiet, gazing over the dark countryside, "it's understandable, I suppose."

"Football doesn't mean anything to me now. Nothing does."

"Your mam would have wanted you to ha' gone back, I reckon, Jacky. Old Johnner, your dad, would. All on uz who've played wi' y' or again' y' in Danethorpe and district would. An' a few million others, I durst bet on that. But I can understand if you don't want to. It's natural enough."

So Bobby Milburne had scored and Jingo Byrnes was magnificent and England were going through to the semi-finals: Mary eyed through her open window the constellations speckling the pale dusk.

Jacky will have to return to America, she decided. Then shuddered in fear, hunched double, arms pressed to her sides, hands protecting her face, voice in her mind shouting no.

Yes, she insisted levelly, he must return.

To murderers?!

The F.B.I. and security guards will protect him.

And Britt Anderson?

I and Jessie shall go with him, she responded calmly. The blonde bitch – her composure broke – shall not come near him! Mary was rational: I shall, in strict confidence, tell Wyckliffe it is my absolute condition for Jacky's return. I shall stop all future contact between Britt Anderson and Jacky.

She gazed westwards: Shades of darkness and summer night, and Jacky training in the marshes.

His whole life was football, since he could toddle. It would destroy him and their marriage if the World Cup passed by without him. He would always regret not going back. At first, he would not reproach her. But later, he would. For she had deserted him in America when he had needed her. She had not realised how immensely. Now, when he was shattered in spirit and needed her as never before, she must not fail him.

Mary, picturing Wolf Wehrman, quivered in atavistic fear. Other assassins would attempt to kill Jacky, herself and Jessie. Oh, she did not want to go back! She did not want to go back!

Sound of Pete Gregg in the room below.

Elspeth Day's grave was covered with flowers, her husband's adjacent, also. A quarter of a mile away, east of where he stood, Jacky stared at the lights of the village's nearest houses, the street lamps' orange aura. When he had been a boy, there had been no street lamps. On the hill ridge above the village, light shone in the front room window of his mother's house.

His head bent and he cried: his mother was not there any more: she was six feet under that flower-strewn earth in a box. Terror at death, then sharpest sadness: memories of his mother, laughing and gentle, playing games with him as a little boy, showing him kindness and generosity and the tenderest affection. "Oh Mam, Mam!" he spoke as if she could hear, he knew she could not, yet wanted her to hear, be alive in spirit, not gone – not for ever, though he knew she was.

He cried even more.

That she was dead made everything meaningless. What was the point of life? To be born to die. Logic told him grief must pass, lessen with years, as it had with Johnner: but he did not feel it. He gazed at his father's grave. Old Johnner. Losing Else was far worse. He had not realised how much she had meant to him.

Memories and emotion kept coming; he could not repress his anguish and tears, did not wish to.

"Jacky," Mary's voice was soft. He turned toward her. Behind her, the gravestones, hedges, bushes and trees were dark blobs in the night. "It's time to go home."

"No."

"It won't help, staying here," she said gently. "You could catch a chill, you've only got your tracksuit on. You've been out training and sweating hard."

"It doesn't matter. Nothing matters now," he said dully.

"Your mother wouldn't have wanted you to be ill over her."

Jacky sobbed, bent double in anguish. Needing consolation and friendship, his hand reached out gropingly. Hers were small and warm round his. "It's alright, Jacky," she said and held him close with his head over her heart. "It's alright, love," she rocked him as one would a little child.

"She's dead," his voice was tiny, grief-stricken. "She's dead. M' mam's dead." And he cried and cried while she stood rocking him, soothing him, murmuring and gentle.

CHAPTER 72

i

Angelo's right shoulder struck the edge of Jacky's right ribs and solar plexus, spinning him breathless in pain, foetal hunched on his side to the turf; he accepted, welcomed his state: an atonement, a punishment for, a clean expression of his repressed agony at his mother's decease.

"The bastard! The bastard!!" Pete Gregg roared, on his feet, fists clenched, glaring at his TV screen.

"Peter! Language! Language!" his wife admonished him.

"Look! the way he did it! The ref.'s not even given him a warning, look! Look at him!" The goat-faced Angelo, compassion personified, was trotting backwards, gesturing regret. "He meant it alright! It's the tenth foul on Jacky!"

"Each time he goes down, Gabe, I think one of those two they're looking for has shot him."

"Britt, honey, neither of those guys is in'erested in your Jacky."

"You said that about Wolf Wehrman."

What did it matter what happened to him? if they kicked him, smashed him about, crippled him. Nothing could bring Else back, nothing. They would be laughing, his sister, the news media and poison pen letter writers who judged him guilty as a heartless, selfish glory-seeker for coming back to the World Cup.

Millions of others did not hate him.

Not Mary.

And Britt did not hate him wherever she was.

Bobby Milburne's leftfooter smacked the juncture of crossbar and post and bounced a yard in front of the goal and ten up in the air.

Sindona's grip on Jim Arrowood's sweating right forearm as they jumped together brought blood, the Englishman's elbow in the Italian's stomach and a foul to Italy.

"Neither the guy here in Washington, Calhoun, nor the New Yorker, Henry Puzenko, had direct contact with Wehrman. Calhoun vanished six weeks ago after talking to some Hell's Angels. And Puzenko went missing last February. The only reason the police are in'erested in 'em is because they once knew Wehrman."

Death's certainty: fear like a hollow roar, endless in loneliness.

Mary's kindness filling the void gave partial relief.

Mary had been gentle and helpful in every way. But not concerning Britt. She refused to talk about Britt – but they must.

It was over with Britt.

Yet above the chasm of death and sorrow, Mary's condemnation and his enemies' moralising hate, he still wanted to make love to her.

Villotti, tackling Jingo Byrnes in the centre circle, kicked late, then, simulating agony, twisted and rolled about at least three times as much as his victim.

Gelli and Bobby Milburne collided when springing at an awkwardly spinning ball: Gelli kneed the teenager in the testicles as they fell, butted him under the chin, and struggled up grinding his elbow into the youth's left kidney.

The Italian defence sprinted as one man. Jim Arrowood about to score from Jingo's through pass, Winston Jones and Curly Greenhalgh were all offside.

Paulo Maccinccussi took the free kick rapidly to Sindona who kicked instantly to his right wing where Fellici running onto the ball centred for Albino Luciani who, at top speed, slashed twenty yards diagonally forward for Bellini sprinting in from the left wing to sway round Eddy

Corelli five yards outside the England penalty area, thus forcing Richard Trelawney to cover and leave a three yard gap for no more than the fifth of a second it would have taken Benny Cawthorne, already moving, to block.

Albino Luciani's eighteen yarder beat Berrigan's dive.

"Italia!! Italia!! Italia!!" Thousands of green-white-red striped flags and chianti bottles waved. Fireworks exploded. In Italy, car horns hooted in near-empty streets mingling with the cheers from millions of windows opened wide in the hot night air.

He should feel desperation at being a goal down in the semi-final of the World Cup, display, like his team-mates, anxious haste to re-start the game, equalise, and win. But Else was dead. As he himself would be. As would the 92,400 crowd about him in the John Fitzgerald Kennedy Stadium, Philadelphia, U.S.A., the millions watching, listening around the world, all life on Earth, the Earth itself, the Sun, everything: it would all vanish and be no more.

Realisation floated terror which to avoid he ran for the centre circle and oblivion in action.

Was Jacky the only man for her? Britt considered, detached. Yes, yes! her yearning replied instantly. She controlled it: play continued quick and complex in and around the South Europeans' penalty area, with eight Englishmen against nine Italians. She had never met a man whose needs and qualities melded so numerously and easily with her own. Life with Jacky was harmony, warmth into ecstasy, balanced tranquillity. She closed her eyes, inhaling delicately, recalling his smell, his presence, their lovemaking, their mutual serenity. Opening them, she watched him dribble round two opponents and pass to Jingo Byrnes. Infatuated bias, she tried to dismiss her feelings. With my background, she thought, cynical yet realistic. Vistas of barren family life. Sexual relief in stunted relationships. The aridity of business success and material wealth. Life wasting by.

Albino Luciani's culmination of the Italian counter-attack bounced off the crossbar: Richard Trelawney out-jumped the Italian to head clear. Fellici half-beat Eddy Corelli, backheeled to Bellini, Benny Cawthorne prodded to Jingo Byrnes who throughballed for Jacky accelerating clear of Angelo outside the centre circle.

Angelo's toecap seared agony near his right kneecap, studs wrenching skin and flesh.

Through his convulsions, Jacky accepted pain as salvation, aware of his sweat and the heat and humidity in the mid-eighties and of his having put England's forwards past the Italian defence.

"He's crippled Jacky!"

The Senator said nothing. On the television screen, Bobby Milburne's goal curved in slow motion. Through the white curtains behind the TV set, Washington D.C. gleamed in the late afternoon sunlight.

Flat on his back a yard outside the touchline, Jacky gasped, wheezing: "It'll be alright! Give it a minute or two, and I'll go back on again." The doctor looked hard at him, the physiotherapist concentrated on his task.

Watching him, Britt yearned to hold him, take his suffering on herself. A close-up of Jacky's grimacing visage, head wrenching aside incised her with apprehension: What if he did not want her?! He had not rung, contacted her – she must meet him! She half-turned her head for aid from her companion – No! I will wait, I should wait, I must wait!

Bobby Milburne, scrambling on all fours after colliding with Sindona near the centre spot, saw the two-foot high ball spin loose toward and across him. He dived to head to Jim Arrowood. Angelo kicked both skull and ball.

"That's more lahk real football, American football," drawled Louella Lyle's father; he popped open a can of beer and sprayed his freshly laundered police uniform. "Goldarn it! All over mah beautiful clean things! Too durned bad it warn't that black was kicked in the hay-ud. 'You sure Louella is sick up in her room, Momma?" His wife, smiling, held up a key. "She ain't a-goin' to no Philadelphia lahk she done told B'lly Joe to see no black. No, sir, bah Gawd she ain't! We done spoiled that li'l' girl of ours, Momma. We sure didn't raise her to run after blacks, no sir! She must have gotten it off o' them god-damned Yankees on the television! Ah don't know whut the world's a-coming to, Momma. The sooner she's a-married to B'lly Joe, the better for ever'body, Ah reckon."

ii

"That bastard, Angelo, eh?! If I get near him, I'll break his facking back!" Benny Cawthorne panted, and swallowed sports drink.

"You alright, Jacky?" Wyckliffe inquired. "Your leg okay?" Jacky nodded, manner untroubled; the cuts stung but were clean and disinfected, tonight the scabs would form, tomorrow his thigh would be bruised – his mother would not be worrying about this injury. Never again. Head bent, left hand covering quick tears, emotional memories, surging, burning, controlled him utterly. "You're sure you're okay?" Wyckliffe was anxious.

Jacky nodded, sobbing. The others were sympathetic or silent. After some seconds, Jacky forced out: "The match! The match, Denzil!"

Wyckliffe analysed, others participated. The Italians had no weakness. England's goal had come from a fast response to a counter-attack. Exceptional speed plus diversity and instant utilisation of quarter-chances remained essential. England were better in the air.

"Poor old Bobby," said Eddy Corelli. Benny Cawthorne cursed and threatened. Jim Arrowood and Curly Greenhalgh expressed their sentiments about the Italian defence and showed their bruises.

Jed Lennox summed up the general discussion: "They rarely do owt the ref. can show 'em a card for, though."

"What about those fouls on Bobby and Jacky then?" Eddy Corelli was indignant.

"They're smart. They t'ke their chances. The ref. has to give 'em the benefit of the doubt all the time."

Sid Garner said: "The left back keeps spitting in my face and insulting me trying to get me mad. But that bloody Italian accent's so funny, it makes me laugh."

"He wants you to hit him," said Benny Cawthorne, "then you'd get sent off."

"I hope Bobby will be alright," said Eddy Corelli.

"They'll be x-raying him now," Wyckliffe frowned, worried.

iii

The sounds and setting and patterns of players seemed a dream no part of him. They were real, himself sprinting over the turf, Angelo's grasp on his shirt, real. His quickness, precision in lifting the ball over Gelli and Maccinccussi to Winston Jones, reflexes to old patterns.

He saw the keeper fumble Winston's hard attempt, Jim Arrowood would score off the rebound.

Jacky felt no elation, let himself hear the crowd: "England! England!" Jingo and Winston and Sid were running to congratulate the goalscorer. The Italians were crowded round the referee, shouting, gesticulating, throwing tantrums.

What did it matter? Jacky stared down at the turf in front of him, seeing the individual grass blades and soil, feeling the heat, humidity, his sweat, scarcely aware of sound. It was only a game. Football. Semi-final of the World Cup: what did it matter?

"You alright, Jacky?" Richard Trelawney's hand touched his shoulder.

Fellici, dribbling swift and dodging against Jed Lennox, backheeled right-angled unexpectedly to Bellini who chipped instantly over Benny Cawthorne for Luciani to volley-curve past Richard Trelawney and force a three yard, one-handed diving save round the post from Joe Berrigan.

"Beautiful," Pete Gregg sighed with relief and admiration. "Lovely football. There's no doubt the Eye-ties can play. But, oh, why don't they do it all the time?! instead of all their dirty little tricks and fouls and chucking their arms about in the air and shouting and gorming like a lot o' bloody lasses!"

"But there haven't been any fouls these past ten minutes since England's goal," his wife protested.

"That's 'cause the buggers are trying to equalise!" Gaze intent on the screen, he exclaimed: "Head it, Jacky!" The Italian high forward pass to the sprinting, unmarked Bellini had England suddenly vulnerable.

Instinctive fear bade no, logic and contempt of brain damage rammed Jacky's forehead at the ball knocking it thirty yards to Sid Garner on the wing and Jacky sprawling, savagely scornful of bodily consequence: his mother was dead, Else was dead, an assassin's bullet could smack his head apart from anywhere around the stadium, his life had been under threat ever since returning to the States; what did brain damage matter? It didn't, nor did getting kicked and knocked about on a football pitch.

"I must see him, Gabe. You must get me past those Secret Service guards."

"You yourself said it would be better to wait till after the tournament," the Senator refused her gently.

"You don't understand, Gabe. There are things you don't know."

"He's got your address and number here in Washington, Britt, honey," he argued rationally.

"He can't ring, don't you see?" Angry resentment began: "His wife's to blame. I hate her! hate her!!" taut in every sinew, Britt crouched forward in aggression: sudden nausea made her rush for the bathroom.

Concerned, the Senator gazed after her.

In less that three minutes, it would all be over, England finalists in the World Cup; emotionless, Jacky sprinted for Curly Greenhalgh's pass, a scoring chance if he outran Angelo and Sindona.

Angelo, half a pace down, tapped Jacky's right ankle as if by accident.

"He's sending Angelo off!" Pete Gregg was amazed, then, laughing, rubbed his hands in glee. "Good old ref! About bloody time! Hurray! We've won now!"

Rob Jarvis and the Swedish Finance Minister would want tickets for the final. Mary would be wondering if he were badly hurt, his mother – never again. Britt – he fled across sorrow –, where was Britt?

He opened his eyes: the referee was motioning that he be carried off; the physiotherapist's cold sponge smoothed and soothed. England supporters were singing, Italian players dancing impatience, screeching for play to re-commence.

CHAPTER 73

i

Science is more important than football, Mary watched her hypotheses sequencing in technicoloured elegance on her computer unit's screen. Resentment over having to subordinate her interests to Jacky's needs seared her upright to gaze from her twentieth storey vantage point over the motley of Philadelphia suburbia.

But football has bought you everything, this computer, access to knowledge, freedom from material want. And science is not truth and goodness unimpaired: it is often otiose; indeed, all too frequently science is a bizarre imbroglio of astute and acute malignance.

Yet football is essentially a trivial pursuit, she persisted, and contemplated Louella Lyle's room window in the low, white annex adjoining the hotel car park.

Jingo Byrnes's £1 million tax-free proposed contract with the Arab oil sheikh that morning and the multi-million pound offers to Jacky and Jim Arrowood the past few days were not trivial. At the moment, Jacky was too grief-stricken to consider them seriously, but with Jim Arrowood joking about making his fortune in Italy, and Beth Langdale telling of its art treasures and the eccentrics and shady characters among her relatives there, Jacky would be nagging her before long.

I don't want to leave home! I don't want to leave Bio-Veracity!

Amid the toy-like traffic, trees, gardens, heterogeneous architecture, Wehrman's friends – and probably others – were planning to murder Jacky, Jessie and herself. A few hours previously, Chinese gangsters hunting Billy Woo had turned up at her and Jacky's home in search of Harry. Mary inhaled deeply to arrest her panic: Jacky and Jessie were safe along the corridor with Joyce Trelawney, Richard, Jim and Beth; Harry was swallowed up by Nottingham. Benny Cawthorne was ringing his Cockney, gangster friends from an outside untapped phone while at the nightclub he and several others were visiting. Jacky would talk to him later that night. *She* did not want to see Benny Cawthorne!

Mary strove unavailingly against abhorring the Cockney – Becky Serene was in Hollyood, had left him for good, she rejoiced maliciously. He had introduced Britt Anderson to Jacky: it was right Benny Cawthorne should suffer!

Louella Lyle's window flashed ajar. Somewhere out there, her Ku Klux Klan cousin was trying to reach her and Winston Jones. Wyckliffe appeared to have abandoned the usual moral tenets: several players had had women in. After the Italian game, half the squad had got drunk. Tonight, Benny Cawthorne and seven others were visiting a downtown nightclub. Anything to relax his players and keep them happy, keep them winning. He needed Jacky.

Louella Lyle's window dazzled. Was Winston Jones visiting her? Wyckliffe would have let Britt Anderson visit Jacky if he had thought it would help.

All my income from the work done for you and the boys is being donated to research into circulatory ailments, Jacky. I want nothing from you, only to give to you, be with you, share all I am with you, my darling.

Mary's fists and face were tight with hatred. The blonde bitch's letters were torn to pieces, burnt, flushed down the toilet the moment after reading them. Her phone calls were refused. Wyckliffe had excised all communication between her and the England squad.

But what if he hadn't? What if he was lying as he had done in Chicago?! What if Jacky was with her that very minute?!

Mary compelled herself to be logical and relax.

Sorrow had riven Jacky wholly vulnerable. He needs me, she thought with relief and satisfaction.

We must talk about Britt, Mary.

We've talked. You'll never see her, contact her, have anything to do with her again. Harsh visaged, arms tightly folded under her breasts, she turned her back. She loathed Britt Anderson with a jealousy approaching hysteria. It's finished, Jacky. I was tolerant once. I know I cannot be again.

The televised chemical reactions and molecules jigged and swerved, spry and neat, engaging her intellect, soothing her. I hate Britt Anderson because I fear her, Mary analysed. She's prettier than I am. My figure's as good. She'll make love better – being a whore. Mary checked her spite, and stayed logical: Britt Anderson did not want Jacky for his money. His fame? Perhaps. The probability which increasingly resembled certainty was that the multi-millionairess, successful business bitch, oft-time whore and worldly wise Aryan goodtime girl had matured into a world-weary woman yearning for hausfrau status with a well-trained family man as her Mr Right.

She's not having Jacky! He shall not meet her, have anything to do with her!

Could she prevent it? Not if Jacky so wished. Would he? Mary fought fear. Not in his current grief. Later? He would not risk losing her and Jessie, she decided. For she would divorce him. Mary glared grimfaced at Philadelphia, the orange and quince sunburst off Louella Lyle's window.

I will not share my husband with any woman.

Behind that glass, Louella Lyle and Winston Jones were –.

Mary turned abruptly aside: her computer was playing the programme's final phase.

She had never made love to any man except Jacky. Sometimes she had wondered: – Jim Arrowood, Richard Trelawney with his enormous – No! Mary pressed her arms tightly against her sides, concentrating on Jacky, Jessie, her home: They mean more to me!

More than your career?

Yes! She wanted to hedge and qualify. Sometimes she really did resent subordinating her work to football and family. Not that Jacky had asked her to. Yes, he had! By wishing to sign for a foreign club. Now the offers were thrusting up afresh, more lucrative than before! She would do everything she could to dissuade Jacky from moving abroad. Besides, he needed peace in his sorrow. And serious interests outside and above football, such as those Robert Jarvis proposed. That was where Jacky's future lay after his playing career was finished, which it would be within the next ten or, at most, twelve years.

Would she have married Jacky if they had first met as adults and not as childhood playmates growing up in the same village? No, Mary was frank. Some fellow academic or colleague would already have been the lucky man. Honest. Outspoken. Virile. A Jacky type whom I'd have been faithful to. I needed a man in my teens!

Euphoria of first love over, affection remained. The daily domestic routines and intimacies. The blending and clash of interests and personalities. Sharing. Jessie. And, soon, hopefully, a little boy.

Life appeared so measured and secure. Yet it was only a concept, fragile in its time and space.

Or not.

For a moment, Mary's perception groped for a timeless spaceless living state.

Then rolled to ponder the familiar intricacies of evolution and natural selection through the generations of her own line via its extinct life-forms and environments, back to Life's origins.

Her existence seemed small, the world, transitory. Her computer programme's conclusions etched sharp and insufficient. The urban landscape was flimsy trinketry, the gaudy flash from Louella Lyle's window a tiny speck off one minor star among billions.

The Nazi killers!!! Britt Anderson!! Harry and the Chinese!

Here in the hotel we are protected, she calmed herself. Benny Cawthorne will apprise Jacky of the Chinese developments so that appropriate measures can and shall be taken if and where necessary. The colour burst ceased: someone was closing Louella Lyle's window.

ii

"How do Ah look, Winston?" Louella, nude, posing legs apart and straight, torso forward leaning, regarded over her right shoulder the unattired negro supine on the bed. "Don't Ah turn you on, honeh?"

"You'll have to come over here and work on it," he leered, penis flaccid.

"You thank Ah could make a living in England as a photo model?" Her left hand stroked blonde locks from over her right ear and neck, her right hand caressed across her backside's smoothness to pluck and friction her genitalia.

"Yer, especially if you let 'em stick a length up you."

She was a trifle offended, confronting him: "Ah ain't no whore, honeh."

She smiled, glancing down to cup and stroke her breasts and belly. "But if Ah lahk a man and he wants to give me a little present, Ah thank Ah might just say yes." Arms at sides, sincerity changed her from a sexually enticing woman into an innocent little girl. "B'lly Joe wouldn't find me in England, and if he did, he couldn't take me back."

"He can't here. He can't get past the guards."

She was fatalistic: "He always fahnds me, takes me back." Her smile showed lively teenager: "But Ah'll apply for a passport tomorrow. Ah'm a-look'n' forward to going to England," she dreamed, "where Ah'll see the Queen." She was anxious: "You sure you'll help me, Winston?"

He said he would. She sat on the bed and stroked his thigh: "It sure must be a lot different than the United States, your Mr Wyckliffe letting me come here with you."

"He's a good guy."

She was curious: "What's it lahk to live in England?"

"How the hell should I know? It's different, ain' it?"

"Do your parents live in London?"

"Dead, ain' they?"

"Ah wish mine were! Ah ain't going back! When B'lly Joe fahnds me, Ah ain't going back with him! Ah ain't!"

"Forget him." Her passion roused his lust. She noticed, and relaxed, smiling.

Knelt between his legs, sucking, licking and squeezing his erection, she murmured: "You're big, honeh, black and beautiful. You lahk this, huh?"

"Yer, it's alright. Sit on the bagger, and get it up you!"

On the lawn in front of the white pillared mansion, dappled in shade from the trees, Momma and Daddeh, gripped captive in the arms of ragged black slaves, struggled, forced to watch while she, their little white naked daughter, took the thick ebony rod of her virile lover, driving glistening tirelessly in and out, turning her over, screwing her from every angle.

This while her daddeh ranted and cursed and wrenched about, helpless to interfere, and her momma cried, jealous of her daughter's taking that big beautiful hard black cock, but momma daren't tell daddeh.

"You are a stud, Winston." She kissed his throat. "A real stud."

"Yer," he relaxed flat on his back, "I might manage to get it up again in anavver few minutes. I like a good fack."

"And am I, honeh?"

"Yer. We've got half an hour before I've to be in bed."

"You could stay in bed here, Winston."

"Not a chance, Louella. When the Boss says early night, it's early night for me."

"Aw, Winston," she pouted disappointment.

"It's my career! I ain't facking it up for you nor for no other bird, neither, Louella! I want to play in that game on Sunday, and I'm going to play in it! And if you don't like it, you can piss off!"

"Ah didn't mean to upset you, Winston, darling."

"Right then," he was somewhat appeased. "Wyckliffe's been straight wiv me, ain' he? Put me right about a few fings, ain' he? Money, and contracts, and fings like that – all kinds of fings. He let me meet you, right?" She nodded, spontaneous and meek. "Yer, right, well then."

"Winston."

"What?"

"You lahk Mister Wyckliffe, huh?"

"He's alright. Straight. Fair wiv you. He knows his stuff," from habit, he begrudged giving praise.

"You-all gonna win on Sunday, now you-all got your big star, Jacky Day, back with you-all?"

"He ain't all that big a star. I'm better'n he is. He's always crying about his mother. She's dead, for Christ's sake! What good's it do crying about it?! Facking baby! I'd have all the goals if they gave me the passes like they give Jim Arrowood."

"His girlfriend's a lady."

"Yer, fack her." He realised, and chuckled savagely in his throat. "I wouldn't mind!"

"Winston!" she protested, "you' got me!" He stroked her left flank and gnawed a mouthful of left breast. She gloated over his blackness, roughness, sank masochistically into the strength of her weakness, degradation, closed her eyes and imagined herself a sex-slave in a little London apartment being screwed and utilised in every way by him, and his black, casual acquaintances, while B'lly Joe searched foggy streets in vain.

iii

Where are you, Benny? You should be here by now! Two players left the England lounge; three more, about to depart for bed, put down empty cocoa cups; three security men, relaxed yet wary, stood imbibing coffee and conversing with two England team officials and Richard Trelawney in the middle of the room; by the wall, Joe Berrigan and another Roman Catholic squad member were in dispute with Curly Greenhalgh about contraception and birth control; Jim Arrowood was approaching Richard Trelawney. The second hand of the clock above the exit leading to the elevators flowed past three minutes to eleven.

"Jacky," he twisted round, eager and tense, then relaxed, "I'll take you up on your offer," Jingo Byrnes spoke quietly. "If your business adviser would negotiate this Arab contract for me, I'd be glad." His delivery continued slow and sincere, his emotions open and honest. "I want m' eldest sister Ethel in Barnsley to get charge o' money. She's got' head for it. She'll not let me starve. 'Cause I'd chuck it away daft and let people swindle me – I always have done. Let your bloke tie it up so as I can't get my hands on it. She'll see me alright. She's on'y one who's ivver bothered about me, her and m' mam. Sin' m' mam died –, " Jingo's shrug expressed sadness and his sister's uniqueness. "Had a rough time on it: her husband walked out on her six year back leaving her wi' two lads. Nivver heard on since, nivver sent her a penny. She's gorr a job at a supermarket cashout. She's good at it. I don't want ought to go to m' other sisters, the two in Australia, ' other in Canada, if ought should happen to me. They're not bothered about me. This contract will be my last chance at big money. Your bloke'll make a good job on it, won't he?"

"He will."

"I've always got on well wi' Arabs. I'm not interested in politics. I don't care what they say," his gaze indicated Richard Trelawney and Joe Berrigan, "I like Islam better'n their religion. They can hate me as much as they like. After ' World Cup, I shan't see 'em again. 'Final on Sunday'll be ' last time I play for England. When I get to ' Middle East, they'll not pick me. After that, I'll be too old. I'll stop out there. Get a job on the coaching and management side. England's finished for me. I've enjoyed playing wi' you, Jacky. I never have to think twice wi' you – I do what's best, 'cause we think alike. You know what I mean?"

"I do."

They stayed silent, remembering, appreciating, contemplative.

"I'd like to score a goal on Sunday," Jingo's tones were carefully free of emotion.

"The winning goal."

"Yeh."

Neither spoke.

Jacky watched Jingo departing, Jim Arrowood sauntered across.

"How'd you like to be best man at my wedding? August."

"Yih."

"Beth wants to go live in Italy and explore its culture."

Jacky's innards lurched at thought of losing his friend and workmate, old dreams of living abroad struck his mind: "You off?"

"If they give us what we want."

"I'll miss you."

"You come, too. We'll sign for the same club."

"They couldn't afford uz both. Besides, Mary won't move. She's got her job at Bio-Veracity, her home, and Jessie, and everything exactly as she wants it." Resentment reared, Britt reaching to console him.

"The richest clubs could. Beth and I can speak to Mary."

Guilt, desolation, and grief bowed his head: "Won't do any good."

"Do you want to go?" Jim's question was direct.

"Yeh."

"Then we'll work her over for you! There must be good laboratories and research facilities in Italy, and she can keep in touch with England by computer, telephone and jet plane. You can rent out your place to go back to."

"She won't have it. I've tried."

"We'll try again. We'll succeed," Jim was sanguine. Jacky looked up hopefully. "Like we will on Sunday, eh, boy?"

Richard Trelawney, in the room corridor doorway, called: "You two coming?"

They were the last left in the lounge. "Soon," said Jacky. Both acknowledged Trelawney's goodnight nod.

Four minutes past eleven – where was Benny?! Had those killers the F.B.I. were hunting ambushed the nightclub group?! They *must* be back by now!

Jim Arrowood took his attention: "I'm on your side, boy, if you want any help. I don't wish to interfere between you and Mary, but I'll stand by you if you need anything. Beth's told me not to interfere. At bottom, she's like the Trelawneys – on Mary's side. As to you and Mary and Britt Anderson, or any other women," Jim shrugged, "I've known you longest and best, so I'll stick with you, even if I don't agree with everything you do – bloody Tory, eh?" he glinted a grin.

Jacky was mild: "What made you come out with this now, Jim?"

"Why, you looked so miserable sitting staring straight in front of you, I thought you needed some moral encouragement."

"I'm waiting for a word in private with Benny – when he finally gets here."

"Wait no longer," Jim stood up, "he has arrived."

"That coffee?" Benny, hand unsteady, poured himself a cupful.

"Not like you getting drunk, Ben, a time like this."

"None of your facking business!"

"If you're like that, I'll talk to you when you're sober," Jacky rose to leave.

"Sit down, Jecky, it's alright. I've been out celebrating. Becky's in Hollywood, about to become a big film star. It's in all the newspapers! Good luck to the girl, she deserves it. She was off to have a kid, you know. Of course you didn't. I thought she might have had it. I'm a no-good bastard, I told her I wasn't good enough for her – but I guess I was. Hello, here's trouble. Now, Denzil, I broke your orders and drank alcohol. Bribed the waiter to spike my tonic water and Coca-Cola. What ' you gonna do about it? Drop me?"

Wyckliffe, serious, considered him for several seconds. "Do we get a repeat performance before Sunday?"

"Nah."

"Since we need you against Barboza, there's not much I *can* do, is there?"

"I'm a cant and a shithouse, but tomorrow I'll reform."

"I doubt it. Becky Serene's in Hollywood instead of coming here, they tell me."

The Cockney turned away, face and manner indicating total disinterest. "Yer."

"Is that your reason for boozing?"

"She's got her career, ain' she? Good luck to the girl."

"I'm surprised to see you here, Jacky."

"I wanted a word in private with Benny."

"I'll let you have it then. I don't need to remind you both we've got some serious training tomorrow."

"Your brother ain't in no danger. He ain't involved. Mister Lee, on the other hand, has done very well to make it this far. He's fighting for his life in the Chinese restaurant bombing war and losing, 'cause the odds and muscle are against him." The Cockney's head moved to look Jacky in the eye: "What I'm about to tell you is best kept to yourself for the time being, Jecky, and I mean yourself – not Mary, not nobody. Right?" He waited for assent or refusal. Jacky nodded. "He's going to be killed. I can't put it no plainer than that. It couldn't happen to a nicer guy." He glanced away, then back: "Your brother's safe. Our agreement wiv Mr Lee still holds good, tell him." He looked left, gazing at the curtained windows. "Little Becky's gone to Tinsel Town to be a superstar on the Silver Screen. I thought she was coming here. But she ain't. I thought she'd have had the kid, though. I was even finking of marrying her – how's that for a laugh?"

CHAPTER 74

i

Noise in corridor. Was it Louella? Billy Joe sped silently to stand in the bright morning sunlight behind the door. The voices passed.

He relaxed. No sense in getting all het up: the bed was made, fresh towels in the bathroom, the hotel staff were finished here for the day. Louella might come back early to get prettied up for her boyfriend. That girl was sick and genuinely needed help. Her daddeh had done the right in fixing things up with that doctor in his sanatorium in Louisiana. He would cure poor beautiful little Louella, with her gorgeous blue eyes and innocent face, her golden hair and lovely figure. Man, she had to be sick, going with the blackest, ugliest, trash she could find ever'tahm she had a fight with her daddeh and momma. This doctor guy would cure all that with his electric shocks and drugs. It would take months. Maybe a year. Maybe two. But in the end, she would not be able to have a black man touch her without screaming.

Poor little Louella. Poor little beautiful sick girl.

When she was cured, he would marry her and they would live happily together all the rest of their days. He could wait. He could wait as long as it took.

Through the venetian blind, he surveyed the sun-thrashed parking lot; his station wagon was parked ten feet below and fifteen yards from where he stood: sixty to a hundred seconds would get her from window to car.

It was not always necessary to use force or drugs on Louella. Sometimes she came quietly when she had had enough of her situation. After he had told her of the new Cadillac convertible her daddeh was going to buy her, the job with the import firm in Jackson her daddeh had arranged for her, and the three month tour of Europe he was sending her on if she behaved and worked hard for a whole year, maybe she would leave quietly without giving trouble. That would be best. He hated using force on little Louella. She was the sweetest thing, except for these crazy outbreaks when she went running off.

ii

Wyckliffe contemplated Benny Cawthorne's out-accelerating Winston Jones over five yards, and thought: tension must have its outlet. The England Manager's own darted, worrying about team injuries, F.A. and news media criticism of his management. Benny's getting drunk the previous night would doubtless be another stick to beat him with at the pre-match Press conference the morrow. The 86°F and 80° humidity simmered Wyckliffe under his straw hat. Let them criticise, he thought determinedly. I'm not a moral crusader. I'm running a team the best way I know how.

"Bobby!" he shouted. "Left!" he stabbed sideways demonstrating how. "Left! Left! And no shoulder-charging nor hard tackles on Bobby, men!"

The Doc and neurosurgeon had pronounced the boy fit, but better to be safe than sorry. Not only did he not wish to risk the lad's health, he wanted the best team possible on Sunday.

He watched Winston Jones complete the move sprinting right and scoring.

He had acted correctly over Louella Lyle.

Tension must out; through sex; physical action: in all the ways it must.

To hell with the chairbound critics and yes-men moralisers, and Howard Vanderskoon's moaning about security risks. The girl had a room in the hotel annex, far away from the England squad quarters. Louella Lyle was no security risk.

He concentrated on the various groups patched about the turf, checking the working of each, scrutinising difficult manoeuvres, analysing details, noting what needed to be done.

Sex in youth is a savage primeval force seeking its exit, he thought, and closed his eyes recalling his adolescence and young manhood, then his early marriage and gradual dwindling of desire with a wife whom he had been unable to rouse. He opened his eyes, unfocussed on the actions of the squad: work had eventually replaced sex, passion for perfection passion. Eighteen years since his divorce. Eighteen! Football, always. Women, few. Hope that one day he would meet a woman who –.

Jingo Byrnes arced and zigzagged hunting possession from the pattern of players encompassing him.

Sex grew quieter with age – in Jingo's case, it needed to! Wyckliffe regarded the thirty-one year-old sprinting at Richard Trelawney: Richard loathed Jingo. His gaze flicked to the far goal, Joe Berrigan, the squad's other devotee: Joe disliked Jingo not only for his pro-Muslimism but also the million pound contract.

Jealousy.

Mary Day.

He watched Jacky wrongfoot three defenders and sideheel inwards for Jingo Byrnes to score past the remaining two.

If ever a man had problems, Jacky has. Wanting to help, feeling he should, knowing he could not, Wyckliffe was concerned but resigned. He wiped sweat from his forehead and face.

Benny Cawthorne dispossessed Jim Arrowood, absorbed Winston Jones's tackle and cleared for Colin Greenhalgh to recommence attack against Benny and Richard Trelawney.

Those two would hold the middle.

Wyckliffe's gaze flicked to the other defenders: How will they fare against the Brazilians? he worried.

Troubles, problems.

Those Nazis!! His attention probed the stands and bleachers. The Secret Service guards were spiderlike in the web of the spectatorless stadium, benevolent predators against would-be destroyers.

Howard Vanderskoon, before breakfast: 'Denzil, we think we have located Calhoun.' John C. 'Death's Head' Calhoun. Former card-carrying Nazi. Ex-Hell's Angel biker. Drugs dealer. Professional killer. Seen two days previously in Miami, Florida, talking to cocaine dealers.

The F.B.I. had as yet no knowledge of the whereabouts of the other Nazi, but they had uncovered his somewhat unusual background. He was the great-grandson of a Polish rabbi whose daughter had given birth to a child the same night and in the next room to her unmarried Ukrainian servant who had died in labour. Only one of the babies had survived the night. Shortly afterwards, the rabbi and his closest relatives had emigrated to the U.S.A. where the little girl had grown up hating her Orthodox Jewish family and believing herself to be a changeling. At nineteen, she had married an anti-communist pro-Nazi Ukrainian immigrant, and died eight months later giving birth in their snowbound cabin in upstate New York.

Tragedy.

Recalling Elspeth Day, Wyckliffe contemplated Jacky afresh.

The motherless half-Jew, Henry Puzenko, had become the Jew-hating, anti-communist, psychotic Vietnam veteran nicknamed in those days 'Himmler' Puzenko.

A top warrior: Vanderskoon spoke. Marksman, weapons expert, helicopter pilot, a man of war, Denzil. And after Vietnam, for a while, more or less crazy – but like a fox. In February, he killed two assassins that the True Maccabee – a Jewish semi-religious-political outfit – sent against him. Since then, he's vanished. The True Maccabee say he has Arab money behind him, and big an'i-Jewish political and financial in'erests in this country. They claim he's done work for the Central Intelligence Agency. The C.I.A. say he's not on their payroll. Their records show he's a one hundred per cent patriot, if a little erratic.

The Secret Service guard on the stand opposite attracted the England Manager's attention by moving quickly, rifle at the ready, to crouch motionless peering at something outside the stadium.

So far we have found nothing to indicate either Puzenko or Calhoun worked with Wolf Wehrman or saw the plans Wehrman sent them.

Psychotic madmen, Wyckliffe thought. The crouched rifleman seemed to ripple in the heat. Tension again:– Put too much, and above all, the wrong kind of pressure on somebody, it warps them, twists them, breaks them. In body, mind, judgement – their whole life. When they cannot get rid of that monstrous tension in a normal way through sex, hard physical or mental work, they do it the only way left them – abnormally.

The guard on the roof, satisfied, began to move.

Wyckliffe turned to watch Jacky, strained to his limit, sprinting for possession: Did I do right in yielding to Mary and isolating him from Britt Anderson?

iii

"It's me, Louella," Billy Joe held the squirming girl firmly, his left hand pressing the inch thick pad over her mouth and nose. "Yew're safe. Stop struggling and keep quiet, 'cause it won't do yew no good – yew know me." The girl went motionless. He released her. "Ah' come to take yew home, Louella."

"B'lly Joe, Ah ain't going back with you."

"Yew don' mean that. When Ah tell yew your daddeh is going to buy yew a white Cadillac convertible." Her eyes widened, her mouth opened in a joyous smile. "Yew are going to have your own apartment in Jackson, and he's gotten yew a job with a company which, if yew can hold down for a whole year without causing nobody no trouble, will win yew a three month trip to Europe paid foh by your daddeh."

"You are lying."

"Cross mah heart," he did so solemnly, "and hope to die, and may Ah never go to Heaven, if Ah'm telling yew a lie."

She sat on the edge of the bed, smiling. "A white Cadillac convertible. Ah thank Ah prefer pink."

"Yew kin have pink, if yew wan' it," he crooned. "Come on, honeh, get youah thengs together. Let's go." He looped a nylon rope round the radiator. "We'll climb out through the window. Mah car's down theah in the parking lot."

She packed her small suitcase: "B'lly Joe? Why can't we go out through the door?"

He explained patiently: "'Cause this here way's the quickest, Louella."

A knock at the door. "Louella, open up! It's me, Winston!"

"Winston!" she whispered, motionless, staring wide-eyed at the door.

"Louella!" The door handle rattled twice, and the door moved inwards a few inches. "Oh! It's open!"

"De-amn!" said Billy Joe, pulling out his .38 Police Special and levelling it at the widely grinning Winston.

"Don't shoot!! Don't shoot!!" Winston, popeyed, had his hands as high as he could get them.

"Ah ought to cut your cock off of yew, but Ah ain't got time! Git out that window, Louella! Close that door behind yew with your foot, boy, that's right, nice and easy."

"Wienston," she explained, "Ah'm going home with B'lly Joe. Mah daddeh's buying me a pink Cadillac convertible, mah own apartment and a three month trip to Europe next year."

"Very nice!" he said fervently. "Congratulations! I'll clear off and leave both of you to it, right?! Right!!"

"Git them hands up!" Billy Joe extracted his switchblade from his right pocket. "Ah didn't tell yew to put them down." Sweat gleamed and streamed off Winston's face, his eyes bulged at the flick-knife's snapping open.

"B'lly Joe! You leave him alone now! 'You hear me?! He's a big sahccer star!"

"He ain't nuthin' but black trash! Whut you, boy?"

"Black trash!"

"Yew say 'Sir' when yew' talking to a white man! Let's hear it."

"Yessir!"

"B'lly Joe, Ah'm sitting on this bed till you put that knife away and promise me you won't hurt him!" The grooved blade gleamed unmoving. "B'lly Joe, Ah'm waiting." The weapon clicked shut. "That's better." Billy Joe returned the knife to his pocket, the .38 remained pointed steadily at Winston's stomach. Louella walked to the window, opened it and tossed out the metal snap-catch holding the looped rope shut. She balanced her suitcase on the window ledge, and, using a chair as a stepping stone, climbed clumsily to sit with legs dangling outside the window. She turned toward Winston: "Goodbye, Weinston."

"Goodbye," he croaked.

"Oh-oh-oh!" Louella, squealing, overbalanced, clutching her suitcase in one hand and the rope in the other, and fell with a ripping of fabric: her dress and panties remained hooked shredded on the window ledge catch.

Men's shouts and women's shrieks came from the carpark.

"Louella, are yew all raht?" Billy Joe gazed anxiously down at Louella curled on top of her suitcase, nude save for her white highheeled shoes.

"No!" she wailed, "Ah've twisted mah foot!" Beefy men in grey suits with handguns out were running towards her.

Winston was fifty yards away along two corridors, ascending his second flight of stairs five steps at a time.

CHAPTER 75

i

As Wyckliffe entered the room, the journalistic assembly howled and brayed a din of questions. The F.A. official administering the meeting waved his arms, his shouts for silence scarcely heard. The Daily Telegraphic freelance belletrist emptied the last drops from his half bottle of gin into his glass and decided to risk breaking wind in the tumult.

Suddenly, silence. Except for the D.T's man. Everybody, turned to stare. Distinctive in his Marylebone Cricket Club tie and blazer, the Conservative Party faithful newspaper writer lolled nonchalantly on his chair, disdainful of his neighbours edging away with estranged countenances: Who were these people anyway? – mere lower-middle class types. The F.A. official began coughing, loudly clearing his throat and stamping his feet whilst turning to check that Wyckliffe and party were in place.

Several journalists bawled and jabbered at once. Wyckliffe indicated his most aggressive critic, the Tory-Mail representative who half-roared half snarled: "The saga of Winston Jones and Louella Lyle continues! Naked women in car parks!! You are responsible for this latest scandal! Letting her stay at the hotel and letting Jones meet her!"

"You must talk to the hotel management about their policy for renting rooms, that's not my business. As to Winston Jones meeting Louella Lyle, why shouldn't he?"

The din of shouted questions and exclamations hit eardrum-hurting levels. The F.A. mediator, smile strained to a grimace, appealed unheeded for order. Through the first decrease in the cacophony, the Tory-Sun questioner stabbed blithely: "Is it true Billy Joe surprised Winston and Louella nude in bed making love?"

Everyone listened, the Daily Telegraphic man, repelled and agitated. "No," said Wyckliffe, "and you know it isn't. The girl and her cousin have already given all the details on American television."

Questions clattered from the assemblage, the Tory-Sun man persisted: "We don't want their views, we want yours!" He was supported by shouts of "Yes, tell all!" "Give us your version!" ribald laughter, "The facts!" "The real truth!" The D.T.'s freelance exclaimed, indignant and very angry: "Disgraceful!"

"Alright," Wyckliffe was decisive, "my view of the whole Winston-Louella affair: They are both nineteen, they like each other. To have banned their meeting would have been wrong. One, because it would have been classified as racial discrimination, and I'd've been whipped for that. Two, we have been under *so much pressure*," his own showed in his voice deepening to a strong growl, "anything – anything that could take some of that pressure off in a reasonable way was welcome, and, as far as I was concerned, warmly welcome!"

The reporters' curiosity and wish for news and controversy swirled and flung: Benny Cawthorne's drunkenness, Benny and Becky Serene, more Winston and Louella, Britt Anderson, Jacky and Mary Day, Jingo Byrnes and young Muslim slave girls and his new bosses, Abdullah the Mullah and the Sheikh.

The Daily Telegraphic belletrist, purple-faced in outrage, was on his feet: "Mr Wyckliffe, Sir, as manager of the England Association Football Team, representing the whole of the English nation, you have an ineluctable obligation to maintain and insist upon the very highest of moral standards for that team! I, Sir, and many anothah of your decent minded countrymen, find you have been singularly remiss in that respect! One scandal following anothah! What have you to say for yourself, Mr Wyckliffe, in your defence?!"

"As to scandals, you people make them!" Uproar, denial, delighted smiles and hand rubbing from some. Delicious! the quarry had turned! roaring in pain? a strong and fighting victim for journalism's jaws to rend and bait and gorge upon for days and weeks, perhaps years, to come. Wyckliffe spoke strong-voiced through the hubbub: "As to being team manager, I put football and fitness and the wellbeing of my players first!" Indignant shouts and jeers mixed with clapping and sounds of approval from supporters. "I discourage anything that can bring discredit on the team!" Shouts of "Liar!" "Not true!" "No!", groans, mocking howls, and cynical laughter of disbelief interrupted him. And vigorous clapping and signs of support also. Wyckliffe resumed: "Concerning the private life of a player, so long as it does not interfere with the team, that's his business!"

Cries of "The Jacky Day business, you mean!" from the Tory-Mail, "What about Jacky Day and Britt Anderson?!" from the Tory-Express, and the Tory-Sun's "Jacky Day and the beautiful blonde!" rose above the rest.

The D.T.'s writer quivered with wrath: "Rubbish!! You have an obligation as manager of the National soccah team to ensure and insist upon the very highest standards from your playahs! They are – whether one likes it or not – the sporting idols of millions, and, as such, should conform to the expectations which ordinary decent people have a right to demand of those representing them internationally!"

"Quite right! I fully agree with you!" said Wyckliffe. "And they do!" Incredulity was rife. Through the hum, Wyckliffe went on: "We cannot expect young men under terrible stress, as our boys have been these past few weeks, to act like perfect saints! But in view of the pressures on them, I think they have been wonderful and have done a magnificent job! They've brought us through to the Final of the World Cup!! And that's what this is all about!!"

Cheers and clapping from a good number, and "Well said, Denzil!" from the People's Mirror sports editor. His questions were loud: "How are your men today, Denzil? Anybody crippled? sick? Any last minute problems?"

The England Manager succinctly reviewed team injuries.

"What're they doing this minute?"

"Relaxing, I hope."

"And Jacky Day?" the People's Mirror inquired.

"Is he with the beautiful blonde?!" the Tory-Sun man shouted, rousing laughter, risqué comments and a change from puce to purple in the hue of the Daily Telegraphic reporter.

Wyckliffe was calm: "Jacky is upstairs in the England lounge awaiting guests."

"Beautiful blonde and friends?!" the Tory-Sun journalist persisted spryly, occasioning mirth and vocal approval.

"His friend and Member of Parliament, Robert Jarvis," continued Denzil, "and Robert Jarvis's friend and Socialist colleague, the Swedish Finance Minister, whom Jacky met in Stockholm, both of whom will be cheering us tomorrow!"

"Socialists!" had the Daily Telegraphic writer's contempt been lethal, socialism itself would have perished.

"The finest of the fine!" boomed the People's Mirror sports editor followed by jeers and cheers, boos and hear-hears.

The Tory-Mail journalist was savage: "More socialist propaganda! We're sick of it! You're turning the national team and England team manager's job into a public relations service for socialism!"

The D.T.s "Hear-hear!" was emphatic, the Tory-Express exclaimed "Too true!", "Complete with sex!" accused the Tory-Sun reporter, scandalised ambivalent.

The Tory-Mail lashed on: "You're a socialist yourself, that's why you actively back and encourage Jacky Day in spouting his socialist drivel! In Stockholm! In Chicago! At every opportunity! If you had not defied the F.A. and let him do the Paddy O'Rourke Show, preaching ridiculous socialism and anti-religious atheism, none of this Nazi terrorist business would have happened! I and millions of others are convinced of that!"

Strong feelings among the journalistic concourse sprayed accusations, counter-charges and epithets splattering and pelting the Tory-Mail and D.T. writers and Denzil Wyckliffe; rival reporters were flogging conflicting ideologies and hobbyhorses.

Denzil Wyckliffe answered: "My sympathies for the Labour Party are no secret! But they have nothing to do with the running of the England football team!"

"Liar!" "Not true!" Rejecting howls of scorn bounced about. And applause and shouts of support for Denzil and socialism.

The American Christian Science Auditor reporter was on his feet: "Jacky Day gave great offence attacking religion and insulting the Mother of God! Millions of Americans were deeply shocked and have felt a real need for an official denial and apology from the English sahccer authorities! Will you give such a denial and apology here and now?!" He received vocal backing from some of his American and all of his practising Roman Catholic colleagues.

"Please!!" Denzil Wyckliffe was near to anger, "this is an Association Football, pre-World Cup Final Press Conference! Not a political meeting! Not a religious seminary! We're here to discuss football!"

The Christian Science Auditor was purposeful in his aggression: "So you agree with the atheistic an'irreligious views of Jacky Day?"

Denzil counter-attacked: "In America, you have freedom of speech, right?! He required an answer from all gathered: "Right?"

The answer came. And it was affirmative.

Wyckliffe continued: "You have freedom of religion in America, guaranteed by your Constitution! I'm here to talk football –not politics, religion – football! You say millions of Americans were offended by Jacky's views – I don't know! But I do know we have received hundreds of thousands, yes, literally, hundreds of thousands of letters and cards and messages wishing him sympathy in his bereavement and difficulties, not only from Americans, but from all over the world! And for all the Americans I have met and had to do with, I have nothing save the highest praise for their warmth, their kindness, their generosity, their help for us in every way! The hospitality which I and every member of the England squad have been given has been magnificent almost beyond belief, and has left us with the deepest gratitude and our sincerest thanks!"

Clapping and good humour suddenly prevailed.

Football and the World Cup competition predominated wholly.

The England Manager and his questioners reviewed past games, analysed incidents and the prowess of players and teams, discussed in detail everything about and around the tournament until, by common consent, nothing remained save the logical finale:

"The Big Game tomorrow, Denzil, how will you stop Brazil? Barboza, Zezinho, Vivi and Dudu and Pedro Maluf," the People's Mirror writer lilted the names, "Lulu and Chico and Lopez, Souza the Black Bludgeon, Rudolfo Soares and Cruz! They've thrashed everybody they've met so far – can we stop 'em?"

"No! They beat you!" "Brasil weell ween!" "Viva Brasil!" "Olé!" the Latin Americans left no doubt as to where their sympathies lay.

"We'll score goals against them," Wyckliffe stated, "that I feel sure, because everybody else has. With a team like ours, an attack like ours, we'll score."

"Brasil score more!" shouted the swarthy chief sports editor of The Daily Brazilian, his country's most popular newspaper, bouncing on the balls of his feet, gesticulating, chin thrust out: "Barboza, Zezinho, Vivi, Pedro Maluf, t'ree, four – each!" Glee abundant; similar exuberant claims from other South Americans roused fighting smiles and grunts from England supporters.

The New York Times journalist spoke: "Perhaps Brazil won't reach double figures, but they've certainly proved they are a formidable goal-getting machine."

"Magnif-i-i-i-fico!!" the Brazilian's powerful baritone interrupted with joyous passion. "Brasi-i-i-i-l-l-l!! Oh, Brasi-i-i-i-l-l-l-l!!" signalling the spontaneous commencement of a handclapping, footstamping, noisy samba from his countrymen and other Latins which continued for over a minute.

The New York newspaperman, smiling, resumed: "How do you propose stopping the – " he glanced at the South American contingent, "magnificent," he let their fresh applause subside, "Brazilians?"

"How do *they* intend stopping *us?*" Denzil countered.

For the next five minutes, the room was boisterous with analyses, provocation and verbal gamesmanship.

In the twenty strong World Cup squad selected by vote of the World's Press covering the World Cup Competition, Brazil had all of four players – Zezinho, Barboza, Vivi, and Lopez the centre back skipper– and three reserves. England had only three: Jacky Day, Jim Arrowood and Benny Cawthorne; with Jingo Byrnes, a reserve. In the betting around the world, odds varied from three to two to three to one on Brazil, in Brazil itself, five to one.

Wyckliffe, pulling out his wallet, amid cheers and laughter, was serious: "How can I get a thousand pounds onto us down there in Brazil?" he asked the smiling but equally serious chief sports editor of the Daily Brazilian. Several Germans and Italians were as keen as the Englishman to wager at odds of five to one: in their native countries and in their own personal book the betting was even money.

The main conference was clearly over. With scores of cameras flashing, the Brazilian handed to the New York Times reporter his £5000 cheque to match Denzil Wyckliffe's stake money already safe in the American's pocket book. White teeth gleaming in savage smile, the swarthy man boomed: "Brasil weell beat you!"

"If they do, they will be worthy champions," said Wyckliffe.

The news media were well content: this conference had provided more than sufficient copy; most were eager to leave, file their stories, and get down to some serious drinking and other innocent fun.

In the jostle and hubbub, the ultra-refined cockney drawl of The Times's Oxford Football Blue elicited an approving smirk from the Daily Telegraphic belletrist: Here, at last, a social equal, even though he had not belonged to the in-crowd at Eton. "Mr Wyckliffe, how do you and your playahs propose to spend this your last evening before, what must be, the most momentous day of your careers?"

The D.T.'s identical tones bantered sarcasm: "No doubt you have arranged to visit some nightclub, or perhaps, a private performance here, with champagne and scantily clad ladies willing to play all your usual games?"

"Beautiful blondes!" the Tory-Sun man relished hope afresh.

Wyckliffe was equable: "The squad will be staying together from dinner onwards. We shall relax with some cartoon films, chat a while, then have an early night," he told the Times writer. "For, as you said, tomorrow is our big day."

The Tory-Mail reporter spoke: "However critical our newspaper may have been of your management, or I of you, on the purely technical footballing side," his appreciation was genuine, "I want you to know I think you have done splendid work, and we'll all be cheering for you tomorrow!" The England and Commonwealth and some foreign reporters applauded fervently.

"Thank you," said Wyckliffe. "I want you to know," he addressed everyone in general, and, in passing, the Tory-Mail reporter and like-minded journalists in particular, "however critical you have been, I appreciate you have had your problems and pressures on you just as I and the squad have. I know, because you need the money, some of you are writing for newspapers whose policies you don't always agree with."

Gazes lowered. The Tory-Express reporter, a secret Labour supporter, bit his lip. Debts incurred for treatment of his paraplegic wife and dead son, the scarcity of suitable positions, and his own age at fifty-three militated against his ever again securing so well paid and safe a post as his current one. "I know a lot of what some of you report often gets re-written upon orders from above." More heads dipped. "And pressures on you and your private problems make you, on occasion, take out your frustrations in ink on some poor unfortunate innocent like me," his listeners laughed, "that you would rather take out in the right way elsewhere. But on the whole, you do a fine job. You are definitely necessary. Ladies and gentlemen – thank you very much!" Wyckliffe prepared to leave.

"Denzil!" Departing through the interior exit, the England Manager paused. The People's Mirror sports editor caught him up: "Do you think I could have a word with Robert Jarvis, the Swedish Finance Minister and Jacky?"

They stepped into the corridor; two armed guards at either end were alert. "Sorry. Not with Jacky. I want him left in peace. He has problems and worries and grief more than enough for one man."

"I nor The People's Mirror would do anything to hurt Jacky, Denzil. He's one of ours," the other reproached him.

Wyckliffe conceded marginally: "I'll speak to the other two, because I can appreciate your newspaper's special interest in fellow Socialists."

Six armed guards reinforced those previously visible. "Goodness!" the People's Mirror man exclaimed. "I've never seen anything like it! It's a veritable fortress!"

"Our protectors are taking no risks. We're grateful for it. Since the Wolf Wehrman episode, we have to assume there are psychopaths out there intent on murdering Jacky."

ii

Late afternoon toy town; the Swede in the chair behind him to his left; Robert Jarvis: "... hundreds of millions starving... diseases... unbearable hardship and poverty..."

Mam! Mam! Else, Monday washday in the old wash-house up the yard scrubbing clothes by hand, Johnner's filthy overalls, kids' shitty nappies, struggling with buckets of water from the forty yard distant pump, himself a little boy helping her, dollying for her in the dolly tub, scarcely able to reach, helping her peg out the clothes, frozen in winter, the cold wet days; living in a damp, dark nineteenth century slum labourer's cottage with only a little coal fireplace in the kitchen for heating and cooking; black-clock beetles, wood-lice, and mice in the pantry. Oh Mam! Mam! his tears had no sound.

"It is a loathsome evil that religious bigots, psychopathic soldiers and politicians, ignorant and corrupt yet cunning and vicious buffoons should rule so much of the world! have so much power!" Robert Jarvis paced up and down. "Children brought up in superstition and prejudice to priesthood and religious power, fear-ridden by Death and Hell fire!"

Else had believed in a hereafter where she would meet the dead she had known in life, all happy and well. The cars down there are so tiny. Mam, Mam. Sorrow numbed life barren, desolation unending. Nothing had substance: everything was an endless, meaningless flux: the traffic, the trees, suburban landscape, sky, hotel, himself. To step through this window, end sorrow and life's futility.

No! His body remained inert, his mind shuddered back from death.

He stared at the panorama, focussing from detail to detail, imagining killers in hiding.

Mary and Jessie were in danger at that local riding school show they had gone to! Fear, mauling his throat and mind, was calmed by Howard Vanderskoon's an hour previous assuring Jessie she could feed carrots to the little ponies, and ride on their backs if she wished, and watch Aunty Beth jumping high fences on a big horse.

..inept and cruel ideas and ways of life sanctioned by religious myths and legends!"

Beth Langdale and Jim viewing religious art treasures in Italy.

".. Backed by huge amounts of money!"

Jim persuading Mary, Beth convincing Mary.

".. by governments!"

Let them succeed, he longed.

".. by tens of millions of devotees in authority in every sphere of life throughout the world!"

But Mary won't leave Bio-Veracity.

"Terrible, isn't it?" the Finance Minister commented drily.

Jacky regarded him oddly, half believing the Swede knew his thoughts.

Robert continued: "The people at that conference had all the right ideas and plans worked out in detail, Jacky, on birth control, education, what land to re-claim, conserve and develop, what industries to set up, institutions and reforms to establish. Some of them are doing wonderful work. But all of them are being hindered by religious, social and political prejudice."

"And lack of money," said the Finance Minister.

"That's why your All-Stars Charity Match for Peaceful Progress is so important." Jacky turned away to stare through the window. "You publicise humane endeavour, combat backwardness, and pump in money where it is needed."

Jacky's voice was low, warped by strain: "I can't, Rob," his bowed head shook in defeat, shoulders hunched, features squeezed squinting at the hotel car park twenty storeys below. "I can't," the sound was small and a sob. "It's too much fo' me," his scarcely audible murmur was distorted by crying.

"Jacky!" Rob Jarvis was incredulous, touched with pity. The Swede, frowning and shaking his head and right palm for Robert to stay still, reinforced his appeal by putting his left forefinger to his lips, counselling silence. Robert was worried and perplexed. After some seconds, he said softly: "We're your friends, Jacky. We're on your side, old lad."

In a tiny, tear-muffled voice, not moving, Jacky repeated: "I can't. I can't, Rob. It's too much fo' me," he began to sob uncontrollably, bowed head and upper body rocking in convulsion, zebra'd in light from the venetian-blind window. Neither of his visitors moved or spoke; Robert Jarvis, anxious to act, the Swede, sympathetic and patient.

After a while, Jacky said: "I can't ring everybody up, and write letters, and talk to 'em –," emotional suffering strangled him for over half a minute before he could continue. "I'd have to persuade 'em – I can't," his bowed head was shaking defeat and denial, "I can't. Organising everything. All that's involved, while m' mam – m' mam –," he was crying.

"Mary said you were going to do it. I thought it was all settled," apologetic, Robert explained.

"What does *she* know?! She doesn't know." Jacky choked, sobbing: "I di'n't – want – to – come – back – here –," weeping hindered him for some seconds. "She got me to – with murderers running after me," he gazed at the hotel annex and car park, the roadway, its traffic, and beyond. "I don't care if they do kill me," he said dully. "That'd be best."

The Swede spoke instantly: "Like Sweden at football," his overweening assertion wholly changed the mood. Jacky jerked his head in astonishment toward him.

"Not at football," Jacky, grief forgotten, was opposed.

The bright-eyed human otter was astonished that Swedish superiority could be questioned: "Oh yes! No doubt about it! The Swedish newspapers this week have been *quite* clear about that!" Jacky and Rob Jarvis regarded him with fascinated disbelief. "Sweden should have beaten England by at *LEAST* four goals in Stockholm!" The Englishmen were grinning. "The Stockholm Evening Express thought six! – but our national team manager went on television and quietly assured the nation that four wass a reasonable number."

Jacky was smiling: "We've come a long way since Stockholm: we're a team now. Denzil Wyckliffe's lived up to his reputation."

The Swede was condescending: "Of course, England and Brasil have done rather well. But the real champions – the *REAL* champions!" he straightened, head cocked to one side, smiling hugely and wide-eyed, right forefinger raised for acclamation. Jacky chuckled freely, completely relaxed by the bright-eyed man's cheerful and outrageous chauvinism. The Swede spoke with friendly sincerity: "We'll be applauding and shouting for you tomorrow, Jacky. Democratic socialists the world over will be, too."

"Except in Brazil," Robert Jarvis was brisk and realistic.

The Swede continued: "When you spoke in favour of reform and enlightenment, and championed the downtrodden and unpriviliged, and told the hard truths that always need telling, you made a lot of friends."

"And enemies. Some want to kill me."

"Nobody will kill you in Sweden," the Finance Minister plucked a visiting card from his inside jacket pocket. "If you want a quiet place to rest and relax after the World Cup iss over," he gave Jacky the card, "I'll guarantee you one. Discreet. Absolute privacy. Anywhere in Sweden, if you don't wish to stay at my country cottage in the Stockholm archipelago."

Rob Jarvis interjected "It's beautiful there, Jacky: good fishing, swimming, sailing, canoeing. Natural forests to wander in. Nobody around to bother you." A knock tapped at the door.

"Come in," Jacky bade. It was Howard Vanderskoon.

The American's murmur gave no echo in the empty corridor: "Britt Anderson is in my office." Shock numbed Jacky's mind so thoroughly that he leant against the wall to his and Mary's room, unconscious of everything except Vanderskoon's words: "No one knows she is there, no one will, if you don't want it. Do you wish to see her?"

iii

"Hello, Jacky," her voice, her loveliness dispelled his intention to stay firm; small, soft hands on his, perfume, smooth cheek against his: he drifted defenceless into tranquillity, eyes closed, imagining sunlit meadows and dappled woods fragrant with flowers: her breasts were hot against his chest; her smooth lips plucked his mouth. He bent her savagely backwards kissing tongue to tongue, right thigh hard between hers.

Coils of ecstasy crescendoed, powerful and delicate, shivering release of tension, doubt and fear, and longing for affection and harmony with the man she was surrendering to.

Jacky, comprehending, held her firmly, watching laughter edged with hurt fashion her features as she curved backwards whimpering in tiny gasps as though in pain.

Eased and glowing, she smiled languidly into his gaze and simultaneously unfastened her dress. Her caress guided him.

"No!" torment and fear wrenched his head aside, yearning kept him immobile. "I mustn't!" his upper body writhed with conflict, visage distraught. "I mustn't!" he turned away, back to her. "Mary would leave me!" the low cry pulsated agony.

Britt was monotone: "Let her." Her voice became soft, pleading, cajoling: "Live with me, Jacky. I love you, my darling. Everything I am and everything I have is yours."

Reason urged he reject her, yet desire to share affection and friendship was strong; he turned to her. Sexual attraction was so intense he could not speak or move: long, graceful legs, pelvis inclined, emphasising pudendum; tiny waist; shapely breasts, taut nipples; slim arms; shoulders partly concealed in wavy blondeness: face, female smooth, symmetrical, wide-eyed sincere child and lovely woman.

Mary raged. Jacky held his breath, bit bottom lip, eyes squeezing near-shut to repress emotion; Mary was at the horse show till after nine o'clock; the squad would be together all evening: he would not see Mary till bedtime. His head jerked marginally left, unable to abnegate Britt's beauty.

"Darling," Britt murmured, body against his, cheek against his.

Memories of past love shared with Mary and their threatened future, her venom, her tears, her unforgiving coldness and total rejection of what he was doing, strove, ferine and suffering, against Britt's proximity, against thought and recollection of the ecstasy which lovemaking with Britt bestowed. Surrendering, he whispered: "No," and the sound, alien seeming and detached, condemned him to fidelity. "No," he spoke firmly and turned away; she clung to him. "No, Britt. No. I'm married."

Endless desolation, no love, only anguish and rejection. The past was barren except of suffering. And I'm pregnant as well! she thought.

Jacky held the sobbing woman close, stroking her head, acutely aware of her softness, warmth and beauty, her need for solace.

Without his consciously wanting it, they began to make love.

Triumphant, self-abasing, infinitely accommodating in voluptuous sexual accord, Britt coiled and shivered in consummation.

Jacky watched the sensations and emotions twitching her features; his body performed remote from his mind. He contemplated the motes in the sunbeams: out there, Philadelphia, and tomorrow, the World Cup Final, zenith of his career; Mary would not forgive him if she knew what he was doing; she need not know; marriage was only a convention, and jealousy was selfishness; Mary would never leave Bio-Veracity no matter how much Beth Langdale and Jim or anyone else persuaded her; Mary always did what she wanted, always got her own way, always had; he could never bear seeing someone who cared for him suffer because of him.

Britt cared for him, loved him, offered everything she had for him to use or abuse.

Affection overwhelmed him.

"I wish we could stay like this for ever," luxuriating in post coital languor and mutual warmth, Britt murmured against his throat, arms and right leg pressing him close.

Jacky considered the dust specks in the sun. Mary will have to know, he thought passionlessly. He wished to go at once with Britt to his wife and explain; but Mary was at the horse show with Jessie, Beth and Joyce: he would not see her till after the squad get-together. Killers were stalking her and Jessie out there. No. Not true. The killers wanted him, not them.

"I'm a wicked, wretched woman," Britt pronounced drily. Jacky eyed her, entranced afresh. "I seduced you." She smiled, near tears. "But I love you," her voice, tiny and breaking, gave the reason. He enfolded her protectively, stroking her hair, acutely sensitive to her. She straightened, eyes six inches from his: "Blame me," she spoke normally. She was sincere: "I had to see you, though it was wrong because you have problems and troubles enough without my adding to them. This makes it worse for you," she could feel he wanted her again. "Don't tell Mary," she ordered quietly.

"I have to."

"No, you don't," she was firm with finality. "In your present situation, you need quietness, understanding, compassion, and encouragement. You have your big match tomorrow."

"My big match," he glanced aside to the sunbeams and windows, then back to her.

Her slender symmetry emphasising the firm curves of her breasts seemed to concentrate and blend in their smoothness and barely tumescent nipples all the primordial power of woman the mother, comforter and protectress with woman the enticer and lover. He touched them, grasped them, enchanted and excited by their tactility and womanliness.

Britt arched and shuddered, sensually totally receptive to him, utterly yielding, aureoles raw swollen sensitive pleasure points accepting and discharging contentment and lust.

"No!" Jacky stepped back, jerking abruptly toward the sun. Britt, ribcage heaving, stayed otherwise still. "I mustn't," his voice was low and distorted.

She realised that additional pressure would break him. His emotional conflict was too intense, too confused, too complex. He has shown he wants you, that is enough for the moment. She fastened her clothing.

"You're right, darling," she was friendly. "You must concentrate on the match tomorrow," her tones and decorous attire calmed him, her practical, analytical, almost aloof demeanour soothed yet amused him.

"You think Brazil will beat us, don't you?" he teased, beginning a smile.

"They're magnificent. But I want you to win."

"You're just like my mother," he grinned, then, remembering his mother was dead, started to weep and turned aside, head bent. Britt put her arm round his shoulders to comfort him. After a while, he quelled grief with despairing bitterness: "What does the game tomorrow matter, anyway? What does anything signify? It's all meaningless."

"It isn't. There are hundreds of millions looking forward to tomorrow in countless ways, some extremely important, especially for the thousands who are very ill and love football and the only thing keeping them alive right now is thought of the Final. For them, it means hope, health, strength, life."

"And death for me if any of those madmen hunting me succeed."

"They can't. The whole power and resources of the United States won't let them," she suppressed her fears concerning the unlocated Henry Puzenko and other potential assassins. "The police have tracked down Calhoun to the Florida Everglades, Gabe told me before I left Washington this afternoon at two o'clock."

"So you're staying with him, like you did with Chuck Bengtsson in Chicago. Make love to him as you did with Chuck? How is Chuck these days?"

She was calm: "You are the only one I make love to, Jacky."

He was cynical: "Yeh."

"I've been staying in Washington because that's where the power and influence are. I've been working for you, Jacky. I've made numerous important contacts and signed several major contracts that should produce considerable revenue for you not merely in North America, but Latin America, the Caribbean and the Far East as well. My only connections with Chuck since leaving Chicago have been on the phone and via telex. He has ordered two dozen bottles of champagne for you and the boys to be delivered tomorrow morning with his good luck telegram."

"I'm sorry, Britt," Jacky was ashamed of his jealousy.

"I love you!" she said gaily, and kissed him chastely on the temple. "How are the boys?" She laughed: "Curly Greenhalgh with his shampoo and hair restorer adverts is a prodigious success! And the coloured pair are earning well. I haven't been able to do much for the others, I'm afraid. But after you win tomorrow–!"

"I'll tell them all tonight. The team's having a final get-together, starting in – " he glanced at the wall-clock, and was astonished, "seven minutes!"

"You can't tell them! I'm not supposed to be here!" They both became serious. "You mustn't say anything to Mary."

"I have to."

"No. If you feel you must, though, wait till you're back in England."

iv

I should tell Mary, apprehension concerning Britt burgeoned suddenly into momentary fear for his wife and daughter's safety at the horse show; around the supper snack table, squad members laughed and chatted, filling paper beakers with non-alcoholic beverages; Jacky watched Jim Arrowood waiting with their cups for a re-fill from the tea urn: Jim and others with women at the horse show are worried, but there's no need. It's me the madmen want to kill – nobody else, Benny Cawthorne stepped jauntily towards some players laughing to talk to him: behind them, a Secret Service guard, putting away the film projector, knocked over the tins containing the cartoons which the England contingent had just finished viewing. Amid the general liveliness and determined relaxation, the clatter passed unheeded by most except Denzil Wyckliffe who, noticing Jacky watching him, communicated a friendly smile and encouraging nods to him before having his attention re-claimed by Richard Trelawney and other religious players at his right.

Half-listening to Richard and Joe Berrigan differing over the importance of God to football, the England Manager regarded the wall clock out of the corner of his eye and Jingo Byrnes in the group on Jacky's left: Vanderskoon should soon be in with news of the horse show party's return and of Death's Head Calhoun – and Puzenko the part-time C.I.A. assassin they've all so suddenly become concerned about.

Rational, Wyckliffe stifled anxiety, considering Jingo while listening to Richard and the heated religious exchanges: I must keep Jingo and Benny – and Curly – away from these boys, he thought.

Britt will be back in Washington now, Jacky closed his eyes: the enfolding clamour became a dell of deafness, memory of Britt a beck of sensations and imagery. I must not see her alone again. He felt guilt over rejecting Britt, and sadness and longing. But I must tell Mary everything. I must! She will understand. But what if Mary didn't? What if Mary cried and screamed at him, refused to let him stay with her the night or ever again, totally rejected him, left him forever? Jacky's eyelids strained apart; his spine shuddered: everything about him seemed garishly unreal and discordant.

"I don't care what them there buggers down in London say!" Jed Lennox's Humberside tones were low and passionate at Jacky's left. "Hull's in Yorkshire, an' I were born 'n' bred there! And I've as much right to weear the White Rose as any on them bastards as nivver played for England!"

"You'd better get the Boss's permission before you put it on," warned Curly Greenhalgh, nodding at the half inch embroidered white rose in the brown youth's pink palm.

My mam's dead, the thought was clear. Elspeth's dead. I'll never see her again. He stood unmoving, recalling his mother, laughing and affectionate, racing against him as a little boy, walking through summer fields, sitting on a sunlit grassy bank making him daisy and buttercup chains. He did not notice he was crying till he tasted his tears.

Winston Jones was overweening: "I don't need no mascot! I'll run rings round the baggers tomorrow! I'll score a hatful!"

"Paulo Souza'll kick your bloody socks off!" Curly jibed. "He'll flatten you! He's not called the Black Bludgeon for nothing!"

"He's too slow! He won't even get near me!" Winston boasted.

"He won't get near you alright, – he won't bloody want to!" Curly was merry, "you'll be shitting yourse'n so much, the stink'll scare him off! Now, me, I'll be whipping past Alberto Cruz, the right back, dribbling round their world class central defender and skipper, Lopez. And Paulo Souza, that Black Bludgeon, will be hypnotised by my brilliance and stand paralysed like a rabbit, while I feint to the right and shoot to the left past the totally beaten Rudolfo the Red Nosed Reindeer Soares, their ace goalie!"

If Mary left him, he would be completely alone. His head bowed, eyes squeezed shut. Terror-riven, falling through black nothingness, he grasped for her to save him, protect him, comfort him; set angry faced, she turned away. No one! No one! he thought in despair. Britt! his eyes opened, her beauty and tranquillity enveloping and soothing him. But only for a moment. Britt was not certainty. She had not lived and shared with him as Mary had. Mary had stood by him in his disappointments, encouraged him, supported him in his need – and he, her. Mary would not fail him now when he needed her most. Yet she had in Chicago. But not now! not now! She would understand about Britt when he told her tonight!

"Jacky, what do you think? Jacky!"

"What?!" Jacky, startled, turned toward his questioner.

"Jingo here should have been in that World Press Eleven instead of Vivi Machado, shouldn't he?" Eddy Corelli spoke. Dave Lewis, Curly, Jed, Winston Jones and Bobby Milburne were attentive. Jingo Byrnes was deadpan.

"We'll know tomorrow," Jacky replied; Jim was joking with Sid Garner at the snacks table; Wyckliffe, listening to Joe Berrigan, observed Richard's, and Jim's accompanying, glance at the wall clock: I must tell her, Jacky thought.

"They say Vivi Machado's dad's so ashamed Vivi's a footballer, he's disowned him," said Jed. "You wouldn"t believe that possible, would you?"

Dave Lewis was factual: "The Machados are the richest family in Latin America, full of generals, admirals, cardinals and dignitaries galore. To be a mere footballer is a disgrace."

"What d'y mean, 'disgrace'!?" Curly Greenhalgh scoffed. "Vivi redeems the rest on 'em! He's the white sheep o' the family!"

"The Brazilians are a right bunch, aren't they?" Jed mused. "Chico, their Indian left back, can't read or write. Lopez their skipper's studied English at university. Barboza's so religious he's thinking of becoming a priest. While Pedro Maluf – did you see that picture in today's papers?" Eddy Corelli deftly opened his copy of the Tory-Sun at a full-page photo of the handsome, toothbrush-moustached Maluf embracing a nude blonde, headlined LATIN LOVER WITH CO-STAR.

"And Zezinho," Dave Lewis rounded off, "is from the filthiest slum in Rio." Jingo Byrnes blinked.

Jacky's reaction was stronger: "He can play football. They all can."

"So can we," Jingo Byrnes spoke low and hard.

"We'll thrash 'em off the park tomorrow!" Winston exclaimed. "They won't get a look-in!"

"Get a hat-trick, will you, Winston?" Jim Arrowood handed Jacky his cup.

"I'll get two!"

"You'll shit wonders and fart miracles," Curly Greenhalgh asseverated.

"I hope my ankle holds up," Dave Lewis worried.

"Let Winston lay his hand on it! Go on, Winston," Curly urged, "you're the wonder worker around here!" The Negro cursed him.

"Get Trelawney to pray over it," Jingo Byrnes was sardonic.

"We won't need no defence tomorrah!" said Winston. "We'll be on the attack all the time! And when we're World Champions, and my contract wiv the Arsenal runs out, I'll make some money! If Jingo there's worth two million tax free, I'm worth at least double!"

Amid the jeering, Jim Arrowood caught Jacky's gaze; they moved a further two yards from the group.

Denzil Wyckliffe watched them: Winston is a braggart, but it's excusable. Parents dead. Dragged up by an aunt who did not want him. Battling to prove he is somebody and not convinced he is. Benny Cawthorne, eying Winston and on his way toward Jacky and Jim, paused to deposit his cup on the table; attention caught by the religious group's fervour, the Cockney began listening intently: Wyckliffe, apprehensive, watched him.

"I had Mary almost convinced Jacky! Beth is determined she and Jessie are going to Italy with us. Beth believes – and I think she's right – that Mary has mainly refused to leave England because of her scientific work."

"She won't leave," Jacky, wanting to share Jim's optimism, was pessimistic.

"She will before Beth's finished! My wife to be is very persuasive, and practical. By the time her relatives have finished, Mary will be able to continue her work in Italy at a good laboratory on her own terms with friendly access to the country's top brains and power centres. The Old Boy network and international social influence do, on occasion, have their benefits, Jacky!"

Benny, smiling slyly, resumed his saunter towards Jacky and Jim. Denzil relaxed: Sometimes I feel like a wild animal trainer, keeping assorted enemy species apart yet hunting as one pack. The whole squad is nervy, tense, but it's a good tension. Not like that malign rottenness of all those madmen out there. The England Manager skewed to the coffee container. Puzenko, protected by the C.I.A. Calhoun. The rest. Black coffee gurgled into his cup; his gaze flicked to the exits seeking Howard Vanderskoon. Puzenko's no threat, Howard says, while the F.B.I. trace him all the way to Alaska then lose him in Pittsburgh!

Denzil, he's no threat, he's a good patriot. His war record shows that, and other things he's done for Uncle Sam since then. We're simply check'n' on him because he knew Wehrman in 'Nam and Wehrman wrote him.

Wyckliffe sipped the black liquid, tepid, bitter strong, he gulped it down.

Denzil, Calhoun's no threat. He's in the Florida Everglades and we're moving in on him tonight. The England Manager re-filled his cup. Everything's under control, Denzil. The England Manager, preparing to swallow the acerb brew, put it down untasted.

I don't believe him. He tells me only what he thinks I know or need to know. Too much secrecy, too many cover-ups, plots and counter-plots – the C.I.A., Nazis, Jewish Intelligence, Arabs, the KGB, the Mafia –, it's a madhouse of rumour and guesswork. The Americans won't risk Jacky or our safety for some underhand reason unbeknown to us, though. Or will they? Roosevelt sacrificed the American fleet at Pearl Harbour to bring America into the War.

Benny was grinning: "I've just heard old Joseph saying he'll have to pray extra hard for us at Mass tomorrah, because the Brazilians are all Caffolics and we ain't. Then Richard says, 'I won't be praying for victory,' he says, 'only for fair play, because the Devil looks after his own.' Joseph didn't know how to take that one! But he gave me a dirty look," Benny's grin widened.

"Will you be saying a prayer for us tonight, Benny?" Jim asked.

"Yer, and touching wood, and keeping my fingers crossed and all. I stand to win a couple of hundred thousand quid tomorrah. I got 16 to 1 on us back in January – let's keep that private, eh?"

"Will Becky be at the match?"

Richard Trelawney's glare dragged from Jingo Byrnes to Benny Cawthorne. "I'm worried about Joyce and the others, Denzil," the England Captain contemplated Jacky and Jim Arrowood. "Vanderskoon said he would personally come tell us the minute they were back," his aversion slashed afresh at Jingo Byrnes.

"I sent her a ticket," the Cockney was cautious. "What about your fiancée? Is she going, or is she stopping here to keep Mary company?"

"Jingo, my lad, Richard's giving you the Evil Eye again," said Curly Greenhalgh. Alarm spasmed Winston Jones's face, his head twisted aside.

"May Allah protect me," said Jingo.

Perhaps Beth has persuaded Mary, Jacky thought. Mary seems to like her well enough.

"That evil eye mumbo-jumbo's all rubbish, Winston," Jed noticed the black youth's fear. "Casting spells and putting the curse on people, it's superstition fit on'y for old lasses like my granny."

"Don't joke about it," the Negro muttered.

"Vanderskoon," Dave Lewis announced the American's arrival.

"I'm going to nip see Beth to check for myself the girls are safe," said Jim. "I'll be back with you boys in a couple of minutes."

I *shall* tell Mary, Jacky resolved. I shall!

"You squeamish, Denzil?" Howard Vanderskoon was serious. In his right hand, he held a large brown envelope. The two men stood alone in the corridor: muted sounds came from the three-yard distant, closed, lounge door.

"Not particularly."

The American gave him the envelope: "Calhoun."

"Oh God!" the Englishman, head twisting aside features screwed up in revulsion, instinctively thrust to arms' length the envelope in his right hand and the objects of horror in his left, two nine by twelve inch sharply focussed colour photos, one of a man's dirt and blood smeared decapitated head, crushed left eye dangling over its cheekbone, tongue fully extended and messily nailed to its chin, the other of the man's eviscerated, castrated body, sprawled in a muddy swamp. The American took back the photos and envelope.

"You okay, Denzil?" The Englishman, regaining composure, nodded. "These ' just arrived from Florida. Seems we weren't the only ones look'n' for Calhoun."

"Who did it?"

"Drug dealers almost certainly. ' Solves one of our problems. Puzenko is still trouble. I want to speak to Jacky about him."

"No!" the England Manager stepped instinctively between the stationary American and the lounge door.

"It'll only take a couple of minutes," Vanderskoon pleaded.

"No! I forbid you to speak to him! On no account!" Voices rose in the lounge.

"But Denzil –!"

"No! He must be left in peace!" Richard Trelawney was as loud for Jesus as Joe Berrigan was for the Pope.

"With Jacky's help, I think we can neutralise Puzenko – Denzil!"

"Can't you hear them in there?! I must get back!"

"But Denzil!"

"I'll see you in my office in half an hour! My office!"

"I don't care what you say about Abdullah the Mullah and the Sheikh who'll be paying my wages, I like Islam better than Christianity! It's not against sex, and it lets you kill your enemies!" Jingo Byrnes, tormented, lashed out. "Muhammad, peace be on him, killed his enemies, took everything from 'em, enslaved 'em – that's a good religion! He *liked* sex with women, not like Jesus, who went and let his enemies do him in."

"That's not religion," Richard Trelawney was intense, "that's Satanism! And you and all else like you who believe in it and follow it will rot in Hell for all Eternity!"

"Hear, hear!" Joe Berrigan was sincere; his co-religionists, also.

Benny Cawthorne was grinning and sardonic: "Christian charity – wonderful stuff."

Curly Greenhalgh was jocular: "You'll have to go to confession, Jingo, and let Father Karol Woytila shrive you!"

"Don't you insult our Pope!" the Liverpool Roman Catholic was ready to fight.

"No!" Curly the coward cried off. "He'd confess Jingo or anybody else if they were sincere, wouldn't he? now wouldn't he?!"

"Aw, religion's all a load o' bollocks," Benny drawled, eyes glinting. Denzil Wyckliffe pushed through the lounge doors. "The Pope and priests are all poofters and wankers who've never screwed a woman in their lives." The Roman Catholics prepared for battle.

Jacky, firm and relaxed, intervened: "Take it easy, Benny." He spoke quietly and with sincerity. "Everybody has a right to their own opinion. They're going to have it anyway, no matter what anybody else says or does, because it suits them. They'll change it when it suits them, and not before." Jacky's reasoning manner diminished aggressions: all were aware of his sadness. The Roman Catholics recalled Benny Cawthorne's fighting skill and their dignity as England representatives. Joe Berrigan and Richard Trelawney dwelt with contempt on the Cockney's intellectual and moral insignificance. "We've all got to live somehow or other," Jacky continued. "If somebody finds a formula that makes life easier for him and doesn't do anybody any harm, and lets that person live with himself, makes life bearable for him when he'd otherwise probably cut his throat, – what the hell – why begrudge him what he believes in? Life's short enough and hard enough anyhow. It's for the living, i'n't it?"

"And for winning the World Cup!" Wyckliffe, loud and leading, seized the chance to divert labile emotions into enthusiasm and common cause. Noisy acclamation rallied forth: "Yerr!" "Right!" "We'll show 'em!" "Come on, England!" laughter, clapping, footstamping curled up and around Winston's declaring: "We'll thrash 'em out o' sight!"

"That's the spirit to finish on, boys!" Ushering the squad towards the lounge door through which Jim Arrowood was entering, the England Manager heightened enthusiasm and firmed resolve: "We'll give 'em a game!"

"Jacky, you were right about Mary," Jim was solemn. "She got mad with Beth." He respired deeply. " But we're not giving up on her, we'll keep persuading her."

Should I tell Mary tonight about Britt? Jacky worried. Can I ever tell her without her leaving me?

v

"I think Puzenko's out there somewhere wait'n' to kill Jacky," said Vanderskoon. "And I suspect he's being helped by people in useful places. And if I can speak to Jacky – "

"No," Wyckliffe refused strongly.

"If I can speak to Jacky," the F.B.I. man continued levelly, "I believe I can stop Puzenko."

Wyckliffe was adamant: "I don't want anyone at all disturbing Jacky."

"That big disaster in the Ukraine the other week, huh? All that talk of environmental pollution, cancer victims. Jack – keen to help, huh? – organise big charity matches, huh? And if he speaks out about democracy in the Ukraine – and things like that –, Puzenko will back off."

The England Manager, intrigued and contemplative, stared lengthily at the American. "No," he finally decided. "No, he must be left in peace. I don't want him worried about anything except the match tomorrow."

"But Denzil – "

"No," the England Manager was firm, turning aside. "Why all this worry about Puzenko? The news media say he's a war hero, a super patriot who's worked for the C.I.A. in Europe, Vietnam and the Middle East. They even speculate that he's dead!"

"He's not dead. He's out there somewhere," said Vanderskoon.

"Murdering Jacky or hurting any of our squad would be terrible anti-American publicity!" Wyckliffe exclaimed. "No American patriot would want that. So why? Until a few days ago, you agreed with the newspapers, assuring me he was no danger, after weeks of saying you'd no trace of him, now suddenly you're making him out a deadly threat!" Wyckliffe, remembering, was shrewd and quiet: "What's that you said about his being helped?"

"The guy has friends. He has favours owing him."

"What friends? What favours?"

Vanderskoon shrugged, non-committal.

"The C.I.A.?" Denzil guessed.

"They've got their best guys," the American pointed at the window, "out there look'n' for him – and they *ARE* look'n', on the direct orders of the President."

"But what – why –?" the Englishman was totally baffled.

"Denzil, I think I'll tell you the whole story," Vanderskoon decided. "After tomorrow, it will be history, and some reporter will eventually root out all the details anyway. Puzenko has done work for the C.I.A. in Europe, 'Nam and the Middle East, exactly as the papers say. The guy's a Ukrainian nationalist, speaks Russian and German. After 'Nam and being discharged from the hospital, he worked for a German import export firm in New York. Killed a couple ' Puerto Ricans in self-defence. Lost his job. The C.I.A. found him another in the Middle East. German owned export-import business again. Some Jews die. The Israelis come look'n' for him. The C.I.A. bring him Stateside and get him a job with an armaments manufacturer since he's – er, useful, huh? The Israelis tell the True Maccabee about him. They try to kill him. He goes missing, and with the New York Police Department and the True Maccabee wanting to talk to him, he stays missing. After the Wolf Wehrman business, we're look'n' for him, too. We're advised not to, but we go on. A Moslem guy he knows contacts him. Puzenko personally, no one else because the proposition he has is delicate. A certain very influential Moslem who hates England and is a very pious man proposes that if Puzenko can take out the atheist Jacky Day, or the whole England team except Jingo Byrnes, and blame it on Jews, he will release some American intelligence agents he has chained up in cellars here and there, and will pay a quarter' million dollars to Puzenko personally into a Swiss bank account. Now Puzenko is crazy, but only in bits and pieces. He knows no way this project will be okayed by the Big Chiefs, and, moreover, it may not be genuine. So he talked to some people he trusts. The proposition is genuine. Three days ago, a half million dollars were paid into a Swiss bank account."

"It's insane," Wyckliffe muttered.

"Sure."

"But it's incredible! It's–it's–it's–," Wyckliffe gulped for breath, suddenly overwhelmed by the scheme's maniac rationality.

"Crazy. Sure. But Puzenko has access to the best weaponry – and he has back-up. Just how good, we don't know. Like Lee Harvey Oswald's, huh? – when Kennedy was killed."

"You mean the people behind Puzenko would betray him, kill him, if – when – after –."

"The guy's hot – too hot. The perfect fallguy, solves everybody's problems, huh?"

"Except Jacky's!"

"That's why I want to speak with Jacky."

Wyckliffe, thinking, stared at him; after some seconds, he shook his head: "No. Jacky mustn't know any of this. Leave him alone. What good would speaking to Jacky do, anyhow? even if he said all you wanted him to, you can't guarantee it would influence – stop – Puzenko."

"We know the guy. Denzil, tomorrow we will need your co-operation. There are going to be last second changes in the route and mode of transporting the team to the ground. Keep that to yourself, huh? We have to block up every possible security breach."

"You think there's been one?"

"Precautions," the American was neutral. "Think about letting me talk to Jacky first thing tomorrow, huh?"

"No! He must be left alone. The whole thing's insane!"

"It certainly is."

"How serious a threat is Puzenko – truly?"

"We don' know. Our security is tight. So maybe he is no threat at all. But the guy is well trained and acquainted with our methods. No security is perfect."

"Even if Jacky said what you want, you can't guarantee reaching Puzenko with it."

"We'll make sure it's on the television coast to coast and on the radio and in the newspapers."

The England Manager, unsettled, half-turned aside to re-consider. "No," he eventually decided, "I don't want Jacky disturbed."

"Think about it tonight," Vanderskoon urged quietly. The Englishman, back to him, walked to gaze through the half-closed venetian blinds at Philadelphia garish and frail in the dusk. "Denzil, I'm sorry your stay in America has been marred by death threats and tight security. America's got more to offer than house arrest and kill-crazy weirdoes. When this is all over, I hope you will come back and pay us a proper visit. That little cabin of mine up in Maine offers you fresh air and freedom any time you want a sample." Wyckliffe, smiling amiably, faced him. "Don't worry about Puzenko and the other madmen." Vanderskoon was reassuring. "They've got the whole resources of the United States of America against them. We'll take care of 'em for you, Denzil. So the Big Day is here. In a few hours' time, you'll be shaking the hand of the President in front of a 93,000 crowd in the John Fitzgerald Kennedy Stadium, Philadelphia, and a couple ' billion or so on television, about to see your boys take on Brazil for the Association Football Championship of the World. How's it feel, Denzil? In spite of the rough spots, pretty good, huh? And when you get back to England, you'll be a national hero."

"They'll pelt me with rotten eggs."

"Make you 'Sir' or a lord, you mean," the American grinned.

"Not me. The knives are already out. When they hear I've given young Lennox permission to wear the White Rose of York on his shorts, they'll be after me with battle sabres."

"You're jok'n'. Sahccer is your national sport. You and your boys'll be heroes."

"For the working man, yes, but not the people in power. England is still very much a class-ridden, class-conscious society with snobbery ingrained to the marrow of the bone. The ruling class and powerful in Engand don't follow football. They look down on it and despise it as lower-class – though they don't all say so aloud. And the middle classes, even if they like the game, still follow their masters' example in order to show that they, too, are part of the 'better' class." Wyckliffe shook his head slowly in amused resignation. "England, oh England! What a country! No, Howard, they'll never make me a lord. They'll fire me the first good chance they get."

"You're a pessimist, Denzil."

"You think so?"

"Sure." Both men chuckled, relaxed and weary. Wyckliffe stood up.

"We're gonna miss you guys," said Vanderskoon.

"You can always look us up in England."

"I might just do that."

Wyckliffe peered at the universe and Philadelphia's evening glowing its patterns of street lighting winked with red, green and yellow traffic signals, vehicle lamps and numerous multicoloured fluorescent advertisements gleaming and flashing. "I don't want to go to bed because I'm frightened of tomorrow," he said quietly. "Will everybody be fit? Will Jacky produce his best? Will young Lewis's ankle hold up? Will our defence be able to keep out the Brazilians? Questions, problems, worries: I'm all knotted up inside. I've done all I can. Yet I feel there are things I should still do. But I can't think of any. I'm forty-nine years old, divorced, no children, no place that I feel is home, no woman to love or be loved by. Only my career, football. Keeping occupied, chasing success – for what it's worth –, getting older, with a touch of arthritis in my fingers, minor haemorrhoids, a bad back on bad days, going grey with a bald spot at the crown of my head, periodic pressure pains and aches in my lower gut and pubic region that make me think I've got cancer. Etcetera. Etcetera. Those stars up there should put everything in perspective. And they do. But I'm still worried about tomorrow."

CHAPTER 76

i

A red, white and blue helicopter painted with a huge star-spangled banner whirled silently for three seconds against blue sky across hundreds of millions of television screens, stilled, vanished momentarily, re-appeared in black and white, stilled afresh, then stuttering sound and vision transformed suddenly into perfect broadcasting: the three-quarter oval John Fitzgerald Kennedy Stadium and surrounding Philadelphia suburbs were neat and small from the air, the near hysterical brass and drums of an American marching band swathed rhythmically through the noise and bustle of the sports crowd and the samba beat from Brazilian supporters. Quick vari-angled close-ups of a line of white-clad, leaping pom-pom girls, then of the prancing, strutting toy-soldier red and blue garbed musicians changing patterns on the green turf as they blared shrilly into 'When the Saints go marching in'.

Brazilian flags and yellow and pale blue and green dressed supporters drummed steadily in the south of the stadium.

England fans with big Union Jacks and sloganed banners were singing.

From his bullet-proof vantage point highest up on the stadium's longside rim, Howard Vanderskoon gazed worriedly at the four hundred yard distant, blue and white, sixty-yard long six storey building to his right. On its ground floor were small business premises, and shops for servicing the personnel in the offices above; its pink and white stuccoed, roof restaurant nightclub, flanked by gardens, dotted with red, white and blue umbrellaed tables, proclaimed in white neon writing, FLEUR'S. Every inch of it had been searched that afternoon. All entrances and exits guarded since then by Philadelphia police. Each visitor was being checked with metal detectors for concealed weapons.

The F.B.I. man scrutinised the crowd, the parking lots, dwelling a moment on the news-stand in the one diagonally to his left. For the past hour, all American news stations had been leading with Jacky's sympathetic views concerning the Ukraine. The crowd roar snatched his attention entirely. The teams were coming out. He focussed afresh on the blue and white block, and on FLEUR'S. He quelled his apprehension. Puzenko was not there.

Puzenko glanced toward the bellowing mass: the J.F.K. stadium and environs were sharp in the evening sunlight, and the cavorting players small through the restaurant windows.

"Your Beefeater gin and English tonic water. You wouldn't be supporting England, by any chance, sir?" the crewcut young barman noted the wavy black hair and gold rimless eyeglasses. The large television screens, one to each wall of the restaurant, silently displayed close-ups of Jacky Day. Approximately half the diners were listening through earphones.

Puzenko smiled, and nodded at the newspaper on the shelf below the fruit juice bottles: "Evening edition?"

"Sorry. That arrives here sometime after eight o'clock, sir."

Had the rogue C.I.A. assassin heard the announcement Vanderskoon had put out? Mary stared at the TV screen. Behind her, Beth Langdale laughed with Jessie over building a toy brick wall. It had been on the six o'clock TV news and on the radio news at six thirty. But not a word so far on this telecast. Surely the football bureaucrats did not as yet control the American broadcasting network. Ah, here it came.

Beth Langdale listened, and, glancing from the TV close-up of Jacky to his wife, thought: It isn't right of Mary to let Howard Vanderskoon go making statements in Jacky's name without their consulting him. She wouldn't like Jim doing it for her. Jessie tugged Beth's wrist for attention. But she's frightened: Beth softened. Frightened of everything.

28°C, 70° humidity, perfect for Brazil: Jacky stood, feeling his sweat, almost emotionless. To his left, Richard Trelawney was introducing the first of England's players to the President. In front, the shirt-sleeved, bare torsoed rows of spectators with their Union Jacks, Brazilian flags and banners waving. Up there, that television helicopter whirring. Mary watching back at the hotel. Britt, somewhere. But not his mother, never again her.

"Cheers, Jacky," Harry Day, near his flat window, raised a whisky glass at the screen. "Your big day, Jacky Day." On the street corner in the lamplight, two Nottingham city policemen: protection against Chinese bullyboys.

Grief snarled at fear.

Let them come! Face savage, he regarded the loaded shotgun against the wall, the naked sabre hung above it, the commando killing knife on the third bookshelf.

Grief powered his hate. Scum had no right to live with Else dead!

Whisky burnt his mouth and gullet and made him shudder but did not touch the cold numbness of his mind.

"Three million bucks tax free signing-on fee, fifteen thousand a month, tax free, a free house, a car, and two return tickets a year to any country he likes for his three year contract," the crewcut bartender commented to a customer along the counter about Jingo Byrnes who was shaking the President's hand.

"He's welcome to it all. He'd sure as Hell better start praying to Allah he stays in top form and gives good value for money, because if Abdullah the Mullah and the Sheikh turn nasty on him, he's gonna need one o' those plane tickets pretty damn quick!"

Puzenko concentrated on the President: Jew lover, he thought. I'd blow you away too, if you weren't the President of the United States.

Listening intently to the barkeeper and the cluster along the counter speaking of the security measures around the World Cup Final and FLEUR'S, Puzenko's impassive gaze switched from the TV screen to the stadium. So the commie bastard and Jones had been disguised as Philadelphia cops and flown out in the chopper he had seen that afternoon while waiting for his three hundred 'n fifty yard potshot from the warehouse.

He visualised the plastic and ceramics sniper rifle and periscope gear in their box in the storeroom cabinet along the corridor to his right, and, in his wallet, the magnetic strip which unlocked all the doors at FLEUR'S. He would finish his drink, then, at his leisure, check up on everything one last time.

The President drawled: "So you're here to win the Sahccer Championship of the World, huh?"

"Football," Jacky corrected him automatically.

"Here in the States, that's another game."

"Gridball," said Jacky. "This is the world game, Mr President. Football. As it has been played and called in England for centuries."

"I'll put flowers on my mother's grave tomorrow, Jacky," Harry Day promised. Sorrow, huge and sudden, broke his numbness. Vivid memories of Elspeth. "I promised you I'd go see her while you were in America," he could not control his sobbing or tears, "but she's dead, Jacky, dead."

"He looks so sad," said Britt.

"Talk'n' to our President would make anybody that," Senator Velasquez remarked drily. Britt smiled. "Did you accomplish what you wanted yesterday?"

"No," she sighed. "How could we?"

"You told him about all the deals you've made for him, huh?"

Britt nodded. "What'd he say?" She smiled wanly. "You tell him about the other?" She shook her head. "You' got to some time," he paused. "Honey, as I figure it, your Jacky on the whole is a straight guy who's been having it rough because of you. His wife is a good woman, they have a fine little girl, are you *sure* you're doing the right thing?"

"I love him."

"He didn't want you, he turned you down, so you had to have him," the Senator accused her.

Britt considered her interlocutor seriously for some seconds. "Initially, perhaps. But other men have rejected me when I've shown willing, and I have not minded. With him, it is different."

"There are plenty of men who are not married who would suit you, Britt, and you could have your pick of them all."

"I'm twenty-seven. I've never met anyone who suits me," she said quietly, "only Jacky. I'm not giving up on him now I've found him. Especially not to a self-centred egotistical little bitch who caught him young and has lived off his back ever since."

The Swedish Finance Minister watched the Brazilian side backheel lobbing from one to the other, not letting the ball hit the ground. The President was making for his seat in the Royal Box. England were sprinting toward the goal backed by the straight-edged stand with FLEUR'S in the distance.

"Mary is convinced Jacky will arrange an All-Stars Charity Match," Robert Jarvis was earnest.

"Oh, look at that!" the Swede clapped applause, the Brazilians were alternating overhead kicks with backheel lobs, keeping the ball aloft. In the centre circle, the referee flipped a coin for choice of ends.

"She's convinced it's best for Jacky. And so am I. He needs to be active, not retreat into grief. Life must go on."

"What beautiful artists they are!" the Swede exclaimed.

"There are so many areas where Jacky could be useful," said Rob. "So very many."

"Quick, Robert! The teams' line-up! Quick! Your programme! Here!" the Swede thrust a pen into Robert's hand. "You check, I'll read!" Intent on the enormous screen at the stadium's curved end, the Swede, stentorian, declaimed through the din: "One, Rudolfo Soares. Two, Albert Cruz. Three, Lopez, Captain. Four, Paulo Souza. Five, Francisco Geremias, alias Chico. Six, Luiz Branco, alias Lulu. Seven, José da Silva, alias Zezinho. Eight, Virgilio Paulo Machado, alias Vivi. Nine, Zé Battist Barboza. Ten, Eduardo Padilha, alias Dudu. Eleven, Pedro Maluf. Substitutes: Jorge Guinle, Manuel Torres, Paulo Guimarez, Oswaldo Fonseca, Carlos Amado. Now England: as usual. Substitutes: Sid Garner, Corelli, Stan Troop, Don Ford," the screen print vanished, "Reginald Sycamore. England to kick off!" the Swede squirmed and wriggled in anticipation.

Left-left-right: Lulu beaten. Left-left-right: Dudu beaten. Jingo running right; Jim ahead right covered by Lopez.

Paulo Souza, the Black Bludgeon, eyes bulging, sweat-shone, blocked goalwards. Jacky was emotionless. Left-left-right, the Bludgeon was kicking, following through, Jacky inside-heeled to Bobby Milburne an instant before Souza's body struck him.

"That's the way, boys! Show 'em straight from the start what you're made on! But you can't afford to miss 'em like that, young Bobby, not even from thirty yards," Pete Gregg eased back from the edge of his armchair in his Trenton farmhouse front room; his wife knitted steadily on the sofa; half a mile away across the fields, lights of a goods train moved steadily in the darkness.

At walking pace, elegantly powerful in ball control, the Brazilian defence utilised their first possession to entice England's forwards in vain chase.

Centre back and skipper, Lopez, right of his centre semi-circle, strolled casually lifting the ball from one foot to the other, apparently totally ignoring Jim Arrowood darting at him five yards away.

Lopez's thirty-five yard forward left lob seethed yellow shirts sprinting and swerving all over the England half.

Pedro Maluf partially beat Dave Lewis, pushed inside to Vivi, thence, Lulu who stabbed for Barboza. Benny Cawthorne flicked from the Brazilian striker's toecap to Richard Trelawney whose pass upfield to Jingo Byrnes was intercepted by Vivi and slashed instantly to the Black Prince.

Jed Lennox's gaze was on the ball: the Prince was committed left, Jed struck the air.

"Go-o-o-o-o-o-o-o-o-o-o-o-o-o-ol!!! Zezinho!!! Zezinho!!! Br-r-r-asil-l-l-l-l-l-l-l-l!!!" The Brazilian radio, and television commentators were in ecstasy. Below them in the J.F.K. stadium, Brazilian flags and banners wagged, samba bands throbbed, and "Br-r-r-rasil-l-l-l-l!! Br-r-r-rasil-l-l-l-l!!" roared and rolled.

The Black Prince closed his eyes amid team-mates' hugs and kisses: in the fine houses he had bought them, his mother and brothers and sisters were dancing, laughing, shouting. Fame. Money. Honour. No more shanty town stench, disease, shanty town death that had killed his twin brother when they were seven, dreaming of scoring for Brazil in the World Cup Final. Winning! Winning!

A few yards to the South American audio-visual journalists' left, their British counterparts were exhibiting dismay, fortitude, criticism and irony: the White Rose of York had brought no fair fortune and ought definitely to have been left in the dressing room. Denzil Wyckliffe had been wrong in permitting the wearing of it. The Chairman of the F.A., it was understood, would be taking the matter further after the match.

In Hull, an old bald black man was near to tears watching the close-up of the sweating, miserable face and dejected stance of his grandson.

"Come on, Jedder!" the picture widened to show Benny Cawthorne's snarling grin as the directional microphone picked up his words. "We ain't facking lost yet!! Not by a facking long way we ain't!!"

In Cockneyland, jubilation and laughter and "Attaboy, Benny!" The B.B.C. streamed abject and profuse apologies over the East Ender's extremely, most regrettable obscenities.

"A bad start, a terrible start!" Robert Jarvis was pessimistic.

"Those who score first don't always win," said the Swede.

One-nil down in the first three minutes, Jacky ran across the centre circle; the Black Bludgeon shoulder-charged Bobby Milburne to the turf and passed for the Indian leftback, Chico, dashing down his wing. What does it matter? Jacky was aware of his sweat, the sultry heat, patterns of movement, his own positioning, the noise of the crowd, Mary at the hotel watching, Britt. His mother's death. These moments, this match, are what I've worked for, hoped for, dreamed of, and now it's happening and I feel nothing. Chico half-beat Dave Lewis, Richard Trelawney won possession but lost to Pedro Maluf and Vivi. Pedro Maluf dribbled round Dave Lewis. Confronted afresh by Richard Trelawney, he stabbed to Barboza for whom Benny Cawthorne was inches too fast.

Jacky sprinted.

The Black Bludgeon's sliding tackle sent the ball to Vivi and Jingo Byrnes twisting awkwardly to the ground.

Oh God! no! no! outdribbled, Jed Lennox deflected leftfooted, spun to give chase, then lost much of his fear: Richard Trelawney's size thirteen foot was as firmly pressed to the leather as Zezinho's.

Two against one, the Englishmen won free, and Richard kicked upwing to Curly Greenhalgh.

The Brazilian right back, Alberto Cruz, retreated warily, impeding the bald man's route. Curly passed inside to Bobby Milburne who touched to Jacky. The Black Bludgeon took ball, felling man.

"Oh Christ," Pete Gregg was moderately indignant, watching the Bludgeon in possession, "why doesn't the referee blow?"

Harry Day drank, mouth and throat warm with whisky. His hands were cold.

"They can't beat Jacky fairly, so they rough him up," he observed bitterly.

The Black Bludgeon tapped to the thin, knock-kneed Vivi.

Army and Air Force generals, admirals, bishops, cardinals and rich and privileged leant forward in their chairs as their man and relative dribbled round Jingo Byrnes, and, confronted by Richard Trelawney, short-passed quick patterns with Pedro Maluf. His unexpected backheeled twelve yard cross to the Black Prince produced ahs and sighs, fierce puffs on Havana cigars, clasped hands from all the clerics and spontaneous prayers from two cardinals whose number would have been three had not the youngest Cardinal Machado reproved himself for lack of seemliness.

Jed's certainty was horror then logic as the Prince rounded him left.

"It should nivver have been a penalty!" Pete Gregg was vehement. "Look at that! – look at it!!" The slow motion repeat showed the Brazilian was inside the penalty area except for his left ankle and foot which the sliding Jed was tripping exactly on the line as Richard Trelawney tackled clear.

The penalty played.

Winning! Zezinho tilted back his head to smile blindly at the hot evening sky: Winning! remembering his dead twin. Winning!

Robert Jarvis pronounced glumly: "We've lost. We'll never pull back from two down against this side. Never."

"Do not forget Dunkirk," said the Swede.

"Poor Jacky," Britt yearned to comfort him. "All the boys," she extended her sympathy. "I did so want them to win, or at least do well, but Brazil are too good for them. I was afraid they would be."

Pete Gregg walked gloomily from his armchair to look across the night fields through his front room french windows where Jacky Day had talked to him many a time when they had played in the village team together, where Johnner, Jacky's dad, had often worked as a day labourer during hay making and harvest times.

The B.B.C. sports announcer's tones dripped sarcasm as bitter as his disappointment was deep: Wycliffe's experiments had been a novelty; he had made lots of mistakes and offended a lot of people, but luck had been on his side and England's which was why they had got this far: the crude, stereo-typed, English, hard-working, pattern-passing type of game with the high ball in from the wings was no good in modern football. You needed technical players, brilliant dribblers, artists like these magnificent Brazilians who were teaching England a valuable lesson English football quite clearly needed to learn.

He moaned on and on.

The big Lincolnshire man could hardly summon spirit to resist. "Aw Christ, shurrup," he grieved. "We've lost – or good as –, so shut your bloody cakehole!"

His wife said: "Jingo Byrnes nearly scored."

"What?!!" He was back in his seat immediately.

Defeat will depress Jacky even further. Mary listened an instant to Beth and Jessie. Jacky had been behind Jim and Beth's nagging her about moving to Italy. I don't want to go! Fear touching her, she stared at Jacky and Jingo Byrnes's short-passing round three Brazilians. What if that was her true reason? fear of the unknown, of failure, fear – the word connected fully with its content. Mary shuddered. Britt Anderson will never give him up. She will follow him to England. Hatred seared laser-like a moment, then turned corrosive as acid in the blonde woman's face.

He wanted a goal! What-did-it-matter dulled and enfolded him, dragging him down. Jacky fought off apathy: This game – football itself! – is Life! He out-sprinted Vivi Machado and passed thirty yards to Curly

Greenhalgh. Britt showed that yesterday, he thought. She's worked for me for nothing. She will do anything for me. Mary always puts her own interests first. Resentment clawed him.

It will be a neat shot: through the restaurant window, ignoring the midgets scurrying about the green turf, Henry Puzenko stared at the drooping stadium flags. He pictured the triple sectioned corridor from the restaurant and bar between the gaming rooms and the toilet facilities, visioned himself opening with his magnetic card the third door, marked PRIVATE: On his left, a small office supplies storeroom, then the secretary's office, the manager's opposite the manager's private elevator – he must remember to press the UP button on his way past. After the manager's office, a cleaner's closet, and, finally, the junk storeroom with one of its windows part-opened for him, the rifle and other stuff in their box in the green cabinet.

Once beyond the PRIVATE door, he would meet no one, they said. How can they guarantee that? he wondered. How had they put the rifle in place? He shrugged aside curiosity. Organisation and planning were covered, which was why he was here disguised as a crinkly black-haired Jew communist with Latin American connections, half of whom were in that crowd.

Shivering, Mary acknowledged her fear by releasing it. Fear. For her marriage. For Jessie: she contemplated her daughter chatting happily to Beth Langdale over the toy brick edifice; Puzenko the C.I.A. assassin, Vanderskoon had assured her, was no danger to Jessie, or herself – only Jacky, if anyone. And almost certainly not Jacky either. The Ukraine announcement was merely a precaution. One additional defence among many. Mary stared at the screen, the Brazilian keeper, Soares, preparing to take a long goal kick, was dwindling in a vortex miniaturising the stadium and environs as the camera back zoomed to its mile high base, a World War 1 Sopwith Camel flown by cartoon character Snoopy the beagle in World War 1 flying helmet, goggles, and scarf. The view dropped to one of the whole pitch, cut to a close-up of the Brazilian team bench then the Brazilian manager's profile, switched to the English bench, retaining the Brazilian's face in the screen's top left corner, showed Wyckliffe's tense visage up close and flipped that image to screen top right as the camera tracked the ball dropping for contest in the England semi-circle.

Wycliffe scrutinised the neat swift patterns midfield: Jacky and Bobby and Jingo Byrnes mostly have the better of it there, he thought. At man-to-man dribbling, Jacky wins each time – though the Brazilians are playing him well. Winston, useless, so far; Jim, neutralised by Lopez; likewise Colin Greenhalgh, more or less, by the right back.

Chico the Indian tackled off Jingo Byrnes and galloped along the wing.

Wycliffe, beneath his analysing and external calm, felt anxiety spurt and spurt again at the speed and direction-changing trickery of the Brazilian attack. Dave Lewis had had trouble each time with Chico, though he seemed to have overcome Pedro Maluf. Jed Lennox had definitely not mastered Zezinho even if he had improved against him.

The England Manager breathed relief as Richard Trelawney out headed Vivi to Jingo Byrnes. Thank God for Richard, and for Benny's outplaying Barboza.

Thirty yards out, Winston kicked the ball an instant before Paulo Souza his ankle. Winston fell, bellowing and writhing.

"It should have been his head," drawled Police Chief Lyle, and chomped on a handful of salted peanuts.

"Honeh," his wife was worried, "you sure we did the right theng with little Louella?"

Watching Jim Arrowood head closely past the post from England's corner, the Police Chief was certain: "Sure we' done the right theng with Louella, Momma. The only wrong theng we' done is we should've done it befoah."

"I'll get that bastard!" Winston Jones muttered viciously, scowling at Souza.

Chico rounded Dave Lewis on the outside. Facking useless! And Jedder had given Brazil their two. Zezinho kept running rings round him.

It wasn't his fault they were losing: if only Jecky facking Day and Jingo Byrnes and Bobby Milburne would give him some decent chances instead of wasting them all on facking Arrowood and Greenhalgh!

Wycliffe squinted, contemplating the goalmouth mêlée with the Brazilian keeper punching Winston Jones's header half clear, Jim

Arrowood out-leaping Lopez and Souza, Bobby's leftfooter ricocheting off two Brazilians and out for a corner: England in possession played well.

Zezinho, what to do about Zezinho? Pull Jacky back to contain him? Switch Dave Lewis for Gerald?

Six minutes to half time.

Jacky beat one man and lobbed over two more to Winston Jones who fumbled the ball. Brazil attacked.

"Vivi!!! Vivi!!! Vivi!!!" chanted through the din. The Brazilian banker's son was surrounded by exultant team-mates, the referee by England players protesting at the goal.

"I'm sorry for Jacky," said Harry Day. "He wanted to win this game." Drunkenness was strong in his body, though not his mind. "What was that noise?! Outside."

"Nothing," his girlfriend, surprised, responded.

Harry prised himself clumsily to his feet from the settee, registering her gasp at the coldness of his hand on her bare thigh.

On television screens around the world, the close-up of the ball in the extreme left corner of the English net cut to one of the Mexican linesman's raised flag as motionless as its bearer in the evening sunlight.

Vivi's military and civilian relatives paused from uncorking champagne bottles, drinking toasts in Napoleon brandy and finest malt whisky, his religious kin from offering prayers of gratitude: the referee was running to consult his dissenting fellow.

Only the policeman on the street corner. No one about tonight. They were all watching the match.

The Chinese were not interested in him.
Billy Woo had said so.
The police had said so.
Jacky had said so.
He himself knew so with his mind and logic.

No need for fear.

Except of death.

Harry shuddered, and drank whisky.

If the ref. gives the goal, we're finished, Jacky thought. Habitual reactions to similar situations ghosted. Yet with Elspeth dead, what did it matter?

IT MATTERS! Britt yesterday showed that. He stared about him at the crowd, and the players. Aware of the noise. Of the heat. His sweat. Britt at the pool in Chicago. Her beauty. He felt afresh the excitement and tranquillity she generated, and his inability to resist. He seemed weightless, floating, strengthless. Mary would leave him.

Everything was in flux, permeated by terror of death.

No Mary for consolation, no Elspeth. Eyes unfocussed, his head tossed fully left, fully right and stayed that way: he saw Jim Arrowood's anxious profile and from Jim's sudden smile and quick exhilaration comprehended the referee's decision.

"Cheers, Jacky," Harry Day poured himself more whisky. "Cheers."

"You're drinking too much, Harry," his girlfriend disapproved.

Tomorrow night, I'll go to Nottingham, Britt thought. Indifferent to the game's recommencing and its vigorous tussles for possession in the Brazilian half, the blonde woman studied Jacky only. I'll find a suitable flat or house, and set up home for us. Eyes half-closed, smiling, right palm unconsciously caressing her flank, left her breast, oblivious to the sprinting, South American attack, she moved sinuously, luxuriously, inhaling long and deeply.

Joe Berrigan, a yard out from his goal-line, was down on one knee, turning, clutching, falling, Vivi six yards away, was horizontal in the air following through after his shot partially blocked by Jed Lennox. The referee, obscured by David Lewis, Jingo Byrnes and Dudu, was frantically dodging about unable to see the action, Zezinho and Richard Trelawney leaping towards the ball were tangled together and falling mid-air inside the goal.

Lulu and Pedro Maluf hurtling in from different angles were a yard away, Barboza and Benny Cawthorne less.

The ball rapped immediately and entirely behind the goal-line an instant before the Cockney's right foot out jabbed Barboza's to flick clear: Jed Lennox whirled booting high and anywhere for touch.

The referee prepared for a throw-in.

The three Brazilians, who had seen the goal, changed from joy to shock then fury.

You could not tell from the replays – too many people in the way. Jacky turned from the J.F.K. stadium's big screen and wiped sweat from his eyes. The Finnish referee was booking Pedro Maluf in spite of the Brazilian skipper Lopez's protests. Useless ever to argue with a referee.

In England, I can't stop Britt Anderson seeing Jacky. Her contracts with him make it worse. Mary pictured hearing of her rival's death, her disfigurement, suddenly imagined the blonde woman chained up and gagged in a rat-rife, plague-infested waterless oubliette in the blackest dungeon of a deserted castle whose massive stonewalls had collapsed and blocked every chance of escape or rescue.

She sobered. Jacky in his present state could in all probability not resist Britt Anderson when the woman pursued him as she inevitably would. Mary fought off panic and stayed analytical. Taking Jacky and Jessie away for a month to a remote part of Sweden would strengthen Jacky, and permit her to assess the then situation.

"Daddy," Jessie, pointing, stood beside the seated Beth Langdale, both were staring at the screen.

Euphoria of perfection, bodiless seeming, dreams from the past that were now: Jacky's speed beat two Brazilians, his swerve a third, Paolo Souza would foul him but be too late.

Horror-stricken, arms outstretched to give help and consolation, Britt sprang forward as Jacky fell squirming and clutching his injured thigh.

Wide-eyed, passionate, ignoring the now Jacky-less screen, she turned in taut, mute appeal to the Senator, then the pastel sky, believing for one all-consuming instant that by her very intensity she could transmigrate to Jacky's side.

Mary, small fists clenched, leant gritting: "Show them! Show them! Finish it for him!"

Jim Arrowood ran clear of Lopez into the left corner of the penalty area and struck in off the right post.

Beth Langdale bounced out of her seat, clapping her hands and exclaiming. She hoisted the laughing Jessie to arms length above her head, then, joyous and hugging and kissing the little girl, danced playfully about the room.

Smiling and indulgent, Mary considered them.

Pain! lunging! rending! She was dead. Jim had scored. One back.

"I'm glad for you, Jacky," said Harry Day. "You deserve something. We all do. If Else had been alive, she'd've been glad, too." He did not realise he was crying.

"Well?" the Swedish Finance Minister was blandly provocative.

Tackled by Jingo Byrnes and Bobby Milburne in the centre circle, Dudu sent to Vivi who sprinted goalwards and through-balled Pedro Maluf. Darting forward left for the return, Vivi overhead-kicked to the Black Prince.

Winning! the glory and joy: Winning! A hat-trick against England in the World Cup Final!

Zezinho leapt high, legs scissoring, hands striving upward to express ecstasy.

In Hull, an old black man was crying with face in his hands, his wife, tearful, comforted him with arms round his shoulders.

Wyckliffe near the touchline was shouting for David Lewis to exchange places and rôles with Gerald Lennox.

I owe Wolfy this commie bastard: Henry Puzenko sipped iced water and stared at his empty soup plate, smelling jungle, Wolf Wehrman's sweat, seeing blood running from Wehrman's shot left forearm, and the bullet hole above his own right nipple as Wehrman laid a field dressing on it, Johnny Calhoun cursing and bandaging his thigh wound. Dead

Cong, eighteen of the motherfuckers, everywhere. Wolfy fixed those motherfuckers but good! Then carried me two miles on his back to the chopper pick-up point with Johnny Calhoun helping him best he could 'cause of his bad leg. Guys! Guys! I owe you this one, Wolfy. I hit those two mafioso wise guys for you in L.A. three years back, Johnny, and you never even knew it was me, never even knew they'd put out a contract on you, you crazy, lawless, fuck'n' son of a preacher man from Alabama, 'greatest state in the Confederacy!'

Now both the poor bastards were dead.

Puzenko sipped ice water, and stared toward the John Fitzgerald Kennedy Stadium.

ii

Denzil Wyckliffe's anxious concentration shifted from Jacky's discoloured right knee and outer thigh's streaked raw meat oozing blood: "You sure you'll be alright?"

"I can play. It's surface." Jacky's nostrils flared, his eyes half-closed as the doctor cleansed and disinfected the wound, sharp pain for justice, part trivial recompense for Else's death.

The doctor nodded. Wyckliffe stared intently at Dave Lewis's grazed and freshly bruised ankle the physiotherapist was attending to.

"Chico missed the right place by three inches. He's trying to get me alright," Dave Lewis stated.

"O' course the ball was in!" Benny Cawthorne, naked, wet from his shower, sports drink in hand, answered Curly Greenhalgh loudly so that everyone in the dressingroom should hear. "But if the ref. don't say it was no goal, it wasn't no goal, was it?! If he don't facking see, that's his business, ain' it?"

Wyckliffe moved systematically and quickly around the room, available, responsive, clapping Winston encouragingly on the shoulder, smiling and giving a thumbs up sign of approval to Jingo before stopping to sit beside a grim Richard Trelawney and a miserable Jed Lennox.

The Black Bludgeon snarled between drinking: "Why' you not cripple Lewis yet?! You had two good chances!"

"I nearly got him," Chico excused his failure.

"Nearly's not fucking good enough, Chico! See how I got Jacky Day? I'll cripple the bastard in the second half! You see if I don't!"

The Brazilian dressing room atmosphere was relaxed and merry, except for Barboza who sat frowning, drinking purposefully to replace lost fluid and to refuel for the second half, his 'mascot', a six-inch long silver and ebony cross on a silver chain, gleamed on his chest in the artificial light. Beside him on the bench, Zezinho, eyes shut, was happily re-living his hat-trick, and anticipating holding aloft the winners' trophy, enjoying his family's pride and love and the squad's return in triumph to Brazil.

Vivi, pensive, re-filled his beaker and regretted his not-given goals.

"I want you to take care of Zezinho, Benny. Play him right out of the game, exactly as you did Barboza the first half. Forget everything else. You've got one problem – Zezinho."

"What about Barboza?"

"I'm putting Gerald on him, and Richard if necessary."

"Don't drink, Harry," his girlfriend implored him. Only one policeman on the corner of the empty street. Different experts analysing the game. Nottingham lights-glow against the sky.

Stars.

Cold space.

Elspeth was dead.

Sorrow. Tears without sound or movement.

Whisky did not bite his inmost, dull sobriety.

Flowers for her grave tomorrow. Something to ease the turbulent, horror-barbed despair disintegrating him. His younger brothers would be suffering. He would see them the morrow, help them all he could. His sister – let her help herself, with her hate and spite over Jacky. Jacky had not killed Elspeth. Cursing him, hating him for going back to play football! What else could Jacky do? It was his life. And they hated him for it. Had tried, wanted yet to kill him.

Harry thrust away thought of Lee Kwang Yoo.

The scum. The vermin. With their vicious newspaper articles and poison pen letters and TV and radio criticism. Jacky was suffering as he was suffering. He would stand by Jacky. Jacky had helped him when he had needed it with the gangster.

He drank whisky and stared at the street.

"Harry!" his girlfriend pleaded.

The Chinese was not after him any longer, logic decreed. But logic meant nothing where gangster prestige was concerned.

Harry raised his glass to drink, his girlfriend coming up behind him stayed his hand. "No, Harry! Please, Harry. No more. Let's watch the match. You'll be too drunk to see Jacky."

Over her shoulder, slow replay of Vivi's disallowed goal. Harry concentrated, the Mexican linesman was perfectly positioned: the offside goal had been exactly that.

Seated, office telephone at elbow, bodyguards playing mah-jong, Lee Kwang Yoo, scowling, longed to turn off the foreign devils' barbarian television football in the cellar club's bar along the passage. Yet he must do nothing to betray his whereabouts. The ASIAN STAR heroin shipment call was due. With it, he would buy himself free of his enemies and take revenge.

Slap of the waves on her hull, wind in her sails, another ten minutes would see her anchored and him rowing ashore in the dinghy in that little cove on the Suffolk coast up ahead with the two waterproof sacks dropped overboard off the ASIAN STAR half an hour ago.

Damn the Chinamen choosing tonight! World Cup night.

Carnival, thought Mary. The highkicking legs and cartwheeling, cavorting, limber elegance of the pom-pom girls sliced gracing the background blare of the red and blue marching band and the light green turf. Gaudy waving flags, motionless banners, spectators in picturesque national dress, white garbed refreshment vendors, bare flesh of men and girls stippled the lively crowd, iridescent in movement and mellow sunlight, whose collective sound rose, smothering, and fell, releasing, the ceaseless rhythms of a Brazilian supporters' samba band.

A close-up of a grossly pregnant young woman in brief white shorts, bra and dark glasses buying an ice cream jerked Mary remembering her own pregnancy, and Jessica and Beth's mission to the hotel shop for soft drinks and lollipops. Fear for her daughter flicked by: no danger here from madmen. Puzenko was no threat, Vanderskoon said, the Ukraine message was only a peripheral precaution. The enceinte girl licked her ice cream. I'm glad I'm not with the child I so fervently yearned for prior to Britt Anderson's soiling our lives, Mary thought. Quelling emotion, she stayed rational. The camera was scanning the crowd, seeking out celebrities. Britt Anderson will pursue Jacky in England. For a moment, Mary, feelings a-riffle, considered escape by moving to Italy. Britt Anderson spoke fluent Italian; her stepfather came from that country. Hate-filled, frightened, Mary fled for the security of home, Bio-Veracity, Nottingham, and Lincolnshire; but nowhere was inviolate any longer. She stared wide-eyed toward the door, frantic for Jessie to be safe and warm against her, for Jacky – she sought him on the screen: the roving camera, registering a flurry in a crowd section, zoomed in. A crowd fight. The picture changed instantly to a nine times divorced, notoriously Zionist, fifty-three year old film star, her twenty-five year younger naturally philistine lover, and her homosexual son in a lemon-coloured suit with an arm round the shoulders of his white buckskin clad boyfriend.

Howard Vanderskoon stared tensely at the television monitors in front of him. At his side, the Philadelphia police captain in charge of crowd security was growling orders into a telephone.

Was this a diversion prior to the main attack? The players would be out any minute. Vanderskoon scanned the parking lots: police on guard everywhere. He eyed FLEUR'S: unease gnawed him. No danger there, he assured himself. It's been checked and re-checked. And this guy Puzenko's no problem. The C.I.A. say so – except the C.I.A. can't guarantee all their people's informal networks. He must have heard the Ukraine announcement by now.

The crowd monitors followed the spreading disturbance. The worldwide telecast concentrated on the Jewish film star and her man friend holding aloft a Star of David banner block-capitaled LONG LIVE ISRAEL!

"Jewish whore!"

The Western trained foreign doctor and the local Army officer stayed silent at Abdullah the Mullah's words. Through the window beyond the television, the desert near dawn was cold and black, the stars were like goblets of quicksilver, and the moon a sliver.

"Would that she were here with those other whores and adulteresses we are stoning to death today! Are the stones ready? Are there enough? They are not too big, not too small?" The Army officer's headshake confirmed that all was according to traditional Muslim law. "The woman who had the miscarriage will be strong enough to be stoned to death with the others?" The doctor nodded, conscience flexible, salary excellent. "They must not die too quickly. Agh!!!" – on the screen, the lemon-suited homosexual was kissing his boyfriend passionately on the mouth. "Such filthiness!!" The picture changed to a head and shoulders view of the film star and her cavalier. "Degenerates! Yankee Western Jewish whores and their filth! It is the will of Allah that homosexuals be put to death! Would that they too were here!"

The soldier said: "His Excellency does not wish the stoning to start until he arrives. Then after that, his Excellency particularly wishes to attend the cutting off of the hands and feet of the two hundred and three petty thieves we have assembled, and the flogging with fifty lashes of those thirty-two foreign workers caught drinking alcohol at their party six weeks ago."

In his sumptuous residence a mile from the mullah Abdullah's abode, the bisexual Mohammedan billionaire dignitary stroked the naked buttocks of his fourteen-year old Circassian slave boy, sipped best brandy, and smiled satisfaction, recalling the 200 million dollar bribe agreed to be paid him by the American-Japanese business consortium for securing, the previous afternoon, their multi-billion dollar building and industrialisation contract.

On the screen, the marching band was leaving the field.

The crowd fight under control, Vanderskoon and his security colleagues, eyeing Brazil and England emerging from the dressing room tunnel, relaxed marginally.

iii

The Black Prince, eager, zigzagged and spurted from the kick-off deep into the England half. Benny stayed close.

Deft and quick, the South Americans tip-tapped and arced near the England left penalty area.

The Prince stayed well right.

Left-left-left-right-left the Prince sprang fast.

The Cockney's gaze never left the ball, his right foot trapped it hard. The contest ranged fiercely for some seconds till Benny prodded wingwards to Curly Greenhalgh.

Denzil Wyckliffe whooshed out relief, then tautened as Alberto Cruz tackled off the bald man and thrust once more to Zezinho.

Benny was as quick as the Prince and beat him cleanly with a sliding tackle shunting to Bobby Milburne.

Fack you, mate! You ain't getting past me, you ain't! Not tonight. You can fack off home for all the good you' going to do tonight, old son.

The Black Bludgeon easily dispossessed the fumbling Winston Jones and sent Chico attacking.

Winston, sweat-soaked, eyes red and glaring, frothed spittle, raging at Bobby Milburne: "What the facking hell do you mean, you cant, never giving me a decent pass?!" He raised his voice at Jingo Byrnes some yards away: "And you, too, you facker!! It's no use asking the great facking Jecky Day, is it?!" he directed his sarcasm obliquely. "Oh no! There's only Arrowood and Greenhalgh for him!"

"Find the space, you'll get the ball," Jingo rejoined briefly, and sprinted away towards the action.

Mother of God, be with me! Barboza prayed. I will burn one hundred candles in Thy honour, O Blessed Virgin! He crossed himself as he ran. Be with me against these Protestant, heretic English!

For an instant, Chico wondered if he should let Lewis make the tackle, then kick his weak ankle when countering, but Pedro and Vivi were too well-placed.

He flicked to Pedro Maluf.

Richard Trelawney charging in hindered Maluf's shot. Vivi breasted the rebound down and darted infield.

Napoleon brandy the wrong way down caused the senior general to choke; the bishops clasped their hands together in fervent instinctive prayer; the youngest cardinal began solemnly to bless what he was witnessing then stopped himself: their relative chipped for Barboza near the penalty spot.

Barboza struck as Jed Lennox blocked; Joe Berrigan, diving the wrong way, watched the whirling, spinning sphere bounce down off the crossbar.

Benny's left foot outreached Zezinho's to concede a corner.

Television pictures around the world vanished as a fuse blew in Philadelphia, leaving only sound.

From radios on remote sheep farms in Patagonia, the Australian outback, forest cabins in the Yukon, jungle and other dwellings in Africa and Asia, research station living quarters in Antarctica, mountaineer base camps in the Himalayas, on every vessel of the British Navy and Merchant Marine afloat the seas and most of the waterways of the world, wherever British ex-patriots had reception, the B.B.C. World Service sports commentator pattered: "A long high inswinger, Trelawney is there! Barboza! Scuffle in goalmouth!" the speaker's voice was high and excited, grabbing words frantically: "It's in! – no! Lennox out – to Lewis – Vivi– Maluf– Vivi –. Jacky Day!!! beats one man, two men, sprinting clear, ball to Jingo Byrnes. A huge and superb rightfooter from Byrnes over the Brazilian defence! Jones is chasing! Paolo Souza! Souza kicks Jones, Jones stumbles, runs on chasing the ball near the Brazilian right penalty area! his voice was so high, it broke: "Only the keeper to beat!"

Space satellite pictures flickered then spat clarity, showing Winston clubbing so hard that he almost fell over.

"Wonderful! Wonderful!" Winston sang as he danced and jumped and waved his arms. "Brilliant!"

Drugged unconscious in her private nursing home padded cell in northern Louisiana, Louella Lyle lay below dreams, beyond rescue.

"Well?" the Swedish Finance Minister murmured slyly and pleasantly to Robert Jarvis.

I won't sacrifice my life and career for Jacky, Mary thought. I won't! He is the guilty one – not I! She glanced with rancour at the jubilant Beth Langdale.

"If you do fly to Notting-haam tomorrow night and set up open house for Jacky, you'll become a worldwide serial scandal," the Senator condemned her. "A muckraker's Magdalene! an open-ended non-stop news item for every junk journalist, candid cameraman and film photographer, all points of the compass! I'm having a hard enough time as it is living with Jacky's anti-Mother of God views!"

"Don't drink any more, Harry, please!" her hand was over his glass. On the screen, recording of Jacky initiating the scoring movement played in slow motion.

"Alright I won't," Harry agreed quietly. He gave his girlfriend the glass and half full whisky bottle. "For twelve months," he decided, purpose hard within him, a declaration of life past grief, his drunkenness an irrelevant annoyance. He concentrated on Jacky with the goalscorer.

Breathing hard, he pulled the dinghy ashore. At least there should not be any trouble with unwanted bystanders tonight, World Cup night.

Where were those damned Chinese? Sitting in their four wheel drive estate car in the spinney by the cart track up there, sod 'em! It was risky having them out here half a mile across fields from a scarcely trafficked Suffolk country road with only that farmhouse for miles around. Chinese! If anybody saw them, for Christ's sake! It would have been bad enough with Englishmen.

He hoisted the first sack onto his shoulder.

"Don't bother, mate. We'll take it from here."

Cockney! Two of them. Dark clad, one holding a radio, listening via earphones to the World Cup Final commentary. "Who are you?" Oh God, he should never have got involved with this! But he had needed the money to buy that kidney dialysis machine to save his wife's life.

"We're the new men. You'll be doing business wiv us from now on. You're getting a raise to your Old Age Pension, skipper – five hundred a pick up."

"Where are the Chinamen?"

"You might say they was unavoidably detained, permanent like. You' got a telephone number we want, skipper. Of a Mr Lee in London who you've got to ring in an emergency if anyfink goes wrong."

"I don't know what you're talking about."

"Let's put it like this, skipper: – we know your name, where you live, and about your wife, right? And you don't want to know the police because what you're doing is highly illegal. We represent the new management what's taken over. So stop facking about and give us Mr Lee's number, right?"

His companion uttered: "Benny's given away a free kick only two yards outside the area! Oh Gawd! Brazil are dangerous from there!"

Barboza crossed himself quickly. I will build a church in Thine honour O Blessed Mother of God, a church for my brother the priest at his jungle mission in Amazonas province, a church with finest stained glass windows, if I score this time.

The paint-daubed and naked Indians gazed at the black cassocked Padre Barboza engrossed in the excited incomprehensible sounds from the thing he called a radio. All about the village, the night sounds of the primeval rain forest.

Fearing both a Brazil goal and for Jacky, Britt concentrated on him in the five man defence barrier. Gabriel Velasquez's carping at her persisted. She ignored him.

"I daren't look!" Beth Langdale, face in hands, bent double. Mary glanced with hatred at her. She had made Jim Arrowood want to go to Italy, brought all THAT rearing to life again!

Joe Berrigan dived and deflected the curving rapid missile against the post. Benny Cawthorne and Zezinho, sprinting in and kicking together, spun the rebound out of play.

"Going to Notting-haam is begging for trouble," the Senator summed up, aggrieved. "It's pure stupidity!"

Britt, lips pressed tight, continued to stare at the screen.

Jessie was tugging at her friend's hands. Mary let reason quash malice: "You may look now. It's a corner kick."

Barboza outjumped Jed Lennox by a foot. Joe Berrigan punched from his high right. Richard Trelawney kicked into touch near the halfway line.

Chico threw to Lopez who headed back to the Indian.

It's gone! My ankle's gone! Dismay ridged Dave Lewis's shock, anger numbed his pain.

Wyckliffe clenched, flinching, apprehensive over his hopping, injured player and the stumbling Chico's accurate pass to Pedro Maluf.

Frustration nearly made the handsome Brazilian complete his shot at the opening being occupied by the leaping Trelawney.

Judgement chipped high for Barboza eleven yards out.

Be with us, O Mary!

The Bomber headed down for Zezinho whose backheel precision lobbed the falling leather over Jingo Brynes for Vivi, inside the eighteen yard line, to volley curve round five players into the near top corner.

"Go-o--o-o-o-o-o-o-o-o-o-o-o-o-l!!! Vivi!!! Brrrasil-l- l-l-l-l-l-l!!!

Six generals and two admirals leapt in the air, jowls and paunches flapping, five others stood at the salute; clerics were on their knees, faces uplifted, smiling beatifically, hands clasped, thanking the Lord and the Holy Virgin; the two younger cardinals among Vivi's relations were on their feet giving blessing, the third, because of his gout, did it sitting down.

In the most palatial mansion in Rio de Janeiro, Vivi's father, with the aid of two sleeping tablets, slept determinedly through the disgrace of having for a son a mere base football player, hero of the scum and rabble, a motherless child who had undutifully and totally without gratitude defied his father's wish for him to become a banker.

"Oh beautiful! There's no doubt it's a lovely goal," Pete Gregg grieved in grudging admiration. "They can play football, there's no doubt. That's football, football at its best – the bastards!"

In Chicago, without recovering consciousness, the policeman, shot four weeks previously by the Nazi killer at the Anglo-American Trade Exhibition, died soundlessly in his private hospital room.

You don't care about me at all!" Fury sieved Britt's restraint. "My happiness doesn't mean a thing to you! Your political career and precious voters are all you are concerned about! Your Roman Catholic bigoted, bullying Church and your smelly little priests, monsignors, bishops, cardinals and grubby old pope! Disgusting, dirty men! – masturbating in furtive secrecy, guilt-laden with shame, copulating with discreet women and prostitutes! Or else privily toying and tossing off with prudently imprudent choir boys, and buggering and being buggered by fellow homosexuals! Obscene hypocrites! Impotent perverts! Immoral virgins! Pandering in piety for power! Abusing the gullible's fear of death, and abject submission through confession, to rule over their religion's adherents and guide them against the rest of humanity!"

"But Britt, honey – "

"Don't you 'But Britt, honey' me! I'm not one of your office staff, nor some political petitioner, lobbyist, businessman or hireling dependent on your goodwill to let you treat me as you like! I trusted you! I thought you were on my side!"

"I am. But be reasonable, Britt, darling," he pleaded.

Jew! Puzenko's hatred seethed at Dave Lewis writhing in close-up. Motherfuck'n' bastard Jew! he longed for Lewis's foot to be broken, his back, his neck. England players were clustered worried about their team-mate. Fuck'n' Briddish! They stopped the Führer in 1940. Gave Israel to the Jews. Hitler would have destroyed every Jew in the world! Envisaging millions of Israelites being mutilated, gutshot, hanged, beheaded, burned alive, buried alive, Puzenko shivered with ecstasy.

The President was leant smiling, nodding, talking to his neighbours. Another ass-licker to world Jewry.

Stretcher bearers were running towards David Lewis.

Denzil Wyckliffe stood very worried in front of the England bench. The television scanned the Brazilian and England players, inserting a half-second full figure display of Vivi, his fifth of a second goal, then Zezinho and his goalscoring, Winston and his, Jim Arrowood's. Jim and Jacky Day walked alongside their crippled fellow.

If it were that communist son-of-a-bitch – Puzenko pictured an injured Jacky Day in the Philadelphia City Hospital, himself in a doctor's white coat. But I'll catch your act soon enough, you commie bastard! Puzenko savoured his bullets ripping Jacky apart.

Wyckliffe instructed Eddy Corelli: "I want you to defend. Not attack! Understand? Your job is to stop 'em, keep 'em out! Remember that, Eddy. Good luck." With a pat on the back, he sent Eddy Corelli onto the pitch and welcomed the stretcher-borne Dave Lewis: "Hard luck, David. Well played." The Brazilians were substituting a defensive midfielder, Jorge Guinle, for Lulu.

"Consider Jacky, Britt," the Senator's insidious persuasion caressed over the TV commentator's analysing the game and individual players; Barboza, thwarted, kicked wingwards.

"You're primarily concerned about your own political and personal best interests, Gabriel, not me nor Jacky," Britt's attention remained on the screen.

"I don't think there's a conflict, honey," the Senator was sincere, "and if there was, I'm still think'n' of you."

"I do believe you, Gabriel. I do indeed."

O Lady, Most Sacred among women, grant me a goal, one goal, I do not ask for more, I Thy most faithful of servants, obedient son of Thy Holy Catholic Church. They are heretics, these English! They do not love Thee, worship Thee, obey Thy teachings, kneel in humble and total obedience to his Holiness the Pope as we, Thy Catholic children.

This heat, humidity! making his poor old bald head feel like a balloon and gut and legs that weak he could hardly stand let alone bloody run. Give him Manchester below freezing point mid-January any day! and pissing it down with sleet and blowing a gale to boot! He would show that little bugger a clean pair of heels then!

Curly Greenhalgh bared teeth in an exaggerated stage grin at Alberto Cruz. The swarthy right back glared hostility, spat, then leered contempt.

They're not as good as I thought, these Brazilians: Eddy Corelli, running well free of Pedro Maluf and Chico, cleared to Jingo Byrnes. Maybe they're tired. Either that, or – he accepted with surprise – it's me.

The Black Bludgeon slammed ball and Jacky, dropping atop him, kneeing his injured thigh, grasping and squeezing and twisting it, using it to push himself off his quarry. Oh God! God! Jacky, head back, moaned through gritted teeth.

He's hurt! Oh please, don't let him be badly hurt! Britt leant forward, face in torment.

"Get up, Jacky! Get up!" whispered Mary, tense. Her husband rolled onto his side, unrising. You must get up.

She was dead! Dead! This pain was clean. He deserved it. He had not caused Else's death, no, but the pain was not unjust.

He forced himself carefully off the ground: on-his-feet-and-play. Play!

"It's the only way they can stop him – by crippling him," Harry Day, beyond bitterness, spoke quietly.

Jingo Byrnes tapped to Jacky.

Smash the Englishman! Lopez's hard though fair charge felled Jacky winded sprawling onto his bad leg making it bleed freely. He scrabbled shakily to all fours, his will to play on immense. Dudu ahead, Jorge Guinle coming in right. Jim Arrowood passing back.

Alberto Cruz, both feet on the turf, coming unseen from Jacky's left, shouldered him off possession and toppling onto his wounded thigh; Paulo Souza kicked the ball full force into Jacky's testicles.

"Oh Jacky! Jacky!" Britt, hands protecting her breasts, shuddered in sympathy.

"They're rough'n' Jacky up pretty good, huh? Nothing to what the English Conservative Press will do to him if you go live in Notting-haam. His mother's just died, tragedy. He needs peace and quiet, you said yourself. He sure as hell ain't going to get it if you live in Notting-h."

Mary let vengeful satisfaction gorge on Jacky's agony, requital for all the pain and misery he had occasioned. She glanced malevolently at Beth Langdale knelt beside Jessica, laughing in noisy dialogue over a picture book. Guilt touched her, then remorse; yet resentment remained: My research IS more important than football!

Here on his back in the heat and sweat and pain with that blue evening sky up there and his mother's grave with the flowers fading beside old Johnner's, what did it matter? What does it all matter?

Mary watching, Britt, everyone. To get up and play the hero, tired, with his bad thigh, why? For yourself, for Jessie, for me, Mary told him. For those counting on you: Britt, yesterday.

4-2 down against Brazil in the World Cup Final, nearly half the second half gone. Wyckliffe on the touchline was holding up numbers, substituting Sid Garner for Curly Greenhalgh.

It's only a game, a meaningless trivial pastime, my career, my life. Life itself. Rob Jarvis and the Swede up there somewhere, all the millions of others, hundreds of millions believe it worthwhile. Mary, Britt. Myself, once, not now.

The doctor said: "There's too much blood, Jacky. We've got to take you off and clean you up and do it properly and see how bad it is."

"If Jacky can't come back, it doesn't matter," said Harry Day. "He's done enough, more than enough. Brazil are worthy World Champions."

Out on the streets, the heroin would buy him free, stave off enough opposition to make deals with the rest.

Above the low grunts and comments of his men at their mah-jong game, the hubbub from the bar along the passageway outside, Lee Kwang Yoo was alert to a sudden rise in volume from the World Cup Final: he glanced at the telephone, wanting its signal to be that sound.

The crowd roar in Puzenko's earphone extruded thinly then vanished amid the rumble reaching the restaurant from the stadium. On screen, Joe Berrigan was full-length on the ground after his save, while, stood over him, an anguished, frustrated Barboza arched backward repeatedly and frenziedly making signs of the cross.

Come on, you bastards! Show us the communist. Is the son-of-a-bitch crippled or what?! If he were, they would use the hospital contingency plan. If not, Puzenko pictured the north west rear entrance of the England hotel: his back-up people guaranteed him an obstacle-free, thirty-second interval. The restaurant wall TV beamed elegant and casual Brazilian superiority with England players being taunted into vainly scurrying hither and yon.

Blessed Virgin, one goal, please! It is not much, not a great thing I ask of Thee. I will do whatever thou wantest of me, O Mother of God. Give me a sign, O Lady! and I will do it! Only, please! please let me score!

Lopez, in the centre circle, contemplating his team-mates' continuing attack in and around the England penalty area, wary of Jim Arrowood and Winston Jones, thought: Tonight, we shall celebrate. All Brazil will go mad!

Tomorrow, the official welcome home, the scenes in his home town, Rio de Janeiro, his wife and family in their luxury house and grounds. And later: his nineteen-year-old mulatto mistress in her backstreet apartment.

Pedro Maluf, cursing, doing the splits, kicked toecap grazing the studs of the nimbly departing Eddy Corelli.

The Brazilian rested knelt on left knee and watched the English right winger, Garner, send Chico the wrong way. It was not important. The match was as good as over. Brazil would win.

Excitement sprang him joyous to his feet. The blonde photo models awaiting him in Sao Paolo! the films he would make! the multimillion-dollar contract he would sign with either Milano in Italy or Barcelona in Spain!

Those goals of his in the first half should have been given! But they had not. Maybe he would get more.

Papa must forgive him now for not becoming a banker. Brasil, World Champions! For with ten men, two goals down and without Jacky Day, England were clearly beaten. They were beaten even with him!

Denzil Wyckliffe, squatted, was attentive equally to his injured player and the game: "They're overconfident, Jacky, and they're tiring. They're open to a fast counter down the right. Can you guarantee the leg will hold, Doc?"

"No, Denzil," the physician continued bandaging. "If it's knocked again, it will bleed again."

"Then nurse it, Jacky, guard it. Stay out of trouble. And the first chance we get – through 'em down the right like a dose o' salts!"

The Daily Telegraphic journalist uncapped his reserve half bottle. England fiasco as usual. Still, what could one expect from lower-order types – no gentlemen there, except, perhaps, Jim Arrowood, though he had not been to any sort of school, had he? Bags of money, of course, but everyone knew that money did not make a gentleman.

Tonight, he would console himself with the sweetest, most darling little black boy he could find, and damn the cost! Maybe he could wangle it out of expenses somehow. Going abroad – even among Yankee savages! – did have its compensations after all.

Britt Anderson peered horrified through splayed fingers at Jacky pushing himself shakily off the ground.

Mary Day perched angry on the side of her chair: Jacky was resting on all fours, head hanging, dazed and weak.

If Jacky could walk, Jacky would play, and while Jacky played, England had not lost.

Gunshot in street? No – a car backfiring. Policeman on corner. Burglar-proof, double-bolted door. Shotgun and cutlery on the wall. The Chinese did not want him.

Benny Cawthorne scowled. Yellow card for Dudu. No blood on Jacky's bandage, so he had managed to protect his bad leg, at least. Brazilians substituting Dudu, the cant.

Right, that was it. Next time they got Jecky, he would have a word wiv Lopez their skipper and let the fackers know exactly how fings stood.

"Is that Brazilian being sent off?" Beth Langdale was uncertain. Jessie, thumb in mouth, dozing, moved in her arms.

"No. Substituted, which gives the new man clean licence to cripple Jacky, you see."

"I think they're being perfectleh beastleh to Jeckeh."

"One becomes accustomed. As you indubitably will in Italy with your husband-to-be. In that land of dead saints and lively sinners, they are exceedingly proficient in mistaking an opponent's head for a football."

London is better than Nottingham, anonymity more or less guaranteed, no scandal, discreet for Jacky, easy for us to meet anywhere anytime, to deepen, diversify, found indestructible our true marriage. Mary Day need not know, and if she does and leaves Jacky – oh, I wish she would! That would make everything so easy: Britt smiled, and closed her eyes, inhaling slowly and deeply, picturing Jacky, herself and their baby in domestic bliss.

Sound of the Senator pouring himself a bourbon from the drinks trolley beside the sofa. Sympathy for Jacky from the TV commentator.

From her chair behind him and to his right, Britt considered her companion, hunched tautly defensive, hurt, angry, sulking, resentful, depressed, fearing he had destroyed their friendship, assessing – if she judged him aright – the damage she could do were she to betray him to his enemies, his Nordic saga princess become a Fury.

Gabe, in his pitiful old man's body, with his ingenuous dream of her innocence and his little boy longing for purity. Gabe the shrewd, the pragmatic, ruthless professional Roman Catholic politico who had long since lost his faith in the religious bases of his power. Lonely in the crowd.

Alone.

As now.

As she had always been before she met Jacky.

Her hand on his arm, lips soft on his cheek coruscated Gabriel's joy mellowly up at her off the polished surface of the occasional table, beside the reflection from the recommencing game.

Jacky flicked to Jingo Byrnes and sprinted forward left over the halfway line for the return.

Denzil Wyckliffe pressed his folded arms tightly to his chest and frowned even deeper: the Brazilians were falling back covering perfectly: there was no way through that defence – none, Sid Garner was making space down the right, Jacky, with a Brazilian about to tackle him, was shaping to pass there.

"What the –!" Wyckliffe's arms came rigid to his sides, hands clutching the bench edge.

Bob Milburne's brief surge tore turf spraying. Jacky's unexpected, technically nigh impossible leftward chip over two Brazilians was creating a defenceless fifth of a second and a yard of space if struck dropping.

"Ye-e-e-e-e-s!!!"

Pete Gregg's massive bellow made his wife jump and protest: "The girls! Peter! You'll wake the girls."

"Brilliant! Aw, fucking brilliant, eh?! Aw, brilliant! There you are, you bastards!! We can play football an' all!!" Then he sobered, the camera was on Jacky, down on his side, right leg stretched stiff, hands clutching above and outside his kneecap. "The bastard, aw, the bastard, he got him," he sorrowed in anger, "he got Jacky."

"He scored! My Bobby scored!" the stout woman hugged herself on the sofa.

Her husband looked impassively at her from his eye corner; through the lace curtains, the orange glow of the street lamp ten yards away, across the street, the mirror row of identical terrace houses. He bent forward to adjust the excited television sound downwards, his whippet's head moved on his foot, opening an eye; he stroked the dog.

"I feel like kicking the buggers myself, boy!" Jim Arrowood, on one knee beside Jacky, muttered.

Grimacing in pain, Jacky indicated to the doctor exactly where he had been fouled.

Thirty yards away, Benny Cawthorne walked his final strides to stand, unblinking, face expressionless, in front of the Brazilian captain. The

Cockney's hoarse rustle was very slow and very clear so that Lopez would understand every word: "If Jecky Day gets crippled out of this game by that bagger Paolo Souza or any others of your lot, we'll lose, and we're not going to lose that way. Not that way. If Jecky gets crippled, Lopez, I'm going to break Zezinho's leg and that of any other Brazilian player who's near enough when it happens – Barboza or Vivi. It'll mean the end of my footballing career and maybe jail. But at least England will have an even chance in this game." Lopez checked his spontaneous savage scorn: everything he knew about Cawthorne evidenced that he would do what he had said. The South American, scowling, motionless, saying nothing, watched the Englishman turn his back and walk away.

Lopez ran towards Paolo Souza.

If Jacky is badly injured – but he isn't! If he were, logic insisted, if he needed half next season to recover, he would have to stay safe at home. From the adjoining room, sounds of Beth Langdale putting the sleeping child to bed. Jessie must come first. Jacky on screen wincing, the referee indicating he be removed from the field of play. Sympathy, regret, vindictiveness, other emotions: Think! Stay rational. Britt Anderson will pursue him wherever he is. He may turn to her. He resents you. She strove against fear and passions almost successfully. More than ever since Jim is leaving. Her glance flicked spitefully to the adjoining doorway. If you go to Italy – opposition surged, she over-rode it –, he will be grateful. Britt Anderson, all other women, will be shut out. The Italian clubs are very strict. I could insist on stipulations in the contract.

Is that what I want? she despaired. To sacrifice myself, my wishes, my career, my principles for a husband I cannot trust and must therefore always watch over?! Outwardly calm, inwardly she was near hysterics.

London, Nottingham, it does not matter where I live, if I can love him, cherish him, give all I have for his happiness, ours: Britt, relaxed in total submission, studying through half-inch eyelashes Jacky limping, pausing, favouring his injured limb, continued to will anodyne, healing forces to encircle him, permeate him, suffuse his injury, transmute tribulation into purpose.

I shall provide a home for him, a family where he shall know only warmth, affection, security. He shall want for nothing within my power. I shall fight the world for him, protect him with my life, my death if needed.

He will be mine, at his inclination, shaped by me, as circumstance decrees, because he is the one man who suits me utterly, no other can blend her being so true to his as I. That woman puts her child, her career before him, intends crushing him to her design as hitherto. The man mature, however, is not the adolescent she latched and leeched upon. The man mature shall be mine entire. I will determinedly and deviously promote her career, thus shifting them apart. I shall carefully, continuously, and unbeknown, provide her with desirable men, suitable lovers, eligible soul-mates. Tantalisingly discreet. Until she chooses.

She watched Benny Cawthorne narrowly outreach Zezinho and prod short of Jacky.

England would lose in spite of the goal. It did not matter. Mentally clear, Harry Day fought whirlpools of drunkenness. Noise in the corridor, not the Chinese. Flowers for Elspeth's grave tomorrow. Jacky! Jacky! he fled grief back to the game.

Lee Kwang Yoo sat upright in his straight-backed chair, unmoving save for the occasional blink: it would have been better to have had two young girls to while away the time with.

But no women for anyone till everything was over and all safe.

Women were weakness, a hindrance, they talked and betrayed. Especially young Chinese girls in England. They had cost several of his men their lives.

Here, he was safe, had no weakness. Only one of his couriers and the English yachtsman knew this number.

O Blessed Virgin, this time! this time! Barboza's twenty-yarder curved for the top right corner.

Joe Berrigan's gold cross touched his lips as he dived, the crucifix blessed in private Vatican audience by Christianity's mightiest representative on Earth, the very Pontiff.

Eddy Corelli crossed himself and toe-ended out for a corner.

Fresh apple drink, strawberries and Devon cream; sailing in Lyme Bay with wind in white sails westward bound for Plymouth, Joyce at his side, a good woman worth more than all the world!

Lord! Lord! Almighty Father! Thank you for this life! For health, for strength, for skill! for being here this day, Captain of England!

Richard Trelawney outjumped the Bomber and Vivi to head clear.

Brazilian artistry: sixty yard curlingly accurate passes, short swift position changing interplay with every type of ball-foot-head combination conceivable, continuous individual mastery and imaginative teamwork. England: flawless in basic skills; effective.

Coffee and the bill. Catch the waiter's eye. Keep it casual. Fingerprints? Only on the cutlery, and he had wiped that with his serviette. The surgical gloves in his jacket lining would keep prints from the office corridor, junk room and rifle. Excitement, huge and rich, licked voluptuously, the terror and power he always felt before a kill.

His leg throbbed. Insignificant. Eleven minutes left, plus injury time.

Jacky watched the Brazilian keeper goal kick to Lopez. Winston Jones had cramp in his left leg, Jim was helping him. Sid Garner was too slow to catch Chico.

Jacky retreated.

If Brazil scored again, it was all over. It probably was anyway.

Heaviness made him want to stop, bow double, lie on the springy turf, hide away somewhere quiet and dark from the present cacophony, heat, humidity, his tiredness, the ache in his leg.

Chico and Pedro Maluf versus Eddy Corelli.

That ache, however, had justice: Elspeth was dead through him; though he was not the cause. Elspeth would not have blamed him.

Eddy Corelli fouled Maluf. Jacky ran for survival.

Chico to Vivi, Zezinho, Benny – Jingo Byrnes!

Jacky sprinted right creating space: the Brazilian defence was too far up!

Jingo Byrnes's twenty-five yard deeply curved pass round three Brazilians dropped equidistant to and spinning away from Paolo Souza who would kick for the injury if he missed his tackle. Let him! Power surged relaxation.

The Bludgeon was a yard too slow, his toecap six inches short. Jacky swayed round Jorge Guinle and delivered for Jim Arrowood.

The England centre forward was scarcely aware of his motion: his being was a thought, an analysis, a coolly laughing rapture veined vanishingly thinly with doubt of failure.

He struck from outside the far right penalty area a bending trajectory wide of the out-rushing diving keeper; Lopez's charge toppled him, Chico at full speed smacked him winded with two broken ribs spinning onto and spraining his right wrist.

Beth Langdale relaxed partially, straightening from her foetal posture, to reveal a contorted countenance, hands and head stretched in taut, soundless supplication.

"Jim's strong," Mary was cynical, "he's hard. He'll have to be when you go to Italy. You'll see lots worse than this." The injured man, face writhing body motionless in pain, endured the patch-up men's careful ministering. "Sprained wrist," she decided. "Broken? Cracked ribs, probably. Six to ten weeks off," she pattered lightly. "Won't stop you going to Italy. 'Almost wish it were Jacky!"

"How beastly!" Beth swung in loathing. "How perfectly horrible!"

"I was joking."

"You weren't! You meant it! You're glad Jim's hurt because he's leaving Nottingham and that makes Jeckeh want to leave as well!"

Mary was calm: "I didn't mean that at all."

"You did! Jim's wanted to leave England, too, and play abroad for a year or so! But he hasn't – because of his father's involvement with the club, and because of Jeckeh. Yes, I *am* to blame for his leaving now! He has to grow up and live his own life sometime. We've done everything we could and bent over backwards to help Jeckeh and you. Jim's been miserable and feeling guilty and talking of not moving because of you and Jeckeh. I won't let him! We're going to live our lives togetahh! So there! You may hurt Jacky and enjoy seeing him suffer, but I'm not having you saying hateful things about Jim!" she was steadfast with angry tears.

"I didn't."

"You did!" Beth Langdale was indignant. "I may not be brainy like you, you think I'm stupid."

"I don't."

"You despise the uppah classes and the aristocraceh."

"The only upper classes are those of the intellect and knowledge, and them I do not despise at all, my dear," Mary was intense.

The Duchess's great-grandchild wafted aside the smaller woman's words: "You know exactly what I mean. You wouldn't go to Italy even though we arranged the most splendid opportunities there for you."

"I don't need you to run my life, nor my husband's," Mary spoke in tart monotone.

"And you shall not influence Jim's either, nor say cruel things about him. I love him, and will do everything to help him achieve the things in his heart – not like you with Jacky, wishing he were injured. Oh, look at him!" she wept freely, biting her lip, intent on her fiancé's televised close-up agony, "poor, poor boy!"

That goal could buy you thirty minutes' extra life, you commie bastard. Bloodlust transmuted his unheedingly sipped bitter coffee to ice cream-sweet and thickly smooth, ethereal fragrant, wholly background: Four minutes before full match-time, he would leave the restaurant. If anybody noticed, good, they would remember the Jew Red fall guy – half a mile away right this moment with a bunch of Latin American commie assholes watching the game on TV, the suckers.

He eyed the close-up of Jim Arrowood, then glanced to the J.F.K. stadium, concentrating on the motionless flags in the windless evening.

If no more goals are scored, I will nurse a brandy and soda and catch the match in the smokers' room next to the office area until four minutes before the final whistle.

He identified where the presentation ceremony would occur.

A neat shot. Ideally, I hit him a frontal gutshot, then two quick ones while he's dropp'n', three when he's down. Medal in hand. Clear of the President. For I must not risk our Jew-lovin' President. With all the firecrackers going off in and around the stadium, smoke bombs in the Coke and Pepsi cans popping off everywhere, crowd leav'n' by all exits, I should be in the basement before they realise what's happened. Straight out through the side exit into the black Tempo with New York plates. Driver gives me the stolen New York detective identification. Car-bomb diversions going off back of us. Switch cars twice; planes once, in North Carolina. Reach the Bahamas for breakfast. Our guys should by then be free from their Moslem hell holes.

He was concentrated, hard with logic, self-restrained save for a vicious contempt for the vermin he was so near to eliminating.

Wolfy, you poor dead American patriot, this'll finish it off for you, even up our score best I can. And make me a sweet half million richer.

Thought of a double-cross gnawed fleetingly: But they won't do that. I've left too many booby traps about to hurt double-crossers – they know it.

Emotionless, he sieved coffee past his tongue. Jees-us! He almost spat out the acerbic brew. What pig's piss *IS* this I've been drink'n'?!

The two man London Metropolitan Police patrol did not pause their measured, heavy tread along the night empty street: the Chinese drinking club back across the roadway was ample reason for the presence of the two climbing out of the rear seat of the grey Toyota: the pair in front were also Chinese.

"Jim can walk, so it can't be serious," Mrs Arrowood embroidered deftly, disregarding the speculative babble from the television commentator.

Her husband was glum: "It's tragic. Just when Jim had equalised!" Shaking his head: "They can't win now. Not with ten men against Brazil in extra time, if it goes that far – ooh! he sucked air through his teeth at the Barboza-Vivi-Barboza attack: Joe Berrigan's two-fisted clearance sprang Zezinho and Benny Cawthorne sprinting.

Mrs Arrowood examined her crewel-work carefully: "He should be fully recovered for his wedding in August. Beth's such a nice girl. Exactly the right sort. I was so afraid he would get mixed up with some female from among those low-bred footballing ruffians he spends so much of his time with."

Zezinho arched in agony as he hit the ground with right leg twisting under the Englishman's weight.

The Cockney, simulating pain, clutched his own left knee.

Vivi and Jorge Guinle rushed to their injured team-mate, other Brazilians toward the referee, pointing in wild anger at the crippler. The official, back pedalling, waved them away, indicating an England goal kick. English players grouped about the Cockney. Jorge Guinle, struggling to get at him round Richard Trelawney, kicked his shoulder.

Jim Arrowood on the right wing near the centreline stood motionless, sprained wrist throbbing, breathing carefully to avoid pain from his cracked ribs. Six minutes left on the clock. Benny had evened things up – the rotten bugger!

Throughout Brazil, police chiefs and militia, prison warders and hard men of every hue wished they had that dog of an Englishman Cawthorne in their power, wouldn't they use the electricity on him! ninety-nine hundredths drown him! flog him on every part of his body! torture him with the most abominable pain conceivable.

Shanty town cursed and grieved.

On the screen, Zezinho, hand over his eyes, was being stretchered off, sobbing.

Brazil's attack probed swift and continuous in and around the England penalty area.

"Go-o-o-o-o-o-o-o-o-o-o-l!!! Vivi!!! Brrrrasil-l-l-l-l!!!"

Generals were on their feet cheering, bishops were on their knees beaming and praying gratitude, even the Jesuits; the youngest cardinal among Vivi's relatives was in a state of grace, the oldest of shock, the middle one –who was very fat and greedy– was choking on a chicken bone.

Disbelief; fury; resignation: the Nigerian linesman was flagging strongly for offside. A close-up revealed three tribal scars on either cheek and noble intelligence in every feature.

Subconsciously, I feared his wish to move abroad was really a wish to leave me: her thought was pellucid.

Richard Trelawney tapped the freekick to Joe Berrigan who motioned his side upfield.

I've been afraid to leave Bio-Veracity, and Nottingham and district, and Lincolnshire because I've feared I may not have the ability to succeed elsewhere. My lab. work is meticulous, my experiments imaginative, but my maths only adequate, not highest international standard.

Sid Garner headed Berrigan's fifty yard pass wide of Jim Arrowood who winced twisting three paces, then stopped: Jim is crippled. Jacky can't use him for one of their customary counter-attacks. Jacky is walking-wounded, too, and tired. They all are. Brazil are fresher.

The yellow-green-blue, white-stockinged figures sprinted, nimble and zigzagging, in and around the England penalty area; Jingo Byrnes hooked direct from Pedro Maluf to Jacky whose volley sent Sid Garner running clear of the Brazilians.

She yearned for a winning goal, compensation against grief, her troubles, a defence against Britt Anderson – a panacea.

Paolo Souza and Lopez outran Sid Garner.

Victory, when it comes, will be Brazilian, she accepted reluctantly.

Once back in England, I can console him.

But could she? Britt Anderson would be there hunting Jacky, a grief-stricken Jacky needing comfort, wanting to escape, to leave England.

Beth Langdale sat legs crossed and arms crossed, elbows in, quiescent in hostile defence, attentive for glimpses of her fiancé.

The openings and facilities her relatives have arranged for me in Italy are impeccable – and mathematically oriented, under the best mathematicians operative in the field. Am I competent to adjust, adapt, work creatively in Italy or elsewhere, to my own capacities and strengths rather than be confined to and by my weaknesses?

Eddy Corelli tackled off Manuel Torres inside the England penalty area and thrust to Jingo Byrnes close by who, with four Brazilians darting at him less than three strides away, looked up unhurriedly and stroked the ball sixty yards, deep into the Brazilian half past Winston Jones.

Winston's face snarled tension in every tendon and exhausted muscle, weeping with frustration and pain while Lopez sprinted by leaving him untouched and toppling with cramp; Jim Arrowood approached to help.

She quashed disappointment.

Beth Langdale, arms and legs no longer crossed, was leant forward, intent on her beloved.

Beth's behaviour was and is justified. I did not realise I was obstructing Jim by insisting Jacky remain at the Forest. She and Jim have a right to their own lives. We all do.

Including Jacky?

His life is with me! she thought fiercely.

Is it? reason was calm. You do not own him.

Our marriage is a free partnership, she admitted. Entered into because we wanted it.

But does Jacky?

She fought off fear, huge emotions. Do I? logic incised, chill and even. All her life, she had had her own way. Mother, placid and fond, father indulgent. Spoilt? Perhaps. She had always wished to be her own person, have her own career.

"Brazil must win," agitation forced Britt up from her seat and halfway to the door, averting her head yet continuing to peep, squinting enthralled. "They must score. Oh well played, Gerald!" wide-eyed, she confronted the set. "He stopped that from a goal. Jacky can't reach it," she took two quick paces toward his image, "he's limping, he looks so tired and frail," she grieved, grasping her chair-back one-handed. "He'll be desperately disappointed. He did so wish for victory!"

"Brazil are going to win this one," the Senator averred. "Here they go again!"

"I wish I could be there tonight to console him," she yearned softly. "He needs! He has suffered so much. They've kicked him and hurt him. His poor leg, see how he's holding it!" her compassion neared tears. "He can hardly walk!"

"Maybe not tonight." The Senator was offhand, dry, almost diffident. "How about tomorrow morning, huh? when I visit the squad to thank them for promoting Anglo-American Trade Relations and goodwill between our two countries, and upon their splendid sportsmanlike performance throughout. 'You want to meet the boys again, huh? honey? to say thanks, and talk business?"

I'm not fooling them I'm crippled, but they've got a doubt in their minds, and that's all I need when Jingo slips it through for me when the chance comes, as come it will! It must! It must!

Stay out!

Keep clear!

Hang free!

If Brazil score now, they're the odds you take! Let Benny and the boys fend 'em off!

The English defence, out-sped and out-thought, strove vainly to clear: Pedro Maluf hit the crossbar, Richard Trelawney did the splits toeing Barboza's header off the line, Vivi incapacitated Eddy Corelli with a fully-kicked ball to the genitals, his rightfooter off the rebound was headed out by Jed Lennox to Manuel Torres whose volley ricocheted via Richard Trelawney's right knee into Joe Berrigan's face, blinding him with pain and tears. Pedro Maluf's stab was parried from the goal area by Benny Cawthorne to Jingo's head thence to Bobby Milburne: Bobby lost against Chico.

"Get that ball to Jacky," Pete Gregg muttered, low and intense.

Jacky darted from beyond the penalty area to fringe the fray: the action shifted distant, goalwards right. Following it intently, he trotted anxiously forward, backed haltingly some yards, then limped sidewards to finish unobtrusively rather upfield left.

Brazilians, nigh all in attack. Leg bleeding again. Ached. Did not matter. Come on, Jingo, let's be having it!

Mother of God! Barboza yearned, heading downwards crossgoal.

"Go-o-o- " In the Amazonas rain forest, bent over his radio, a cassocked priest closed his eyes in prayer over his famous brother's triumph and happiness.

Benny Cawthorne sliding on one knee trapped the ball against the post, Pedro Maluf's kick spun it up gyrating in, Benny, toppling forward, headed out, Richard Trelawney slashing for touch angled high off Jorge Guinle towards Manuel Torres and Sid Garner.

Pete Gregg was in an agony of tension: "Get that ball to Jacky," his voice, normal volume, squeezed ordering, begging.

"They'll score!" Robert Jarvis keened, face puckered, head half-turned away, scarcely able to watch.

Vivi took possession.

"Go-o-o- ," the ball was aiming for the net's top right corner, the whole of the John Fitzgerald Kennedy Stadium a-roar with sound.

"Ye-e-es," Pete Gregg growled deep in his throat through clenched teeth as Berrigan's one-handed save deflected towards Jingo Byrnes.

Mary Day leant forward, eyes wide, fists clenched: Now!

Jacky sidestepped Manuel Torres's lunge, swayed right and went left past Jorge Guinle, chipped left and sprang free of Vivi's tackle.

The field stretched ahead, vast and green and empty save for two Brazilians and Jim Arrowood out on the far right wing. A third Brazilian in the middle was sprinting parallel.

An eagerness, a zest, awareness of the turf's springiness under his studs, hurt in his thigh stabbing each stride, part payment for indulging in other sensations than grief's.

But Else would have cheered this! And Johnner.

Mary, yearning him on to triumph: For my sake – or hers?

Britt!?!

Cruz up ahead, Lopez falling back in the middle, Jim running crippled and chased by Chico cutting in from the right.

Score, for me! – for us, Jacky! If we win, you'll *WANT* to stay in England!

Britt Anderson's features etched commiserative horror: "Oh, look at his leg! It's a river of blood!"

"Honey, he doesn't feel a thing – he's going for touchdown!"

Scarcely audible in the standing, object brandishing gesticulating tumult, Robert Jarvis and the Swede were on their feet. "Come on, Jacky-y-y-y!!! Come on!!! Come on!!!" the English Labour M.P. kept bawling hoarsely.

The roly-poly Swede was punching both fists skywards, shrieking "Hey-a Yackeey!!! Hey-a!!! Hey-a!!!"

Upright in his armchair, eyes gleaming, lip curled, Pete Gregg growled repeating hard and measured: "Goo on, boy! Goo on!"

"So you attempt the hero's rôle, Jacky," Harry Day was the cynical intellectual, "though they will chop you down. You must, however, try. Run it, Jacky. Run it."

The Cantonese chucker-out at the Chinese drinking club begrudged leaving off viewing to answer the door, but his boss had ordered him. The two little men with Vietnamese accents both had membership cards, so were admitted hastily.

The Englishman Day was moving so fast, swaying so far down left with his whole body and left shoulder, the ball sent left –: Alberto Cruz, trying to change direction, teetered unbalanced sitting down as Jacky swayed right.

"Hey-a Yackeey!! Yeer yernet, fer fa-a-ahn!! Po dom bahra!! Hey-a!! Hey-a!!"

Rob Jarvis wondered what his chubby companion was yelling but dispensed with translation by shouting his own as Jacky turned space to past.

Wyckliffe noted that Paulo Souza would reach back-up position if Jacky delayed over Lopez.

Jim Arrowood was marked by Chico. Winston hopping about with cramp. Bobby Milburne outspeeding everyone except Jacky, catching Paulo Souza but not fast enough. John Byrnes and five Brazilians. Sid Garner was too slow.

Jim was out of it. Beat Lopez, then there was only the keeper. Pain in his leg was worse, but with it he outweighed grief to justify joy, old habit of triumph.

Lopez wanted him away from the middle.

He would comply.

Mary's excitement and urgency passed into calmness. Irrelevant if Jacky beat Lopez or not, evaded the Black Bludgeon or not, scored or not, England won or lost. She loved him. All the things they had shared, the many moments of mutual tenderness – by a hoar-frosted kale field hedge-side in snow-squalled Trenton, on a crowded summer beach at Cleethorpes, in and around Nottingham, and at home.

I do not wish to lose him.

Britt left unheeded the television cacophony behind her and relaxed into the established continuum: power pulsed optimising him, protecting him against all except his own wish.

A swerve would not beat Lopez: it had to be trickery and reflexes.

Throughout Brazil, each football patriot felt proof.

In England, likewise, plus the parts of the world graced or afflicted by her breed.

Lopez lunged right, Jacky flicked through his legs and went round staggering as the Brazilian clipped his heel. He regained balance four yards nearer the ball than the speeding Paolo Souza.

Malevolence hurled shrieking and multiform from infinite evil all around.

Gentle and invincible, Britt dispersed it harmless.

Only he himself could hurt himself.

Mary relaxed: he would survive the Black Bludgeon's foul: he would score.

Pete Gregg gritted out, whispering: "Goo on, boy!! Goo on!! Don't fall!!!"

Pain tore and punched in his thigh but Souza had missed his target by an inch – he could still run.

He sprang to possession a yard inside the penalty area, the keeper was nearly on him, he kicked the ball right and arced left, the Brazilian lunging sideways missed his left foot parry and struck Jacky on his bad thigh, bringing him down.

Breath gulping in, heat, sweat, pain dulled in repose. Evening blue sky direct overhead, doctor at work on his leg, players standing about. Crowd sounds; England supporters singing "You'll never walk alone": odd, it was the first time he had heard them sing that tonight.

Jingo would be alone when he took the penalty.

Benny Cawthorne was asking if he was alright.

He grinned and winked affirmation at the Cockney, then closed his eyes, re-living around his pain the run, its sensations, remembering his mother was dead, Mary consoling him, believing in him, encouraging him, loving him – yet, as always, solidly refusing to leave England, as always, ultimately, putting her own desires and interests first.

Not like Britt.

He opened his eyes.

Britt loved him, too. Defiant, he strove against guilt, remembering more strongly than the previous day's intimacy how she had encouraged him, stressed how vital this game was.

And it was!

Urgent for action, he propped up on his elbows. The Finnish referee, insisting he be removed from the pitch and ignoring English protests over his leniency towards the goalkeeper, was beckoning for a stretcher. Brazilians jostled about, shouting and frantically tapping imaginary wristwatches. Pain stabbed and stung; he bore, almost welcomed, it. The physiotherapist held him steady with one hand on his shoulder.

Richard was denying Jingo the penalty!

"But it's all agreed! I take penalties when Jacky can't!"

"Not this one you don't! Anyone but you!" The England Captain ordered Arrowood to take the kick: "Jim."

"Look at Denzil over there! He's going off his head shouting it's Jingo's!"

"If you can't, or won't, I'll take it myself!"

"Stop. Give it here."

Not looking back, Jingo Byrnes walked away, disappointment so immense, hatred for Richard Trelawney so venomous that he yearned to gouge out his eyes and crush his skull.

His cracked ribs stabbed, but it was only four paces and he would hold his breath.

Everything seemed so still except the goalkeeper's bobbing and swaying.

Okay. Let's do it.

"Look at that goalie!! He's yards out!" Denzil Wyckliffe was on his feet, head thrust gazing at the Brazilian keeper at least two paces off his goal-line as Arrowood kicked.

"He's saved!! Magnificent!! Wonderful!! He's saved" The radio commentator's words brought relief to the priest Barboza in Amazonas.

Pete Gregg was angrily triumphant as the referee took the ball from the protesting goalkeeper: "I should bloody well think so, ref!! He was miles off his line! If you'd ha' let that stand, it would ha' been a travesty of justice!"

Yellow smoke puthered from a smoke bomb near the Brazilian right corner flag. Two policemen were attempting to extinguish it. Scores of their colleagues tussled vigorously with the pitch invaders who had breached the thousand strong police barrier in front of the ululating Brazil crowd section.

Vanderskoon anxiously considered the phalanx protecting Jacky. Fireworks, exploding haphazardly about the stadium, kept snatching his attention. He gazed towards FLEUR'S. Check it again! He reached for the phone. No, it was clean. Under constant surveillance.

The Philadelphia police captain in charge of crowd control worked methodically utilising the television monitors' information.

The worldwide telecast showed Jim Arrowood adjusting the ball's position on the penalty spot: a small insert, top screen left, focussed on Denzil Wyckliffe; at top screen right, the similarly tense Brazilian team manager; bottom right, Joe Berrigan, forehead against goalpost, back to the field of play, stood praying; Jacky Day, propped on elbows, stared nervily in the remaining insert.

The Brazilian spectator samba bands ceased drumming. The stadium appeared almost silent.

Vanderskoon gazed at the scene below.

A firework exploded. Instinctively he eyed FLEUR'S.

"Ye-e-e-e-e-e-e-e-e-e-e-e-e-s!!!"

Jim Arrowood stood motionless in a delirium of happiness. His initial shock lessened enough to let him feel his broken ribs, sprained wrist, hear the crowd and be aware of team-mates running to congratulate him. He stuck out his elbows and held his left hand up, palm and head pivoting warning off all physical contact with him. His gaze focussed on the crippled Jacky: Jim's left arm raised and straightened, forefinger directing honour where most due.

Jacky, hands shielding his eyes, sat bent sobbing, grief-broken: his mother healthy, laughing, playing with him as a very little boy, reading to him, baking him his own jam pasties, taking him for walks, shopping in Danethorpe on market days, eating in the luxury of the Silver Grill restaurant for less than fifty pence the two of them, teaching him to ride her woman's bike down River Lane when he was six, buying him a new pair of boots at the Co-op, a new suit, always shopping around first to get the best bargain because they were poor and had to make ends meet. His mam scrubbing other people's floors, washing windows, doing seasonal work on the land, anything to earn an extra honest pound to augment Johnner's inadequate labourer's wages. Giving him her own pocket money to go out with the other boys when he was thirteen-fourteen-fifteen.

Oh Mam! Mam! Why are you dead?!! Why did you die?!! Why?!! Why?!!

Harry Day was crying also.

Observing the other woman's intense commiseration, compassion dispersed Beth Langdale's reserve: "I'm sorry I was so harsh, Mary," she conciliated her softly.

"My fault." The surrender was brusque. "I was cruel." Mary twisted to face her: "Jim was very brave just now, wasn't he? – and noble," she smiled, unstable.

"Yes," Beth's mood swayed to Mary's.

The small woman strove for nonchalance: "I've been under so much pressure lately. It's been – " emotion, inordinate and suddenly irresistible, chopped her sobbing and convulsing doubled over with tears a-gush.

Beth, one hand on Mary's shoulder, wept as well. So lovely, so vulnerable: The Senator, relaxed on the sofa, regarded Britt beside him leant almost rising in her concern for Jacky. Harder'n steel, laser quick slicing you up and dousing you in poison. Female! he sipped bourbon and branch, and blinked, eluding the brown blotches of old age on his hand but not the hollow chill anguish over lost physical powers, his body's ever increasing debilities and decay, Death's tightening proximity: Britt knew where to put in the barbs, wrench raw the pain.

Exhaling part aggressive trepidation, part-sigh at Jacky's disappearance from the screen, Britt considered the yellow-shirted figures sprinting deep into the England half: If both Gabe and Chuck insist on seeing Jacky tomorrow, Mary Day can't hide him from me. "Oh no!" eyes squeezing shut, she swivelled away from Eddy Corelli's fouling Vivi near the England penalty area.

"Sir!"

Passing the almost deserted bar, Henry Puzenko paused.

"Latest edition," the crewcut young barman proffered the newspaper. Puzenko shook his head. "The Brazilians have scored every time from that position," the bartender nodded towards the restaurant wall TV and stadium. The referee, encircled by protesting England players, was booking Eddy Corelli.

"Say, buddy, gi' me another, huh?" the drunken bass rumbled from a muscle-bound colossus at the corridor end of the counter; a gaily dapper, middle-aged androgyne, daintily sipping a green chartreuse, moved to sit beside him. "And put your radio onto station P.H.P.A. They ' got the sports news on. Maybe they can talk about somethin' other'n this god-dehmned sahccer." He mumbled, mostly to himself: "Ah cain't un'erstehnd what she sees in him – a skinny li'l' guy Ah could break in two with one hand!"

If they scored, he would go straight to the smokers' lounge. Maybe he should do that anyway.

"That ain't Radio P.H.P.A.! I wan' the sports!" the inebriate, deep tones submerged the announcer speaking of democracy versus communism.

"This is Radio P.H.P.A., sir. The sports news follows next," the bartender was cheerful.

Beside the linesman with flag horizontal aloft, Jacky Day stood freshly bandaged, urgent to re-enter the game.

If Brazil score, you' got one more half-hour of life, plus six, seven minutes, max. Bloodlust gouted imagery of Jacky Day gutshot, lungshot, face and half his skull and brains smashed away, crumpled twitching and crimson. Elbows on the bar-counter, Puzenko leaned back, eyes half-closed, exalted, delicate with enormous power, with the clarity of death-terror rampant yet totally controlled.

"But Ah won't lay a finger on him," the muscleman's bullhorn rumble crunched inaudible the newscaster save for stray sounds and half words. "Ah ain't no lumbering monster lahk she says. Sure Ah'm a big guy – six eleven, three hun'ed 'fifty pounds. Ah can run a hun'red yards in 10.1. Her skinny li'l' guy can't do that!"

"–Ukraine." At the newscaster's word, Puzenko became wholly alert, head fractionally and discreetly turned to hear every syllable.

"But she don't care," the giant's powerful tones gravelled the radio unintelligible.

" – the right –"

"'Your neck's bigger'n mah waist,' she says."

" – to choose capit–"

"And it is."

"The Ukrainians –"

"'You're too big,' she says."

Son-of-a-bitch! Puzenko stared at the referee single mindedly supervising details around the free kick. He longed to be let listen in peace about the Ukraine, but that would alert the smart-ass college kid barman too much.

"'Go way!' she says. 'Ah don' want you!' she says. Aw Gawd!" the resonant bass tones slurred sundering; Puzenko turned enough to note the giant drooping his face onto his forearms on the counter.

"– freedom –"

"Women sure are Hell!"

"–Independence, and democratic capitalism –"

"But Ah love her," the bullhorn gravel-grinder articulation disintegrated into rumbling incoherence.

"And those were the views of the man of the hour, Jacky Day."

Puzenko twitched instinctively turning, then went rigid, fingers clenched white, forcing himself to remain still and staring at the Brazilian starting his free kick. Two men sprang sprinting from the England five-man defence wall. The Brazilian broke off his run-up. The referee intervened. The English captain, shouting urgently, trotted towards him, pointing at the linesman with the raised flag. The referee beckoned Jacky Day onto the pitch.

Puzenko half-turned.

"Women can be bitches," the spruce androgyne's very light tenor lilted consolingly, his gold wrist chain gleaming as he squeezed the muscleman's shoulder. "They don't always appreciate men – real men. Another drink?"

"What was that about Jacky Day on the radio just now?" Puzenko, casual, asked the barman.

"Jacky Day and the Ukraine? It's been the leading news item since six o'clock, sir. The evening paper contains all the details, sir."

"You should have backed your judgement about Brasil scoring from that freekick!" the Swedish Finance Minister jibed.

"I'm a pessimist," Robert Jarvis answered. "Not only that, I didn't want them to score."

"Well, they didn't," said the Swede.

"Oh-ho!" the Englishman agonised, "here they go again!"

"They'll not score. England are going to win," said the Swede firmly. "And I've thought of a cause for Jacky – street children; the orphans, the homeless, unwanted, friendless, defenceless kids all over the world sent out to starve, steal, slave, prostitute themselves or die."

"Yes," Robert mused, "he probably would go for that. Yes, he might indeed."

"They're not playing extra-time, are they?" Mrs Arrowood, intent on her embroidery, wondered.

"What? No," her husband squirmed as Barboza, twenty yards out, came free of Jed Lennox.

"I could almost wish" – Benny Cawthorne confronted the yellow-shirted attacker – "that Jim had not scored at all. It will mean so many more of those grubby, drunken scandalmonger press people at his wedding," Mrs Arrowood's needle plied carefully.

Benny Cawthorne had possession. "It will anyway, with Jacky Day as best man," said her husband.

"I find that hard to forgive Jim. He had the choice of a duke, a marquis and three earls, and yet he picks that – " she laughed humourless contempt "I-don't-know-what. Such a common little communist really."

"That's it! Finished! Over!"

"Pardon?!" Mrs Arrowood, exceedingly indignant, relaxed. "Oh, that."

From the bar room, loud jubilation, disputes, disappointment, glee: bet money changing hands over the result of the game.

The two little Chinese from the grey Toyota, grinning drunkenly, staggered left from the wash room instead of returning to the bar room. At the end of the short passageway was another corridor terminated by a top-and-bottom bolted heavy street door. Two rooms on each side of the corridor, the far left was open.

At sight of the diminutive drunks in the doorway, the smaller lolled grinning over his companion's shoulder, the three disgruntled room occupants and the fourth merry over his winnings became alert and menacingly silent.

The winner stuffed his gambling gains into his pocket and gripped his gun. "Bar's the other way," he growled. The first drunk stepped aside: his comrade's silenced automatic was steady. The winner's hand jerked in his pocket. The phut-phut from the tiny visitor's weapon was scarcely audible above the small colour TV in the room corner and the hubbub of the bar. Blood and brains splashed the corpse's three associates flinching, jerking their hands instinctively upwards in surrender.

"Which is Mr Lee's room, and what is the entrance signal? How many are with him? You. We only want Mr Lee. No one else."

"Four men. That room. Three knocks, wait two seconds, then one knock."

"Undress naked. Fast."

Twenty seconds later, Lee Kwang Yoo's men were spread-eagled face down on the floor, trousers tied over their heads and faces.

The first bullet knocked the door-opener backwards with a broken right arm, the second exploded Mr Lee's stomach, the third felled his best bodyguard via his right lung, the fourth, fifth and sixth disintegrated for ever Mr Lee's skull and dreams of vengeance and criminal riches.

"That's right, Mr President. You step down there to gi' the boys their medals," said Pete Gregg. "They've earned 'em. Folks'll criticise, though. I can hear 'em already."

"Mary will be pleased it's all over," said his wife. "She'll be glad to be getting back home. It's been a very trying time for her."

Pete Gregg became serious: "Ay. Poor old Jacky's mam dyin'. A bad job. Tragic."

"I was thinking more about that woman Jacky got in with over there, and all those awful death threats! And Wolf Wehrman and Death's Head Calhoun – and the other one they still haven't found yet."

The rifle sight crosshairs descended the white shirt's belly sweat stain to centre on the stomach muscles ridging the clinging cloth. I could blow you away now, you commie bastard! Aggression was ecstasy, sensuous, ethereal. He respired deeply, precise and controlled. Prone, he glanced up from the periscope-cum-support-and-trigger to the rifle barrel whose muzzle tip rested beyond view on the windowsill. In front of him on the floor, the flat fifteen by twenty centimetre electronics screen imaged the officials preparing the presentation ceremony. Not long now, Wolfy! Not long you guys toughing it out in Moslem shitholes! Not long now before I'm enjoying six months of sun and fun in the Bahamas, with a half million buck sweetener piling up interest in Switzerland! Those F.B.I. jerk-offs think they could sucker me into quitt'n' on this job – they ' picked the wrong guy! Thrustingly cynical, he cuffed aside fractional unease concerning the Ukraine announcement.

Crowd rumble bunched up dulled and compact from the stadium, filling the storeroom and making him strain for sound of its door opening, for noise in the corridor. No problem, he soothed himself. The back-up boys are taking care I won't be disturbed. What if the stuff in the paper was true? doubt flickered.

No way! Who do those bastards think they're kidding?! Rage curled his visage snarling and his right forefinger flexing alongside but not touching the trigger.

But if it *were* true?

No way!

But if it were?

Else is dead. She can't see me, hear this crowd. Jacky stared about him, noting each England squad member, the Brazilians, the stadium, the sky, each detail disparate and forever unique, changing. Hollowness inside him ghosted feelings numbed incomplete by anguish.

It's an F.B.I. shrewdy to stop me. The flat screen showed the President approaching the presentation table; the rifle crosshairs held steady on the sweat stain.

Jacky Day is in the best Anglo-American tradition of the Founding Fathers, the Bill of Rights, the Rule of Law: the newspaper article stuck deep and clawing.

Son of a bitch! he squeezed against the floor, trying to discharge his tension.

– In the Paddy O'Rourke Show, he spoke out against Soviet and Communist oppression –

It's a trick! A smart-ass fucking trick to stop me! Puzenko, countenance a-snarl, writhed in frustration, forefinger stiff straight alongside the trigger.

But what if it isn't? What if every word of it is genuine?

His professional instinct struggled cold and ferocious, and temporarily successfully, against the tormenting rationale attempting to destroy his mission: his forefinger crooked gently round the trigger.

What if you kill him, then find he really is a friend of the Ukraine and championed things you've believed in since a kid?

The crosshairs moved with the stain. The flat screen depicted the President presenting the World Cup to the England Captain.

Puzenko, in torment, kept the crosshairs steady on target. It's a bluff! A god-damn' bluff!

Jacky watched Richard Telawney turn holding the Cup high, the President was smiling, adding his clapping to the crowd's acclamation. Joe Berrigan beside Richard was beatific. I understand their belief in Heaven: Jacky, imaging his mother laughing and happy in God's endless love and truth, yearned for it to be so.

Reality, however, was her grave in the cemetery's darkness.

He stared at the shirt-back in front of him, recalling his sorrow, death's certainty, fear; and Mary, comforting him, her perfume and the scent from the wreathes and bouquets mingling.

Mary, persuading him to return to America though she was terrified.

Jealous of Britt.

Who was watching him now.

Kill him! The urge danced maniac and lush, trance-like.

Wait.

Kill him! Free all those guys locked up! In chains! Tortured, maybe!

Think: he cautioned himself.

I have a contract! professionalism insisted. All the planning and back-up guys and big money needed to put me here'll spit blood ' I don't hit him!

Think. – Think, god-damn it! If that guy is for the Ukraine, he can be the best mouthpiece we' ever had. Sure, a hit here can free our boys, but there are other ways. There are always other ways.

"Congratulations on a glorious game. So you won your Football World Championship after all," the President's handshake was firm, his smile broad.

I could blow you away so easy, Jew-lover! The crosshairs centred the smiling profile.

"That run of yours sure was someth'n'! 'Hope the leg's not too bad?"

"It aches, but that'll pass."

"There's speculation you might return to play in America."

"It's a thought."

"If you do, I'll try and take some time off to watch you! Congratulations again. And good luck."

Kill him NOW! bloodlust surged, then suddenly frosted: a hit right now on the communist would look like a missed hit on the President.

Jingo Byrnes's hand, reaching for the coveted treasure, was knocked hard aside by Richard Trelawney's elbow as the England Captain swivelled and galloped off.

"The bastard!" Curly Greenhalgh, running up, exclaimed.

"It's alright," Jingo sluiced joy over bitterness, "I've got this," he looked sideways down at the World Championship medal in his left palm.

Curly, though jerky with anger, lacked valour: "I'm gonna get Jacky and Benny!"

The billionaire Mohammedan dignitary smiled benevolently at his pretty little thirteen year old wife, pregnant with his ninety-third child, and fed her a piece of Turkish Delight.

Yes, he ought to buy one or two more of those players, Brazilians and English. It had been a very enjoyable game. A truly exciting game.

Soon be time for the stonings, the amputations, the whippings. Delightful.

Yes, he would definitely buy some of those players. He would order it done today.

Religious bigotry, inequity and cruelty: Jacky gazed at Richard Trelawney and Joe Berrigan behind Jed Lennox who was between and two-handed relieving Eddy Corelli and Bobby Milburne of their held-high trophy; Winston Jones was being hindered by others in the surrounding cluster which Benny, Jingo and Curly were fast approaching: Joe Berrigan suddenly stared up at the electronics display showing full screen a six inch silver and ebony cross on a long silver chain against a Brazilian shirt. Richard Trelawney glanced also, scowled, and became vehement. Joe Berrigan replied angrily.

Jacky turned: Barboza, pious in defeat, stood second after Lopez to receive his silver medal from a sympathetic President.

The President's bodyguards edged restlessly vigilant.

Puzenko and other would-be assassins cannot reach us here: fear touching his spine, Jacky stared at the crowd, ten yards to his left, Denzil Wyckliffe was surrounded by well-wishers, officials and non-playing squad members. Tomorrow, we shall be safe back in England. Mary will be glad.

Jim at his side chuckled, wincing: "That Winston!"

Chased by Benny, Winston was zigzagging and leaping, exultantly brandishing his glimmering booty. Joe Berrigan was halfway to Barboza.

Jim in Italy. No Elspeth at Trenton, Mary at Bio-Veracity, self-indulgently well content with *her* life and ways, for ever stopping him and crushing him down.

Rage and resentment imploded so total and sudden he almost fell over. Remorse and guilt held him upright: he loved Mary, needed Mary, their life together, she really did care for him, had persuaded him to return, had come back with him though she was terrified.

Britt's image appeared: Because she realised she did wrong deserting you in the first place and leaving you to me.

No!

"Win-ston! Win-ston!" chanted through the crowd's laughter and cheering.

She was afraid for Jessie.

For herself! Britt was scornful. She puts her own interests first and yours and everyone else's a long way second!

Mirth and applause swirled over-topping the crowd's "Win-ston! Win-ston!" – Benny was half goodhumouredly half angrily contesting possession.

"Jacky, Jim," Denzil Wyckliffe's greeting was quiet.

"Ben-ny! Ben-ny!" The stadium screen was one vast Cockney grin.

Watching in her Beverley Hills luxury apartment Becky Serene cried, depressed and despairing.

"To think the chairbound hacks wanted me to drop you because you're a Socialist and you spoke out for your beliefs," Denzil Wyckliffe's soft-spoken intent was clear. "You can't organise your All-Stars Charity Match, Jacky? I'm a good organiser. Say the word, you've got it. Well done, boys," he turned to the rest of the squad running up.

Disproportionately affected by Denzil's friendliness, with emotions as intense and chaotic as the events around him, Jacky stared about. In the general jubilation, Brazilians were sad, some crying. On the big screen, Barboza's raised crucifix was motionless between his bowed head and Joe Berrigan's.

"Popish mumbo-jumbo!" Richard Trelawney, breathing hard, growled.

"I think they're saying the Lord's Prayer in Latin, Richard," Jacky conjectured. The Methodist preacher's contempt vanished. "Ask the Brazilians to run a circuit of honour with us, with them holding the Cup the first half, and us all together the second. Tell them we'd be honoured."

"Fack 'em!" part jocular but mostly sincere, the Cockney stepped aside, hugging his triumph close. "It's ours! We won it! Fack 'em!"

"Yours, completely on your own, out in front, leading us all, for the second half lap, Benny, if you want. Ours the first."

Lopez stared at the England captain.

"For the good of the game," said Richard Trelawney.

"Tomorrow morning, you should tell him."

"I'll select my time and my place when we are safe back in England." Britt shuddered at the panoraming aerial view of the John Fitzgerald Kennedy Stadium and environment viscid with people and vehicles, the yellow and white clutch of players forming on the green, the pink and white nightclub glinting FLEUR'S: "They look so vulnerable, so unprotected, down there!"

"What if he denies it's his?" Vengeful, he ignored her contempt. "What if he rejects you entirely? won't have anything to do with you? His wife will certainly insist on that."

"Her!"

"She'll definitely say it isn't his. She will maintain it is Chuck Bengtsson's, or mine, or somebody else's. She will paint you the dirtiest of prostitutes possible. She will fight tooth and nail to keep him from you."

"That bitch! She's not worthy of him!"

"Are you?"

"I love him! I'll do anything for him!"

"You idealise Jacky, and you misjudge yourself. You, a domesticated housewife, utterly submitted to one man?! No more travelling all over the world, no more of the fast and high life, the wheeler-dealing! Goodbye independence!"

"I'm of solid German hausfrau stock – remember? I want to settle down. In two months, I'll be twenty-eight. I want this baby. If Jacky does run back to that gold-digging careerist, I can wait, and meanwhile take care of his interests, and those of our child. The factors which brought him to me are still at work. She will not put him first. She might for a time, but not long. Having Jacky's baby sets us on even terms."

"Alright. You're beautiful, relentless, you get what you want. He leaves his wife and little daughter to live with you and you discover he is not the man you thought. You kick him out. You've ruined his life, broken up a family, for nothing."

"He is the man I want," she was quietly certain. "To live with, share with, do everything for."

"And after a while, he leaves you for another woman, like he left his wife. Maybe hates you, despises you."

"Then I'll still have the memories, and our child, or children. My life until I met Jacky was barren. Without him, it would be barren again. I want him in my life on any terms."

"Even as no more than a memory?"

"Jim's not going to run with the others," Beth Langdale realised. "His cracked ribs and injured wrist must be too painful for him, poor darling."

With Jim off to Italy, Jacky will really resent my hindering him! At present, I can control him because he needs me. But, if Britt Anderson keeps pursuing him, he may turn to her, or even to other women! fear a-flutter, Mary stared at the screen; behind the loping, waving players, smoke bombs amid the crowd were discharging thick yellow smoke, and fireworks started crackling about the stadium as if on signal.

Puzenko! Assassins! No, not here with all this security: she calmed herself. How did they bring in the smoke bombs and fireworks, though?! she worried afresh.

A three-second close up of Snoopy, the cartoon character beagle, highflying in his Sopwith Camel, changed to an aerial view of the stadium and its traffic filled environs: columns of yellow smoke and red smoke smeared the busy car parks, except around FLEUR'S.

Whining from Jessica twisted Mary toward the sound. Beth rose: "Stay. I'll go."

Jessie must come first, Mary thought. We should move to Italy, help Jacky escape and become the old Jacky he was before all this mess began. She fought off fear of change, resentment at personal submission, despair over forfeiting the revolutionary discoveries she felt herself verging upon at Bio-Veracity and the loss of research momentum and time which removal to Italy implied.

"Jessica's sleeping," Beth Langdale announced softly. "Goodness! What a lot of smoke!" Police were struggling with spectators in the crowd. An aerial sequence showed smoke thick and drifting about the car parks and roadways near the stadium. A lorry and trailer were slewed blocking the main thoroughfare. The area around FLEUR'S remained clear.

Scowling and apprehensive, the President's bodyguards bunched round him as he paced briskly from public view into the stand's interior.

A grim faced Secret Service bodyguard was talking urgently to a serious Denzil Wyckliffe at the England bench, his gestures clearly revealing he wished the players off the pitch immediately.

Puzenko! No – that Ukraine announcement stopped him! Some other assassin?! No! There is no danger now! There cannot be!! must not be!!

A cop caught using a firearm built into a billy stick! Tense, Howard Vanderskoon stared through his binoculars at the struggling knot of policemen in the stadium section beyond the players: Is it Puzenko? The F.B.I. man gazed aslant at the crowd surveillance TV close-up jumbled with bucking figures overpowering the would-be assassin.

"Let's assume that guy is not a real cop," Vanderskoon told his Philadelphia coadjutants. "Check with all our crowd control personnel to ascertain no other phonies are among our boys out there! And check that guy on our computers – now!"

Vanderskoon stared at the vehicles blocking the roadway, the scores of turbid, tumbling smoke columns, the clear area around the blue-and-white office block, and FLEUR'S with its part-open window sunflecked at one cornertip. Pre-timeset smokebombs in Coke and Pepsi cans. It was all too well planned and co-ordinated.

"Ask for reports on any odd or unusual incidents – especially around that smoke-free office block area and parking lot."

Puzenko was a pro. His back-up people, top quality. Big, anti-Jewish money behind him.

Maximum chaos. A clean, quick hit. A fast get-away. His connections bribing, blackmailing, using Mob threat and influence to move him in and out of that office block.

Vanderskoon stared at the pitch, the players, Jacky, the crowd.

In that mass were perhaps would-be killers with weapons disguised as flag sticks, walking sticks, telephoto lenses or whatever, compressed spring guns, gas shooters puffing poison plastic darts or pellets, or weapons smuggled in piece by piece, then re-assembled inside the ground. He longed to have the pitch cleared immediately.

Should I send bodyguards to protect Jacky?

Why just Jacky? Why disregard the hundreds of celebrities, dignitaries and politicians here, all potential targets?

Puzenko. Because of Puzenko.

Tranquil, totally self-controlled, the marksman contemplated the flat screen. No clear shot there. Those soccer suckers assing around for the crowd are sure giving you plenty of time to decide if you want this hit or not, the Moslem's half million or not.

Elephants asleep in darkened Africa; Arctic reindeer feeding under an all-night sun; the Earth a green blue white luminous ball swung fragile round an atomic fire in blue-black space with fleeing galaxies, time an idea as depthless as length and breadth. His mother was somewhere!

Jacky's upward gaze and being were a dream in reality, the pain and bleeding in his leg mundaneness. Else gone forever. I shall never see her again. All this gaudy pageantry is meaningless, life in vain, death inevitable.

Terror at his own impending decease, revulsion from his mother's annihilation, rejection of his own, shuddered him jerking and staggering.

"Alright, Jecky boy?" Benny Cawthorne, alongside, wondered.

Jacky nodded, aware of the converse and behaviour of players running about him, the stadium and sky; of each thing insubstantial in flux, substantial in balance: existence in continuum.

Elspeth is not lost, he reasoned. Her life had meaning, is part of the inextricable totality, in every extricable detail. Her life was its own meaning. Each life is its own meaning.

His was this – was Mary, and Jessie. And Britt who had told him that this was worthwhile.

"I'll never promote atheism and socialism!! Never play in any charity match set up by Jacky Day!!" Joe Berrigan savagely spurned Jed's tentative query.

Mary's jealousy cauterised him rivuleting into despair. Resentment saved him.

She always gets her way! She's used Jessie, her studies, research work, her scientific projects, anything and everything to twist things to how *she* wants them!

What *I* want is important, too! *My* career is important! Football is! To hundreds of millions, thousands of millions! I want –! I want –!

He visioned Jim and Beth, departing for Italy, himself confined, never able to escape. Despairing, he fled for habitual consolation to Elspeth. Sorrow, immense and enervating, staggered him toppling, stumbling, in agony.

"I play, Gerald. Me," indifferent to and ignoring Joe Berrigan, Vivi Machado was nodding, tapping his chest with right forefinger. "I play weeth Jackee Day, eef 'e want. Other boys, too, I theenk."

Vanderskoon squinted at the consecutive close-ups on the crowd monitor: arrest of another fake cop with a fire-armed billy. Two God's Huntsmen, one to each long side of the stadium, because this other man had to be a God's Huntsman also. He scanned the computer print-out concerning the failed assassin. Were there more of them? Those trick billies and false police rôles demanded high quality skill and planning.

He scowled at the scanty information: God's Huntsmen, a secret society with sacrificial killing – perhaps murder – as an integral part. Their sole informant, an interviewee during the investigation concerning the unsolved homicide of a Jewish New York game warden two years back, had blown his own head off the same night. Official verdict: suicide. The fake cop had been a suspect in the hunting knife butchery.

Was Jacky the target? Was he?!

The police captain said: "We have a report of an incident in the office block parking lot. Approximately a minute before the end of the game, the two officers guarding the lower east entrance to the block were asked by a Philadelphia police sergeant, not personally known to either man, to watch for a black haired Caucasian male pickpocket, age about thirty, hiding in the parking lot. Five eight, hundred-forty, 'fifty, pounds, wearing dark trousers and medium gray sport jacket. He had stolen over twelve thousand Canadian and U.S. dollars off a guy from St. Catharine's, Ontario, Canada, won at stud poker on the bus ride down here today with fellow sahccer enthusiasts. Three, four minutes later, the officers saw a suspect, not fifty yards away, and went to get him. Wrong man."

"They left their entrance unguarded!" Vanderskoon condemned. "Check that sergeant out! Meanwhile we search those offices, and make it noisy, huh?! so if there is anybody there, they'll know we're look'n'!"

No President: Jacky saw. They're afraid of assassins. Hearing the rifle shots that were fireworks, he glanced dully at the red, yellow and grey vapours blotching the stadium, tendrilling the pitch, and at the varying countenances and actions of the players, the police, the antics of the crowd. A Secret Service bodyguard was running from the England team bench toward Richard.

Jacky welcomed a bullet, wanted it to smash him into instant oblivion. Maybe he would see Else: he let himself think like her. She had been afraid of suffering after death. If they had hurt her –! Gigantic with will to protect his mother, he was ready to tear Almighty God Himself off tormenting her, though he knew by definition such could only be by the Almighty's Own permission.

Else is safe and God only an idea in the mind, he accepted. Else feels no pain. She feels nothing. She does not exist. When the body is dead, there is nothing to feel with. Individual annihilation. Oblivion, complete.

Jecky is suffering: Benny Cawthorne stood two yards distant. Other players were slowing, most waving to the crowd. Richard Trelawney and Lopez were alternately pausing and walking a few strides, the Cup aloft for photographers and spectator applause. Winston Jones, that facking idiot, five yards in front of his nearest player, was bowing low, then standing erect, stiff wide-legged and straining both fists at the sky. Smoke was gushing from scores of smoke bombs about the stadium, fireworks banging in all crowd sections. Exit gangways were full of spectators seemingly reluctant to leave. My Uncle Ralph is dead, like your mother, Jecky. Poor old bagger. He would've liked to have seen this. Me wiv my medal! Gravity momentarily diminished elation: Becky, the bitch. The stupid cow. Women!

Then, exalted by the rowdy vitality about him, Benny let triumph at ambition-achieved prevail.

I shall go to Italy: the thought slid up. Sign with Jim's club if possible, with some other if not. Mary will go mad. I shall do everything reasonable to satisfy her. But I am going!

Utterly rejecting Mary's initial refusal to transfer to Italy with him, he visioned himself running with a ball across fields, through coppice-woods and glades, training alone for hours, giving her time to adjust.

And if she still won't consent?

I'll leave and stay in Nottingham.

Panic wrenched him. He longed to abase himself, beg her forgiveness. Reason held him steadfast: If Mary does not want me, but only what she can get out of me, our marriage is finished anyway.

"It's great, ain' it?!" Benny's joy, distinct and immediate, seemed from a separate universe. "What an atmosphere! Come on, Jecky! It's yours as well! That's the stuff!" he encouraged him. "And tomorrah night, London Town, here we come!" Beaming, right fist raising, the Cockney challenged the sky.

Britt.

Offering everything.

His to take.

Yet it was not another woman he wanted.

It is my life I want: he realised. My life! Mine! with absolute right to live my life as I, I myself, ultimately decide!!

He's there! Vanderskoon concentrated on the pale blue and white edifice topped with the pink and white FLEUR'S. Fatalistic, he scanned through his binoculars the third floor office windows, most obscured by venetian blinds, curtains, or shadowed with decorative foliage. Stay in the pack, Jacky! Don't give him a clear shot! Figures moving behind a window tensed him motionless unbreathing a fifth of a second till he identified their blue uniforms.

He focussed on the fourth storey: glimpses of the police.

"We should search FLEUR'S, also, to be on the safe side," the Philadelphia police captain admonished Vanderskoon. "Look at that window sparkl'n' at us, almost invit'n' us in."

"No top assassin is gonna shoot from that window, Captain. An open window is the one place we watch like hawks, and any marksman smart enough to breach our security knows that," the F.B.I. man was definite. The two men stared at the nightclub, and the office block. "FLEUR'S has been thoroughly checked and guarded these last four hours, everyone entering searched for weapons with metal detectors. They have their own security people inside who have just told us nobody has entered the club these last ten minutes – that eliminates our police sergeant. No top assassin is gonna shoot from that window, Captain. If we send a bunch of uniformed policemen bursting in there right now with drawn guns, some drunk, or a nervous cop, could make a wrong move and innocent people get hurt."

Is Puzenko the sergeant? Vanderskoon conjectured worriedly. Was the sergeant a real Philadelphia cop? the pickpocket and stud poker story genuine? Is it another decoy like the smoke bombs and the slewed truck and trailer? Is it connected with God's Huntsmen? A slaughtered Jewish game-warden – Puzenko, a Jew-hater. Big anti-Jewish money. Rogue C.I.A. expert back-up organisation and planning, could have would have decoy, red herring, sucker bait and contingency hitmen alternatives for Puzenko, especially after all the publicity on Puzenko.

Vanderskoon eyed Jacky amid the straggle of players sauntering, jogging here and there, pausing, waving, with the Secret Service bodyguards attentive among them. Jacky had to be the target. Had to be! Vanderskoon scrutinised the applauding masses, turgid in the gangways: The identified God's Huntsman had almost certainly been aiming at Jacky. That had been confirmed. How many more God's Huntsmen or other would-be assassins were in that crowd?

The sun-flash window-dazzle stabbing his eyecorner, Vanderskoon walky-talkied his F.B.I. subordinate nearest the office block: "Take two plainclothes men with you and check out that open window at FLEUR'S."

The samba rhythms throbbed and beat. England fans were singing "You'll never walk alone." Clapping and cheering and shouting, fireworks exploding, different coloured smoke wreathing, a mélange of gladness and goodwill. No danger here! No killers! Not in this festivity, with all the fantastic security clamp-down! His dad would have been happy to have seen this! Poor old Johnner! And Else. He transformed grief into her joy. Harry would be laughing in Nottingham. His two younger brothers as well. Not Joanna, blaming him for Else's death. Poor Joanna.

Somewhere in that main stand, Rob Jarvis and the Swede would be smiling and glad. He would take Robert up on his offer. He would do good works the rest of his life. That would please Mary. He waved to two Robin Hoods in Lincoln Green holding a white banner with his name in block capitals over a white football marked '1', then bobbed and weaved, changing position as he had just been advised.

"Curly!" trotting towards Jacky, the Cockney urged, teasing. "Curly, Curly, come on, Curly! Come and hold hands wiv little Jecky!"

The bald man, grinning with fear and shaking his head backed even further away.

"Shut your big mouth, Ben," said Jacky, "and go get the Pot!"

"Come wiv me."

"I'm not allowed to run out in front, even if I wanted to, which I don't."

Winston Jones, twenty yards ahead of everyone else, completing a somersault along the ground, leapt punching upwards in glee.

"We'd never catch that bladdy clown anyway!"

Vanderskoon's anxiety fixed on Jacky observing Benny Cawthorne approaching the team captains. The F.B.I. man eyed the crowd.

Puzenko can't be here! No hit on Jacky could succeed here. The window's cornertip glimmered: No! Not there. If they try now, it will be between here and the hotel; at the hotel; somewhere, tomorrow. Or back in England, where protecting Jacky will be out of our hands.

He loved Mary! She would understand! She would!

I'll do anything to satisfy her, help her career! – But I am going!!!

And Britt?

A by-product. A might-have-been.

He yearned momentarily, then insisted: Because Mary does love me! She will go! Ultimately, she won't fail me! She won't! She won't! She never has. Not ultimately.

When Jacky Day gets to hold that Cup up for the crowd, as he surely will any time now, then, right then, at *THAT* moment, Henry Puzenko, old buddy, old pal, that is your Decision Time.

Vanderskoon's attention flicked away, from the gleaming prize Lopez was hugging, to the little yellow glint off the distant, slanting pane: No assassin there, he soothed his unease. The only possible danger is in this stadium: apprehensive, he scrutinised the crowd for flag sticks and telephoto lenses. Benny Cawthorne, left hand extended, approached the Brazilian captain.

Maybe I've been too smart in presuming FLEUR'S open window safe. Vanderskoon's doubt-streaked judgement rebelled against the notion; recollection of criminal ingenuity spurted doubt into fear. He could be there – and if he is, it may now be too late to stop him.

Fatalistic, the F.B.I. man fixed on the bodyguards near Jacky who was observing Benny Cawthorne, left arm extended holding the trophy which Lopez retained close to his chest while conversing with the Cockney. I promised the President – and Denzil – everybody –, we would protect Jacky: he thought, and remembered his daughter that morning from her hospital lab. in Seattle telephoning her pride in him, her love, urging he let nothing harm Jacky.

Vanderskoon's eyes closed: his daughter, thirteen, her brother, fifteen, sobbing, clinging to him beside the open coffin of their cancer dead mother. The desolation of that time numbing life meaningless except for their need of him. His daughter, scoured of all religious belief, dedicated to fighting cancer. His son, a rigid Calvinist, corporation lawyer: I, for one, Father, shall consider it God's Justice, if you fail to protect your atheist, socialist charge from assassination.

God, thought Vanderskoon, I sometimes wonder whether He exists at all, or whether He's just the invention psychologists say, as Jacky said on that Paddy O'Rourke Talk Show that started all this madness.

Vanderskoon eyed Jacky before concentrating on the crowd.

Insane, Denzil said about the Puzenko plot: Unbelievable! Too incredible to be real! Denzil, reality is more improbable than you can imagine, in this kill-or-be-killed crazy world where perverted scum rise to the top and whitewash themselves legitimate with the money and power they've gotten through murder, theft and swindling – or politics. Then use weirdos like Puzenko – or maybe God's Huntsmen – to help do their dirty work. And for every one we catch or stop, he thought grimly, there is an unending line to fill that never empty place.

He watched Benny Cawthorne take sole possession of the Cup, briefly raise it two-handed aloft, then pace offering it to Jacky.

If they succeeded in hitting Jacky now, it would be perfect timing, he mused sombrely. A hero's tragedy in triumph, with the whole world watching, a quick clean end to all your grief and problems, Jacky. Stay in that pack, stay shielded! Don't give anyone chance to draw a bead on you!

The sunfire off FLEUR'S open window dazzled Vanderskoon afresh.

Jacky accepted the Cup Benny was gravely almost ceremoniously proffering.

But what if Mary does fail me? Does refuse to come with me? Leaves me? With the other players moving aside, and the guards reluctantly likewise, he displayed on high the trophy for the near longside crowd.

"Ja-cky-y! Ja-cky-y!" England supporters began, the Robin Hoods' banner wagged and swung.

She won't! Never! Men's movement enmeshing the area to his left and right, bodyguards shifting protective behind him, he saluted the stadium's curved short side, spectators everywhere rising to him.

"Ja-cky-y!! Ja-cky-y!!" the measured chant was drowning the samba bands.

But what if she does?!

She won't!! She won't!!

"Ja-cky-y!!! Ja-cky-y!!! Ja-cky-y!!!" two-thirds of the spectators had it now.

The third, the long side, with its Royal box and no President: Jim on the bench – standing up, and joining in, the bloody fool! Jacky was near tears. And Wyckliffe and Dave Lewis! And the V.I.P. section with its representatives and celebrities from the Football Associations of every nation in the world. Overcome by the distinction being sincerely accorded him by the game's foremost connoisseurs, Jacky was weeping: Benny and the boys there, grinning, clapping, chanting, the daft buggers!

"JA-CKY-Y!!! JA-CKY-Y!!! JA-CKY-Y!!!"

I'm going to Italy, too, Jim, boy.

And if Mary won't?

I'm going anyway. I must! I must! He was crying hard. It's my life!!

He turned to the final, the short, straight side, its spectators rising like a wave that stayed crested: "JA-CKY-Y!!!! JA-CKY-Y!!!! JA-CKY-Y!!!!"

It's my life, Mary: my life: his summary was humble, and total.

With emotions so intense and vast they included almost every beneficent nuance within human register, his sobbing body and head went back to weep laughing up at the golden symbol and infinity.

Four hundred and fifty yards away, in untrammelled straight line, sunlight glinted off a part-opened window at FLEUR'S.